MW01488493

THE
GLASS LETTERS

S.A. Gensch

The Glass Letters by S.A. Gensch
Published by S.A. Gensch
sagensch.com
Copyright © 2021 S.A. Gensch

All rights reserved. No portion of this book may be reproduced in any form without permission from the publisher, except as permitted by the U.S. copyright law. For permissions contact: gensch.samantha@gmail.com

Cover by: aaniyah.ahmed@99D

ISBN: 978-1-7372607-0-7

Printed in The United States of America

Edition 1

-1-

Aiden stayed still on the floor. He refused to stand up. His body wouldn't stop shaking. Was it from the chill of the white tile or from the events that had taken place seconds ago? He wasn't sure. The embarrassment, the shock, the pain, both physical and mental, kept him in place. Had he imagined it would go this way? Of course not. But now that it had, he was too scared to get up. There was a pounding force around his face, yet felt numb. He wasn't sure if he should open his eyes. Could he even open his eyes? He would have to in order to make sure his apartment was empty. He couldn't remember hearing the door open and shut, signaling the departure of his assailant. If they hadn't left, were they waiting to go after him again the second he tried to get up? It didn't matter; he couldn't get up. He couldn't open his eyes. He couldn't take that risk.

The deliberation inside Aiden's head continued until there was a knock at the door. His eyes flew open. Even with that being an indication the perpetrator must have left, there was a weight still holding him down. He silently begged for whoever it was to leave. The sound of keys began entering the door, causing Aiden's heart to jump into his throat. It began opening. The panic pushed the weight off as Aiden jumped up from the kitchen floor and hurried to his room.

"Hey, Aiden!" a voice called out. "Are you home?" It was Jaxie.

"Jaxie, don't come in here," Aiden begged from the other side of his bedroom door. "You need to leave!" Part of his plea was because he wasn't sure if the attacker was still in the apartment and could harm her too. Another part was that he didn't want his little sister to see the damage to his face.

"Why?" Jaxie asked, not the least bit worried by Aiden's tone. "What's...Aiden, is that blood on the floor?"

"Jaxie, just leave!" Aiden choked out.

Hurrying across the apartment, Jaxie began knocking on the bedroom door desperately. "Aiden? What's going on? Open the door now." When there was no response, Jaxie let herself in. She wasn't willing to wait for him. Aiden stood at the other side of the room, turned away from her. His shoulders were trembling.

"Don't look at me, please," Aiden begged with an unsteady voice.

"Are you kidding me right now? Aiden," Jaxie walked around him, trying to get him to look at her. He didn't make it easy though as he fought hard to hide, using his hands to block his face. He knew he wouldn't get her to leave anytime soon. Not while he was acting like this.

"Alright, alright!" he finally gave in. "Alright...I'll show you. Just...look and get out, okay?"

Jaxie impatiently waited as Aiden removed his hands from his face and turned to show her. She felt her stomach surge up to her throat. Aiden's face was discolored, one of his eyes was nearly swollen shut, his lip was busted with blood trickling down the corner, and his cheek looked like a balloon.

"What happened to you?" Jaxie asked with tears filling her eyes.

"I said to just look and leave," Aiden said, turning away again.

"Who did this to you?" Jaxie repeated, watching Aiden fall onto his bed. "Aiden, if you don't tell me, I'm going to have to call the police."

"No."

"How do I know you weren't walking here from the store and got mugged?"

"I didn't."

"Then tell me what happened."

"I can't."

"Then how do I know I don't need to call someone or bring you somewhere?"

"Because I'm telling you!" Aiden yelled, sitting up on the bed. "It was my fault anyway."

"How?" Jaxie asked, "Did you start a fight somewhere?"

"No! I-I just can't tell you."

Jaxie was becoming livid, and she didn't take well to being mad. She didn't take well to seeing her older brother hurt. She struggled to comprehend what he could have done to someone for them to do this. Aiden wasn't the type to get in trouble. He didn't get involved in much for anyone to have a reason to get upset with him. The truth needed to come to light, but Aiden wasn't breaking. She went for a different approach to get the answer. Taking a seat on the bed, she looked at her brother. They were close, they always had been. They told each other everything.

Someone hurt the person she considered her best friend and she wasn't about to let that go so easily. "Aiden, please talk to me. Who did this?"

Aiden looked up at her and could see the hurt in her eyes. She wanted to fix this right now. How could he tell her it would never be fixed? He had messed up. Very badly. He messed up so bad it wasn't going to go away, ever. She may even want to knock his head loose after she hears about everything. Then again, he didn't want her to hear it from anyone else. She'd get the worst impression of it that way, and he couldn't risk losing her, too. It was bad enough he already lost the person who caused all this.

-2-

Three months earlier

Aiden Cooper was in a panic. He hadn't comprehended what just happened. Maybe it was a dream. He begged for it to be a dream, or rightfully a nightmare. There was no telling how to handle it if it were reality. He was truly lost in what to do.

"Okay, okay, okay," he said to himself, running his hands through his hair. "Don't freak out. Just take a breath and figure out your next step."

Taking his own advice, he closed his eyes, stood still, and slowly inhaled. His mind had to get straight if he was going to fix this. He had to be rational. "It's not what you think it is. It is not that." He slowly let the air out. Even with the self pep talk, Aiden couldn't seem to decide on a

5

logical move. He needed some help. He knew one person he could call who may be able to soothe his worries. Gripping his phone harder than he intended to, Aiden dialed the number and waited for the answer. Each ring seemed to go through his ear slower than usual.

"Hello?" a voice answered on the other end of the call. It was Aiden's best friend, Brett Glenson.

"Hey." Aiden felt his fingers ache as he grasped his cell phone, talking in a low voice like he had a secret. He was getting himself worked up and tried to hide it.

"What's up?" Brett asked, noticing the tone coming from his best friend. "Are you okay?"

"Yeah, I was just...well, I was going to ask..." Aiden sighed. "No, I'm not...I'm not okay at all. Can you come over? I know it's late, but I need someone to talk to. I need someone to come calm me down."

"Yeah, yeah sure. Want me to bring anything?"

Aiden groaned, "How about some whiskey?"

"Done. Be there soon."

As soon as the beep signaled the end of the call, Aiden let his phone fall to the couch. There was another person he should be trying to call, but he knew his attempts would be ignored. He immediately felt bad for asking Brett to come over, but he didn't know what else to do. Sitting in silence was only going to drive him mad.

It wasn't long before there was a knock at Aiden's door. His and Brett's apartment buildings were close to each other, and the liquor store was right between them.

"Hey," Brett said as he walked in, placing a case of beer and a bottle of whiskey on the counter. Aiden and Brett had been best friends since middle school when Aiden's family had moved from Colorado to Minnesota. At twenty-six, they were as close as ever and even had the same job. They were bartenders at RN's Bar and Grill where they have worked since their junior year of high school when they'd been hired to do grunge work around the place. Brett had become the manager who now runs the bar. They were both good-looking guys too, which brought in a good crowd every night they worked. Aiden was more mysterious in his appearance with short black hair and a goatee, and dark eyes that anyone could get lost in. Brett was the celebrity type of attractive with blond hair and light blue eyes, and a more social personality. He could hold longer conversations with customers and make friends with anyone. Aiden was quieter. He couldn't help but blame that characteristic of his for what had happened today. It could be part of the reason things ended the way they did. Being "the quiet type" didn't always come off as very manly.

As Aiden walked into the kitchen, he snatched the bottle of whiskey. "Thanks for this."

"No problem." Brett watched as Aiden grabbed a glass from the cupboard and filled it with the liquor. "Don't you want ice?" Aiden answered the question by taking a quick drink of the whiskey, feeling the liquid tighten his chest. "Wow, alright. It must have been a bad day. What's going on?"

"I don't know. I'm sorry for making you come over like this." Aiden reached into his freezer and grabbed a few ice cubes before going for his second serving of whiskey.

"Well, you seemed off. Did something happen today?" Brett asked, opening a beer. Aiden responded by strolling into the living room and slamming onto the couch. He began swirling his drink, making the ice clatter against the glass. Brett made his own way into the living room and took a look around. The atmosphere was uneven and could make anyone feel on edge. It wasn't hard for him to begin to put the pieces together and start to get an idea of what may have happened, but he didn't want to believe it. "Where's Courtney?"

Aiden took a long sip of his drink nearly emptying the glass again. "Do you believe in that theory that if you drink enough the alcohol will just burn your feelings away and you won't care anymore?"

Brett stared at Aiden, getting the vibe of what was about to come out of tonight. "Where's Courtney?" he repeated.

Aiden waved his hand around the room, "Gone."

"What do you mean gone?"

Getting up from his spot, Aiden clutched his drink as he marched down the short hall and opened the doors to the bedroom and bathroom. "She ceases to be here."

"She's actually gone? Like gone gone?"

"That's what gone means," Aiden said softly, leaning against the wall and looking down to the floor.

Brett was in disbelief as he slowly sank into the armchair. It was understandable for him to be in such shock. Aiden and Courtney had been in a relationship for nearly five years and had moved in together a year ago. They both talked about the rest of their lives like it was clearly in the cards for them, so her leaving was comparable to a head-on collision for Aiden.

"I don't understand," Brett went on. "What happened? Have you guys been fighting lately? Maybe she just needed to get away for a couple days."

"Nope. No fighting at all. I have no idea what happened. I really don't."

"Well, okay. Then take me through what went on today."

Aiden glanced at the clock. Courtney had only been gone for three hours now, but it felt like three years. He checked his phone for the thousandth time, but there were no messages or calls from her.

"I got home from work and she had a lot of her things packed up. I asked her what was going on and she told me that she decided this wasn't what she wanted anymore."

"What wasn't what she wanted?"

"Me. Us."

"Why?"

"I have no idea, Brett. I kept trying to figure it out, I kept asking her, but she wouldn't give me an exact reason. She was just...she was just done."

Brett didn't say anything. He just stared at the beer in his hand as he had no idea how to fix this. He could sense Aiden barely hanging on, though, so he had to try and do something.

"Aiden," Brett shook his head, "I'm so sorry. That's really rotten of her."

"Yeah, it was. I'm sorry I dragged you over here at such a late hour over relationship drama."

"Hey, that's not what this is," Brett stood up. "This isn't some petty girl drama. This is someone you were planning to spend the rest of your life with. You guys talked about wedding stuff before you even put a ring on her."

"I was saving up to do that," Aiden said, chugging the last drops of his drink.

"What a bitch. Where did she even go?"

"I don't really know. I asked her...well, I'll admit I begged to know where she was going, but she wouldn't tell me. She didn't want me to follow her I guess," Aiden turned away, wanting to hide himself. "I just wanted her to give me some answers. I wanted her to give me a chance to fix it. She wouldn't give me that."

With that statement, Brett knew Courtney had found someone else, but he wasn't going to say that. Not right now. He could tell Aiden was trying to fight the emotions about to fall down his face and wouldn't be able to handle hearing that. Even he knew alcohol couldn't bury the pain his best friend was feeling. "It's all hitting hard right now, ain't it?"

Aiden slowly nodded, "A lot."

Brett stayed over until three in the morning. With the help of the whiskey, Aiden eventually insisted he was a grown man and could take care of himself. Brett willingly went home knowing the drunkenness would knock his best friend out before he could go knocking on every door to find Courtney.

Aiden was alone again, he laid in his bed, but he didn't sleep for a minute. It had been a long time since he had slept in a bed by himself. That was uncomfortable in itself. Knowing why he was alone made it tougher. He'd feel himself sink into a slumber, roll over, and expect a body there to lean against. Once his arm dropped straight to the mattress, he'd spring back awake. Aiden went back and forth with that all night and it didn't phase him when the sun was peeking into the window.

As the morning turned to the afternoon, Aiden sat in his bed, unwilling to get out. His eyes stayed glued to his phone screen, but there was nothing from Courtney. He was begging for something, anything from her, but his expectations were sinking. Even when there was a knock on the door, he strongly assumed it wasn't her, so he didn't bother rushing to answer it. The knocking persisted. Whoever it was wasn't leaving.

Letting out a loud groan, Aiden rolled out of bed. He still felt quite buzzed from all the whiskey, so he knew the hangover was only going to hit him later, and hard. On the other side of his apartment door was his younger sister, Jacqueline, or Jaxie.

"Good morning," Jaxie said as she walked inside the apartment. Jaxie was twenty-one, had long hair that she dyed black, and bangs that hung down over her forehead. She was loud, confident, willing to speak her mind, and extremely protective of those she loved. Aiden often envied the confidence of Jaxie and Brett.

"Morning," Aiden rubbed his eyes.

"I'll make some coffee. You'll need it later."

"Is it that obvious?"

Jaxie laughed. "I know your hangover look."

"Joke's on you, I'm not hungover yet."

Jaxie rolled her eyes as she grabbed the coffee tin.

"What a night you must have had."

"What are you doing here anyway?"

"Wow, I love you too, cranky."

"I wasn't expecting you here," Aiden said, softening his tone.

"Brett called me this morning. He told me what happened," Jaxie explained, pouring water into the coffee maker.

"Well then, you know the answer to any questions already." Aiden sat down on the couch, clearly not wanting to talk about it.

"I don't understand, Aiden. She just decided to leave?"

"Exactly. She didn't give me any type of explanation."

"Had she been acting differently?"

"No. I mean, I hadn't noticed her acting weird."

Jaxie was quiet for a minute, thinking. "Have you considered that maybe she found someone else and just fell hard for them?" Aiden looked up at Jaxie with an annoyed look. "I'm sorry."

Aiden turned away as he admitted, "I had thought about that." He hated to say it out loud. He didn't have to look at Jaxie to know she had a soft look on her face, but deep down she was boiling with rage. "What can I say? Being in your younger twenties is different than being in your older twenties. You want different things. She may have met someone and decided she still wanted to have fun. The idea of settling down and having a family wasn't good enough for her. Maybe it's never what she wanted."

"That's what *you* want though, so, then, you aren't meant for each other. You can't change what you want for someone else. You'd just lie to yourself for her and that wouldn't be fair. You'd resent her."

"I was saving up for an engagement ring, Jaxie."

"Well, it's good you didn't propose. Now you can put that money towards something else."

"It's not that simple!" Aiden suddenly barked, getting to his feet. "Physically yes, I can spend that money on something else. Emotionally no, I can't. There was a lot coming for us, and now I have to just throw those ideas out."

Jaxie sighed. "I know, Aiden. I'm sorry. I know a lot of change is about to come in your day to day life and it's going to be far from easy." She walked into the living room and wrapped her arms around her brother. "I'm here for you though. Brett is here for you. Mom and Dad will be here for you in their own way."

"Oh God, everyone is going to find out and try talking to me about this. Please don't tell Mom and Dad. I'm not ready to go through that kind of questioning."

Jaxie understood what he meant. Their parents were very traditional with all aspects of life, and that included relationships. They made it known that they had high expectations for Aiden to tie the knot with Courtney after their relationship hit the two year mark. Aiden kept Courtney moving in with him a secret for the first six months because he knew the nagging would only get worse. It was a timely process, especially when Courtney came from a much different background. With the way their parents were, Jaxie kept most of her own relationships a secret.

"I won't tell Mom or Dad anything. Either way, you don't have to talk to anyone about anything if you don't want to. If anyone asks, just tell them straight up to mind their business."

"I'm not as good at that as you are," Aiden said, rubbing his temple. The hangover was starting to hit.

"Then I'll do it for you," Jaxie stated. "You know I don't care." It was true. Jaxie wasn't afraid to put her foot down with people or hurt feelings. She wasn't rude about it, but she had boundaries that she wanted others to respect. Aiden thought it was easier to say whatever people wanted to hear.

"I know you don't."

"Do you want me to hang out here? I have the dinner shift at the restaurant, so I got time."

"Thanks, but I just want to go back to bed."

"Are you sure you want to be alone today?"

That word felt like a knock to the head. Alone. Did he even know what it was like to be alone anymore? Aiden groaned as the sunlight became an ache to his head. "Yeah, I'm sure. I'll call you later, alright?"

"Okay, well, come drink this coffee and don't puke on the floor."

"Thanks."

"I love you," Jaxie said, opening the door to leave. "Don't forget to call."

"I won't. Love you too."

As he had planned, Aiden spent the rest of the day in bed. He slept on and off. He'd pull out his phone and scroll to Courtney's number, only being one button away from sending a text or calling her. As desperate as he was to hear her voice, he knew she would only say things that would hurt. He kept going back to yesterday morning before they parted ways for work. What did he miss? Was she acting different like Brett and Jaxie implied? How was she saying things? Aiden couldn't remember. It didn't matter. Whether she was acting different or saying things that should have been a red flag, Aiden missed it. If there was a chance to fix anything, he let it slide away.

13

It wasn't until the evening hit that another knock on the door came. This time Aiden got up, wondering if Courtney came back. She had her own key, but maybe it was too awkward for her to walk back in. His hope was short-lived once he answered the door and Brett stood there.

"Oh, it's just you."

Brett put a mock-hurt look on his face. "And it's just you."

Aiden smirked. "Sorry. For some reason I thought maybe she came back."

"I'd rather be spending tonight with a girl too, but I guess we get to deal with each other."

"That's just fine with me. I'm done hanging around by myself anyway."

"Good, because I thought we could have ourselves a little fun. You've had a girl living with you for about a year now, so it's been a long time since we got to do an actual guy's night over here. I'm sick of my apartment always being the one getting messed up."

"That's very true," Aiden agreed.

"So, here's my beer and more whiskey for you. Get on the phone and order some grub," Brett nudged Aiden. The next couple hours consisted of playing video games and willingly making a mess with pizza and wings. Once their stomachs began to rumble from all the food and alcohol, they decided to step out onto the porch for some fresh air.

"That hit the spot," Aiden commented. "Once I smelled those wings, it struck me that I hadn't eaten today."

"This should help settle it all," Brett reached into his pocket and pulled out a carton of cigarettes.

"Brett," Aiden shook his head, "I haven't smoked in a long time."

"Yeah, you quit for that horrible woman, so now you can have one to settle the score some."

14

Aiden couldn't help but smile as he took one. "It does sound relaxing. I know I'll regret it later, though." "No you won't." Brett smirked. Aiden took a long inhale, letting the smoke fill his lungs. He hated to admit Brett was right. It was satisfying to be smoking after he went through a tough road of quitting for the woman who ditched everything else they had been through. "Has she talked to you?"

"No," Aiden said, blowing out a long line of smoke.

"Have you tried calling her?"

"I've wanted to, but no. I know she won't answer. Even if she did, I know she wouldn't say anything I could handle hearing right now."

"Do you think maybe you should try?"

"No. You weren't there when she was telling me all of this," Aiden fiddled with the cigarette between his fingers. "I don't know why it was so sudden, but she was done. She has been for who knows how long. She ain't suffering either, she's moving on. It may have been sudden for me, but it wasn't for her."

Brett shook his head. "Whatever. If she can live with that, fine. She doesn't deserve you."

"Sure. I just know if she hasn't tried contacting me, then that's all the answer I'm getting."

"Yeah. Well, enough of this sappy girl trouble. Let's go eat some more. Then I'll kick your ass in some more games and pass out on your couch."

It had gotten late and the two men slouched on the couch, the drunken words beginning to spill out.

"I think I'm going to feel better tomorrow. I can move on just fine," Aiden slurred.

Brett shook his head, knowing that was the alcohol talking, not logic. "I mean, if you can keep the whiskey flowing all the time, you'll feel great."

"I can't just sit and cry all the time. That just gives her satisfaction that I'm hurting."

"Well, I don't know about that. I don't think she cares either way." Aiden was quiet as he stared into his glass. The ice was almost melted, watering down the liquor that was keeping him leveled. "I think you should go to bed."

"Yeah, I should. Thanks for coming over tonight, Brett. It means a lot for you to be in my life."

"Of course, man. But that's all the sappiness I'm allowing for today," Brett chuckled as he began spreading himself across the couch. He let his legs settle onto Aiden's lap, indicating he would be asleep in seconds.

"Alright, alright." Aiden slowly got up, heading down the hall. "Here's to another painful morning tomorrow."

"It'll be worth it," Brett muttered.

-3-

The rest of the weekend was mostly a blur for Aiden. He worked on Saturday and Sunday which helped pass some time. That was all he could really recall from those days as he mostly stayed in bed when he wasn't working. As the first week as a newly single man went on, he began smoking and drinking a lot. Courtney never called, and she hadn't gone back to the apartment. Aiden hoped each day would help push her away, but he felt everything was just being shoved in his face instead. He kept going back to that day and attempted to answer his own questions, but he wasn't satisfied. He really felt like he had meant nothing to her. To top it off, it was becoming difficult to be alone and let his mind wander, so he spent any time off work with Brett.

Watching Aiden sulk at his apartment wasn't cutting it for Brett. He would try to get Aiden to go out for some sort of distraction, but he struggled to have the desire to leave for anything other than work. It was bringing Brett down. All he wanted was to help Aiden get through this rough patch. It wasn't going to be a quick fix, though.

Friday was a weird day. For some reason, everything was hitting Aiden extra hard. He was feeling angrier, more anxious, and would cry without warning. There was a feeling hitting him that he was truly at his rock bottom. Everything he had imagined for the next sixty years was being forcibly rewritten and it was making him feel uncomfortable. His stomach was torn between begging for food and wanting to throw up anything that entered. Whenever he tried to relax, his body couldn't manage to sit down for a second. Anytime he tried, his fingers began moving and he felt the need to grab something and mess with it. His body didn't want to stop being in motion. He couldn't figure out what was going on with him or how to stop it.

From the direction the day was going, Aiden was feeling rather sick. He didn't want to call out of work, though, as he could use the distraction. He stood in his kitchen leaning against the counter, thinking about staying home versus going to work, when things suddenly became a rush. Out of nowhere, Aiden felt like he had to get out right now. The apartment walls felt like they were closing in on him. His chest was sinking in and staying in. There was a dense pressure against his lungs. Something was wrong. As he hurried to the door to leave, his knees got weak. His muscles were giving in and he wouldn't be standing much longer. Aiden placed his hands against the door for guidance as he slowly sank to the floor. He couldn't breathe. His eyes watered from unclear pain. He looked up the lining of the door to get to his escape, but the handle seemed too far away. Instead of reaching upward, Aiden turned himself around and leaned against the door. He looked around but couldn't get his eyes to focus on anything. Color appeared to be fading from the room. The shapes of his furniture began blending together and he couldn't make out anything around him.

There was too much going on for Aiden to keep up with. Slamming his eyes shut, Aiden tried to focus on his breathing. He had to manage one breath before he went mad. Keeping himself still, Aiden counted to three, and forced himself to take a deep breath in. It did not feel like the simple task he had been doing his entire life but he managed it. That breath helped Aiden calm down enough to open his eyes. He looked around and saw the apartment back to normal. The color wasn't running and his furniture was still. There was no explanation for what happened and he didn't dare wait around to figure it out. Scurrying to his feet, Aiden flung the door open and got out.

Walking into RN's and seeing Brett behind the bar wasn't as relaxing as Aiden would have hoped. It only caused the anxious feelings to rise, and he was unsure how to handle it. This was unknown territory. He tried to have faith that mixing drinks and hearing rowdy talk and laughter would calm his nerves once the night got going. Aiden didn't want to talk about what had just happened, and thankfully Brett was too busy with the mindless small talk of customers to notice that anything was amiss.

As Aiden expected, the night started picking up once the game came on. It was getting close to the colder season, so they were expecting weeknights to get busier with the multiple sports happening. It was always the best time of year for Aiden and Brett to make extra cash.

Unfortunately, Aiden found he was wrong about work being a distraction. The thoughts became worse, the discomfort turned to pain, and the anxiety was knocking at his head. He wasn't hiding it well either. His usual quick wits at making drinks from memory were now taking time to remember. Aiden knew Brett had noticed because his friend was jumping in more than usual before Aiden could mess anything up. When the rush calmed, Brett left the bar to a third bartender and pulled Aiden outside for a breather.

"You are quite out of it tonight," Brett said as he lit a cigarette.

"Yeah, I know. I'm sorry."

"What is it?"

"It's just been a really bad day," Aiden admitted.

"How?"

Aiden couldn't try to lie if he wanted to. He began pacing as the words raced out of his mouth. "My mind has just been running all day. My stomach has been in knots, and even when I think they can't possibly get any tighter, they tighten up and squeeze my insides. I don't know whether to eat or throw up. I wanted to lay down and sleep, but I couldn't shut my mind off. I couldn't stop moving either. I had to be up and doing something, anything all day long. My chest felt like it was under constant pressure, and when I couldn't find the room to get a breath, I fell apart. I collapsed and lost it. It was...my God, it was an awful day and I don't even know what was actually going on and—"

Brett stopped Aiden in his path. He tossed his cigarette aside and placed his hands on Aiden's shoulders. "Aiden, breathe."

"What?"

"Slow down. Breathe."

Aiden did as he was told and took a slow breath in, then let it out. It was still crazy to him to think back to earlier when his body seemed to have forgotten *how* to breathe.

"Better?"

"A little," Aiden nodded.

Brett squeezed Aiden's shoulders and let go. "Good, now I want you to go home."

"Huh?"

"Go home. No offense, but you're not helpful tonight."

"Come on, Brett, I'm fine."

"No, you're not. I want you to go. Henry and I got the rest of tonight fine."

Aiden shook his head. "Look, I appreciate your concern, but I don't want to be alone the rest of the night. I was looking forward to work tonight just to be out."

Brett lifted his wrist to check his watch. "Okay look, the game will be over soon and I'll come over. I can have Henry take over and I'll come in early tomorrow to catch up on my stuff. We can talk when I come by, alright?"

Aiden knew he was defeated. He didn't want to admit how terrified he was to go back to his apartment. He was afraid his feelings could end up in an ugly episode like earlier. There was no more room to argue, though, and he turned towards the parking lot to leave. He hoped the knowledge of Brett being over later would make the time go a little faster.

"Promise you'll come by?"

"I promise."

Even with that commitment, Aiden couldn't get himself to drive home. His hands kept turning the steering wheel down another road, getting further away. It was keeping his head calm for the time before Brett would be by. It wasn't until he figured Brett had to be heading out that he drove back to his apartment. As Aiden opened his door, he peeked inside with half-closed eyes. Everything seemed to be in place. He was able to breathe fine.

"You're still up."

Aiden jumped as he turned and saw Brett behind him. "Oh, hey."

"What are you doing out here?"

"Um," Aiden pushed his door open all the way and took a small step inside. "Nothing. I just got back is all."

"Where did you go?" Brett asked, following Aiden's slow pace inside.

"I was just driving around."

The two friends walked into the living room. Aiden sat on the couch, Brett in the armchair. They were silent for a moment while Brett looked over his best friend. He could tell Aiden was exhausted, but could also see his mind was spinning fast.

"How was the rest of the shift?" Aiden asked, trying not to make it obvious he was looking around the apartment like it was new. However, he was looking for anything unusual. Something that would prove he wasn't imagining the earlier events. If he did tell Brett about it, he didn't want to appear too crazy.

"It was fine. Busy without you there, but it was also smoother."

"I'm sorry."

"Don't be sorry. It was just an off night for you."

"Yeah."

"What are you doing?"

"What?"

"You keep turning and looking around. Did something happen before I got here?"

"No, no. Sorry, it was just a bad day, so I was...I was having a hard time coming in here."

"Talk to me, Aiden."

"About what?"

"You know about what."

"I already told you everything."

"Well...how are you feeling about Courtney right now?" At that question, Aiden repositioned himself on the couch so he wasn't facing Brett. "Hmm?"

"I miss her. I thought I was mad enough to not, but I do."

"What else?"

"Come on, Brett."

"No, I want you to keep going and get everything out. You have a lot going on inside of your head, so let's do this. Let's get it done with. Spill everything."

Aiden sighed, trying his hardest to keep the tears away. He thought he had cried all his tears, but there were still some threatening to be seen. "I...do miss her."

"I don't doubt that. What else do you feel?"

"Sad."

"Obviously."

Aiden didn't say anything else. He didn't want to show more weakness. By anyone else, he was sure he'd be told his reactions were coming off as ridiculous.

"Aiden, I want you to talk. Say whatever comes to mind. Yell, cry, throw something if you have to."

Aiden took a deep breath, "This might sound weird, because I didn't expect to feel this, but I feel kind of worthless."

Brett furrowed his eyebrows in confusion. "Worthless?"

"Because of how much feeling and energy I had put into my future with her, and it wasn't good enough for her. All of a sudden it wasn't enough. *I* wasn't enough. I put everything into this relationship, and for what? Nothing. How can anyone expect me to do that ever again? How can anyone expect me to put all that emotion, time, or feeling into another relationship? All for someone else? I wasn't good enough for Courtney, I won't be good enough for someone else."

"No one is going to expect that out of you right now. You need to get past her first and you clearly need some shoving to make that happen." Aiden didn't say anything to that. Brett leaned back in the armchair and let out a small groan. "Give it some time, a lot of time, and you could feel differently. This will be a life lesson. For another girl, for the *right* girl, it's going to be worth going through it all again. It'll be effortless."

"Well, now, that's a whole other thing. How can I trust anyone else? If I get in a new relationship, all I'm going to do is question if it'll last, or if a new girl will truly feel the same way about me as I do about her."

"Yes, you will question it. Even after you're completely over Courtney, you'll question any other girl. You'll ask me a million times if you should trust her or if I think she's the actual one. You'll drive yourself nuts. You'll drive me nuts."

"So how will I know?"

"Whoever the girl is that's supposed to be for you, she'll figure out a way to prove it to you. She'll show you the unconditional love you're supposed to get from a significant other."

Aiden took a hard swallow, barely moving the lump in his throat. He was happy to have Brett around, but struggled to feel better. The answers he was giving were hard to accept. He forced himself to keep talking to avoid bawling. "I'm also angry."

"At her?"

"Yes, for putting me through this. I thought I'd just have a couple bad days, but so much of my everyday life has changed. It's hard. It's a lot harder than I thought it'd be. I've realized how long of a road I have, and I don't even know where to start. On top of that, she...she's probably not suffering at all. She knew what her next step was, so she's good to go. I had no time to prepare. She hasn't checked in on me. Nothing. She left me to go through this while she moves on. She's just fine," Aiden turned back to face Brett, "She should've been a bigger person. If she loved me like she claimed she did, she should have broken up with me a long time ago. Once the feelings were going away and once she realized she was looking into other options, maybe unintentionally looking...either way, she should have told me! She should have been honest with me! We could have taken a break

24

from each other and both figured out if we were right for each other or if we should move on. But no. She took a selfish route. She went on and figured out her next chapter in life before ending this one. She didn't see my worth in that little bit of decency."

Aiden couldn't help it anymore. The tears flowed down as he stared past Brett. It wasn't like the little cries he had throughout the day. This one hit hard. His eyes flushed out fast. It was a cascade of emotions down his cheeks. His body shook as his crying became audible. He knew this was what Brett was aiming for. Getting him to talk to the point where he couldn't help but cry. He was a little annoyed that it had worked. But it pissed him off more knowing Courtney wasn't going through anything like this.

Brett stood from the armchair and joined Aiden on the couch, placing his arm around him. "Just let it out. That's going to be the first step to getting better."

"So manly of me, huh?"

"No, but no one else is here to know."

It didn't seem possible, but Aiden depleted himself even more. He didn't mean to, but he fell asleep against Brett. It was a comfort being against him during such a rough time. The rhythm of his breathing rocked Aiden into a slumber his body and mind desperately needed.

The next morning, Aiden turned over and looked up at his best friend's sleeping figure. There was a feeling of serenity he had been reaching for as he stared at Brett. This man had dropped everything and was being there for Aiden as much as he could be. He was being Aiden's rock right now.

As much as he didn't want to leave Brett's side, Aiden got up from the couch and went straight into the shower. The hot water felt refreshing. He could feel his muscles finally relaxing. Glancing down, Aiden watched his cries, worries, and anger begin to disappear down the drain. He didn't care how long he stood in there. It was a rejuvenating moment. But his rejuvenation came to an abrupt halt when he heard an unsettling noise. He wasn't sure what it was so he turned the shower off to get a better listen. Through the walls, he detected mumbling. It couldn't have been Brett on the phone. There was too much conversation for it to be one-sided. Grabbing a towel, Aiden did a lazy dry off and threw on some clothes. The noise was getting louder; the mumbling turning to rough voices.

He walked out and stopped cold in his steps. Brett was up and was face-to-face with Courtney.

Aiden felt himself choke as the feelings came back up the drain and flooded him again. "Wha-What's going on?"

"She helped herself in," Brett said with frustration.

"I still had a key. I was just going to drop it off and leave, but Brett's getting involved," Courtney snapped.

"No!" Brett barked. "You owe him an explanation."

"I don't owe him anything. I broke up with him. That's it. That's how breakups work."

"That's not 'it,'" Brett said, putting air quotes around his last word. "You left him with nothing. You dropped everything you guys had been through and were about to go through. You owe him a reason."

Aiden didn't want to be a part of this. So much time had been spent begging for answers, but now that this was in front of him, he realized he didn't want them anymore. He just wanted her to leave. He did what he needed to last night. That was supposed to be it. He was supposed to be able to move on now.

"Brett, please..."

"No, Aiden. She can be an adult and talk."

"But, Brett, I don't want to hear it."

"He doesn't want to know, so butt out of it, Brett," Courtney said. "I'm out of here. Have a nice life you two." Brett was about to argue more, but the look on Aiden's face shut him up. "At least take all your crap." "I don't want any of it," Courtney said as she walked out, slamming the door behind her.

"I can't believe her," Brett muttered. He glanced at Aiden, and saw he was about to fall apart. "I'm sorry, Aiden."

"It's not your fault. You didn't know she was going to show up."

Brett walked closer and placed a hand on Aiden's shoulder. "Just don't worry about it. Don't let her ruin what you accomplished last night."

"Thanks," Aiden said as he pulled away. "I'm sorry for falling asleep on you. You could've woken me up and gone home."

"You didn't want to be alone. You really needed me here. I could tell."

"I did. Thank you," Aiden said, sensing a little bit of peace coming back again, "for everything."

-4-

Nearly two weeks had passed and Aiden wasn't
pleased to still be feeling as lost as he did when Courtney
had first broken things off. There were times he regretted
not pushing Courtney more for an answer, but then he'd
realize he wasn't feeling as desperate for that answer. He
had to figure out how to finally take that next step to
moving forward, and Brett was ready to be there to push
him.

They had arrived at Aiden's place after an afternoon
shift. They were going to take advantage of having the
evening off and go to an indoor batting cage. During work,
though, Aiden told Brett how he wasn't feeling progress
being made. Brett was now looking around the apartment
ready to throw reasonings at him.

"You know what the problem might be? You're still
surrounded by Courtney," Brett said.

"What do you mean?" Aiden asked.

"You still have pictures of her around," Brett said, pulling a photo off one of the corner shelves. "You need to just trash these."

Aiden quickly grabbed the photo from Brett, "I can't do that."

"Why not?"

The pictures Aiden had around held a lot of memories. Years of memories. Moments and milestones that he hadn't realized were going to be limited. Aiden looked down at the frame he held. It was a picture of him and Courtney from a concert they had gone to when they had just started dating. It was a big night for them. It was when Aiden began realizing his attraction towards Courtney.

"You going to keep them forever?" Brett asked, breaking Aiden out of his trance. "Even when you do find a new girl, possibly your future wife, you're going to keep these pictures of your ex forever?"

"Well, no. I just..."

"You've said it yourself: she has moved on. She's probably deleted every picture of you off her phone."

"I just need time, Brett."

Brett shook his head. "How about just one? Every day you get rid of something that reminds you of her."

Aiden looked at Brett. He wanted to argue but knew Brett's idea was a good one and would help him. "It doesn't seem like she brought any of the pictures with her. She only packed up her personal belongings. Even when she came by to drop the key off, she didn't grab anything else."

Aiden looked up towards the ceiling, "She didn't pack the necklace I bought her. She didn't even bring the couple of shirts I bought her."

"Exactly my point. Are those shirts still in your closet?" Aiden didn't answer as he kept looking up, hoping the ceiling would cave in. "Jesus, Aiden. It's been what? A few weeks now." Brett began walking towards the bedroom.

"What are you doing?" Aiden asked, marching down the hallway.

"The one thing you're getting rid of today is those shirts," Brett grabbed three shirts from the closet. "You still holding onto these is a little depressing. Don't take this the wrong way, but it's also pathetic."

"I just haven't gotten to it."

"Aiden, this is stuff people do when someone really close to them dies. They struggle to get rid of their personal belongings. Courtney ain't dead. Although it'd be nice if she were."

"Shut up, Brett. You think I'm being dramatic, fine. I'm just telling you I haven't gotten to it."

"Uh huh," Brett shook his head. "Come on, let's throw these in the dumpster." Aiden stood where he was, biting his lip. "Come on man, you've got to do it. You need to start somewhere."

"I just...don't know if I can get myself to do it."

"That's okay. I'll help you."

Aiden watched Brett exit the closet with the shirts. If it were up to him to decide on the right time, Aiden knew the right time would never come. He was hoping he wouldn't have to watch, but he was forced to follow Brett out to the dumpster. This was going to be one of many gateways to the finish line, but that wasn't comforting enough for Aiden to jump on it. Standing next to the big metal bin had an unrewarding sense to it. The shirts may have been lifeless, but Aiden might as well be throwing Courtney in the dumpster with how much significance they had to him. Brett didn't wait as he held the clothes out towards him.

"Do I have to?" Aiden asked, trying for one more chance to get out of it.

"Yes. You have to do it. It won't have the same effect if I do it."

Staring at the clothes, Aiden began counting in his head. It took him a good twenty seconds to count to three before he gripped the clothes, looked away to the side, and quickly tossed them into the dumpster. He didn't even wait for Brett as he hurried back towards the apartment.

"There, that was something at least," Brett said as he closed the door behind him.

Aiden sat on the couch and didn't respond. He wasn't mad at Brett but wasn't sure what to say next. Brett stayed by the door and waited for a minute, but knew he wasn't going to get anything else out of Aiden for the day. He knew they wouldn't be going to the batting cage either. Aiden was waiting for Brett to try and make him talk, but that didn't happen. Instead, he watched as Brett began walking around collecting other things that were Courtney's. He didn't throw anything out. He just gathered them onto the small table in the dining room. Aiden didn't intervene. As flustered as he was with it all, Aiden was grateful for all Brett was trying to do. He was being forceful but understanding in his attempt at getting Aiden to move along.

"I'm sorry we didn't go batting," Aiden said later that evening.

"Don't worry about it," Brett said. "Anything you want to do tonight?"

"I don't have the energy to do anything."

"Well, we can just sit and watch TV then."

"You don't have to stay here, Brett. I can sulk alone."

"You don't want to be alone."

"I appreciate that, but this is my problem. You don't have to deal with all this."

"You obviously need me to deal with it *with* you."

Aiden didn't let it show, but he was happier than he was letting on that Brett was staying over. He didn't mind if he was alone for the night, but he didn't want to make it weird by saying he just wanted to be around his friend. After falling asleep on him the other night, Aiden felt a new comfort level with Brett. He found himself wanting it to happen again but tried to ignore it by accusing the current situation for his emotions.

That night, the two of them were watching TV, not much conversation going on, when Brett's phone began ringing. Aiden listened as Brett talked to whoever was on the other line. His heart sank slightly when Brett said, "Yeah, I'm on my way."

"What is it?" Aiden asked as Brett hung up from the conversation.

"They need me to come to work for a bit. There was a problem."

"How long will you be?"

"Hopefully not long," Brett said as he slipped his shoes on. "I'll come back, alright?"

"Okay..."

"I'm just going to be a little bit."

"Yeah, yeah. I know."

The moment Brett shut the door, Aiden looked around the empty apartment, unsure of what would happen. Earlier he felt okay telling Brett to go home. Now he wasn't so confident. He didn't know what caused the change. Reaching for the remote, Aiden turned up the volume as a distraction. He couldn't keep his eyes focused on the screen as he constantly looked around for the walls to start moving again. He knew that was ridiculous. Walls couldn't move from their spots. They weren't supposed to, yet, Aiden was sure they did that one day. His mind was being far from rational, but he couldn't seem to reason with it. It was alarming how quick his anxiety began attacking him then. The pain came back. Hard.

"What is going on?" Aiden stood up and gripped his hair. Why was this happening again? He couldn't seem to get air down his throat as his body seemed to have forgotten how to breathe again. Time slowed to a stand still, not letting Aiden past the moment. His mind began convincing him that Brett wasn't going to come back and he'd have to deal with his anxiety alone. Questions began spinning in his head. Was Brett noticing the clinginess Aiden was showing towards him? What if he was at work until a late hour and decided to go home? Would he even tell Aiden?

His chest began to hurt from the lack of air. His first instinct was to check the medicine cabinet. It seemed stupid, because he had no idea what would be in there to help him breathe. He should be going to the hospital, but he wanted to wait for Brett to come back; he needed him there. He knew it would go away if Brett would just return.

After shuffling things around and knocking a couple bottles over, Aiden was surprised to find something else Courtney had left behind. Her sleeping medicine. She had had it prescribed to her earlier in the year after going through the trauma from her grandmother's passing. He had completely forgotten about it, but now was glad it was in the cabinet. Quickly getting the cap off, Aiden spilled three pills on top of the counter. His unsteady hands managed to grab one and toss it in his mouth. It slid down his throat a lot easier than air was willing to. Knowing he had taken a pill that might help him sleep off the anxiety seemed to calm his head. It was more reassuring than the unknown timing of Brett's return.

He wasn't sure how strong they were, so he hurried the other pills back into the bottle and put them away. The combination of the anxiety, the adrenaline, and the pill were taking over as a faint feeling came over him, so Aiden hurried back to the couch. He closed his eyes and waited. He wasn't sure if it was the pill working, but he began

33

feeling weak and light-headed. It didn't bother him as he gave in to the oncoming sleep without concern if he'd wake up.

Brett returned and found the door still unlocked, so he let himself in. He found the lights still on, the TV still going, and Aiden fast asleep on the couch.

"Hey," he said quietly, shaking Aiden's shoulder. Aiden didn't move. "Aiden?"

Brett was relieved to see his best friend getting a break from reality. Although, if he was being honest, his concern was beginning to grow. Aiden seemed to be doing better about Courtney, but he seemed to be on edge about other things, but Brett couldn't pinpoint exactly what those things were. Not wanting Aiden to wake up alone, Brett turned everything off and made himself comfortable at the other end of the couch for the night.

Aiden slowly opened his eyes at the bright light fighting to get through his eyelids. The second he realized it was the morning, his eyes flew open. How had an entire night gone by? It freaked him out to realize he had slept the night away without waking once, but he was admittedly glad that the pill did its job and that he had escaped from the panic attack quickly. He didn't find much else to concern over since the pill didn't seem to cause any effects other than a deep sleep. His happiness grew when he looked over and saw Brett asleep next to him again.

"Hey, Brett." Aiden nudged him. "Brett, wake up."

Brett sat up, rubbed his eyes and groggily said, "Good to see you up."

"When did you get back?"

"I was only gone for like an hour," Brett replied.

"Was it only an hour? There's no way." Aiden shook his head. He couldn't hold it together for only an hour?

"Yeah. I came back and you were out cold. I couldn't get you to move at all. I'm glad you got a good night's sleep though."

"Me too."

"Were you okay?"

Aiden nodded as he lied, "Yeah, yeah. I was just really tired."

Brett studied his friend's face. "You're just worrying me is all. The vibe you were giving me last night just made it seem like something was wrong, maybe some other things going on."

"No. I think I'm fine. I'm sorry I worried you."

"You don't need to say sorry. I just wanted to make sure." Brett stood and stretched the kinks out of his neck. "I'm going to go home and take a shower. I got to go into work a little early. I'll see you tonight though?"

"Yeah, I'll be there," Aiden said quietly. As soon as Brett left, Aiden wasn't willing to take a chance on another anxiety episode. He got ready for the day and decided to spend it with Jaxie.

"I feel like it's been forever since we've hung out," Jaxie said.

"I know, and I'm sorry. I thought this would have gotten easier by now, but it's a slow...*very* slow process," Aiden said as he followed Jaxie through the mall.

"I understand. What have you been up to to pass the time?"

"Just hanging with Brett, having some guy time. He's been helping me. He actually made me get rid of some of Courtney's stuff yesterday."

"That's good! You probably needed to do that."

35

"I know I did. I don't realize it yet, but I know I did. He's been spending some nights with me. It's really hard to be alone," Aiden admitted. "I get really anxious and feel stuck."

"What do you mean? What kind of anxious feeling?" Jaxie asked.

"It's mainly my body. I can't breathe or relax. Like last night, Brett was over but he had to run to the bar for something and I couldn't relax after he was gone. I was freaking out. It's, um...not the first time it's happened either."

"What did you do about it?"

Aiden sighed as he formed a partial lie, "I just took some nighttime cold medicine. I didn't know what else to do, so I took it to help me relax and get to sleep."

"So that's why you asked to hang out today? You didn't want to sit at your apartment by yourself?"

"Yeah, I guess so. I didn't really think of it that way, but my subconscious probably did."

"Maybe it's just because of Courtney. You haven't lived alone for quite some time. When does your lease end? Maybe you need a new place where she hasn't been."

"Not anytime soon. I don't have the money to break it early, at least not to make it worth it. I'll just have to bear it."

"Alright. Want to get a pretzel?" Jaxie asked, pointing to the pretzel stand.

"Sure. I feel like you come to the mall just for the pretzels. You get one every time you come here."

"Well, they are the most delicious food."

The siblings got a couple warm pretzels with sodas and sat at a small table. As she ate, Jaxie thought about what Aiden had said about his problems at home. "So, can I suggest something with these panic attacks you've been having?"

"Sure."

36

"If you have to stay at your apartment and it's not feasible to break the lease, which I do agree with you on, why don't you go to the doctor?"

"What for?"

"This problem sounds serious, Aiden. You might be able to get something from a doctor to help keep your mind from...I don't know, messing with you or pushing you over the edge."

"Like what? Get told to go to therapy like I'm a mental case?" Aiden asked.

"No, but there's medications."

"I'm not a crazy person."

"Aiden, people who need help are not crazy. It's not just for people who regularly deal with it. It can be a temporary thing, too. I think you should at least go talk to a doctor and see what they say. If you're not comfortable with a pill, they might suggest something else. Yes, that might be therapy but that doesn't mean you're a mental case." Jaxie stared hard at Aiden with that last sentence. "It wouldn't hurt to ask."

"Maybe. I'll think about it."

"I mean, Brett can't always be with you, and I can't always be with you when Brett isn't around. You'll need an alternative to help you get through the lonely moments."

"It just sounds ridiculous that I can't handle things. I'm a grown man!" Aiden said, frustrated. "It's the fear a five-year-old has for God's sake."

"But it's understandable. You had that first panic attack for whatever reason, and you were probably alone when it happened, so now, anytime you're alone, your mind automatically begins to freak out because you go back to that initial panic attack. It's not an irrational thing for you to go through."

"I understand that, Jaxie." Aiden tried to focus back on his pretzel, but could feel Jaxie's stare as she waited for his answer to her suggestion. "Look, I appreciate the idea. I might try to give myself a couple days and see if my mind settles down. I just didn't expect it all to affect me this much."

"I know, I know," Jaxie grabbed her brother's hand and gave it a squeeze. "I love you."

"I love you, too."

After the mall, Jaxie headed home to get ready for work and all the while the things Aiden admitted to her wouldn't leave her alone. She sighed to herself knowing that Aiden very likely wasn't going to make the decision to get help from a professional. That wasn't okay with her. She was too worried about him and decided to give him a little push by getting Brett involved.

"Hey, Jaxie," Brett said when he answered the phone.

"Hi, Brett, how are you?"

"I'm good. What's going on with you?"

"Well, Aiden and I hung out today. He was telling me some stuff that has me worried."

Jaxie heard Brett let out a deep sigh. That wasn't a good sign as he didn't seem shocked by her statement.

"I've been worried too. Something seems off with him. What did he tell you?"

"He was telling me he's been having panic attacks. He's having moments when he can't function. He's been trying to spend time with you to keep it from happening. Did you know that?"

"I mean, not to that extreme. I kind of caught on there was something going on. He's always wondering when I could go over there and stuff. I didn't realize he was having panic attacks over it. I think he told me about it one time, but I didn't realize at the time he was telling me it was a panic attack. He may not have known it was."

"Yeah, so I'm concerned. I'm even more concerned if there's more to it, but he may not be spilling everything. I brought up going to the doctor and talking about maybe getting on something. I don't know. I just think he needs to talk to somebody. He seems unsure though, so maybe you could give him a nudge to do that."

"Yeah, sure. I think you're right. I'll talk to him at work tonight."

"Thanks, Brett."

When Aiden arrived at work that evening, Jaxie's words about meds for panic attacks were still weighing on his mind and were making him feel down about himself. He knew something was wrong, but he didn't like the thought of admitting he could be mentally messed up. Medication seemed like a simple solution, but it was difficult to accept that he'd need it just to get through the day. It was easier to think he just needed sleeping pills to get a restful night.

"Hey," Brett greeted Aiden, "what were you up to today?"

"Spent time with Jaxie."

"How was that?"

"Fine. We went to the mall. I watched her pick out clothes and other junk."

"Sounds so fun," Brett said sarcastically, stifling a chuckle.

"I guess."

Brett watched as Aiden got the bar ready. "So, how did Jaxie convince you to tag along to the mall with her?"

"She didn't. I called her to see what she was doing and I decided to go with her."

"You didn't just want to chill at home?"

Aiden shook his head. "I wanted to catch up with her."

"At the mall?"

"Sure, why not?"

Brett looked at Aiden disbelieving. "She called me, Aiden."

"Okay?"

"You're in some trouble it seems."

Aiden rolled his eyes. "You knew about this stuff."

"I sort of knew. I didn't realize you were having panic attacks when I wasn't around."

"Maybe a couple."

"You haven't told me about them. I was spending time with you to keep you busy and get your mind off Courtney. I didn't know how bad this really was."

Aiden sighed in defeat, "I'm sorry I didn't tell you. It wasn't really your problem."

"Okay fine, but I think Jaxie is right. You should go to the doctor and get some help."

"And I think you guys are being a little dramatic."

"Are we?"

"I told Jaxie I was going to give it some time, alright? Now can we just work?"

"Fine, but I'm not done talking about this."

Aiden didn't end the conversation out of annoyance. Sure, he didn't love the fact that Jaxie had called Brett about his panic attacks, but that wasn't really bothering him. He had other things on his mind and couldn't focus on the topic. As Brett walked around grabbing materials, making drinks, and socializing with everyone, Aiden couldn't stop glancing at him. He kept telling himself to stop, but he just couldn't.

As the night was coming to an end, all the other employees had left, and it was just Aiden and Brett finishing up and closing down the bar. There was an eerie feeling creeping up Aiden's spine. Flashbacks from his attacks were nudging at his brain ready to strike. And then visions of Brett began flooding his head, alleviating the threatening flashbacks. The feeling of falling asleep against Brett brought chills. It was too much for Aiden to process as he started planning a way to avoid going home alone with the thoughts.

"Do you want to come over once we're done?" Aiden asked Brett.

"It's almost two," Brett pointed out. "Aren't you gonna go to bed?"

"Well, yeah, eventually."

Brett gave him a look, knowing the truth deep down. "Just admit it. You don't want to be by yourself."

Aiden shrugged. "Not really."

"Will you have another panic attack if you are alone?"

"Come on, Brett..."

"Well?"

"I don't know. I hope not."

"I think you should try and go to bed. Just sleep on what me and Jaxie told you."

"Yeah, yeah. Fine."

As they began closing up, Aiden continued to watch Brett out of the corner of his eye. He desperately tried coming up with a new plan to get Brett over. He needed that moment of falling asleep on him again. The thought made Aiden's heart beat fast.

In a quick turnaround, Aiden's mind cut out the fantasy of being next to Brett and began focusing on the apartment closing in on him. The day he sat against the door, begging for air.

"Alright," Brett abruptly said, breaking Aiden from his thoughts. "I'm going to finish up some stuff in the office. You can head out if you want."

Thankfully, Brett's sudden words caused Aiden's mind to stop stirring. He was able to focus on what was going on around him again. Taking a deep breath, Aiden hoped that meant he could leave and go home without any worry. He continued to straighten things up, then he wiped down the counters. He moved some things around. He wiped some liquor bottles. He wiped down the counters again. He straightened things up again. His stomach began hurting whenever he'd look towards the doors, so he kept finding something else to do. Then Brett walked out, locking the office door behind him.

"You're still here?"

"Yeah." Aiden shrugged. "Got caught up in organizing."

Brett walked up and placed his hands in his pockets. "Everything was already done. Just go home."

"Yeah, okay."

Aiden walked out from behind the bar and followed Brett. The lights were turned off and the door was pushed open. Aiden felt his feet stop as he stared at Brett holding the door for him to walk through. Brett didn't appear surprised that Aiden wasn't moving too fast. "Ready?"

The walkway through the door triggered Aiden. He wanted to avoid leaving, but was trying to calm himself to go home. He didn't want to go home and risk having thoughts or...

"Hold on," Aiden gasped out as he turned and ran for the bathroom. He shoved a stall open and got sick in the toilet.

"See? This is what Jaxie and I were worried about," Brett claimed as he entered the bathroom.

Aiden didn't want to admit it, but his best friend and sister were right. This was becoming a problem. He wasn't even having these attacks over thoughts with Courtney, he was only feeling this way over thoughts involving Brett, or more accurately, thoughts of not being around Brett. He just couldn't stand being alone. He was scared to sit in his thoughts and let them run him crazy. He was also longing for those moments with Brett, the ones that have happened and the ones he had only fantasized about. Those were thoughts he couldn't even explain to himself, much less to Brett. Aiden slowly stepped out of the stall, went to the sink, and began splashing cold water on his face.

"Explain it to me. Why don't you like being alone? Do you just wish Courtney was there?"

Aiden looked up at himself in the mirror. How was he supposed to explain it? "Not exactly."

"Why did this start then?" Brett asked. "Why did being alone suddenly start causing all of this?"

"I wish I knew," Aiden sighed.

"Sometimes this stuff happens from deeper issues. You need to get past this. It's becoming a pity party. I'm sorry to say that, but it is. You're going to the doctor to talk and figure out what to do to help. You need to fix this. You need to get on meds to keep you from becoming a psycho with this stuff. That's the end of it."

"Yeah, yeah. Okay, fine. Just give me a sec and I'll be back out," Aiden said, looking down at the running water. Once he heard the door shut, he glanced up to look at his reflection again. He could almost see a new formation taking place. It was making him very uncomfortable.

Aiden knew Brett and Jaxie wouldn't let this go, so he went to the doctor's a few days after his episode at work. He was thankful the waiting room was fairly noisy as he couldn't get control over his tapping foot. A plan formed in Aiden's head that he didn't have to do this. He could leave and lie about the appointment to Jaxie and Brett. Each glance towards the exit door brought him closer to getting up from the chair. Then the nurse called out Aiden's name, breaking him away from his plotting. It took everything for him not to leave the building right then and there.

43

While Aiden talked to the doctor, he only went into detail about his anxiety from the breakup and new living style. He didn't elaborate about the fantasies going on in his head. The doctor didn't make Aiden feel like he was a crazy person, so that made the acceptance of medication easier. They ended up prescribing him two types of meds for his anxiety. He had to take the first one every morning. It was a stronger dosage to help him manage his anxiety throughout the day. The second medication was a smaller dose that Aiden could take any time if he felt a panic attack coming on. Aiden was relieved to hear he was only going to be on the medications for three months and then have a follow-up with the doctor on how he was doing. Even though he was originally against the appointment and use of medication, Aiden was thankful to hear how simple it was to try helping his anxiety. He only hoped the meds would start blocking out the fantasies and rewire his thinking too.

-5-

There were some good and not so good changes that came in the first month on the medications. Aiden took the first pill in the mornings and it was helping him get through most of the day. He didn't feel as panicked when Brett wasn't around. There were certain times his anxiety kicked in without warning, and he had to take the second pill. These were typically moments when he was alone at his apartment in the early hours of the evening. Sometimes it became too much and Aiden would really break and take a sleeping pill to knock himself out for the night. What Aiden considered to be the worst part—but also sometimes the best part—was that his fantasies over Brett hadn't stopped. He didn't want to think about him that way, but it was relaxing to do so.

Aiden had experienced some other noticeable changes, too. He got rid of every last one of Courtney's belongings without fret, besides the sleeping pills. He wasn't waiting for her to call or text him. There was no care anymore. He deleted her number, and had felt a decent weight lift from his shoulders with that last move. His daily texts or calls were now with Brett. The unfortunate thing, though, was that it was now October, so Brett was becoming busier with the bar, including having to work during closed hours. Aiden didn't like getting the busy responses, but soon enough he came up with the plan to go sit around the bar while Brett worked.

There were nights where Aiden would lay in bed, feeling relaxed and letting his head rest against the pillow. Calming thoughts would slide into his head. He'd think about how him and Brett spent time together. Then he'd start imagining what else they could have done together, especially in times of comfort. Sometimes Aiden would catch himself imagining these thoughts with customers at the bar too. Male customers. He was becoming more aware of inner feelings that were starting to surface. Even though they didn't cause panic attacks, Aiden would take a sleeping pill to stop those thoughts if he felt they were getting out of control.

Aiden's head was beginning to spin with his newfound feelings towards Brett. He didn't know what to make of them, or whether to even admit them. Whenever they would hang out or were at work, Aiden was watching Brett more and more. He was finding a spark of attraction in Brett's movements, his facial expressions, his words when he was comforting Aiden through anything. Aiden wasn't sure if he liked where it was all going, so he'd try telling himself that he needed to take some time away. It didn't happen though. Once the morning hit again, he was back to asking Brett what his plans were for the day. It was a rollercoaster of Aiden arguing with himself on what Brett was beginning to mean in his life.

It wasn't long before Aiden could tell Brett was trying to figure out why he was acting the way he was, especially when there didn't seem to be a problem anymore. Brett didn't think it was all necessarily a bad thing, but he thought the medication would have helped Aiden's loneliness. One day at work, he tried to convince Aiden to try and get out to meet some people. Clearly, the intention being to get Aiden a new girl in his life.

"It doesn't even have to be serious," Brett said as he was taking inventory. The bar wasn't open, but Aiden was spending time there anyway. He knew that had to seem at least somewhat desperate since Brett was bringing on this conversation.

"I know."

"You just have to get yourself out there, go out on some dates. Don't even try to look for the potential second date or third date or whatever. Just go with the intention of having *fun*. Girls won't know you're available if you're around me all the time."

The idea that Brett could possibly see what was going on in Aiden's head terrified him. He looked to the floor, hoping one of the tiles would open and he could abandon the conversation. Brett's intention seemed like a ridiculous thing to argue, but Aiden didn't want to agree with him either. "Am I getting on your nerves or something?"

"No. You're my best friend, I don't mind you wanting to hang out so much. You should try and explore other options though."

"I don't know if I'm ready."

Brett accepted that with a nod and changed the subject. "How is the medication working for you?"

"It's been good. I've been feeling better. The nights can get rough sometimes, but I manage okay," Aiden told him, downplaying the true difficulty of the evenings. "I guess it's just hard to tell."

47

"What do you mean?"

"It's hard to tell you're feeling better."

"Why?"

"Because you're still acting the same, mostly. We always have fun together of course. It just worries me that you might still really be struggling but won't admit it."

"I'm not having panic attacks over things anymore."

"Well, I'm glad the medicine is at least helping that. Do you still not feel right being alone? I mean, you're here at work right now, but don't need to be. Any other time, you'd be home on your couch just watching TV or something."

Aiden didn't know how to explain it to Brett. "Maybe it just became a weird habit to not be by myself."

"Maybe." Aiden didn't know what else to say as he fell silent. "I'm not trying to question it all or anything. I just wanted to see how you were feeling."

"Yeah, I appreciate it."

"Keep taking your medication. You'll be back to your old self in no time." Aiden knew he wanted him back to his old self soon. There was a clear understanding that Brett was wanting this done and over with.

As Brett began walking to the other side of the bar, Aiden was unable to take his eyes off of him as he quietly said, "Yeah, I don't know about that."

A few nights later, Aiden was sitting on his couch by himself. He was feeling exhausted as his mind seemed to finally be taking a break from everything. For once he felt relaxed without the help of extra medication. That was a nice change of pace. Maybe too relaxed. He wasn't focused on the images going across the TV screen. His brain was playing its own entertainment. Unwanted entertainment. Not wanting to risk his mind wandering too much, Aiden turned off the TV and went to bed. As soon as his head hit the pillow, Brett popped into his mind. Thankfully, there were no signs of a panic attack coming on from it. Instead, other feelings were hitting harder. He began feeling physical changes coming with the visuals, and he tried to fight them off by thinking about something else. As most guys go through, though, his body was winning over mind. Aiden rolled over to his stomach with the hope discomfort would stop the quick bliss. He wasn't willing to wait as he snatched the bottle of sleeping pills on his nightstand and hurriedly slipped one between his lips.

The sleeping pill didn't help to its usual effect that night. Aiden fell asleep fast, but the dreams he had were unsettling. They weren't about Brett this time. They were about another man, but Aiden didn't recognize him. He may have been someone he served a drink to or passed by at a store. The dream seemed still. Aiden couldn't speak or move, but he wasn't panicking. There was peace with a sign of arousal. When he woke, he felt rattled by the dream. But not because he didn't know who the man was. It was messing with him because Aiden had been in this battle for some time, but wouldn't acknowledge it. He couldn't express the peace and joy from his dream into his reality. He didn't think he could run out and make it happen. Not yet. Not when it was being shoved down as a lie he was keeping from himself. It didn't seem right. Maybe it wasn't but after that dream Aiden realized he had had enough. He couldn't take lying to himself anymore or hiding it from Brett. He was going to tell Brett that night. He had to. Maybe he wouldn't get to have the fantasies with him, but he didn't want to hide wanting that fantasy with another man.

After spending the afternoon at an indoor golf center, Aiden and Brett stopped at the gas station on their way back to Aiden's apartment. He was planning to tell Brett everything, and the closer they got to his place, the more nervous he was becoming. They were grabbing drinks and snacks, and Aiden also grabbed a pack of cigarettes for himself, knowing he may need quite a few of them.

As they walked back to the car, Aiden couldn't help but notice a couple standing outside. It was two men in each other's arms. Aiden was sure it wasn't the first time he had walked by a same-sex couple, but he had no reason to notice before all this. He didn't mean to keep looking back at them while stepping into the car, but he hoped them being there at this time was a sign.

"I can't believe they can just do that in public," Brett commented as he closed his car door.

"What do you mean?" Aiden asked.

"Just being all over each other like that."

Aiden felt that little bit of hope slip away, "Uh..."

"Disgusting," Brett muttered under his breath.

Aiden sank back in the passenger seat. "You don't...hate them, do you?"

Brett turned the key as he shook his head. "I know you're not one to have strong feelings towards this sort of stuff..."

"I'm not?"

"You never talk about them."

"Should I?"

"You really don't pay attention to some of the things talked about at work, do you?"

"I'm busy working," Aiden said matter-of-factly.

"You're not social," Brett corrected.

"This is the type of stuff you and customers talk about?"

"Sometimes, among other things. Why do you think their type doesn't come into RN's?"

"Well," Aiden paused, "I guess I haven't had strong feelings towards it before."

"Right. You should if it's ever going to get fixed. You should care for things to be the way they're supposed to be."

"Fixed? There's nothing wrong with it though."

Brett simply shrugged. "Not unless you want to answer to the big man upstairs later on." He started his car and looked at Aiden. "First they'll have to answer to the people who are going to tell them what's right."

Aiden felt sick then. He didn't usually let these types of things get to him, but he didn't know these were the conversations happening right in front of him. He hadn't even come to terms that he broke any rules that his very-religious parents had constantly told him to follow. His parents would recite the Bible's wording of relationships being only a man and a woman, but Aiden never thought much of it before. Then again, he never thought he'd be in this position.

Now he wasn't sure what he was worried about more: Brett disapproving of his new desire, or God disapproving.

Aiden didn't tell Brett anything that night.

Aiden was now getting himself in an uncomfortable situation as more days passed by. It was clear to him that there was no chance of being in any kind of relationship with Brett, at least not further than friendship. He was struggling to convince himself that Brett would accept him that way. Brett had no idea what Aiden had gone through to accept this of himself. He had no idea what Aiden was still going through. There was still joy anytime he got to be around Brett, but Brett still didn't know the deeper meaning of that happiness. Aiden tried brushing it away many times, he really tried, but it kept nagging at him. He even thought about his next move if he couldn't push himself to come out to his best friend. It was always the scenario of being with another guy that Aiden's mind went to. He wanted to make it reality. There would be a brief confidence that Aiden could reveal his new sexuality, but that would get sabotaged by Brett's comments at the gas station. It wasn't long before he wanted to give up on telling Brett at all. Instead, Aiden thought that maybe he could have a relationship with someone without Brett ever knowing.

All of the back and forth battles with himself caused Aiden to become a pro at ignoring his feelings around the right audience. He was close to accepting the lifestyle of being two people: the straight guy around his best friend and the gay guy around potentional companions. But that all changed one day, and without warning.

Sitting on his couch, Aiden had a staring contest with his phone that sat on the coffee table. His knee bounced up and down. He had made the decision that today was the day to tell Brett. He couldn't let another day pass without Brett knowing the truth. The first move was to get him over there, and that was proving to be more difficult than it had ever been.

He sat there, changing TV channels back and forth for a long time before finally picking up his phone. Then he put it back down. He took a shower to calm himself, then returned to the couch. He picked up his phone a second time, held it longer, but put it back down again. That's when he got frustrated. Brett's comments towards the same-sex couple at the gas station were running through Aiden's mind, and that was the chain holding him back. Aiden tried convincing himself that it didn't mean Brett would think any less of him, but he wasn't sure. Nothing he told himself was releasing the mental constraint.

"Five..." Aiden began counting down, "four...three...two..." Before he could mutter the final number, he grabbed his phone and swiped for Brett's name at lightning speed. He didn't want time to think. Once Brett answered, Aiden invited him over for the night. He quickly ended the phone call as soon as Brett agreed. There was no mention that he needed to talk to him about anything.

Well, this was it.

"Hey," Brett said, walking inside.

Aiden felt his heart begin to race. He was surprised he could even mutter out his own greeting. "Hi."

"I decided we needed to do something different tonight, so I stopped at the store and bought a new video game for us to try. We can go back to our middle school days, huh? I think..."

"Wait..." Aiden blurted, not actually meaning to.

"Huh? What is it?"

"Um," Aiden ran a hand through his hair, "I actually...well, there's a reason I asked you to come by..."

"I've been here plenty of nights for the past few months," Brett chuckled, "Now you think you need a reason for me to be here?"

Aiden smiled. "No, no. I just...I need to talk to you about something." He looked Brett up and down. Goosebumps came across his skin. Different reactions that Brett could have ran through his head. He was excited and fearful all at once.

Brett could read the worry on Aiden's face. He set his things down and gave Aiden his full attention. "Alright. What is it?"

"I...I don't really know where to begin."

"Did Courtney call you?"

"No. I think I've pretty much forgotten about her."

"That's good, isn't it?"

"Yeah, it is. I mean, I think about her sometimes, but the feelings have changed."

"To what?"

"I don't know. Instead of being angry or feeling worthless, I just feel...nothing, I guess. I'm not worried about her anymore."

"That's great though!" Brett said. "So what did you want to talk to me about then? Did your panic attacks start acting up some?"

"It's nothing like that." Aiden opened his mouth to continue, closed it, and opened it again. "This is really hard for me."

"Just tell me."

Aiden looked up at Brett. He knew, or least presumed, he could tell Brett anything, but now he was about to find out if there were limitations to what he could accept. "You're my best friend. I mean, we've been friends for a long time. I just went through something that really turned my life around. It was painful, I had bad days, and then I had really bad days. I yelled, I cried, I went through every emotion every single day."

"Yeah, I know."

"Well...you were there for me. You did everything for me. There were so many days I had no idea how I was going to get to the next day, but you'd be here bringing me to that next day. You...you did so much for me. You did more for me than Courtney ever did. You did more for me than maybe anyone ever will."

"You needed someone to be here," Brett said, "of course I did all that. You'd do the same for me. I know you would."

"Of course. Man, you even checked me back into reality sometimes. You didn't sugarcoat everything to make me feel better. You were real with me." Aiden wondered if that was going to come back to bite him now.

"You needed someone to be real with you."

"Yes, I did, but...things have sort of...changed."

Confusion fell over Brett's face. "I'm not following. What does that mean?"

Aiden bit his lip. "Things sort of changed...changed for me."

"Good?" Brett asked.

"That's good?"

"I guess. I'm just not sure what you mean."

"I just...God, this is so hard to explain to you. I...I started wanting to be around you. I knew if I was spending time with you, I'd be happy."

"Well, I knew all that, Aiden. You had us hanging out whenever there was a chance. I understood though. We talked about that."

Aiden shook his head, turning his back to Brett. He wasn't going the right direction with this. "No, no. It wasn't just that. I wasn't just *happy*. I was...pleased."

Brett didn't respond and the confusion on his face turned to a look of being completely lost. He waited for Aiden to continue his explanation.

After a moment, Aiden turned back towards Brett's silence as he came up with another way to expound on his confession. "It got to a point where I wasn't feeling sad anymore, at least whenever I was around you. If I'm honest, it became kind of...addicting."

"Okay..." Brett slowly nodded.

"And I started seeing you in a different way," Aiden began staring hard at his shoes, ready to let words flow. "I became curious about you. I was looking at you differently. I was looking at all...all...guys differently."

Aiden didn't see it, but Brett's expression changed drastically. He became impatient, and got frustrated by what Aiden was saying. "What are you talking about?"

Aiden felt himself jump a little at the tone that was so unlike Brett. He had anticipated this possible reaction, but it still startled him.

"Answer me, Aiden. What are you talking about, man?"

Aiden slowly looked up. "I..."

"Spill it." The sharp words tore right through Aiden's skin.

"Are you mad?"

"I need you to be specific." Brett uncomfortably shifted himself. "What are you trying to say?"

"I saw you differently," Aiden quickly repeated. "I see you differently. I felt differently about you. Hell, I feel differently about myself. I couldn't figure out what it was at first. Then when I thought I had it figured out, I argued with myself. I had to fight with myself every time we hung out."

Brett rubbed the back of his neck. "What is it? I need you to tell me what it is, no bullshitting. I need reassurance that it's not what I may be thinking."

Aiden gulped, "I became more curious about you...as...as a..."

"Hold on," Brett suddenly blurted. "Are you...do you think you're gay?"

"I...yeah, I..."

"No, you're not. You don't just become gay. You're just confused. We'll figure this out and fix it. We have to fix this."

Aiden could sense Brett's rage as he stated the need to fix the supposed problem, but was willing to try talking him through this. "No, I'm not. I mean, I thought I was confused and that everything with Courtney was messing with me, but it's not. I've...I'm into men now. There, I'm just going to say it. I'm interested in being with guys." Aiden said the last part with more confidence. He felt he could redirect Brett's feelings and views if he didn't cower away.

"No! You're not."

Aiden felt himself jump back at the bark. Brett's guard was up and ready to resist anything thrown his way, but Aiden attempted to recover himself as he continued. "I am, Brett! I don't know why you're getting so mad..."

"You know I ain't about that life."

"No, I know that. I mean, I kind of knew you didn't really like seeing guys..."

"You *kind of* knew? You know exactly how I feel about those people."

Aiden shook his head. His voice was getting shakier as he went on. "I just want to tell you everything, alright? Maybe you'll understand. Just hear me out. I was feeling different and thinking about things differently, so I wanted to tell you. I'm not expecting you to...want anything with me. I wasn't going to have this conversation with that intention, but..."

"Of course I don't."

"That's okay..."

"No, none of this is okay! You think I want to watch you do those disgusting things with another guy? How can I even be around you knowing what you're doing alone with guys?"

Aiden's mouth hung open for a second. He was losing his briefly won confidence. "Brett, you're my best friend. Are you saying you won't be anymore?"

"Not if you're deciding to be gay. I don't want to be around someone who is picturing...whatever it is with me."

"I'm not..."deciding" to be gay, Brett," Aiden snapped back, putting air quotes around deciding. "It just...happened. I don't know, after everything with Courtney and everything you did for me, that's just what changed for me. I thought it was maybe a phase with my feelings being all over the place, but it's not. I can't deny it anymore. I just can't. I have to stop lying to myself, and I don't want to keep hiding it from you. I don't want to hide it from everyone."

"Aiden, I swear to God, if you choose to be gay over being friends with me..."

"I'm...not. You're making me choose? You'll only be friends with me if I lie to myself about who I want to be with?"

"You're going to get yourself into a lot of trouble with this, and I ain't going to be around for it. I ain't going to be sticking up for you when you get what you deserve."

"Brett!" Brett ignored the call as he turned for the door. He had made up his mind and was done with the conversation. Aiden couldn't let it end this way. Something was telling him everything would be over if he let Brett walk out. "Wait!"

"Just back off," Brett said, reaching for the handle to leave.

"This is not what real friends do, Brett! You can't just leave me like this!" Aiden begged. "This isn't right."

"Stop talking to me."

Aiden walked over, forcing the tears to stay away. "Brett, please. I'm trying to come out to you and..."

Brett spun around fast, and his fist connected with Aiden's face. Before he could straighten himself up, another blow landed near his eye and he was shoved to the ground.

-6-

"Brett," Aiden quietly responded to Jaxie. "Brett did this."

Jaxie didn't say anything. She was stunned and angry, but she waited to ask any further questions. She left Aiden on the bed and went to the kitchen to wrap some ice. Glancing down, she saw the red spots on the tile. It made her nauseous and livid. She couldn't begin to decipher what happened between her brother and his best friend. No friendship was perfect but for one of them to physically assault the other was baffling. Before going back to Aiden's room, Jaxie locked the door and turned off the lights. There was no way she'd be leaving him alone tonight.

Aiden held the ice to his face for a few minutes before uselessly tossing it towards the bathroom. He didn't bother asking for anything else. He felt like he'd be passing out any second. Jaxie got in on the other side and lay next to her brother. She scooted close and wrapped her arm around him. They went to sleep, not saying anything else.

The next morning, Aiden stayed in bed as long as he could. He knew Jaxie was in the living room waiting for him, but he couldn't bring himself to face her. Humiliation was coming over him and he couldn't talk to her. He couldn't admit what had happened with Brett. Last night was a big deal, though not in the way he had hoped it would have been, but Aiden began to feel like he'd overreacted towards his sister. He didn't have to make it obvious that it was a big altercation. He didn't have to scare Jaxie. The back of his mind was telling him he should've handled everything differently. He should have hid it better. Not just the fight, but being gay. As much as he wanted to let go of his dramatic performance and pretend it never happened, he knew no matter what he said Jaxie wouldn't leave easily. He knew she wasn't going to ignore it.

"Morning," Jaxie said softly as Aiden walked out of his room. "I made you some coffee."

"Thanks." Before she could interrogate him, Aiden grabbed his cigarette pack and walked out to the porch.

"You're smoking again?" Jaxie asked, following him outside.

"I don't know. Brett thought I'd want to have a couple after Courtney left," Aiden replied, taking an inhale of the smoke.

"Oh. Are you going to keep doing it?"

"I don't want to," Aiden admitted, "but I kind of need it right now."

Jaxie nodded. "I won't bug you about it then, not yet." She nudged him with her shoulder. After a few minutes she asked, "So what happened last night?"

"Jaxie, I'm sorry. I know you're worried, but please just let it go. It's my problem, I have to take care of it."

"That's fine, but you're still going to tell me what happened."

"No, I...I can't."

"You can't be serious. We tell each other everything."

Her words echoed loudly in his head. He thought he could tell Brett anything too, but he had been proven wrong. "I am serious," Aiden said, flicking his ashes, "I can't risk what I already risked last night. Look where it got me."

"What risk? You're not making any sense."

"I was being dramatic last night. You came at a bad time. I hadn't had time to calm down and think about it all."

"I saw your face. I see it right now. Brett messed you up pretty good. Now tell me what happened, and *I'll* decide if you were being dramatic."

Aiden glanced over at his sister, blowing out a long line of smoke. "Why did you come over last night?"

"Oh, so now I'm being questioned?"

"I wasn't expecting you."

Jaxie rolled her eyes at her brother's attempt to redirect the conversation. "I had a bad shift at work. I decided to stop by and see you. I figured it'd help me feel better."

"I'm sorry you walked into this instead."

"Now your turn. What happened last night?"

"No, Jaxie. End of conversation. We're moving on."

"Fine," Jaxie said, storming back inside. She couldn't hold in her patience anymore.

Aiden quickly tossed his cigarette over the porch railing and hurried in behind her. "What are you doing? You don't have to leave. Tell me what happened at work."

"Someone is going to tell me," Jaxie said, grabbing her keys and ignoring Aiden's last sentence. "If you won't, I'll make Brett tell me."

"No!"

"Then tell me, Aiden!"

"I can't!"

"Something serious happened! I can tell! I'm finding out from one of you, so you decide how I find out."

Aiden was cornered. He didn't want Jaxie finding everything out from Brett. She didn't need to hear any awful things Brett would say about him, even if she ended up on Brett's side of the matter. She could end up hating him as much as Brett did, but Aiden knew she needed to hear the truth from him.

"Sit down," Aiden said with a heavy sigh. He held his hand out towards the couch and Jaxie sat down in a huff. Aiden could tell she had reached a point of combined distress, annoyance, and impatience. She wasn't happy about his attempt to keep this from her, but she was also really worried about him. It made him feel bad for believing she would hurt him the way Brett had. She didn't deserve him to hide the truth.

"Last night...I called Brett over because I had to talk to him about something. I had to...come clean about something. When I did, he wasn't happy about it. He was," Aiden gulped as he remembered the events of last night, that now seemed like forever ago. "He was really angry with me."

"Well, I got that," Jaxie said, rolling her eyes, "Why though? What did you say to him?"

Aiden turned away, wanting to hide the wave of shame washing over him. "God, Jaxie...I can't have you mad at me too. I couldn't bear to lose you."

"Well first of all, you'll never lose me. We're siblings, and I don't care what's going on. Second of all, you don't know if you've lost Brett. Maybe he's cooled off and..."

"No, Jaxie. You weren't here. You didn't hear what he said to me, you didn't see..." Aiden trailed off as he remembered the look that had been in Brett's eyes. They weren't just full of rage; they had been full of hate. Even after he hit Aiden, there wasn't a smidge of resentment. "You didn't see the look he was giving me."

"As he beat you up?"

Aiden shut his eyes tight. He still ached from Brett's fists.

"Aiden, please. What did you say to him?"

"Do you swear nothing could make you hate me?"

"I swear."

"I'm serious, Jaxie. Think hard, of all the things I could do, or say, or be, nothing could change our relationship?"

"I'm serious, too. I don't need to think hard about that. I know."

Aiden slowly turned to face his sister, "I...I told Brett that something has changed about me."

"Like what?"

Aiden looked at the floor. It was now or never. He just had to say it. He had to count to three and just spill it. "I'm gay, Jaxie."

"What?" Jaxie's tone made Aiden's shoulders sink a little. He hadn't even realized he had been tightening his back up as he spoke. It wasn't anything like Brett's tone, but he still didn't feel good about it.

"You heard me. I said a lot more to Brett, but that was what I had to tell him. I developed these feelings towards him, and then I started checking out other guys. I thought maybe it was just from everything that had happened with Courtney and then the panic attacks and me having this comfort with Brett all the time. But then I...I just finally admitted to myself what it was. I couldn't argue it anymore. I'm sorry. I'm so sorry this happened."

There was no hesitancy as Jaxie stood up, walked over to her brother, and pulled him into a hug. "Oh, Aiden. I love you."

"I...love you too, Jaxie." Aiden squeezed her tight as slow tears made their way down his cheeks. They were silent for a few minutes, just hugging each other. This was what Aiden had hoped for from Brett. He didn't need Brett to try a relationship with him, but he had at least hoped that his best friend would accept him and continue being by his side.

When they finally broke apart, Jaxie looked up at him. "Brett...he really hurt you over this?"

"He said he doesn't associate with *that* kind of person."

"That kind?" Jaxie asked in disbelief. "Being gay is a kind?"

Aiden shrugged. "He said I was just in a weird place, which is what I thought at first too, but it's not. I know it's not. He was trying to convince me I wasn't right in the head or something."

Jaxie shook her head as she placed her hands on her hips. "I can't believe him. That's where he draws the line on friendship?"

"I guess."

"When did you really start noticing this?"

"Well, some time passed after Courtney had left and I hadn't heard from her. I had some horrible days and nights. I was struggling really badly. Brett was there for me. He was taking care of me a lot. And...I don't know...I started seeing the things he was doing as things a significant other would do. He was showing how much he cared for me and I didn't know if anyone else would do that. I doubted I'd ever find anyone to be what Courtney was to me, you know? But Brett made those doubts sort of

64

go away. Then I was catching myself actually checking him out, so I thought maybe I was going through a weird thing with that and I tried taking a few days to myself. That didn't work because I would text Brett anyway. Just having a small conversation with him made me feel really happy. Then, whenever I went out or was at work, I noticed I was checking out other guys. I wanted to talk to them, get to know them. I started talking to guys at work in a way I really hadn't before. I have been spending weeks now trying to figure this out, and eventually I came to this conclusion."

Jaxie couldn't help but smile. "Well, I'm really happy for you."

"Thank you, Jaxie."

"But I'm super pissed at what Brett did. It disgusts me actually. How are you feeling about it?"

Aiden sighed. "I'm really hurt. I feel kind of stupid."

"Why?"

"Well, I guess I just never noticed his feelings towards gay people. There was one night he made a comment towards two guys outside a gas station. I couldn't really tell if he was just uncomfortable or really hated them. I should have seen it though. I should have noticed. He even told me about conversations he's had with customers at work. I'm stupid for not putting it all together."

"Maybe, but it wouldn't have been easy for you to accept anyway. You would have convinced yourself that it wasn't true."

"You're probably right."

"It's wrong though. I don't see how people can have such deep feelings towards it. People have a right to love who they want to love. It's ridiculous to hear about the hate that others are willing to spew towards them."

"I just didn't think this new thing about me would throw all of our memories out the window. I didn't know

65

how I would get through the Courtney situation, but that seems like nothing compared to this. Now I'm worried about how I'm going to fix this. We've been best friends for years."

"You don't know if...I'm not trying to give him excuses for what he did, but just give him time."

"I don't know, Jaxie."

"Well, how did you expect him to take the news?"

"When I was going over everything I was going to tell him, I was picturing him turning me down as a partner. I would have been more comfortable trying out these curiosities with him, so it would have hurt for him to do that. I would have accepted it, though."

"You didn't consider he'd have the reaction he had?"

"No. Not that far. Again, maybe that's my fault."

"No, don't be blaming yourself. Don't be sorry for any of this."

"It's hard not to. Last night, after it all happened, I kept trying to change back. I know that sounds ridiculous, but I told myself I messed up and I needed to stop myself from going down this route. I just can't."

"Then don't. He's the one that's wrong. Not you."

Aiden shook his head, "I just can't believe he could be completely out of my life like Courtney."

"Slow down. You haven't talked to him. Maybe he does have strong feelings towards those who are gay, but maybe his best friend coming out will change his perspective. I know he left a big verdict here last night, but you never know. You may not have lost him."

Aiden understood what Jaxie meant, and he wasn't about to argue it. He was sure he knew the truth, though. "I have a long road ahead of me, don't I?"

"I mean," Jaxie shrugged, "yeah, probably. There are plenty of people who have the same opinion as Brett. I'll be here for you through it though, okay?"

"I know you will."

"Don't let Brett scare you out of how you feel. Don't try lying to yourself. If this is who you are now, then it's who you are. Don't let Brett keep you from telling people or being true to yourself."

"Oh, Jaxie, speaking of telling people...don't tell Mom and Dad."

Jaxie understood what Aiden meant by that. Their parents would not approve of this. Not in the same way Brett didn't approve, but they'd still be upset. They were deeply religious and very old-fashioned. If he was a minor admitting he was gay, they'd be sending Aiden off somewhere to learn of the "righteous ways of life." It was beyond obvious they weren't ready to hear about this, if there was ever a right time to tell them.

"I won't tell them," Jaxie promised. "I mean, I won't tell anyone anyway. That's up to you."

"Thanks. You know, you always hear about how it's lifting for people to come out and tell the world about this stuff. I'm not feeling that way, even after telling you."

"Uplifting, but they all go through some sort of hardship. I'm sure they've all had some sort of Brett in their coming out moments. Just take things slow for now. Don't rush anything or rush Brett, just take some time to yourself with this new part of you."

"I'll try. Thank you."

"When do you work next?" Jaxie asked.

"I work tonight, but Brett doesn't."

"So, you should be okay tonight?"

"I think so. We're both supposed to work tomorrow night."

"Maybe you should try talking to him before then."

"I can try. Even if he won't talk to me, I'll see him at work so we can talk face-to-face."

The siblings spent most of the day talking. Jaxie avoided asking question after question so Aiden wouldn't feel like he was being interrogated. He appreciated that more than she realized. There were moments they were laughing, moments they were angry, and moments they shed a couple tears. It was tiring, but it was also a relief for Aiden to have someone ready to support him through everything. As it got later in the afternoon, Jaxie left and Aiden got himself ready for work. He was nervous. Even though Brett wouldn't be at the bar, that didn't mean he hadn't tried to turn anyone else against him already. Aiden also had the feeling that the world could just *tell*. He had admitted the change in himself out loud to two people, and somehow that made it feel as obvious as though he'd tattooed it on his forehead. Even as he drove, Aiden felt everyone's eyes on him, making their judgements.

Aiden lit a cigarette as he passed the final traffic light before reaching the RN's parking lot. He took a few long inhales to get his nerves under control. He parked his car and sat still for a moment. This was it. He was taking the chance. Turning the key, Aiden felt the slight shake of his car turning off. Silence fell around him and the cigarette dangled loosely from his lips. With one more huff, Aiden stepped out and tossed the cigarette to the pavement, then walked determinedly into the building, ultimately expecting the worst. He got the usual glances, everyone checking to see if he was a customer. No one stared at him or was looking at him any differently. That was a good sign at least.

"Hey, Henry," Aiden quietly greeted the other bartender.

"Hey, Aiden," Henry returned the greeting, "How are you tonight?"

"F-Fine. How are you?"

"Good. Whoa," Henry gasped as he got a good look at Aiden, "What happened to your face?"

"Oh..." Aiden had forgotten that Brett's fist had bruised him. He hadn't looked in the mirror, so he wasn't sure how it looked. "Nothing important."

Henry looked slightly concerned. "Are you sure?"

"Yeah, it's nothing. Don't worry about it."

"Alright, if you say so."

"Have you talked to Brett?" Aiden asked, curiously.

"Not today, no. Why? Is there something we got to do tonight?"

"No, no. I was just wondering."

"Did something happen between you two? Something that brought up that shiner?"

Aiden shrugged. "Nothing to worry over."

Throughout the shift, Aiden couldn't help watching his back. He couldn't shake the feeling that everyone could tell what he had admitted in the last twenty-four hours. As soon as he'd set a drink down for a customer, he'd walk away trying not to listen to what they would be talking about. Anyone's movements made him wonder if they were going to hit him. He felt like there was a billboard outside the bar that said 'Aiden's gay.'

Aiden didn't hear from Brett the next day, and he held out hope, however foolish a thought it may have been, that maybe Brett was feeling guilty and wanted to work things out in person. That hope was crushed, though, by the hurt he felt knowing that Brett was disgusted with him and the fear he had that Brett might not let Aiden through the doors at work. Aiden was petrified to find out, but he wanted to stick to what he had told Jaxie the previous day. If Brett wasn't willing to talk to him before work, he'd make him talk in person. They had to clear the air between them. No matter Brett's feelings, Aiden was hoping that at the very least they could take the "agree to disagree" approach. Brett didn't have to agree with him being gay, but that didn't mean they had to throw away years of friendship over it.

Unfortunately, it appeared that battle was going to be difficult to even kick off. The aura between outside the bar and inside was black and white. The second Aiden glanced towards the bar was the second Brett looked away. It wasn't a guilty type of looking away, it was pure disappointment. The tension was heavy, and Aiden felt it bearing down on his shoulders. Something was telling him to leave. There wasn't going to be a happy ending to this; not today. Even so, something else was telling him not to run away from someone giving him a hard time. There could be multiple instances of that coming his way. That's not how he was going to come out strong in this. He knew he had to stand his ground, no matter how difficult or out of character that might be.

Aiden walked behind the bar to prepare for the night. Brett's back was turned towards him. Some of the other employees looked at them. It was unusual for the duo to not be talking up a storm the second they were together. Everyone could tell something was off. Aiden knew that by the end of the night there would be more than one story floating around about who had messed up his face and the reason behind it.

"Hey," Aiden said, quietly. Brett didn't respond and that scared Aiden more than he thought it would. "I guess we're not going to work things out then, huh?"

Brett continued going over some of the paperwork in his hand.

"Come on, Brett," Aiden said, quiet enough that only Brett could hear him. "Are you really going to do this to me?"

Brett made a quick turn and brushed past Aiden. "Just stay out of my way tonight."

Aiden couldn't believe it, nor did he want to. The disappointment he was feeling got in the way of the sorrow. The sorrow of the truth. He knew that would hit later.

The rest of the night was long. As the bar had gotten busier, Aiden had hoped that would make it easier not to worry about Brett. He was wrong. Despite his request, Brett was the one getting in Aiden's way. He was trying to take complete control over the bar, barely letting Aiden make any drinks or socialize with any of the customers. He knew why Brett was doing this, and it wasn't improving the situation for either of them, or the customers. Even though he was angry, the anger wasn't strong enough to push Aiden to fight back. He wasn't willing to bump heads. It was easier to stay out of Brett's way and work at the other end of the bar.

While Aiden was cleaning some pitchers, he took a good look over at Brett. Those fantasies he used to have weren't coming to his head this time. He knew Brett saw him as worthless now and that shattered Aiden. He wasn't sure he could go on like this. There was no way this was how it had to be. He had to try again.

"We need to talk," Aiden said as he approached Brett, trying to stand tall as he spoke.

"We're busy. Get out of my way."

"When it dies down, we're talking. You owe me that much."

"I don't owe you anything."

Aiden opened his mouth then closed it again. He was slipping back into old habits and was ready to step down. Swallowing his fear, he forced his voice to speak again. "N-No," Aiden managed to stutter out. "If you're such a man, then talk to me face-to-face."

That seemed to flip the switch. Taking the bait, Brett agreed to step outside. Aiden tried to keep his confidence up, but that proved challenging. He tried to remember the guy that had been his best friend for years; maybe he was

71

just scared. Any other time, any other situation, Brett would be there for him. He wanted to remind Brett of all this. He needed Brett to see him as his best friend again.

"What do you want?" Brett snapped. He wouldn't even stand near Aiden.

"Brett, please. You can't be serious about this," Aiden said. "What do I have to do to help you with this? Are you just scared of everything I admitted to you? It took a lot for me to come out to you like that. I was so scared to do it, but it wasn't because I was scared to get hit in the face. I hadn't even thought of that happening in the first place. I didn't expect you to react like this. I didn't know that me being gay was the drawn line for our friendship." Aiden stopped as he felt the air take a turn. He glanced behind him and saw a couple customers standing in the parking lot. They didn't try to hide that they were listening to the conversation. Aiden timidly turned back to Brett, lowering his voice. "I couldn't imagine being this way towards you if it had been you that was—"

"Don't even say it," Brett said, crossing his arms, "I wouldn't dare do that."

"Okay, that's fine. I'm just saying that I must be dreaming, because I can't believe how this is actually playing out."

"Guess you didn't know me as well as you thought you did."

"Brett, come on...you're forgetting everything we've been through."

"Are you done?" This wasn't working. Brett already knew what he was going to come back with regardless of what Aiden was trying to say. Without a response to the question, Brett muttered, "Good."

Brett saying the word 'good' didn't just mean it was good Aiden was done with the conversation. He was also meaning it would be good if Aiden was done trying for anything anymore. That realization seemed to light a little spark to finally push Aiden into defense. "No."

"What did you say?"

"No. I'm not done talking. I don't want to lose you as a friend."

"Are you going to quit trying this whole gay thing? You don't have to do this just because you don't think you can get another girl."

"Damn! You really aren't listening! It's not that! It's not a phase! It's not some crazy thing I'm trying to work out for something else! It's real!"

Brett stared at Aiden, trying to intimidate him. Aiden didn't want him to know that it was working.

"Goodbye, Aiden."

Aiden's mouth dropped. When Courtney had said that sentence, it was a knife slowly cutting through each of his heartstrings one by one. It was happening all over again now that Brett said it. He couldn't believe how powerful two words could be, especially coming from certain people. "That's it?"

"You heard me."

"What about here? This is how it's going to be at work now?"

"I'll make sure we don't work together anymore," Brett said as he walked towards the door. Aiden watched him walk back inside, signaling the completion of their friendship. He stood unmoving, staring at the closed door. It would have felt good to cry then, but he was too dumbfounded to do so. That battle was over and Aiden lost.

-7-

The end of the shift arrived and Aiden was beyond grateful. All of the customers had left. Their interactions with Aiden had changed after his talk with Brett outside. There was no mystery as to how that happened. All the employees were now focused on cleaning and closing up their areas while Aiden was focused on making a choice about work. He knew Brett couldn't get him fired over his sexuality, so that was a safe haven. But work could become extremely awkward if Brett let something slip to the other bartenders. Although, maybe none of the others would care and would be on Aiden's side. That might mean work could still be manageable. On the other hand, what if the other bartenders or customers became uncomfortable around him and wondered if Aiden was checking them out? What if they thought of him as some animal who couldn't control himself? Even if Brett couldn't fire him over this, he could still stir the pot and say horrible things. Aiden knew he would get his answer soon enough, but he really hoped it wouldn't make him want to quit. He had been there for so long; it was like a second home, a second family.

Aiden tried distracting himself as he walked into the back to count liquor bottles. The biggest favor he could do for himself right now was to finish his work and get out of there. He began moving bottles, taking stock of what was there. He hadn't heard Brett come up behind him. He was nudged forward and dropped a bottle of tequila, smashing it all over the floor.

"Clean it up," Brett said. Aiden bit his tongue as he grabbed a broom and dustpan. Maybe that was his answer right there. If he were about to be harassed at work, there was no way he could safely stay. He wasn't sure how far Brett was willing to go. Once the glass was cleaned up, Aiden grabbed a mop to wipe up the liquor.

Brett walked by again and commented, "Don't let that happen again."

Aiden stared at Brett in shock. Brett had sought *him* out in the back room, not the other way around. He shook his head in disappointment and turned back to his mopping. "Leave me alone."

"Don't talk back to me."

That was it. Aiden was done. He dropped the mop, walked up to Brett and shoved him. "You're not going to talk down to me, Brett. The next time you make me drop something, you're going to clean it up." He had never treated Brett like this before and Aiden could feel the regret as the words left his mouth. Even though he was trying to stick up for himself, he felt he was the one in the wrong.

Brett did a quick turn, grabbed Aiden by the shirt and pulled him up close, their faces inches from each other. "Listen to me because I'm only going to say it once. I told you I don't associate with your type. They're not worth anything because they are doing it the wrong way. A lot of people are going to think you're trash now. You keep your mouth shut if you know what's good for you."

Letting go of Aiden's shirt, Brett gave a shove and watched him fall to the floor.

"What century do you live in?" Aiden asked. "How can you feel that way?"

"Did I stutter?"

Aiden couldn't say anymore. The tears were threatening to take over, but he wasn't going to give Brett that satisfaction of seeing them. He hurried to his feet and stormed out, refusing to take a look back. The drive home was a blur. He slammed his brakes when he reached his parking spot and rushed inside his apartment. His lungs were expanding as much as they could, but the air wasn't flowing. Collapsing to his living room floor, Aiden began screaming. He didn't like that Brett and the hate was getting control over him like this.

"How does anyone do this?" Aiden cried to himself. "Why is this happening to me?" Aiden believed coming out was the way for him to start moving forward, to truly start a new life. Now he felt he was being punished. He was starting to believe he had committed a major sin and God was going to use the people in his life to punish him, showing him he couldn't truly be happy this way.

There was no telling when, or if, his cries would cease. He had endless questions and no answers. He wanted to know what his future would hold if he kept treading on this path. There was no telling, and he didn't know if he was prepared to take the risk. Aiden took his stronger anxiety medicine for the second time that day and popped a sleeping pill. He needed to shut down his mind for the rest of the night.

There was a light musical tone trying to get him out of the deep slumber. Aiden woke up to the sound of his phone ringing. He felt woozy as he rubbed at his eyes. Taking a strong anxiety pill and a sleeping pill left an unsettling feeling in his stomach. When he answered his phone, his boss, the owner of RN's, was on the other end calling him in to talk. It was no secret what it was going to be about. There was the consideration of not showing up and never returning there again. It sounded favorable in that moment, but Aiden knew that would have been a bad idea. He started to consider that maybe talking to the boss meant things might improve for him. Maybe he could tell his boss what happened and he'd enforce a zero tolerance for the harassment. Maybe Brett would be fired.

After his internal argument, Aiden decided he had to go in and see what would happen. He got dressed and headed to RN's, though, he regretted not taking care of the ache crawling around his gut first. There was a fire going on as his stomach hated not having food in him after the drugs it had endured. On the other hand, last night's events were causing a sickening feeling at the idea of eating at all. The unknown matters of this meeting pushed him to smoke a cigarette, but that first inhale nearly caused him to pull over and vomit out the door. The drive was hell. The only element that seemed to put a bit of relief to the internal chaos was that he didn't see Brett's car in the parking lot.

Before going into the office, Aiden walked behind the bar to get a cup of water. It was the only thing that could soothe his stomach. The last thing he wanted to do was get sick while discussing last night, which was highly possible.

"Morning, Aiden."

"Good morning, Travis," Aiden greeted the owner as he entered the office.

"Take a seat."

Aiden slowly sat down. Since he wasn't there, Aiden had to assume Brett must have told Travis everything, at least everything from his point of view.

"Brett talked to me about an altercation last night," Travis began.

"Well, yeah..."

"Do you want to tell me what happened?"

"He made me drop some liquor and then he shoved me to the ground. He had been ignoring me all night and was making the whole shift difficult for me."

"He told me something's come up and it appears it's going to affect things around here beyond my control," Travis explained. "Not only that, but I'd guess you don't feel comfortable here after last night either. I think the easy decision is you leaving. It's only best for all parties involved if you willingly quit."

That was not how Aiden pictured this conversation going. There had to have been follow-up questions, but none were asked. A verdict was already made. It was obvious it had been made no matter what Aiden said about the situation. That's why Brett wasn't there. "Wh-What? But he started this. *He* shoved me."

"Aiden, I'm sorry, but I heard all that I needed to hear. Brett runs the bar. He makes the call, runs it by me to make it official, and that's it. The decision has been made. Brett made it clear it wasn't going to work out if you were employed here anymore. He's sure it's not safe for you here, and quite frankly, customers just don't come here for that," Travis went on as he folded his hands on the desk, not defining what he meant by 'that.' "I'm sorry you have to end your career like this. You were great at your job and I hope you find what you're looking for. Just give me some time to finalize things and I'll mail you your final check."

"I can't believe...I don't even get to tell you my side of it?" Aiden asked.

"Aiden, whatever your side is, it won't change anyone's mind. Now please, let's leave on peaceful terms."

This didn't feel like peaceful terms, but there was nothing he could do now. He didn't want to argue and possibly have Brett become part of the conversation. Aiden stood up, placed his hands in his pockets, and left.

"That's discrimination," Jaxie said. "They can't fire you because of your sexuality."

"I don't know if I have an argument. Brett made a big issue about it, but I can't really prove Travis fired me over it. He didn't say anything about it. For all I know, Brett said I started the fight over something else."

Jaxie crossed her arms. After his conversation with Travis, Aiden had driven over to her apartment. Aiden could tell she was feeling helpless and wanted to fix it. She had always been like that, especially if there was a problem involving her brother. "Jaxie, please relax. It's not like I can't get another job. Besides, I'd probably have to quit anyway. It was going to become toxic one way or another. He probably would've turned the other bartenders against me or something. I'll admit it would have been more gratifying if I had quit on my terms."

"It's just not fair."

"I know, but I'm trying not to dwell on it, alright? I just can't believe he took it this far. Gays have the right to be married and stuff, you know? I didn't realize there was still so much hate towards them."

"Aiden, just because they get the rights doesn't mean everyone changes their minds about them. You get what I'm saying?"

"Yeah, I guess you're right. Brett's just...I mean, he's made some remarks about them, but I didn't realize deep down he had such a passionate hatred for them. He really believes they have no worth."

"Well, he's never had a reason to show you his true feelings, not to that extent."

"Or I was being naive about it."

Jaxie bit at her nails, clearly fighting the urge to go confront Brett herself. "Are you upset about the job?"

"Of course I am! I've been revisiting all our memories there together, along with every other memory we've had, and it's killing me that this is it. It's over. It all is. Two very important people in my life just aren't a thing anymore," Aiden said, shaking his head.

"For what it's worth, I'm still here. I always will be."

"I know. I appreciate that more than you know right now. I need to try and not think about Brett. I don't want to revisit where I was a couple months ago with those panic attacks."

"And I don't want to see you like that again. Just try not to worry about him. Maybe he'll come back into your life and maybe he won't, but don't focus on that. Take this day by day, and keep up on your medication," Jaxie suggested. "Tomorrow you can focus on looking for a new job."

"Yeah. You haven't told Mom or Dad, have you?"

"No, of course not. Why?"

"I just haven't heard from them in awhile."

"Aiden, you only came out a few days ago."

Aiden thought for a moment on the past three long days. "I guess you're right. Those days sure felt like years."

"I haven't heard from them either. That's not really unusual, though. You're just overthinking it because you know what you're hiding from them."

"Yeah, I know."

"Maybe we should go see them for dinner tonight?" Jaxie offered.

Aiden groaned. "I don't know if I want to." Aiden loved his parents. He knew Jaxie loved them too. They were just hard to be around, regardless of Aiden's new lifestyle he'd have to admit someday. "I have to tell them about Courtney, because she won't be with us."

"Just leave it at that. You don't have to tell them you're gay, you don't even have to tell them you lost your job. They'll only pry about as much as you tell them. Besides, it would be easier for you to tell them little by little instead of one day having to spill ten life changes at them. And I do mean easier on you, not them."

Aiden sighed. "Alright, I guess it couldn't hurt." He paused for a moment, staring at his feet. "Jaxie, do you think God is punishing me? For the medication and for being gay?"

Jaxie shook her head. "No, of course not! Some people may tell you otherwise, like everyone else in our family, but I don't like their version of God. Him being some sort of punisher doesn't sound like love."

"I hope I can believe that soon."

The siblings called up their parents and mentally prepared themselves for an evening with them.

"Aiden!" Lauren Cooper smiled at her two kids standing on the porch, "Jacqueline! I'm so glad you both called for dinner tonight."

"Hi, Mom," Aiden said as he walked inside the house.

"Hey, Mom," Jaxie smiled, giving her mom a kiss on the cheek.

"We are just getting the table set so go ahead and wash up."

Aiden looked around his childhood home. Nothing had changed. It never had. As usual, his mom put a lot of time into cleaning and organizing the house, making it presentable. He peeked into the living room before going into the dining room. The couch and armchair were in their perfect positions, the coffee table was cleaned with its items organized, and every decoration piece on the mantle was in its carefully-considered order. This was how the living room had always looked. Every room in the house always stayed the same. The last thing Aiden spotted was the Bible at the corner of the coffee table. Aiden felt a shiver as he looked towards the ceiling, wondering if he was being watched and judged.

Once everyone was seated at the table, Dalton Cooper said their blessings and everyone began passing food around. The siblings knew the questions and conversations about what was new in their lives would begin. It never ended with all of them being happy.

"Aiden, where's Courtney?" Dalton asked.

"Oh now," Lauren sighed with a forced smile, "we could try asking how he is first."

"It's okay, Mom," Aiden said. "Courtney and I actually broke up." That was the easiest he had ever spoken about it.

"What?" Dalton asked. "What did you do?"

"Wow, Dad, how is it automatically Aiden's fault?" Jaxie asked.

Dalton shrugged as he reworded his question, "What happened?"

"Honestly, I don't have much of an explanation. She just broke up with me. It was out of nowhere. One day she decided she was done and wanted to move on to something else."

"That's not how relationships work," Dalton went on looking at his wife. "Kids these days give up so easily."

"I wasn't the one who gave up," Aiden explained.

"You're saying she moved on, so you're not exactly trying to get her back either."

"Dad. She doesn't want me. Why would I try to get her back?"

"You guys put five years into your relationship. You moved in together! You're meant to go through these things with one woman. You're meant to be with only one woman the rest of your life, and she was it."

82

Aiden shook his head as he tapped his fork against the food. "I'm sorry, but she's not coming back. It wasn't my decision."

"Go fight for her. Fight for what's right."

"Dad," Jaxie butted in, "maybe Courtney wasn't right for him. What if getting back with her means Aiden isn't happy the rest of his life? Wouldn't that be reason enough not to get back together?"

"I just don't understand," he went on, ignoring his daughter's questions. "You two seemed so happy all the time."

"I thought so too," Aiden said. "Like I said, it was out of nowhere. I didn't see it coming. I thought we were happy, but apparently she wasn't happy enough."

"Stop," Jaxie said. "You didn't do anything wrong, Aiden. Dad, you could try asking how this has all been affecting him. It hasn't exactly been easy."

"He seems to be doing fine. He didn't call me or your mother about it, so he apparently didn't need our support."

"If you have no support to give then just move on."

Aiden glanced over at his mom at the end of the table. She was quietly eating her food. That wasn't unusual. He felt bad, knowing she didn't like it when Jaxie got into it with their dad. There wasn't any stopping them once they got going. Jaxie got her strong boundaries from their dad, but their views were too different for either of them to give in.

"Jacqueline, you don't need to get so uptight about it," Dalton said. "I asked him questions. Sorry if they were the wrong questions."

"Just move on, Dad. You could ask me about my life."

"You aren't in a relationship."

"I prefer my men for one night," Jaxie shrugged.

"Jacqueline!" Lauren snapped, nearly choking on her wine.

"Don't you dare talk like that here," Dalton firmly said.

"You know I don't like it when you joke like that," Lauren said, "It is very important to save yourself for that one man."

"I know, I know. I am," Jaxie said, winking towards Aiden.

"I'm sorry I've disappointed you guys," Aiden said, feeling uneasy that they didn't even know half of it.

"You didn't," Lauren smiled. "I'm sorry you and Courtney are going through a rough patch. Your father and I will be praying for you to work things out."

Aiden didn't respond to that, and he was thankful Jaxie kept any more comments to herself.

"It's okay," Jaxie said as they drove back to her apartment, "We got through another delightful dinner."

"I can't believe Mom said she'll pray for my rough patch. This isn't a rough patch. We're done."

Jaxie let out a small laugh. "I still can't believe they think I'm a virgin."

"You don't take home that many guys, do you?"

"No, but I do like to have a little fun every now and then. I don't care to settle down yet." Jaxie smiled at her brother. "Now we can check guys out together!"

"Oh stop," Aiden laughed, unable to hide his blushing, "They also believe Courtney and I never slept together, even though we lived together."

"Yeah, Mom and Dad are very, very old school," Jaxie lamented, shaking her head. "So! Do you want to hang out some more?"

"No, I'm really tired. I just want to relax and drink myself to sleep. I got a busy day ahead of me tomorrow."

-8-

The next morning, after a restful night's sleep, Aiden came to the realization he had been worrying too much about what was happening and if he was being punished for it all. That wasn't going to continue into today. He needed a break. The job hunting was going to be put off. He had to treat himself a little, and that was something he hadn't done since the breakup with Courtney. He was going to do that by going out for the night.

The plan brought some spirit to Aiden. He drove to the store and picked out a new outfit. *New clothes, new man,* he had thought to himself. His plan was to go to a new bar that night and relax. Maybe he would meet somebody, someone who could be a friend or potentially more, but he wasn't going to make that a priority. Aiden laughed to himself as he tried to remember the last time he had gone to a bar just to have fun. He couldn't remember when that had been, so he was looking forward to it. Typically, he didn't care to go to bars since he spent so much time working at one.

As the evening drew closer, he got himself ready for the night. He showered, did his hair, trimmed his goatee, and put on his new shirt and jeans. He had no idea where he was going but he liked that. He just wanted to go somewhere new and be around some new people. The first thing Aiden saw when he got in his car was his pack of cigarettes. His jumpy nerves were saying to smoke one before he entered any establishment. The vision of Brett, though, made him pick up the pack and toss it in the backseat, hoping to forget about it.

After driving around for a half hour, Aiden found a place he hadn't seen before. That was good enough for him to check out. It was a smaller place hidden off the main road. It was called The Color Band. Aiden wanted to give it a shot. He had been driving around for longer than he had hoped, and he knew if he drove around too much longer, he would lose hope and go home in a slump. He parked his car and suddenly felt vulnerable. He felt like everyone would know that he was gay and that some people wouldn't be okay with it. Reaching into the back, Aiden grabbed a cigarette and lit it. He only took a few small puffs before shaking it out and placing it back into the carton. Now he at least tricked himself to believe he was relaxed enough to step out and begin walking towards the building.

As he entered The Color Band, Aiden expected accusatory and judgmental stares. No one batted an eye at him. That was slightly comforting and he let out the breath he'd been holding in. There were small tables and chairs spread around, stools at the bar, a small stage that was being used for karaoke, and a pool table.

Aiden walked in further and picked out a barstool at the end of the bar not seated next to anyone. There was a lot of chatter going around. It seemed a lot of them knew each other, or maybe it was just that welcoming of an environment. He didn't know what to expect from the night. The moment he was settled in his spot was when he had no idea what the rest of his plan was. He just knew he wouldn't be ready to try and mingle until there was some alcohol in him.

"Hey buddy. What are you drinking?" the bartender asked Aiden.

"Just start me off with whiskey and soda, lots of ice, please," Aiden responded. Once the bartender brought over his filled glass, Aiden immediately got into it. The chill mixed with the alcohol was soothing, but he couldn't get himself to really look around the place. The longer he sat alone at the bar, the quicker his confidence from earlier in the day had begun to fade. He still felt like he was being watched and the drink wasn't helping to relax him as quickly as he had hoped. He did the typical move of looking through anything on his phone. It didn't work well to force him out of his comfort zone. Out of frustration he pushed his phone to the side. He came out to enjoy himself, have some therapeutic time for himself, but he was struggling to do any of that. If anything, he felt he was being pushed a step back.

Aiden hadn't realized he was having a hard stare down with his drink when someone suddenly said, "Hey."

Aiden looked behind him and noticed that the greeting had been directed towards him. He saw a man taking the stool next to him as he responded, "Hi."

"You've been sitting by yourself for quite some time. I assume no one is sitting here?"

"Oh no, you can have it. I'm here alone."

"Are you new around here?" the man asked. Aiden could tell right off the bat this guy wasn't shy to start up a conversation. Maybe that's what he needed someone to be.

"Not this town, no. I don't live too far, but I've never been to this bar before."

"Yeah, it's sort of hidden away. It's nice when a new face shows up every now and then." The man smiled.

Aiden smiled in return at the man's contagious grin. He extended his hand and introduced himself. "I'm Aiden."

The man accepted the handshake as he responded, "Jack. So, what brings you in here, Aiden?"

"I needed a night out."

"Yeah, that's why I usually come out here," Jack said, holding up his bottle. "Hey, Toby, can I get another beer?"

"Are you here with friends?" Aiden asked.

"Not tonight. Sometimes I just come here for a couple drinks after a long day at work."

As Aiden continued talking with Jack, he started feeling himself loosen up while the tension released from his back. He could also credit the alcohol for that. Jack Blakemis was twenty-eight years old and was a tall man with a strong build. He had brown hair and bright green eyes. Aiden wanted to keep looking away to hide any awkwardness, but also couldn't help and keep looking at those eyes. Not that he minded, but Aiden had assumed Jack was just introducing himself and would move on to something else. He didn't though. He had stayed put, ordering drinks and talking to Aiden. It wasn't until he finally took a close look at the bar that he realized why.

"Oh God," Aiden commented, leaning his head into his hand, "I feel stupid."

"Huh?" Jack asked, confused, "Why?"

"I should have caught on by the name of this place," Aiden ran his hand down his face. "This is a gay bar, isn't it?"

"It's geared towards us queers, yes," Jack laughed. Aiden went into brief shock as that word flew from Jack's mouth without hesitation. "You didn't come in here in search of someone, huh?"

"I..." Aiden slowly shrugged. "It wasn't my initial reason for coming out, no."

"Let me rephrase, you didn't come here looking for a man to sweep you off your feet?"

"Oh," Aiden cleared his throat, "Um, I mean..."

"Shy all of a sudden?" Jack winked.

"No, I'm sorry, I'm not usually this naive about flirting or anything," Aiden said nervously, downing the rest of his drink. "I'm bad at this apparently. Can I get another?" he asked the bartender. "Less ice, more whiskey this time."

"It's okay. Don't need to get anxious over me. Just talking," Jack shrugged, "Want some food?"

"Uh, yeah, I could eat."

"You like wings? They have the best wings here."

"Yeah, sure. I love wings."

"Great. Hey, Toby, can you put on a couple baskets of wings. Extra hot for me."

"Thanks," Aiden said. He took a long sip of his refilled drink before blurting out, "I am gay."

Jack chuckled, "You've had quite a bit to drink."

"I'm sorry. I don't know why I said that. I guess I didn't catch on that you were flirting with me, so I wanted to make it clear that I'm accepting of it if that's what you were trying to do," Aiden explained, "I'm very new to this."

"New to flirting?"

"I guess that's the way to word it," Aiden admitted.

Jack shrugged as he smiled. "Just relax. We're just two guys talking and eating."

As they ate their wings, Aiden started feeling more comfortable. Jack was an easy guy to talk to, and he wasn't doing it in a purely flirtatious way. He didn't make Aiden feel pressured to go any sort of direction with the conversation they were having.

"How were the wings?" Jack asked.

"Delicious."

"I told you. So," Jack sipped his beer, "what else do you have planned for tonight?"

"Oh, I don't know."

"Just seeing if you're going to ditch me anytime soon," Jack jokingly said.

"I really am enjoying this, too. I probably should go soon though. I gotta get up early and go job hunting."

"Oh really? What do you do?"

"I *was* bartending," he said, staring into his drink.

"Really? I think Toby is actually looking for a bartender here," Jack said waving Toby over.

"Oh, you don't have to do that," Aiden insisted.

"It's not a problem. You'd be doing me a favor by them putting a cute bartender back here." Aiden looked away as his face went hot by the comment. It was like hanging out with Jaxie with the quick comments that clearly held no shame. "Hey, Toby, you still looking for a bartender? Aiden here is looking for a new job."

"Oh yeah? How much experience you got?" Toby asked.

"Well, I was at the same place for the past ten years. I started as a host and waiter at sixteen, then became a bartender there once I turned twenty-one."

"Wow, ten years?" Toby asked. "Why did you leave?"

Aiden stirred the straw in his drink. "Just got let go for some reasons."

It was quiet among the three. Aiden could feel Jack and Toby staring at him. He felt like they could almost see the conversation he had had with Travis.

"You can tell us," Jack said. "What happened?"

91

Even though Aiden had become more talkative in his conversation with Jack, he really hadn't gone below the tip of the iceberg. He hadn't opened up about anything personal. However, it seemed Jack and Toby already knew, so that made it easier to tell them about the altercation. Giving a soft shrug, Aiden explained, "Well, I came out to my best friend, or the guy who used to be my best friend, anyway. It was only a few days ago actually. He's pretty much forgotten all about me at this point. We worked together, and we got in a fight. He caused it, but he got the boss to fire me anyway."

"We know what that can be like," Jack said, putting a hand on Aiden's back.

"Why don't you come by tomorrow and we'll talk?" Toby offered. "Can you come around ten? I'll be here stocking before we open for the night."

"Yeah, sure," Aiden smiled. "Thank you. I should head home then and get some sleep. Here," pulling out his wallet, he turned to Jack, "I can give you some cash for the wings."

Jack looked at the cash in Aiden's hand as he took a long drink of his beer, clearly not intending to take any money. "How about you give me your number and we're even?"

Aiden felt his stomach leap and couldn't keep a smile from growing on his face. That was probably enough of a sign that things could be turning around soon, and things did seem to be hitting off between the two. "Okay, yeah."

"Sweet. I'll text you then, and I expect a response." Jack winked.

"Yeah, definitely."

"Have a good night, Aiden."

"You too," Aiden smiled as he stood from his stool. "Thanks, Toby. I'll see you tomorrow."

As Aiden stepped outside, he saw the first snowflakes beginning to fall. The feeling of hope from earlier was coming back, and it was stronger than ever.

Aiden didn't sleep too well, but this time it was for a good reason. He had really enjoyed himself, and he was glad he had met Jack. On top of his good night, Aiden found he hadn't needed any medication to help him get to sleep. He wasn't sure he wanted to sleep. He didn't mind tossing and turning as he thought about the night over and over again. The next morning he got hot coffee in him and was walking tall out of his apartment.

Despite his experience with bartending, the nerves were kicking in. Aiden had only been to one job interview in his life. Skipping out on his morning medication wasn't helping, but he realized that mistake a bit too late. He simply didn't think about taking it with how good he felt. When he pulled into The Color Band's parking lot, he took a few moments in his car to collect himself. A few deep breaths and reminding himself of his skills as a bartender seemed to do the trick.

Toby turned out to be a really nice guy which eased Aiden's self-doubt even more. He was laid-back but professional, keeping the interview about Aiden and his skills behind the bar.

"When can you start?" Toby asked.

"Anytime."

"Want to start tonight?"

"Really?"

"Absolutely. I think you'll do great here."

"Thanks, Toby. Yeah, I can be here tonight."

"Good. Be here at four, so I can show you around and everything before it gets to the busy hour. With your background you'll catch on quick."

"Great. Thank you so much."

Aiden couldn't believe his luck. Once he was back in his car, he pulled out his phone and opened his contact list. He froze as he thought about who to call. He couldn't call Brett. He knew Jaxie would be happy, but he didn't want to tell the entire backstory and he knew she'd ask. He reluctantly decided to call Jack. As the first couple of ringing tones passed, Aiden considered hanging up, thinking this was too odd. Jack easily held a conversation and asked for the number exchange, but he had also been drinking.

"Hello?"

"Hey, Jack. It's Aiden." Aiden drummed his fingers against the steering wheel to get past the jitters. "I hope it isn't weird for me to be calling you, but I was excited and wanted to share: Toby gave me the job. I'll be starting tonight."

"That's great! Not weird at all, I'm glad you called."

"Yeah, good, me too." Aiden shook his head at himself for being awkward on the phone.

"Hey, I want you to come by. I want to do something for you before you go in tonight."

"Oh okay," Aiden said, unsure what he meant. "When?"

"You can come now. I'll text you my address. It's not far. See you soon."

The bittersweet jitters hit Aiden harder. He was excited about getting the job, but anxious about seeing Jack again, let alone at his house. He drove slower than the speed limit, though that didn't help matters, but he finally made it to Jack's neighborhood and found his house. It was a nice little home with a black truck in the driveway. The fresh blanket of snow made the house stand out.

As Aiden stepped out of his car and stood at the end of the driveway, the nerves hit him again. Of course Aiden wanted to see Jack, but those butterflies were flying around his stomach and reaching his throat, making it dry.

Now he was *really* regretting not taking his medication that morning. Maybe that would help Aiden get out of this? The excuse was right there for him to grab and use as his escape.

"No, no," Aiden leaned his head side to side to pop his neck. He fiddled in his pockets and quickly pulled out his carton of cigarettes. "You don't need the pills." Closing his lips around one, Aiden shakily lit the end and slowly inhaled.

"Hey!"

Aiden jumped at the interruption and looked up. Jack was standing at the front door waving.

"Hey, Jack," Aiden replied, trying not to let his voice shake. He took one more long drag before tossing the cigarette into the snow.

"Come on up. I'll show you around. Do you want coffee or water or something?"

Aiden took a deep breath and let it out slowly before taking tentative steps up the driveway. "Water's fine, thanks."

"Cool. I'm glad you were able to come by."

Aiden stopped at the porch and glanced at his feet. Jack stepped to the side, holding the door open. Slowly, Aiden walked up the two steps, looking past Jack and into the house. As he brushed along to walk through the door, he felt his heart jump. There was no turning back now, but he was almost sure he was okay with that.

The front of the house had an office area and stairs off to the side that went to the top floor. Going down a short hallway, Aiden found himself between the living room and the kitchen. The rooms looked bigger than the outside of the house let on, and Jack made them look real nice. "Oh wow!" Aiden exclaimed, taking a look around.

"Like it?" Jack asked.

"Yeah. It looks small on the outside, but you certainly know how to make the space look really good."

"Thanks. You haven't even seen the basement yet. Come on and I'll get you that water. Looks like you could use it."

Aiden groaned, not even wanting to think about how flushed his face must look. "Is it that obvious?"

"You look a little tense," Jack said as they walked further into the kitchen. "Coming on too strong for you?"

"No, no."

Jack gave Aiden a look as he handed the glass over. "Don't hide it. It's good to talk about your feelings."

"Yeah. I don't know, I'm just not the most social person. And you're clearly a people-person. You made me feel really welcome last night though. I had a lot of fun."

"This is just a lot for you?" Jack asked.

Aiden took a long sip of water, thinking. "Maybe, but I really wanted to come over and see you again."

Jack's smile that came across his face then brought an assuring feeling for Aiden. "I'm glad."

"Why did you want me to come over anyway?"

"Follow me downstairs."

Aiden was confused as he watched Jack walk out of the kitchen towards another door. "What?" he asked.

"Just come on. I promise this isn't the part where you find out I'm actually a serial killer and you're trapped in my basement forever."

"Comforting," Aiden awkwardly laughed. Even though he was unsure of the intentions, Aiden followed Jack downstairs. He was right about the basement looking even better than the upstairs. The basement was clearly the hangout spot for company. The furniture and technology made it evident Jack had some money and put some thought into the layout. There was a flat-screen TV mounted on the wall, a pool table, a dart board on the wall, and a poker table. In one corner was a small bar counter with a mini fridge and drink glasses behind it. The decor screamed man cave.

"This is awesome," Aiden commented. "Makes my apartment look pathetic."

"I try," Jack motioned towards a room. "Come in here." Aiden followed him into the small room and saw a setup that was similar to a barbershop. There was a big mirror on the wall, a big chair, and a black sink. At the other side of the room were some shelves with shampoos, conditioners, hair color, and other materials. There was a sliding table with combs and a hairdryer.

"Have a seat," Jack patted the black chair. Aiden sat down and took a glimpse at his reflection in the mirror. He quickly looked away, feeling a sudden shame wash over him. There was still slight discoloration from Brett's hits. He had forgotten about them; Jack never mentioned them. Maybe he already knew like he seemed to know why Aiden was let go from his last job. After everything with Brett, Aiden wasn't sure if he liked the man he was seeing in the mirror anyway. "Alright, let's get you washed up."

Aiden leaned back in the chair and felt the warm water slide down his head, soaking the strands of his hair. Jack's fingers sliding through, massaging around his head, brought up goosebumps all over. It was soothing. He had to continuously fight the anxiety that would threaten to overcome the relaxation. Jack appeared to be the type of guy who wouldn't judge the anxiety, or the medication that helped run Aiden's life the past couple months, but it was still a struggle to feel okay about it. Once Jack was done washing his hair, he sat Aiden up in front of the mirror. He grabbed the blow dryer, a comb, and some bottles of product. Aiden was thankful when Jack walked in front of the mirror, blocking it.

"So, is this what you do? Like, for work?" Aiden asked

"Oh no," Jack said, "I'm actually in IT. That's what pays for this house."

"Very nice."

"You could consider this a side hustle. Just something I like to do and seem to have a talent for. I have this friend, Lydia, we've been best friends forever. Her girlfriend, Avy, loves to try new things with her hair. She gets to be my guinea pig a lot," Jack explained. "Alright, let's fix this hair a little."

"Is something wrong with it?"

"Well no, I mean, I obviously already find you cute since it was me that approached you last night."

"I thought you came up to me because I was new to the bar?"

"That was certainly a good excuse, too. Your looks may have had something to do with it as well," Jack winked.

Aiden shook his head as he remembered some of the stupid things he had said last night. "Do straight people ever go into that bar?"

"Yeah sure. Toby is straight."

"Oh...did you know I was gay before you started flirting with me?"

"I didn't know. Took my chances though."

Aiden couldn't help but smile. He was glad Jack had taken that chance.

"Anyway, if I'm going to be looking at you serving me drinks, I have some preferences." Aiden watched as Jack combed some of his hair back. He took some gel and slicked the front slightly upwards, then used the blowdryer to get it to stay in place. "That's better. Do you like it?"

"Yeah, I do. I never thought of doing it this way before. Thanks."

"Of course." Aiden stood up and began opening his wallet, but Jack stopped him. "You don't owe me anything, Aiden. It barely took ten minutes. It was my pleasure."

"I could have done this myself. You didn't have to."

"Yes, you can easily do it yourself."

"Then why did you do this?"

"It was an excuse to see you."

Aiden let out a low chuckle. "Still, you paid for my wings last night."

"I got your number for it."

"I appreciate it, Jack, but...it'd make me feel a little weird not to give you something."

"Why?"

Aiden tapped at his wallet. "Listen, it's just that...I only recently admitted to myself I was gay. I mean, I told you last night I came out a few days ago. This all started because I got left by a girl I had been with for nearly five years. Then things started changing for me. I haven't actually been with a guy yet or anything. I told you I already told my best friend and he's done with me. That's why I'm uneasy, this is all still new to me. I finally stopped fighting the fact that I'm gay, but I'm still...figuring things out I guess."

Jack nodded. "You need things to move slower?"

"Kind of. I don't want to feel like I owe anyone anything right now."

"I get it. It's hard at first. You have to admit it to yourself, then you admit it to others, then you try to meet somebody. It can be a lot."

"And I guess I should be honest with you that if you are looking for that special someone, a serious relationship or whatever, I'm probably not the right guy. I still have a lot of work to do with myself."

"I ain't looking for anything specific right now. I am perfectly content with us just hanging out and getting to know each other." Jack took the wallet from Aiden and replaced it in his pocket.

"Are you sure?"

"I'm sure."

Aiden watched as Jack began cleaning the sink. Luck was truly on his side with getting a new job and finding a decent person to bring into his life who was willing to just be a friend for now. "When did you realize it? That you were gay?"

"I sort of knew it most of my life. I had this feeling before I even realized a relationship was a guy and a girl, generally. Then when I did figure that out, I learned quickly that society said guys don't be with guys. So, I kept it to myself. I had no idea what to actually do about it."

Aiden looked down at the floor, "Did you lose any friends?"

"Oh yeah. Lydia and I both did. Before anyone knew we were gay, kids in middle school and high school would bug us to date, because it just seemed like one of those obvious things I guess. Like we were supposed to be together. It was basically like this: in our own minds, we knew we didn't want to date, because, even if we hadn't admitted it, we knew we were gay. However, I also thought that in her mind maybe she didn't want to date because we were too good of friends, and she had thought that about me too."

"You guys were friends for that long and it took you forever to come out to each other?"

"Yeah. Like I said, you go through the process of admitting it to yourself first. That takes some people longer than others. Then you know, you go through the fear of what your best friend, family, and others close to you will think."

Aiden nodded slowly. "For me that did not end well."

"I know, and I'm sorry that's how it went down. I really am," Jack said. "Anyway, it was the beginning of our junior year. I had come to terms with myself by then. I hadn't dated a guy yet, but I was ready to get to that chapter of my life. I knew I wouldn't be able to do that without being honest with Lydia first. So, I invited her over to my house to hang out. I let it out, and her reaction was

'Oh thank God, that makes this a lot easier.' I was confused and asked her what she was talking about. That's when she told me she was gay too. It was such a surreal thing for us."

Aiden felt tears brimming in his eyes as he imagined what it would have been like if Brett had reacted that way instead. Not admitting he was gay too, but just the surreal feeling Jack was describing. He quickly blinked the tears away. "That sounds amazing. I wish Brett would have said nothing would change between us. We could still be best friends."

Jack put a hand on Aiden's shoulder and gave it a squeeze. "I know."

"It hasn't even been that long, but I've argued with myself a million times about why I came out."

"Would it have been worth it not to have come out? Would you rather still be best friends if you had to lie to yourself the rest of your life? If you couldn't have the true life partner you wanted?"

Aiden shrugged. "It's hard to answer that, you know? I feel different about it every day, even every hour."

"I get it. Just know that it's not fair to you if you have to lie to yourself to be accepted. I had to learn that when I lost some friends. It meant that they weren't supposed to be in my life. It's hard to move on with that lesson sometimes; it's hard to accept, but it's true."

"Yeah. I hope I can become more confident in my choice like you."

"Hey, I haven't always been like this. It certainly took some hardships first."

"Hard to imagine. You come off as so upbeat and full of life," Aiden smiled at Jack. "Thanks again."

"No problem."

Aiden looked over at the reflection of himself in the mirror, not shying away this time. "Seriously. Not just for the hair, just thanks for making me not feel so bad about myself."

Jack glanced at Aiden with delight. "Anytime."

The first night of work was going great for Aiden. He was plenty busy, and everyone was very welcoming. It was a refreshing atmosphere to be in.

"The majority of our guests are regulars," Toby explained. "We're all just a big family. We all take care of each other."

There were regulars at RN's too, but there was a larger share of random people that came in. Unlike there, though, a lot of the customers at The Color Band wanted to get to know the new bartender and make him feel at ease. After only a few hours into his first night, Aiden could feel he was going to grow into this place.

"Having fun?" Jack asked while Aiden handed him his beer.

"It's going really good, actually," Aiden said, smiling.

"Good. I have someone for you to meet," Jack said, putting his arm around a woman beside him. She was a short woman with dark brown hair. She wore a long necklace and had a lot of bracelets on her wrists. Just by looking at her, Aiden could feel the bubbly personality she was about to show. "Aiden, this is my best friend Lydia. Lydia, this is Aiden."

"Ooooh! *This* is who you were telling me about," Lydia smiled. "It's nice to meet you, Aiden."

"You too," Aiden said, shaking her hand.

"You were right, Jack. He's cute," Lydia said. "He'd do good for you."

"Oh boy," Aiden said, hoping his face didn't look as red as it felt. "You need a drink?"

"I'll just take water please, thanks."

Aiden took his time getting the water, waiting for his blush to fade away.

"Hey, Aiden," Jack said when he returned, "remember I told you about Avy? Lydia's girlfriend?"

"Yeah."

"She's up on stage about to do some karaoke. You have to listen to her pipes," Jack commented.

Aiden glanced behind him at the stage where a woman in a jean jacket stood. She had half her head shaved and the rest of her brown and blonde hair was swooped to the side, in a short half mohawk. She looked like someone you wouldn't want to mess with, and Aiden wondered if she had the same sparkly personality as Lydia.

"You did that hairstyle?" Aiden asked, surprised.

Jack nodded. "Pretty badass, huh?"

"That's amazing. You really do have a talent for that."

Even while distracted by work, Aiden felt goosebumps as Avy began singing. He couldn't help but pause on occasion to watch her. Aiden wasn't even really catching the lyrics to the song but was mesmerized by Avy's performance. She really did have talented pipes.

"I'm going to go sit up there," Lydia said, "It was nice to meet you, Aiden."

"You too," Aiden said, turning towards Jack. "She's really nice."

"I love that kid. She's awesome. Don't tell her I called her 'kid' in front of you. She likes it to be known that she's a month older than me even though I tower over her."

Aiden chuckled. It was clear Jack and Lydia had a deep bond. It made him wonder if they ever had similar conversations or did similar activities that he had done with Brett. "You were right about Avy. She can really sing."

"Yeah, she can. I can't wait for you to meet her," Jack said. "I've got to head out, though. What's my damage?"

"Sixty-two dollars," Aiden answered.

Jack tossed a one hundred dollar bill on the counter and stood up. "Keep it."

"Oh, Jack, come on," Aiden insisted.

"Not hearing it. Have a good night," Jack said as he threw his jacket on and turned for the door. Aiden tried not to make it obvious, but he couldn't stop watching Jack until he was out of his sight.

-9-

Aiden began feeling that things were falling into place. There was no word from Brett, so he assumed that was it for them. Brett was moving on just as Courtney had and he was done with Aiden. It was still difficult to accept—he and Brett had been friends for years, after all—but he had helpful distractions. He had his new job at The Color Band keeping him busy and he met some great people there who made working more like a fun night out. Then he had Jack, and although they were keeping things on a friend level, Aiden was feeling more connected with him.

Most of Aiden's interactions with Jack were while he was working at the bar, except for the couple times he had gone over to Jack's house. In no time at all, Aiden noticed he was developing the same feelings he had thought he had for Brett. The somewhat obsessive feelings were now craved interactions with Jack. It made him nervous, even though Jack clearly wanted the same, if not more, with Aiden. After the way things had gone with Brett, though, Aiden wanted to be extra careful about how he approached things.

It had reached December and the weather had become cold and snowy. Aiden's mind had been buzzing after Thanksgiving at his parents' house. He realized even though the past few months had been rough, he had new things in his life for which he was truly thankful, even if he didn't share them with his parents or Jaxie. With that thankfulness in mind, he wanted to take a leap. Aiden decided to invite Jack over to his apartment, and Lydia and Avy, too, to get to know them better. Serving drinks to loud customers and trying to hold a conversation wasn't always the easiest combination.

Jack arrived before the girls. He pulled Aiden into a brief hug as he walked inside. Aiden could have stayed in that hug. It gave off those little vibes that things were going the right direction, even though he did still question if there was a hidden punishment for this life he was now living. Aiden was also going through the internal argument if this was the right time to be trying to meet Lydia and Avy on such a personal level. He's known Jack for a month. That seemed dragged out to have him over for the first time since he had been to Jack's house. Was it weird to invite the girls over for the first time too? Jack, Lydia, and Avy seemed to be their own group. They knew a lot of people at The Color Band, but they were their own circle. Aiden didn't want to appear to be pushing himself into it or cross boundaries, even if he was desperate for friends.

With the questioning on his good intentions, Aiden snuck one of his anxiety pills. He wanted to be relaxed and avoid overthinking things during the night. He wanted to have fun and he intended to make sure Jack had a good time as well.

"Aiden, this is my girlfriend Avy," Lydia said in a formal introduction. "Avy, you've seen Aiden behind the bar."

"Yes, you've made me some good drinks! It's really nice to finally meet you, Aiden." Avy smiled. "I've heard a bit about you from Lydia, but I've heard lots about you from Jack. All good things, I promise."

Lydia Hamilton was twenty-eight years old and was just as animated as she appeared to be at the bar. She wasn't loud by any means. She simply loved being around people and making them smile. She was ready to be anyone's biggest supporter. Avy Parton was twenty-nine years old and walked confidently. She sang with a purpose and she carried that attitude when she spoke too. They had been in a relationship for two years and anyone could feel how much they adored each other. Aiden couldn't help to compare his relationship of five years with Courtney wasn't anything near the passion Lydia and Avy had in only their two year relationship.

"I hope they were good things," Aiden chuckled at Avy's comment. "I've heard great things about you, too. The biggest is that you can obviously sing. You are amazing up at the mic."

"Thanks! I'm glad you enjoy it."

"Avy actually has an album coming out early next year," Lydia said with a big smile.

"Really? That's incredible."

"It's going to be released during our spring event in April," Jack chimed in as he handed Avy a beer.

"What event?" Aiden asked.

Jack handed Aiden his drink. "Avy's album is titled 'He Still Loves Us.' That's what the event is called."

"What does that mean exactly?"

"Let me ask you something," Avy began. "What is the biggest argument you think we hear from people on why same-sex couples can't be together?"

Aiden thought for a minute. "I mean, because they are the same sex?"

"And why do people use that argument? Where was it first placed that couples have to supposedly be man and woman?"

"The Bible," Aiden answered, his parents quickly coming to mind.

"Exactly. People will tell us we aren't true Christians and that we'll be judged and damned, because we aren't following the true way of Jesus. The righteous way if you will. So the title 'He Still Loves Us' gives us the voice to tell people Jesus does still love us. We are still His children and He still loves us no matter what."

"Wow. That...that's actually really comforting to hear. Honestly, I had started questioning how God feels about me lately on a lot of things. I was raised Christian. Very strict to the exact word of the Bible type, you know? So, I haven't dared come out to my parents. I have no idea how they'll respond. They already think I went against God's ways because I was living with my girlfriend before we were married."

Avy set her beer down and took Aiden's hand. "All I can say, Aiden, is pray about it. Just because you're gay doesn't mean Jesus still won't listen and help guide you."

"Thank you, Avy," Aiden smiled. "That's reassuring to hear someone say it out loud."

"Good," Avy smiled.

"And we'll pray for you too," Lydia said as she put her arm around Avy. Praying for him. The structure of the sentence Lydia had said compared to his parents held different intentions. Lydia simply stated they would pray for Aiden to receive guidance. His mom, on the other hand, had said she'd pray for things to work out for him and Courtney. It was two people praying for him, but for different types of outcomes. With Lydia's blessing, Aiden could already begin to feel the repair on his faith.

"Thank you," Aiden said, taking a drink of his whiskey before he could get too emotional.

"Alright, enough sap," Lydia clapped her hands together, "let's have a fun night."

"I agree. I brought the cards and chips. Let's set this up," Jack said. The four of them spent the next couple hours playing poker. Lydia and Avy were very welcoming and interested in the guy who could potentially become their friend's new boyfriend, which was relieving to Aiden. Avy talked about some of the songs she had written over the years and sang a little. Aiden was feeling touched by them. They weren't just about relationships or same-sex relationships. They were simply about life. Aiden felt he was hitting it off nicely with everyone and he was thrilled to have found people who truly accepted him for who he was.

After poker, the girls left for the night. Aiden wasn't feeling tired enough to go to bed, and, if he was being honest, he didn't want to be alone yet. The events of the last few hours would end up running through his head and he would question if he had done or said anything stupid in front of everyone. He also wasn't ready for Jack to leave. He kept thinking about if he could get in another hug as he watched Jack clean up the cards and poker chips. He knew Jack would easily do it, but Aiden didn't know how to make it happen without stupidly asking.

"You have a poker table in your basement," Aiden began while refilling his whiskey. "Do you usually have people over for a game?"

"Yeah, from time to time," Jack replied.

"That's cool. This was fun. I can see why you talk so highly of Avy. She's incredible."

"She really is. She's very inspiring."

"So, what is the event you guys were talking about?" Aiden asked, trying to keep any conversation going along.

"She's going to be performing songs from her new album. It's just a way to bring people together and remind them that Jesus is about love. He loves all of us."

"I hope my parents can remember that when...if I ever come out to them."

"What if you wind up in a serious relationship?" Jack asked. "You don't think you'll tell them?"

"I'll want to, but it will be so hard. I wanted to tell my best friend for so long, but it was really difficult to get myself to do it. Then I did, and, well, you know the rest. I've told my sister I'm gay, but I don't even know when I'll tell her about you." Aiden looked up at Jack, realizing how that sounded. "I don't mean any offense by that."

"Hey, there isn't any. Stop acting like you got to be sorry for how you're handling things. I shouldn't and I don't expect anything out of you."

Aiden ran his hands down his face. "I just feel mentally exhausted from coming out to a couple people, especially after Brett's reaction. I don't know about telling my sister I'm spending some time with a guy I like. I know she'll be happy for me, and she'll be excited. Too excited. I don't think I can handle it right now."

Jack smiled, clearly elated that Aiden had admitted he liked him in that way. "Do it on your own time. I'm a patient guy. If we're meant to go further, we'll figure it out."

"Yeah."

"You know," Jack cleared his throat, "now you've kind of set me up to sound really pushy."

"What? Why?"

Jack sighed as he threw his beer bottle away. "I was going to see what your plans were for Christmas in a couple weeks."

"Oh...um, Jaxie and I go to our parents' house on Christmas Day. Christmas Eve was spent with Courtney's family the past few years." Aiden shrugged. "That plan has changed, obviously, so now I have nothing going on."

"Well, if you don't end up doing anything, want to come over?"

"You don't have usual, annual plans for the holidays?"

"I'll go to my mom's house on Christmas Day. Christmas Eve changes every year. Sometimes I can sucker Lydia and Avy to spend time with me. I'm sure they're sick of me crashing their alone time."

"Oh, well..."

"Look, don't answer now," Jack said, putting his hands up. "I don't want to pressure you if it seems too fast. I'm not looking to make it a serious holiday together. Just let me know, alright?"

"Okay," Aiden smiled, "thanks for the offer, Jack."

Jack gave him a small smile in return. "Certainly. Well, I should get going. I'll talk to you soon?"

"You mean you'll text me once you're laying in bed?"

Jack slowly opened the door and turned to Aiden with a smirk. "You caught on to my habits, huh?"

"Yeah, maybe a little. Thanks for coming tonight. It was a lot of fun with you guys."

"We had a lot of fun," Jack said as he stepped out the door. "Oh, looks like you have something out here."

Aiden peeked past Jack and saw an envelope sitting on his doormat. "Thanks. Have a good night, Jack."

The first thought that ran through Aiden's mind was his mail got put in the wrong slot and someone brought it for him. It happened from time to time, but the late hour was odd. Confusion hit even more when he didn't see anything written on the envelope. Not his name, not a return address, nothing. Aiden opened it slowly and pulled out a folded piece of paper. It was incredible that after so many good things were happening, one word could trample over it all. Scribbled on the paper with black sharpie was the word 'Faggot.'

Aiden's throat went so tight he wasn't sure how to react. He wanted to turn away but he couldn't take his eyes off the word that seemed to jump at him from the page. He had forgotten that word existed, let alone how it would affect him. That was a word he heard thrown around among people, but usually in a joking way. Was there ever a time he heard it said towards a gay person or in a derogatory matter? He wasn't sure. His lips quivered as he looked over to the window. The feeling he was being watched came to him again, like someone in another building knew what was going on. That was the excuse he wanted to believe when in the back of his mind he knew who really left the note.

He scattered across the living room and closed the shades. Gripping the paper tight, Aiden fell back on his couch. His eyes couldn't resist looking at the word over and over again. His mind wandered with the definition. He wanted to convince himself that there wasn't anything demeaning about it unless he believed being gay was demeaning.

The moment his phone went off was when Aiden's heart seemed to reset. He walked to the counter and picked up his phone. There was a text message icon. He expected the word from the paper to have somehow hopped to his phone screen. There was hesitancy as he swiped the screen to open his messages. His guard dropped some when he saw it was from Jack.

Miss you already. It meant a lot to me for you to meet Lydia and Avy.

They were awesome. I'm glad I met them.

Aiden didn't mean to be short in his response. He was distracted as that word kept echoing in his head. Jack appeared to be able to read through the phone with his next message.

Was that letter anything important?

Aiden peeked back at the paper that sat on his couch. He could see the black lines that formed into letters. Jack could probably help, but Aiden didn't want to bother him with it.

Naw. I'm about to fall asleep. I'll talk to you tomorrow. Good night.

Aiden left the note where it was and went straight to bed. He didn't feel himself begin to cry, but the tears flowed down, staining the pillow beneath his head.

The first thing Aiden did the next morning was pick up his phone and dial. He didn't even get out of bed as he listened to the ringing, unsure what his plan would be if this fell through.

"Hello?"

"Hey, Jaxie," Aiden said, clearing his throat. "Can you come over? Or are you working?"

"I have to head to work in an hour. I'm pulling a double and I'll be there until close. I can swing by real quick though. Is everything okay?"

"Yeah, I'm fine. I'll just stop by your work and have some lunch, alright?"

"Okay, sounds good. I'll see you in a bit."

Aiden placed his phone back on his nightstand. He didn't immediately move. He was having a mental debate with himself. Last night was full of so much joy. Was he going to let it go to waste because of a mysterious note? He didn't want to. He couldn't. It was hard not to. If Jaxie could tell him it was nothing, then he would feel a little better. When Aiden managed to roll himself out of bed, he went straight into the shower. He did his hair how Jack had done it, grabbed the letter, and drove to Jaxie's work for lunch. She worked at Audrey's Diner, a little restaurant with a 60s theme. Aiden walked in and saw Clarice waiting at the front.

"Hi, Aiden," Clarice greeted him with a smile. She worked with Jaxie and was also one of her good friends. "Are you looking for Jaxie?"

"I'm actually going to grab a bite, so if you can put me at one of her tables. I'd appreciate it."

"Sure, just follow me down," Clarice walked towards some booths. "You haven't been here in awhile. Been busy?"

"Yeah. How have you been?" Aiden asked as he sat down.

"Same old, same old."

"I hear ya. Wait...what's that?"

Clarice glanced down at her hand. "Oh, that?" she asked innocently, a smile creeping to her lips.

"Yes that. Did Trey propose?"

"Yes, he did," Clarice said excitedly, the smile fully spread across her face now.

"That's awesome! Congratulations! Why didn't you say anything?"

"Well, Jaxie told me about you and Courtney. I didn't want to flaunt it, you know?"

"Oh, don't worry about that. You should be bragging, that's amazing. I'm really happy for you," Aiden stood up and gave Clarice a hug.

"Thanks, Aiden. I'm trying to bribe Jaxie to be my maid of honor."

Aiden laughed as an unfamiliar image of his sister came to mind. "You're going to get her to wear a dress?"

"We'll see," she shrugged. "Maybe you can help me think of a way to get her to do it."

"Yeah, that's a tough one. She might ask to be a groomsman instead," Aiden sat back down, chuckling. "Did, uh, did Jaxie tell you anything else after me and Courtney's breakup?"

Clarice furrowed her eyebrows, confused. "No, nothing really. Why?"

"Nothing, I was just curious."

That was when Jaxie walked over to the table, nudging her friend. "Is she bugging you?"

"No," Aiden shook his head, "she told me her big news though."

"Yeah, she wants me to dress up for it too," Jaxie snarled playfully. "She's so needy."

Clarice laughed. "I got to get back up there. It was nice catching up, Aiden."

"You too, Clarice. Congrats again."

"Want a soda?" Jaxie asked.

"Yeah. And put a cheeseburger and fries in too while you're back there."

"Cool. I'll be right back."

It wasn't long before Jaxie returned to the table, taking a seat across from Aiden with his drink. "Here you go. I like your hair by the way. When did you start doing it like that?"

"Recently. I do it from time to time," Aiden simply answered, "Just trying something new."

"It looks good. What did you need to talk to me about?"

"I wish it was just me asking for some simple advice, but there's been some complication thrown at me."

"What do you mean?"

Aiden slid the note to Jaxie. He looked down at his lap as he waited for her response.

"Did someone give this to you at work?" Jaxie asked with a disgusted look on her face.

"No. Someone left it in front of my door."

"*What*?! Are you serious?"

"Yeah. It was there late last night," Aiden stated, not feeling confident enough to bring up Jack or the girls being over.

"Brett?"

"Maybe."

"Seems obvious."

"I know, I know."

"What are you going to do about it?" Jaxie asked.

"Nothing. I'm not going to sink to his level. Not that I have the balls to."

"Do you think he'll do anything worse?"

Aiden shrugged. "If he leaves notes at my apartment, then I just deal with being annoyed. At the end of my lease, I can move and that's that."

"Yeah, I suppose. I'm sorry it happened though."

"It kind of freaked me out when I found it last night, but I felt a little better this morning. It's not really a threat, you know?"

"I guess not."

"He hasn't tried talking to me or anything. This was just kind of sudden, kind of weird, you know?"

"Yeah. It pisses me off, but like you said, don't sink to anything low over a note. It's not like he hit you with something personal. Anyone would know to use this word to hurt someone who's gay." Jaxie shook her head. "He turned ugly so quick."

"He really does have strong feelings towards this. If he really did leave this, I guess he realized this wasn't just a stunt I was pulling as a pity party and now he's mad.

Maybe I should have expected this. Maybe I didn't take his comments towards gay people seriously enough."

"Don't start, Aiden. Don't go on with that again. I'm not going to listen to you blame yourself."

"I'm not blaming myself."

"You're trying to find excuses for his actions," Jaxie groaned in frustration as she shoved the note back to him. "I'll go get your food."

As Aiden expected, it took her some time to return, longer than it should have. He knew she was calming herself down. A few years ago, Jaxie would've continued on and let anything spill from her mouth. She still did that to people she didn't know well enough or care to upset. Around Aiden, though, she began the habit of stepping away to calm down before saying anything too hurtful.

"Here you go," Jaxie said, placing the food down and retaking her seat.

"I'm sorry, Jaxie."

"You don't have to say sorry."

"No, I am sorry. It's hard for me not to try and figure this out though. It's not like I can just kick him out of my life."

Jaxie's mouth hung open from the statement. "Is that what this is about? You want to save your friendship with him, don't you?"

"I don't know." He took a bite of his food and took his time chewing it as he tried figuring out his words. "I'm not blaming myself, but if I can fix this or change his mind then..."

"You won't change his mind, Aiden."

"But, Jaxie..."

"Aiden!"

"No, hear me out. He left this note, right? But he hasn't tried to talk to me since we got in the fight at work. If our friendship really was over, then he'd just leave it at that. But he's trying to get my attention or something."

"Attention for what?"

"Maybe he misses our friendship. He doesn't want it to be over. He—"

"But you literally just said he probably did this because he's mad that you're gay."

"That doesn't mean he doesn't miss our friendship. That could eventually push the anger away and change his thinking or..."

Jaxie slammed her hands on the table. "Aiden."

Aiden swallowed hard. He hadn't meant to upset Jaxie this much. It was obvious she didn't think this note meant nothing like he had hoped. "What?"

She let out a deep breath. "Nothing. Since you don't want to listen, it looks like you'll have to figure it out for yourself."

Aiden didn't like he had made Jaxie so flustered. If he was being honest with himself, he was still trying to understand what he had attempted explaining to her. He had been grasping at straws; justifying something he knew he should let go of. He really wanted to believe that Brett missed their friendship, but also knew that he wasn't the type who would be willing to step down and admit he was wrong in how he had handled the situation. After he finished lunch, Aiden found himself mindlessly driving to Jack's house. Maybe he would tell Aiden the note meant nothing.

"Hey, Aiden," Jack said, surprised to see him at the door. "Nice surprise."

"Oh, I didn't even call, huh? I'm sorry for just showing up."

"No, it's fine. I'm just working."

"Really? Sorry. I can go..."

"No, no come on in. I work at home from time to time," Jack said as Aiden walked inside. "What brought you to my neck of the woods today?"

"I was...just hoping to talk to you about something. I sort of need your help."

"Okay, on what?"

"So, that letter left at my door," Aiden began, "it was kind of a hate note."

"Yeah?" Jack asked, not seeming surprised, "What did it say?"

Aiden reluctantly handed it over. It wasn't as easy as letting Jaxie read it. Jaxie didn't have any emotional ties to the word. He wasn't sure how much it could hurt Jack to see it.

"I've seen lots of these," Jack commented calmly. "Was it Brett?"

"I guess, maybe," Aiden said, "It seems like it would be, but I don't know for sure."

"How did it make you feel?"

"It scared me at first because I wasn't sure of the intention. After sleeping on it, though, I felt a little better. I mean, I shouldn't take it as a threat, right?"

Jack sighed as he took a seat at his computer. "I don't know, Aiden."

"I just came to ask because I figured you'd have an idea of what I should do."

"It's hard to say. I've gotten comments, or the coward notes, that meant nothing. Sometimes they mean something more."

"Like what?"

"It just depends how much Brett wants to get to you, you know?"

"Well...I didn't expect this from him. I just...I figured he wanted me gone from his life, so I assumed that'd be it. I'm gone and he could move on."

"And maybe that's what happened. Maybe this wasn't him at all and he did move on. Maybe it was someone else, someone you don't even know, just someone who wanted to get under your skin." Jack took a deep breath before continuing, "And then...maybe it was Brett, and he is looking to make your life hell."

Aiden took a hard swallow. Jack didn't hold back from letting that sentence flow, but it seemed harsh. "What if it's like...he's blowing off steam, because he just misses the friendship we used to have, you know? Does that...?"

Aiden didn't even finish his question as he saw Jack's facial expression. That said it all.

"Just be careful, Aiden."

Both conversations with Jaxie and Jack were not easy to have. The answers he had hoped to get didn't happen. In the end, it took Aiden four days to throw the note away. He was waiting for anything else to happen just in case he needed evidence. When nothing else did, he took it as a sick joke and tossed it. Maybe it was Brett, and maybe it wasn't. Aiden knew he may have to live with the fact that he'd never know. He wasn't sure how seriously to take Jack's concern either. Jack had clearly been around the block before and knew what could be coming for Aiden. It didn't have to be true though. Not for everyone.

-10-

Before Aiden knew it, Christmas Eve had arrived.

He never made a decision on whether to spend it with Jack or not. No plans had come up, but he hadn't tried to call Jack, assuming that he would have made other arrangements by now. Especially since he didn't see him at The Color Band that evening.

"Have a Merry Christmas, Aiden," Toby said as they closed up the bar for the night.

"You too, Toby. I'll see you in a couple days."

Aiden sat in his car for a few minutes. He lit a cigarette, waiting to warm up before driving away, but he also sat in a debate on if he was going to go home or see what Jack was up to. Fate appeared to have an answer for him when his phone began ringing. "Hello?"

"Hey," Jack said a smile in his voice. "Did you fill your Christmas Eve schedule?"

"Uh no, I didn't. Did you?"

"Nope. I kept it open. Do you want to come by and play some cards?"

Aiden tried not to sound too excited by Jack's question. "Yeah. I'm just leaving the bar, I'll be by soon. Want me to grab anything?"

"I got plenty. See you soon."

Aiden couldn't keep the smile from his face as he hung up the phone and pulled out of the parking lot. He was happy an answer came to him on its own. He only hoped that whatever came out of tonight would accommodate what he may encounter for Christmas Day tomorrow.

"It's cold out there, huh?" Jack asked as Aiden walked inside his house.

"It's freezing," Aiden said. "I've never been a fan of snow."

"Well, I have great news then," Jack said, removing Aiden's jacket. "The fireplace is going, so go warm up before we get cards going. I'll get your whiskey."

"Ah, see, now *that* will warm me up real good," Aiden laughed, taking a seat on the couch. He let out a contented sigh; he was glad not to be spending the rest of the night by himself. Being alone on a holiday sounded depressing.

"What did you end up doing with that note?" Jack asked, handing him his drink.

"I finally threw it away after a few days. I got sick of looking at it, so I got rid of it."

"Good deal. Has anything else happened?"

"No," Aiden shook his head.

"That's good to hear." Jack took a long sip of his beer before asking, "Now can I ask you to stop doing something purely because it's bugging the hell out of me?"

"Okay?"

"Would you stop smoking before you come here? I can't be making you that nervous every time we spend time together."

"Oh," Aiden chuckled nervously, "sorry. I know it's a bad habit."

"It's a gross one. I never see you smoke at the bar."

"I can admit I do it in tense situations. I haven't always smoked. I used to be really bad. Courtney made me quit, and it was fine. Then when she left, Brett sort of got me back into it. I know I should stop again and not rely on it."

"I don't mean to sound picky, but that'd be nice. Have all the whiskey you want instead."

Aiden nodded with a smile. "I'll probably have to take you up on that."

"Now to a brighter note! I know you wanted to take things slow and all, which is fine, but I did get you something for Christmas. Actually, it's a rewrap of something I've had, but it'll be good for you."

"What? Really? Why did you do that?"

Jack shrugged. "Why not?"

"No, I can't. I didn't get you anything."

"I wouldn't have expected you to. Don't even think of this as anything more than a friend looking out for a friend," Jack said, handing Aiden a wrapped gift.

"A friend looking out for a friend huh?"

"Yeah of course."

Aiden looked at the gift, shaking his head slightly.

"Are you okay? Did I say something?"

"No, Jack, you didn't. It's just..." Aiden couldn't finish his sentence as he set the gift down.

"I get it. You always had Brett as a friend. You never thought you'd ever call someone else a friend, at least not with him out of the picture or in the content I just said."

123

Aiden smiled as he looked up at Jack. "It's like you've gone through this before."

"You could say that."

"Well, Lydia is your best friend right? You didn't lose her."

"You're right. I'll always be grateful for that. We did lose other friends within our circle though."

"That's one downfall to me not being very social. I didn't really have a circle. Brett had other friends he'd hang out with, but I really only had him." Aiden sighed. "When did it all stop hurting?"

"It didn't," Jack admitted. "It's gotten better. I've met new people, experienced new relationships, learned more about myself. Sometimes I think back to the old days and miss them. Sometimes I think about trying to reach out and see if things have changed, but then I remember the hell they put me through. I'm just not willing to risk going through it again, not after how much I've grown."

"I don't know if I want to know what they put you through."

"And I hope you don't have to go through it either," Jack said, patting Aiden's knee. "Now come on, open it."

Aiden slowly opened the present and held a book in his hands.

"This book helped me a lot in the beginning. It helps you learn how to love yourself first before you move onto loving anyone else. It's specifically for the homosexual community."

"Thanks, Jack. This means a lot," Aiden said as he flipped through some of the pages. They were definitely worn, as if Jack had read through it many times. "I'll be reading this. I'm sure I could use some guidance."

Jack put his arm around Aiden's shoulders and pulled him close. "I'm glad."

"Have you ever been in a serious relationship with another guy? Did this book help you with that?"

Jack thought for a minute then said, "I don't know if I'd say serious. I've dated around, sure. I haven't been in a relationship like Avy and Lydia are, though."

"Is there any reason why?"

"Just haven't found someone to be serious with."

Aiden set the book down on the couch. "Well, thank you again. Ready to play some cards now?"

The two went downstairs to Jack's poker table. Aiden couldn't remember the last time he had been in such a relaxed atmosphere. They were drinking, playing cards, watching TV, and eating food. He did these simple things with Brett, but he went through lots of anxiety with his secret. There were no expectations with Jack. They were simply enjoying each other's company. It was bringing Aiden back to the night he met Jack, when there was only simple conversation going on between them. That night when he couldn't stop looking deeper into his green eyes. It was just two guys talking as Jack explained it. No worries of sexual preference and Aiden was sure Jack would be that way even if he found out Aiden was straight. He had been, and continued to find himself, getting swept up in Jack's positive aura. There was the simplicity of being Jack's friend and there was a craving Aiden wanted to keep feeding.

"If only I could be doing this for Christmas tomorrow," Aiden commented.

"Not looking forward to it?"

"I don't know. I'll be hearing all the questions about Courtney. Again. My parents don't know about the fall out with Brett, obviously. It's definitely not the time to come out, not in front of everyone."

"I wouldn't have suggested that anyway. What about Jaxie?"

"She won't tell anyone about Brett or about me coming out. I know I can trust her."

Jack tapped the stack of cards against the table. "You still don't want to tell her about me?"

Aiden couldn't respond to that. Him and Jack had definitely grown closer over the past several weeks and things were looking great, but part of him was afraid to admit someone else was important to him in the way that Courtney had been, or the way he wished Brett could have been. They both had broken his heart and he didn't want it to happen again.

"You don't have to, Aiden."

"I'm sorry, Jack. It's not fair to you. I trust Jaxie with everything; I should tell her."

"It's really okay. If things get that far, I'd love to meet her. She sounds really important to you."

"She is. We've always been close. We've always been there for each other, especially with our crazy parents."

"Bad home life?" Jack asked as he shuffled the cards.

"No, I can't say it was bad. They were just very strict. They stuck a little too close to the word of the Bible when raising us, and it kind of drove me and Jaxie away as we got older. It was too much. I told you Courtney and I moved in together? Well, my parents were disappointed in me for our breakup because, to them, I had made a vow to make her my wife by having her move in," Aiden explained. "I did have that intention, but then she left without any reason."

"And your parents still expect that the two of you are going to get back together and you'll make it work?"

"Yeah, pretty much. I'm sure you can guess how they feel about same-sex couples."

"Oh yeah."

"They had told me and Jaxie about how God sees gay people, but we never took it to heart since we weren't in that boat at the time," Aiden chugged the rest of his drink. "Now I can't help but wonder if my parents will disown me if I come out to them. What happened when you came out to your parents?"

"My older brother and I were raised by my mom. My dad was very sick when my mom was pregnant with me. He died shortly after I was born, so I never knew him. I was sort of forced to come out to my mom and brother about six months after I came out to Lydia."

"Forced how?"

"Just things that happened at school. To answer your question, they were very supportive. I wasn't sure what to expect, but they helped me a lot."

"Have you told your mom or brother about me?"

"I haven't told my mom. I've told my brother a little bit," Jack said. "I watch my niece sometimes, so you came up in conversation with him."

"I wish it could be that casual with my family," Aiden said softly. "I'd love to tell Jaxie about this, about us, but any time I start to, I back out. The questions she would ask run through my head nonstop. I feel like I'd be pressured to make this serious if I tell her. Don't get me wrong, she wouldn't push me to. I just get overwhelmed."

"I know. Like I said, I'd love to meet her some day if that's in the cards for us."

Aiden felt his heart skip a beat. He wasn't sure why, but suddenly his desires were peaking. They gave him a slight scare as he tried to push them down by redirecting the conversation. "How old is your niece?"

"Five. Her name is Marissa. She's a sassy little thing. She might get it from her uncle," Jack winked.

That wink didn't help matters. Aiden could feel his temperature rise as he awkwardly looked at his phone. He needed an escape. "I should leave and get some sleep. It's gonna be a long day tomorrow."

"Alright. Thanks for coming over and giving me a little company." Jack walked Aiden upstairs. Aiden threw on his jacket and boots, trying not to stare at Jack. He could feel himself begin to blush slightly anyway. It didn't help when Jack pulled him into a tight hug. In that hug, his reason for needing to get home melted away and he found himself almost wanting to let the desires run free. He didn't want the safe, warm feeling of Jack's presence, of his arms around him, to end. As Jack backed away, Aiden forced himself to look to the floor. He didn't know what he'd do if he was pulled into Jack's gaze right now. He only knew he wasn't ready to find out. "I'll see you soon?" Jack asked.

"Yeah...yeah, of course." Aiden turned towards the front door. He headed out into the snowy wonderland, the snow dropping heavier than when he had left the bar. He certainly wasn't feeling any chill, though.

Christmas morning used to entail Aiden and Courtney waking up, feeling drained from events on Christmas Eve, and making their way to the Cooper household. Aiden would tend to himself as he caught up with family members while Courtney would hide away with Jaxie. With Courtney growing up in a different background, Jaxie was typically the easiest family member for her to connect with. Jaxie and Courtney did have a respectable bond. Courtney didn't get in the way of Jaxie's relationship with Aiden, and Jaxie didn't get in the way of hers. Now that things were drastically different, it didn't truly feel like Christmas. Aiden felt like he was going to a basic family meeting instead of a joyous family get-together.

Standing outside his parents' door, he took a few deep breaths to prepare himself for the day ahead. Even though he had a great time with Jack last night, he still didn't feel ready to tell Jaxie about him. She could be like a battering ram when it came to questions, especially when it was happy news, and one thing he knew for sure was that he had no idea how to answer them. His feelings were all over the place about it. Especially after his episode of fighting what his body wanted to suddenly do with Jack last night.

"Hey, Mom," Aiden said distractedly, hugging her when he walked in the house.

"Merry Christmas, Aiden!" Lauren smiled.

Aiden walked into the living room. It was full of family: his grandparents, aunts, uncles, and cousins. He immediately regretted being there. Although it was probably obvious since she wasn't there with him, he wondered how much his parents had told everyone about Courtney and the reason behind her departure.

"Oh my gosh, what took you so long?" Jaxie hissed in his ear when she hugged him. "I was about to go crazy with grandma."

"Oh yeah?" Aiden laughed. "Sorry, I slept in."

"Oh, did you have to work late?"

"Yeah," Aiden lied. "By the way, do Mom and Dad know about my new job?"

"I mentioned you got another bartending job. I didn't tell them why. I wasn't able to tell them where though. I didn't realize until they asked that you never told me where you're working now."

"Oh, well that's another conversation for us to have alone," Aiden said, giving her a look.

"Okay, gotcha."

"Do you know if Mom or Dad told everyone about Courtney?"

"Yeah," Jaxie rolled her eyes. "That's why I was getting annoyed. Grandma was asking me a bunch of questions and then egging me on to find my forever guy. You know who she should be picking on?"

"Don't get on it, Jaxie," Aiden said, turning to walk into the kitchen.

Jaxie followed him as she certainly did get on it. "She should be bothering Jessica. She's thirty and hasn't gotten married yet. They all think she's such a saint."

"Jessica puts on an act," Aiden said as he poured himself a drink. The first of what he knew would be many. He wasn't a fan of the liquor his parents kept, but he was desperate enough. "The only time I'm willing to drink vodka is here."

Aiden ended up drinking more than he had planned to. Everyone asked their questions about Courtney and he was getting sick of repeating himself. He started wondering why he didn't make a presentation and tell everyone at once. He was also put in the awkward position of listening to the Lord's way of life and the path He has for him. Everyone in his family had the same point of view and would very likely have loud, ugly opinions if they knew the truth about him now. These conversations reminded him why he was thankful he wasn't the confrontational kind. He wanted to let them know they were wasting their time preaching to him, but it didn't push him enough to say anything.

"Don't worry, I got him," Jaxie said to her mother as she helped Aiden out to her car. "We'll get his car in the morning."

"Maybe you guys can stop by and have breakfast then," Lauren suggested. Aiden half-crawled into Jaxie's car. Once she closed the door, Lauren continued talking to her daughter. "He seems to be going through a lot. He drank too much and he was quiet."

"Maybe that had something to do with everyone talking his ear off about Courtney," Jaxie responded. She walked to the other side of her car to get in the driver's side. "Merry Christmas."

"Should I expect you guys for breakfast?"

Jaxie didn't answer as she closed her car door.

"Sorry," Aiden slurred as Jaxie drove him to his apartment. "I went overboard."

"It's fine. You're just lucky I held back on *my* drinking so we both weren't stuck there for the night. Why can't you just drink beer? You wouldn't be so bad off."

"I hate beer."

"Yeah, yeah, I know." Jaxie took her brother's hand and gave it a squeeze. "So, where are you working now?"

"A bar called The Color Band."

"Oh, I've heard of that place. Are you liking it?"

"It's going great actually."

"So..." Jaxie glanced at Aiden with a curious smile.

"Shut up."

"Well, it's a gay bar. Have you met anyone there?"

"Naw."

"You got your eye on anyone there? Anyone cute?"

"Oh, Jaxie, I ain't whoring around," Aiden leaned against the car window.

Jaxie laughed, realizing her brother wasn't going to be able to have a stable conversation at the moment. Once they arrived at his apartment, Jaxie walked Aiden to the door, finding an envelope there.

"Really?" she muttered. "On Christmas?"

"Hmm? What is it?" Aiden mumbled.

Jaxie didn't answer him as she picked it up, unlocked the door, and helped him inside. "Here, lay down," she said, letting him fall to the couch. She opened up the envelope and read the folded paper inside.

There is a place you will go if you live a sinful life. God only forgives those who deserve it. He can't protect you from anyone who wants you dead.

"What a coward," Jaxie commented, ripping up the paper. She looked over at her brother, thankful he was

131

already passed out on the couch. She was hurting for him. He had tried to convince himself and her that Brett was only doing this to rekindle a friendship in a nasty way. She knew the truth. Anyone else could tell what the truth was. Once that truth hit Aiden, it would hit him hard, and she was worried about that.

Aiden woke up the next morning still on the couch. His head was pounding. He was still in yesterday's clothes. There was drool coming out the corner of his mouth, leaving his throat feeling dry. He groaned as he turned his head and saw Jaxie in the kitchen.

"Good morning," she said.

"Don't talk to me."

"Struggling? You ought to be with the way you drank yesterday."

Aiden shook his head. "That was rough. Did you sleep here?"

"Yeah. You weren't moving from that spot, so I used your bed," Jaxie said, bringing two cups of coffee with her to the couch. "You got new sheets. They were very comfy."

"I felt like it'd help me sleep some," Aiden said as he slowly sat up, holding a hand to his head. "Oh my God. This is why I only drink whiskey."

"Here you go," Jaxie handed the cup over.

"Thanks," he softly said, taking sips of the hot coffee.

"Have you made a doctor's appointment?"

"Huh? For what?"

"I saw your medication was almost gone. Aren't you supposed to go get reevaluated?"

"I guess so. I don't know if I'll need a refill."

"Really? So, you're feeling better?"

"I think so. I have skipped some mornings. I still get anxious, but I haven't had any panic attacks for quite awhile."

"I'm really glad to hear that," Jaxie smiled.

"I still have the other medication too, so I might just hold onto that and see how things go."

"Good. Are you ready to go get your car? Mom invited us to breakfast, but we don't have to do that. We'll just get the car and go."

"Yeah, alright. Then I am coming back here and going back to sleep."

The beginning of the drive to their parents' house was quiet, mostly because Aiden was focusing on not getting sick in Jaxie's car. Then something began bugging Aiden and he had to ask her about it. "What did it say?"

"What?" Jaxie asked, unsure what he meant.

"The letter. What did it say?"

"How do you even remember..."

"I wasn't blacked out from what was going on. Tell me."

Jaxie sighed in frustration. "It just said something about you living a sinful life."

"Really?" Aiden rubbed his temple. "I felt like I was yesterday. All day as everyone was talking to me about relationships and everything, I just knew they all meant with a woman. If I would have said otherwise, they would have had something to say about where I'm meant to go in life."

"Don't even start, Aiden."

"Brett's not as religious as Mom and Dad, so why would he bother sending that letter?"

"He knows it'd be a good scare tactic against you," Jaxie pointed out. "Just let him burn himself out. He'll get bored and move on."

Maybe Jaxie was right, but Aiden also considered what Jack had said. Maybe Brett wouldn't go any further than this, but maybe he would.

-11-

Aiden was spending New Year's Eve at Jack's house. He had received two more notes from Brett since Christmas. One was at his door again and the other was on his windshield at The Color Band's parking lot. Brett knowing where he worked made Aiden nervous. It was a new territory of harassment as he felt like he was being followed. This time the notes weren't religious wordings. They were on a more personal level as if it was Brett talking to Aiden himself. One said how their friendship was a lie and Aiden meant nothing to him anymore. The other was the first one that came off as a threat, telling Aiden he will get his ass kicked soon. Surprisingly, Aiden was more affected by the one stating he was nothing anymore. It hurt him so much that the idea of him getting his ass kicked wasn't phasing him. He hadn't told Jaxie or Jack about those notes. If he ignored it, maybe Brett would stop.

There was a good crowd of people at Jack's house, including Lydia and Avy. There were quite a few people Aiden recognized from The Color Band. If Aiden didn't know any better, he wouldn't have thought Jack went through any hardships being gay. He was surrounded by a lot of people who cared about him. He seemed to be a pretty popular guy.

The basement was full of laughter and people playing pool or poker, and while he was having a good time, it was a little out of Aiden's comfort zone. He was used to being surrounded by people at work with a bar between him and the customers. A house party was entirely different. He tended to shy away from more intense social interaction, especially when everyone was brand new to him. Aiden passed on a round of poker and took the opportunity to go upstairs to give himself a break.

"Are you having fun?" Lydia asked, joining Aiden in the kitchen.

"Yeah I am. Just needed a breather."

"I hear ya. I'm glad you came. Jack's really glad you came."

"Are any of these people old friends of yours and Jack's?"

"Yeah, a couple."

"He was telling me how a lot of friends at school kind of unfriended you guys after coming out."

"A lot of them did, yeah," Lydia confirmed. "Unfortunately, it wasn't just us not being friends anymore. We got our asses handed to us."

"What...kinds of things did they do?" Aiden asked, although he was still scared to find out.

"Well, we both went through different things. I got comments from guys who wanted to watch me do things with other girls at school. They'd say I should take off my shirt and not wear a bra, you know, be a guy because I'm not trying to attract guys anyway. The meaner girls would wear provocative clothes on purpose and then ask if I liked what I was seeing. One of our old friends had a one-on-one talk with me. She asked me if I felt I had to be gay because I couldn't get boyfriends as well as she could. It was all verbal and visual bullying to me. Sometimes I'd get the ones who would brush past me aggressively so I would drop something, but I could handle that."

The one-on-one comment brought Aiden back to Brett. "My old friend told me I only thought I was gay because of the breakup with my ex-girlfriend. He thought I was going through some pity party, and he told me to snap out of it."

Lydia nodded, "People can definitely be cruel."

"But how? I just don't understand it. After being friends with someone for so long, how?"

Lydia looked at Aiden with empathy, "Because some people have their limits to friendships, whether they realize it or not. They don't unconditionally love their friends, not even their close friends. They have a large circle of people they know, so they can bond with new friends whenever they lose other ones. Jack and I coming out as gay was a limit to some of those friends. They didn't believe gay people had rights, they didn't believe a girl can love another girl like she can love a guy and vice versa, they weren't comfortable being around us. Some people can change a lot with things like this. Some of them can just move on and never acknowledge your existence again. And some of them feel like they have to do something about it, like you betrayed them in some way. They do crazy things."

Aiden didn't want to ask, but he had to know. "You said you got visual and verbal bullying. What happened to Jack?"

Lydia's expression shifted. She went from understanding the hurt someone was going through and now feeling the hurt of someone else. "He got notes left in his locker. They were calling him names, giving him death threats. Guys would say sexual things to him. He got beat up. There was this one guy, he wasn't a friend of ours or anything, but he had a real hatred for any guy he found out was gay. We had seen it on another kid at school, but we didn't think he'd care about Jack since they didn't really know each other. We were wrong. This guy had a younger brother who was a freshman. When he found out about Jack, he kept threatening him that if he looked at his younger brother in a certain way or if he had thoughts about his younger brother, he was in trouble. Jack never went after anyone anyway, and I didn't either. We knew trying to actually date would be too dangerous, so we just didn't. That guy would claim over and over again that Jack was wanting to...do things with his little brother, and he'd beat Jack up. Not just a shove to the ground or a quick pound to the face. He got his buddies together and they'd really hand it to him. This went on over and over again. No one would do anything either. According to a lot of kids, Jack was asking for it."

Aiden shook his head, feeling a heavy pit form in his stomach as he imagined it all. "Jack didn't deserve that. He's such a great guy."

"He really is. If he hadn't been with me through all this, I don't know what I would have done." Lydia looked at Aiden sadly.

"I just...I don't get it. In my head, I know Brett is done with me and wants nothing to do with me. In my heart though, I'm trying to make reason with his acting out as a way of missing me or something."

"I get that. Jack and I went through our denials too. You'll figure out the truth soon enough."

Aiden didn't like hearing that phrase again. He wanted one person to tell him that his theory was possible. Instead, everyone was looking in clear water, trying to show Aiden the truth right before them. He was at the other end scooping through mud trying to find validation for his reasoning. "I don't want to believe that." He fell silent for a moment, then looked at Lydia with a small smile. "Well, let's get back downstairs before Jack thinks I'm stealing all his whiskey."

As they approached the stairs, Lydia grabbed Aiden by the arm. "Jack really likes you, by the way. I hope things work out with you guys."

"Thanks, Lydia. I do too."

"Even if they don't, I hope things work out how they're supposed to for you."

Before long, the countdown to the end of the year came. Aiden had dreaded it all day and had been hoping to find an excuse to leave early, but he had lost track of time. His stomach was doing somersaults. He wasn't sure if Jack was expecting them to kiss. Maybe Aiden had given him that impression by being here and staying for this moment. Everyone was beginning to count down in chorus. Some were holding their drinks in the air and some were holding their loved ones close. Time had slowed down and it was the longest countdown Aiden had ever heard. He was watching everyone call out the numbers, and it seemed to be an eternity for each one. Jack had come over and put an arm around Aiden. That's when he decided to prepare himself. Jack really liked him, and he really liked Jack. He knew he did. If Jack leaned in, he wouldn't stop him. He would let it happen. Aiden quickly tried convincing himself that he wanted to share his first kiss with Jack, there and now.

Once the number one was shouted, Aiden felt himself chickening out. He could feel his head lowering slowly, not daring to look up. Cheers went around the room, but Aiden was still in his spot. No movements were made. He wasn't pulled closer in any way. With that, Aiden decided to take a peek. He saw Jack out of the corner of his eye taking a drink. He hadn't tried to kiss him. Part of him was relieved, but he also wondered if him lowering his head made Jack think that he hadn't wanted it.

As the party wound down, Jack continued mingling with everyone not really making eye contact with him. Aiden couldn't stop himself from overthinking the whole night, and he wondered if Jack was upset with him. Eventually, the guests started to filter out the door and Aiden waited until everyone had left to talk to him.

"Did you have fun?" Jack asked as he collected empty cups around the kitchen.

Aiden felt his anxiety rise now that they were alone. He needed to start moving if he was going to have any sort of conversation. Quickly, he grabbed the garbage can and began cleaning off the counter. "Yeah, it was a lot of fun."

"Good."

They were quiet for a moment. As much as part of him was trying to avoid it, Aiden had to ask about the countdown. Maybe it didn't bother Jack as much as he was thinking. If he didn't find out, though, he knew he'd toss and turn all night trying to figure it out. And that's when the worst case scenario would creep into his mind and possibly cause a panic attack. Aiden didn't want to risk that, no matter how uncomfortable he felt, he needed to know, if only for his own peace of mind.

"You...didn't try to kiss me?"

Jack stopped moving for a second. "Did you want me to?"

Aiden silently cursed at himself. "I just expected you to when you came over and pulled me close to you. I was kind of preparing for it, but then I chickened out at the last second."

"I didn't think you were ready for that. Sure, I wanted to, but I know better. Besides, I really want you to read that book first."

"I think I should too."

"Do you think you still have feelings for her?" Jack asked suddenly. "Maybe not in certain ways anymore, but do you miss her?"

Aiden was surprised to hear that question. Mainly because he hadn't thought about it in a long time. He also hadn't expected the conversation to take such a hard turn. "Maybe." He shrugged. "I went through this weird thing where I really wanted her back in the beginning. Then when I started noticing my personal changes, I realized that I wanted what I had with Courtney, but with Brett instead. Well, now not with Brett anymore. So I guess the answer is I miss what I had with Courtney, but I don't miss it with her. Not the way I did." As Jack turned to continue cleaning, Aiden saw a quick glimpse of a smile on his face. It warmed his heart. That was confirmation enough that there were no hard feelings.

"Hey," Jack said, pouring two more glasses of champagne. "One more drink."

"Please don't twist my arm," Aiden smirked, accepting the glass.

Jack raised his drink. "Here's to a new year. A new you." Aiden tapped his glass against Jack's and took a sip. "You're spending the night by the way."

The liquid did not make it far as the statement caused his throat to close up. He should be expecting the quick wit statements from Jack by now, but it still caught him by surprise. When coughing subsided he asked, "What?"

"Relax, I'm not talking about *that*. You've had a lot to drink. You can stay in the guest room downstairs."

"Well...yeah, that's probably a good idea. I've been drinking a lot lately."

"Holidays," Jack simply shrugged.

"Very different holidays, that's for sure."

"And if you have nothing planned tomorrow, we can go grab some breakfast or something."

"Yeah, that sounds great!"

Aiden was relieved with the way the conversation about the night had gone. He should have known that Jack wouldn't have held anything against him for the countdown moment. It was starting to come around to him that he truly could discuss any thoughts or feelings. It made him feel confident in talking to Jack about so much more, especially with the help of that final glass of champagne. "Hey, I was talking to Lydia and she told me some stuff. It sort of got me thinking."

"What stuff?"

"About when you two were in school."

Aiden was surprised to see Jack straighten up. That was the first time it looked like a nerve had been struck with Jack, as if he was scared of something. His usual confidence seemed to slip away. "What, um, what did she tell you?"

"About what happened to the two of you after coming out. She said you got beat up, especially by one guy who thought you were after his little brother or something."

Jack slowly turned to begin washing some dishes. He didn't say one word.

"Jack, I'm sorry. I didn't mean to bring up bad memories..."

"What did she tell you exactly?" Jack interrupted.

"Nothing more than that. She just said you got beat up," Aiden quickly answered.

"She didn't tell you specifics?"

"No, not really."

"Okay," Jack said quietly. "Listen, I can get the rest of this. Go on downstairs and get some sleep."

Aiden slowly turned away, realizing another side of Jack was coming out. It only proved why he usually kept his mouth shut. "I'm really sorry Jack, if I..."

"It's fine, really. Just go get some rest, alright?"

142

"Okay." Aiden left it at that and hurried downstairs faster than he intended to.

Jack didn't continue cleaning after Aiden left the kitchen. He stared at nothing. Memories flooded his mind, causing him to feel scared and angry. His legs became unsteady as he slowly sank to the floor. He hadn't expected to be confronted with those memories. Not today. And not from Aiden. He had planned to talk to Aiden about his experiences eventually, if they got as close as Jack wanted, but not yet. Jack was angry, sad, overwhelmed, and he couldn't calm himself. He took out his phone and called Lydia.

"Hey, Lydia."

"Hey, is everything okay?" Lydia asked, unsure about the late call.

"You told Aiden about our school days? Really?"

"I didn't tell him the details of what happened. He asked what we went through so I gave him a basic outline," Lydia explained. "If it makes you feel better, I told him more details about what happened to me."

"Lydia, how would that make me feel any better?" Jack asked. "He doesn't need to hear that stuff."

"If you want something to develop with him, you need to be honest about your past. Your experiences may help him cope better with all of this anyway."

"He didn't need to know yet. You know I don't like to talk about it with anyone, no matter how I feel about them."

"Jack, calm down. It kinda seemed like you mentioned it to him for him to ask me what happened."

Jack shook his head in frustration. "He hadn't asked me about it. I had mentioned it in passing. It was mainly to warn him about Brett. I really don't appreciate this."

143

"You are overreacting and—"

"He's already asked me more about it, Lydia! Now he's going to expect me to—"

"He won't expect anything! Look, I'm sorry. I didn't tell him specifics. You are worrying over nothing, I'm sure. Just get some sleep and call me in the morning."

"Fine," Jack said, hanging up his phone. He got up from the floor and marched upstairs to his room, leaving the rest of the mess where it was.

Aiden went upstairs as soon as he got up. He wanted to check on Jack since he was still kicking himself for bringing up the conversation with Lydia. Even knowing Jack wasn't the type to hold this against him, Aiden was still nervous about what he'd say to him once he got up there. The way the conversation went was causing Aiden to back away from his curiosity of wanting to know any more details of the past.

Entering the kitchen, Aiden saw Jack sitting with coffee in hand. "Morning sunshine," he greeted. "Want some?"

"Yes, please," Aiden said, relieved to see him more like himself. "Are you feeling better?"

Jack nodded. "Yeah. I'm sorry I was short with you last night."

"No, I'm sorry I brought it up. You're a very open person, so I just assumed you...it doesn't matter, I shouldn't have been asking Lydia about anything. I wasn't trying to pry."

"No, I know. It's okay. It's a sore topic. Maybe we can talk about it someday. Just not yet."

"Of course." With that comment alone, Aiden could tell that something traumatic had happened to Jack. His warning to be careful and not take Brett's notes lightly made far more sense now.

"Alright, it's a new year! We aren't starting it off by sulking. So! I have tickets to the hockey game tonight. Do you want to go?"

"That sounds fun. Jaxie and I go quite a bit. She loves hockey," Aiden said, and then it hit him and his face fell. "Oh shoot."

"What?"

"Oh no. I'm a lousy brother." Aiden threw his head back, looking at the ceiling. "It's Jaxie's birthday. I always call her once the New Year hits to say happy birthday. Oh boy, she's not going to let me live this one down."

"You're in trouble," Jack teased.

"Looks like I may be taking her to the hockey game." He bit his lip as he thought of the predicament he put himself in. "I guess it's biting me in the ass now that I haven't told her about you."

"Aiden, no. Don't look at it like that. You're handling it fine!" Jack smiled as he slid the tickets across the counter. "Go ahead and take her."

"I can't take your tickets."

"I was planning to go with you, so there's no point in me keeping them. Just go and have fun."

Aiden reluctantly picked up the tickets. "I owe you later."

"I'll accept that," Jack winked. "You better call her though."

"Yes, I should." Aiden walked out of the kitchen with Jack behind him. Jack didn't know it but Aiden was worrying over what excuse he was going to tell Jaxie for not calling her. "Thanks for the coffee, the food, all that whiskey, the party," Aiden said as he backed up towards the front door, "Did I miss anything?"

"Hmm, the bed."

"Yes, and thanks for the bed. I'll talk to you later."

Aiden walked through the snow to his car. He began dialing Jaxie's number as he took his brush to clean the light snow off his windshield.

"You are eleven hours late," Jaxie said when she answered the phone.

"I know, I know. I'm sorry. Happy Birthday, sis!"

"Not good enough. You owe me."

"You are now twenty-two years old. You get the adult treatment for your birthday which means you're lucky I still call you every year."

"It actually means you're taking me out for drinks then," Jaxie corrected.

"Yes, at the hockey game. Wanna go?"

"Absolutely!"

"Okay, I'll pick you up around four. We'll grab some dinner and head downtown."

"Cool! What is your excuse for not calling me for the first time ever?"

"I went to a little get together with some coworkers and, I'll admit it, I completely forgot."

"Hmm, did you forget because you were *busy* with someone at the ringing in of the new year?" He could hear the smile in her voice.

"No. Just hanging out with some new friends."

"Well, I can forgive you then. Did you have fun?"

"Yeah, I did. I'm going to get cleaned up and ready, so I'll come pick you up soon. Love you."

"Love you, too."

As Aiden hung up the phone, he looked down and noticed something on his windshield. It was another envelope. At first he was irritated. By now, he was beginning to see Brett's behavior as pathetic. Then he realized something: he wasn't even at his apartment. Brett had to have followed him to Jack's house last night, or maybe he found him that morning. Aiden took a look around, but didn't see Brett's truck anywhere. He quickly grabbed the envelope and got into the car. He ripped it open. This time there were pictures inside. Aiden began flipping through them. There was a picture of him and Jack standing outside The Color Band, a picture of Jack walking outside his apartment complex, and a picture of his car outside Jack's house from last night.

"You can't be serious," Aiden muttered to himself. Reaching inside the envelope again, he pulled out a small white paper.

Is it worth it getting hurt and your parents knowing about this? No one is going to protect you.

Aiden felt his stomach flip. Brett was attempting to blackmail him now. This is what Jack was talking about. Brett wasn't going to burn out of this or get bored when Aiden didn't react. He wanted Aiden to suffer, and he'd make sure it happened.

The afternoon came and Aiden picked up his sister for their night out. She had on one of her many hockey jerseys and hat.

"Everytime we go to a game, you act like it's your first one," Aiden laughed as they drove to dinner.

"It's always exciting!" Jaxie said cheerfully. "Thanks for getting us tickets."

"You're welcome."

"I haven't talked to you much since Christmas. How are things going with you?"

"Fine, for the most part."

"Has anything else happened with Brett?"

"Unfortunately. It was just notes directed at me, and I didn't really care about that, but the note I found this morning was about telling Mom and Dad. Then it

147

mentioned no one protecting me." Aiden said, keeping the details about Jack and the pictures to himself.

"I swear to God if he...why does he want to mess with you so bad?"

"I'm trying to ignore it. I don't think he'll stop though."

"Do you think you should report him to the police or something?"

"He's not really threatening me," Aiden partially lied. "He's trying to scare me and stuff, but my life isn't really in jeopardy." He wasn't sure whether he was trying to convince Jaxie of that or himself.

She sighed with some annoyance, clearly wanting Aiden to do more to defend himself. "You're right, sort of. But still, it's frustrating. Maybe from now on you don't open anything from him? Just throw it out right away. That's one thing you can do."

"Yeah, I will do that. That's a good idea. Better than getting worked up over his pathetic scare tactics."

"Exactly. Anyway, let's enjoy tonight. I'm pumped!"

Aiden enjoyed hockey games, but the best part of them was bringing Jaxie to hockey games. She was entertaining to be around when it came to the game. There was so much energy she brought. She never sat down and was always yelling. Aiden decided to sneak a small video of Jaxie's antics at the game and send it to Jack with a text.

This is what you may have to deal with.

She looks like a lot of fun. I'm glad you put good use to the tickets. I miss you.

Aiden was thankful Jaxie wasn't looking at him. He was sure she'd be seeing a silly grin on his face as he responded to Jack.

I miss you, too.

A couple nights later, at a typical late hour after his shift at the bar, Aiden had reached his building and started trudging up the stairs to his apartment when something caught his eye. He stopped mid-step with his foot hovering over the step in front of him. Through the stairwell, he could see a figure outside his door.

It was Brett.

Aiden was frozen on the spot, his adrenaline rising. He wanted to leave and go back to his car, maybe drive over to Jaxie's apartment. But he knew he couldn't. That wouldn't stop anything, it wouldn't make it better. He made the indecisive decision he wasn't going to be scared of Brett over the notes and pictures, no matter the level of the threat. He didn't even know why Brett was there. Maybe he was coming to apologize or try to talk things out. Aiden would never know if he didn't confront the opportunity right before him. On the other hand, he thought of Jack's words telling him to keep his guard up.

Aiden reached the top of the stairs, and Brett looked at him. As much as Brett had hurt him, Aiden couldn't help feeling a little happy at seeing his best friend and hoping there was a chance that he had come with good intentions.

"You didn't bring your boyfriend home tonight?" Brett asked with a snarky tone. The comment made Aiden step back. His heart sank, the truth quickly coming to light. This wasn't about Brett making amends. Now Aiden had to watch his back.

"I don't," Aiden paused as he took a hard swallow, gathering any courage he could muster, "have a boyfriend."

"You better stop this nonsense before you get in some real trouble. I know you got my messages," Brett said, taking slow, deliberate steps towards Aiden. "Just

149

drop this little act and we can move on. No one will hurt you then."

Aiden's heart sank further. He wasn't sure if he should take that as a warning or not. "It's not an act. How can you say that to me?"

Brett took Aiden by surprise as he pinned him to the wall and threw a punch at his face. Quickly, Brett took off down the stairs while Aiden fell to the ground. His body was trembling. He hadn't expected something like this to happen and he was scared it may not be over. He fiddled his keys out of his pocket and hurried inside, locking the door. His body wouldn't slow down as he ran to the bathroom to check the damage. Blood was running down from his nose.

"Damn," Aiden said, his heart trying to break through his chest by now. His breath was coming in gasps and tears tried to fight their way down his face. It looked like Jack was right, and after what just happened, Aiden was going to have to admit it. Brett was going to make his life miserable and make him regret all of this.

"Okay, maybe now we call the police?" Jaxie suggested. Once Aiden got the nosebleed to slow, he called his sister to tell her what happened.

"I don't know. I can't think about that right now."

"What do you mean? He hit you, again! That's assault."

"Jaxie, I'm just trying to process this, okay? This wasn't about leaving me notes to scare me or whatever. He wants to hurt me!"

"Exactly! All the more reason to get a restraining order or something," she said. "Are you worried the police won't help?"

"I just...I don't know if I can go through with it. I don't know if I can press charges against my best friend, or whatever the hell he is!"

"Why not? Why can't you do that?"

"I don't hate him," Aiden admitted. "I think he's right. I'm just asking for trouble."

"You can't be serious."

"Look, I have to think about some things, okay? I'm sorry I called you late. I just needed to talk it out for a minute. I'm going to sleep on it."

Jaxie didn't respond right away. He heard her let out a long sigh. "I don't like this, Aiden."

-12-

The first thing Aiden did in the morning was call the doctor for his reevaluation. He knew what was going to come along in the approaching days, so he knew he would need to get back on track with his medication. The doctor was going to have him continue taking a pill every morning and having the backup pills for sudden episodes. Against his sister's wishes, going to the police wasn't part of Aiden's plan. He spent all night tossing and turning trying to come up with a different solution. Although he didn't figure out a way to protect himself, he did come up with another arrangement to make sure Brett couldn't take things too far. Aiden had other means of protection to take care of and it was a tough decision for him to make. He didn't want Jack to get hurt or involved in his mess. Jack had already dealt with this stuff, and Aiden cared about him too much to let history repeat for him.

He decided he had to stop becoming personally involved with Jack.

Aiden couldn't get himself to come clean about it either, because he knew Jack would fight him on it and then he'd give in. He couldn't risk that happening. It had to be the band-aid getting ripped off technique. If he quit Jack cold turkey, the quicker the wound should heal. Aiden didn't want to hurt Jack by ending what they could've had, but he was scared what could happen if he kept him around. He also didn't like the approach of ghosting Jack, but it was easier to come off as a rude person than watching him become heartbroken. Aiden assumed Jack would move on easier that way if he gave the impression he was an asshole.

This all made for a long couple of weeks. Aiden's focus was on moving forward with his life. He had to work on being the best version of himself, by himself. More importantly, he had to put an end to the problems with Brett before bringing another man in his life. Maybe that meant Jack and maybe that meant someone else. Aiden couldn't worry about that detail right now. He depended on the medication to make the pain stop, even if it was only temporary. Unfortunately, sometimes that meant taking extra to get through the day. Jack would call or text, but Aiden ignored him. On the nights Aiden worked, he wouldn't interact with Jack. He'd try to have another bartender serve him or he'd avoid conversation beyond his drink order. Aiden enjoyed The Color Band too much to leave, and, besides, he did hope to maintain a friendship with Jack someday, when the deeper feelings killed off. It hurt Aiden more than he realized it would, but he thought it was for the better, even if he was taking more of his pills than he should have been.

During the time this went on, Aiden believed it was working, as nothing was coming from Brett and he imagined Jack was giving up on him. The tactic didn't last long though. Aiden was trapped when Jack randomly showed up at his apartment one night.

"Jack," Aiden said, surprised to see him standing at his door.

"Aiden," Jack said as he raised an eyebrow. "Can I come in?"

"I...Yeah, sure." Aiden looked to the floor, feeling the guilt hit him like a wave. He was cornered. There was no avoiding Jack now, and he'd have to explain himself.

Jack walked inside and was quiet for a minute. "You've been ignoring me." Aiden put his hands in his pockets. He didn't know what to say. The feelings he had hoped would start becoming less and less haven't budged.

"Why? Did I do something?"

"No, of course not."

"Then why are you ignoring me?" Jack asked with a demanding tone. "You won't even acknowledge me at the bar. What is it? What's going on?"

Aiden expected to have kept his cool. He thought he would have been able to stand his ground with his decision but he couldn't do it. Everything came tumbling out. "Brett showed up here a couple weeks ago. He was here waiting for me. He knows about you. He left me pictures of us together and me at your house. He left me a note about kicking my ass. He kept telling me I'd get hurt. He...hit me. That night he was here, he hit me. I freaked out. I was scared because he knows who you are. He could hurt you and I wouldn't be able to forgive myself if that happened." He looked at Jack with misty eyes. "You were completely right about him. He wants to hurt me. He can't just stop being friends with me. He wants to make sure I don't live happily. I couldn't risk him hurting you. I...I didn't want to ignore you, but I had to protect you somehow. I..."

"Okay, okay. That's enough," Jack said, pulling Aiden into a hug.

"I just want him to leave me alone."

"Shh, be quiet. Don't say anything else," Jack said, pushing Aiden's head against his shoulder. "I knew something was up when I saw your nose all swollen a couple weeks ago."

Aiden leaned into Jack and quietly cried. It felt good to be near him again. His heart slowed as he felt Jack's strong hands run through his hair, aiding to soothe the worries. Aiden felt himself sink into an alternate universe where all his problems with Brett vanished. It was just him and Jack alone. He didn't have to overthink anything anymore. They could do anything together and it was all going to be okay.

When Aiden finally backed away feeling a little more collected, he continued, "I know you've already been through a lot. I didn't want to put you through that again."

"Aiden, I told you I didn't want you to go through anything that I've had to go through. That also meant going through it alone," Jack placed his hands on Aiden's shoulders. "Hey, look at me."

Aiden slowly looked up at Jack. It didn't matter what he was about to say regarding the situation. All Aiden could think about in that moment was how much he missed him.

"How do you think I came out of the situation I was in? Hmm?"

"I don't know."

"I came out of it wanting to make sure it wasn't the norm. I want to be there for anyone who needs it. I want to be there for *you*. Brett, or anyone else that comes your way, isn't going to scare me away. I care about you too much."

"I care about you too. But I've been awful to you. You should be pissed at me."

"I wasn't happy. I'm here trying to figure it out though. I want this to work."

"I'm so sorry I ignored you. It's actually a relief that you still want to be around me. I wouldn't have blamed you if you decided to get away."

Jack shook his head. "No way."

It was quiet for a moment. Aiden had no idea what he had done to deserve Jack and his kindness. He just knew he couldn't let that get away, even if Brett was telling him that his worth should be nonexistent to everyone.

"Can you hang out here? I really missed you," Aiden admitted.

"I was hoping you'd ask." That smile Aiden was begging to see again appeared on Jack's face.

For the next couple hours, Aiden and Jack had the TV on, but they weren't watching much. Aiden lay against Jack and they talked. They were talking as if they hadn't seen each other in years. It was mostly Aiden venting his thought process to Jack on his decision. He made Aiden feel a lot better. It was evident Jack wasn't the least bit worried or intimidated by Brett. He was more than prepared to stand his ground and to help Aiden stand his. As Jack spoke, Aiden felt himself becoming more relaxed. He felt protected in Jack's arms. Aiden hadn't realized how much he wanted to lay in Jack's arms until it was finally happening.

"I really hate to do this, but I should get going," Jack said, running his hand through Aiden's hair. "I gotta get up early."

There was hesitancy as Aiden lifted himself into a sitting position. "Alright. I'm sorry again for what I did, but I'm really glad you came over and made me face it."

"I'm just glad I hadn't done anything wrong," Jack said as he stood up. "Do you work tomorrow?"

"Yeah."

"I'll see you there then, *actually* serving me. Maybe even talking to me?" Jack winked. The flutters went through Aiden's stomach. He missed how good those

156

winks made him feel. He missed seeing a lot of the little things Jack did.

"Yes, absolutely," Aiden said, smiling weakly.

After Jack left, Aiden got himself ready for bed. As he walked past his dresser, he saw the book Jack had given him. He picked it up and flipped through the pages as he fell back to the bed. Now seemed like the best time to begin reading it. Aiden opened it to the first page, and read it until he couldn't keep his eyes open.

The next night of work was an energetic one. Aiden was ecstatic that things worked out with Jack. His attitude was instantly better and everything seemed to sit right again. The concern level for Brett's threats went from Aiden recoiling himself to play Brett's game and now were at moving forward with his life as he should be. He was grateful Jack hadn't held this odd, standoffish behavior against him.

"We're closing up now," Aiden said to Jack as the stragglers still at the bar were paying their tabs and leaving.

"I want to wait here. You owe me a lot of missed time," Jack said, tapping his fingers against his beer bottle, "which brings me to a question."

"What's that?"

Jack tossed back the rest of his drink before asking, "Want to go to dinner with me tomorrow?"

Aiden was silent as he wiped down the counter. Why couldn't he just accept an invite to go out on a date without overthinking it from every angle? He was becoming increasingly frustrated with himself. He had fantasized about these situations with Jack, normal date-type outings and being in public, but was now chickening out when the opportunity presented itself. He was hating the feeling that he could only be with Jack at one of their homes, as if he was committing a crime and had to enjoy it in secret.

"No expectations," Jack added.

Aiden looked up at him and nodded, forcing the fears aside enough to answer. "Yeah, I'd really like that."

"Awesome." Jack smiled. "Finish up, I'll walk you out."

As Aiden and Jack walked outside, they saw Avy and Lydia standing in the parking lot.

"What are you guys still doing here?" Aiden asked.

They didn't respond as Jack said, "He said yes."

"Yay!" Lydia gasped as she gave Aiden a hug. "You're going to have so much fun!"

"He was nervous to ask you," Avy said. "He was sure you'd say no."

"I was terrified to answer," Aiden admitted, running his hand down the back of his neck.

"Now that that's out of the way, we need to get going." Lydia smiled, unable to contain her excitement for her best friend. "I can't wait to hear how it goes for you guys. Night!"

As the girls drove away, Aiden turned to Jack. "She's pretty happy for you."

"Yeah, she is." He smiled at the place where Lydia had just been standing. "Well," he turned his attention back to Aiden, "I better go get some sleep. I'll pick you up around six?"

"Okay." Aiden smiled as he turned for his car, although his heart was pounding with nerves, he was feeling proud of the step he was taking.

The next day, the excitement had flipped to fear. Time could not have gone by any slower and Aiden not doing much had made it worse. Multiple times he wanted to text Jack and cancel their date, but he couldn't get himself to do that. He wondered if Jack was as scared as he was. Jack was the most confident person he'd ever met, so Aiden had trouble imagining he would be on edge over going out on a simple dinner date.

Aiden wanted to go on this date, he knew he did, but he didn't know what it was going to be like and that caused his mind to run with ridiculous scenarios. Between 5:02 and 5:56, Aiden sat on his couch, staring straight at the wall, unable to keep his feet still. As soon as there was a knock at his door, he rushed to the kitchen to swallow his backup anxiety pill. He followed Jack out to his truck with ease and begged for the rest of the night to be that way.

"Don't be nervous," Jack said with a smile as they sat at the table in the restaurant. No matter how good Aiden felt he was at hiding his feelings, Jack always seemed to know the truth.

"I don't know why I am."

"Because we're spending time together in a public place that isn't The Color Band."

"Yeah." Aiden let out a long breath. "Just feel like I'm being watched."

Jack glanced around the restaurant. "Some people may be looking and wondering, but they don't all have the same agenda as Brett."

"I should know that."

"And I know you wanted things to move slow, but I did want to do something a little special."

"I'm glad you did. I really am." Aiden smiled but then it faltered. He couldn't help but think about how much worse it could be right now if he hadn't taken one of his medications to keep his head leveled. Right now he was simply nervous, but he could be having a true anxiety episode if he hadn't taken a pill. He still didn't like that that was the way to keep his days smooth, but he was more willing to take them than he was before. "I want to talk to you about something though, you know, in case things do get more serious with us. I should get it off my chest."

"Okay, shoot."

"So...while I was going through the stuff with Courtney, I began having these anxiety problems. I just...I had these...panic attacks. They got really bad. Brett and Jaxie made me go see a doctor and I was put on a couple medications. I have to take one every morning and I have a backup one that I can take if things are getting, well, scary. They help me a lot. After spending some time with you, I skipped some days of my medication, which was good. I didn't initially go to my reevaluation because I didn't feel like I needed it. Then things got a little ugly, and I tried keeping you out of it, out of my life, so I went back on the meds to try and help with that. It's just been a very, very, very crazy ride for me. I'm still trying to figure out how to manage any panic attacks without taking a pill, but I haven't yet. I took one before this date."

"Do the pills help?"

Aiden nodded. "Yeah. I guess I just felt like you should know what you could be getting into. Some days I feel completely fine, days that I'm sure I could have gone without my morning pill. Then there are days I'm sure I would have had panic attacks or something if I didn't take it."

"You can't be ashamed of something like that. Who knows where you would be if you didn't ask for help, you know?"

"I don't want to know."

"I think everyone has something that helps keep them grounded, you know? Some people have medications. I play with these." Jack slid a blue rubber wristband off. He wore six of them on his left arm, all different colors. "They each have a Bible verse on them. Sometimes I just start messing with them if I need to get distracted from reality."

"I wish I could have something as simple as that."

"Maybe you'll get there. It doesn't matter either way. I'm glad you felt comfortable enough to tell me, but whatever you have to do for your own health, don't ever wonder how others will perceive it. It's not even my business. Just do what's best for you."

Aiden shook his head with a smile. "I don't know what I ever did to deserve you in my life."

"I ask myself the same thing." Jack smiled, putting a hand on top of Aiden's. "Does Jaxie know you're here tonight?"

"No." Aiden shook his head. "You know, I feel like it really bothers you that I haven't told her. You bring it up enough."

"Do I wish I could meet her? Sure, but I'll handle it on your time. Honestly, you coming out to dinner with me means a lot more than you understand."

While they continued talking and eating their meals, Aiden felt the tension loosen up. He realized he had stopped caring about whether anyone was looking at them or what was going through their heads. His attention was focused only on Jack. Nothing could seem to tear him from it. He felt in control and confident for the first time in a long time.

Suddenly, Aiden's pocket vibrated. Assuming it was a text from Jaxie, he took a quick glance at the screen, but then couldn't look away.

Jack saw the sudden change in Aiden's face. "What is it?"

"It's Brett," Aiden said quietly. "I deleted his number, but...I still recognize it."

"What did he say?"

"He wants me to come outside and talk."

"He's here?"

"I guess..." Aiden said, beginning to stand up.

"Wait a second," Jack grabbed Aiden's arm. "What are you doing?"

"He says he wants to talk. That's a good thing, right?"

"Aiden, think for a minute. He followed you here. That doesn't seem like he's here to make amends."

"Well...maybe he didn't follow us. Maybe he was coming here anyway and saw I was here."

"Aiden, be logical..."

"I'll just step outside. I won't go near him," Aiden assured him.

Jack wiped his mouth with his napkin and stood up. "Well then I'm coming with you."

"No. I'm not putting you in the middle of this. It's between me and him. Just please, sit down."

"You're not going alone," Jack said firmly. "I'm at least standing by the door."

Aiden sighed, knowing he wasn't getting out of this. "Fine."

"Look," Jack said as they walked towards the door, "I know part of you still wants this to work with him, that you still want to have the same relationship you had before, but he's just using that as his advantage to mess with you. It's blunt, but you need to know that. You need to understand that."

Aiden didn't respond as he walked outside. As promised, Jack stayed inside the building. This could not be a wasted opportunity for Aiden, no matter how much Jack was against it. Aiden was scared, but he felt he had his guard up better than before, and could keep himself from getting hurt this time. He didn't see anyone at first, so he made his way towards the other side of the parking lot.

"Wait, what are you...?" Jack said as he watched Aiden walk further away, "Damn." As much as Jack wanted to jump out and intervene, he knew it'd just make

Aiden resent him, but what he knew was about to happen made him sick to his stomach.

Aiden got around the restaurant and looked among the cars for Brett's truck. "Brett?"

He barely got it out before he felt himself get tugged to the side. Tossed to the wet street, Aiden felt the blows and kicks begin. It happened so fast, Aiden had no time to react. He put his arms around his head as much as he could while hard kicks were connecting with his stomach and back. Even though it felt neverending, the attack only lasted seconds. Jack had rounded the corner and pulled one of the assailants off, shoving them away. He grabbed the second jumper and threw him to the road. Aiden was trying to catch his breath as he kept himself covered, expecting more hits to come.

Jack flipped his knife out and held it for the two guys to see. "Come on! Let's do this big guys!"

No one was going to get into anything further as a truck came down the parking lot. The truck slammed on its brakes and let the two guys hop in. Jack felt his rage begin to fly as he walked up to the truck, not intimidated in the least.

"Some man you are!" Jack yelled. "Can't even fight your own fights!"

Aiden finally came out of his hidden shell as he peeked up and saw Brett's truck driving away, Jack yelling any profanity he could think of at the taillights. The world began to shake as Aiden tried his best to hold the cries in but failed. His shoulders dropped and the signal finally hit his brain that he was cold sitting in the snow, but he was too ashamed to get up.

"Hey," Jack got down and pulled Aiden close. "Are you okay?"

"Get off me." Aiden shoved Jack away. "Please just go away. I want to go home."

"You don't have a car here," Jack said, looking down. "I'll go pay the bill and drive you home, alright? Just come inside..."

"No," Aiden interrupted.

"Alright. Here, take the keys and go wait in my truck. I'll be back in a minute."

Once Jack was gone, Aiden got up and brushed himself off as best he could. Even though he saw Brett's truck drive off, he had a feeling that it wasn't over. As he made his way across the parking lot, he kept his eyes peeled for anyone else coming towards him. He kept picturing someone else coming up and pulling him down, their advantage now being Jack inside the restaurant. Taking one last look around, Aiden grasped the passenger side door and opened it. He got in and started the engine, his body now begging for some heat. Whether the shivers were from the cold or the fear, or both, Aiden pulled his knees against his chest. There was a harsh pain throughout his torso as he did that, but he didn't care. He buried his face, scared to look out the windows. He wanted to sink down as much as possible. All the things he imagined Jack was going to say rang in his head. This was an easy opportunity for him to rub it in Aiden's face. He hated that Jack had been right again. He hated more that he didn't learn from the altercation in his apartment hallway.

The driver side door started to open, causing Aiden to jump. To his relief, Jack got in the truck without a word. Even as he began driving, he said nothing, instead letting Aiden sit in silence.

"Where are we going?" Aiden asked, noticing Jack wasn't heading to his apartment.

"The hospital. You're really hurt."

"Take me home, Jack."

"Aiden, please just let them check..."

"No! Take me home!"

164

Jack immediately dropped it. Much to his dismay, he turned the truck around. Once he pulled up to the apartment complex, Aiden was quick to grab the door handle.

"Don't storm out," Jack said, grabbing Aiden by the hand. "You should at least fill out a police report."

"For what? I don't even know who those guys were. Brett didn't do anything."

"Go get a restraining order then. Please. It killed me to watch that, and to see you like this now."

Aiden didn't promise anything. He stepped out of Jack's truck and hurried up to his apartment. He didn't want to think about what happened or what he was going to do about it. All he felt was embarrassment, and a little stupid. If it were up to him, he wouldn't relive it ever again. The quick solution to this was for him to take one of his anxiety medications and a sleeping pill to knock him out for the night. There was a part of him that hoped he wouldn't wake up, or if he did, that he would wake up to the jumping being a dream.

-13-

Unfortunately, it had not been a dream. Aiden was in a lot of pain when he woke up. He went to the bathroom and stripped down to look at the damage for the first time. His face was the least of his worries with a few minor scratches. There was bruising around his torso where he was kicked. And he could feel the damage to a few of his ribs. His back was killing him, and he could barely walk without making it obvious there was discomfort. The first person that came to his mind was Jaxie. There was no way he'd be able to hide this from her. Even if his face showed easy-to-cover damage, he wouldn't be able to hide the pain from his upper body. Once she did find out, there was no way he'd be able to convince her the authorities' help wasn't necessary. Aiden felt he was at a dead end, and he knew Jack was right. He needed to look into a restraining order for his own safety. In addition to doing that, he would at least have a settling way of telling Jaxie what happened once the time came.

Once Aiden got himself cleaned off as best as he could, he got dressed in fresh clothes and drove to Jack's. He wouldn't willingly go to the police, but he knew Jack would help push him there.

Jack opened his front door, relief clear on his face at seeing Aiden, "Hey, are you okay?"

"It hurts," Aiden said, walking into the house.

"I believe it. I'm so sorry." Jack's face fell as he watched Aiden hold a hand to his abdomen.

"No, I'm sorry. You didn't deserve me to act like that. You were right and I should've listened to you."

Being aware of the injury, Jack hugged Aiden gingerly. "I know it's hard to accept. I know it's also hard to listen to reasoning when you so badly don't want it to be true."

"Yeah. Anyway, I wanted to see if you'd come down to the police station and help me file all this. I can't do it by myself."

"Sure, if you can wait until later," Jack nodded towards the kitchen. "My niece is actually here."

"Oh, I'm sorry I had no idea. I can come back later."

"No, no. Come on, you should meet her."

"Oh. Alright, sure."

Aiden followed Jack, finding a little girl coloring at his counter. She had long, braided brown hair and was wearing a purple dress with unicorns on it.

"Hey, Marissa," Jack said cheerfully, "this is my friend, Aiden."

"Hi, Marissa," Aiden smiled, hoping his appearance wouldn't scare the little girl.

"Hi," she said, not bothering looking up from her paper. "Wanna color with me?"

"Sure," Aiden said as he grabbed some paper, "What do you want me to draw?"

Jack chuckled. "Well, she told me to draw a football stadium, which is proving difficult, so maybe you can do better."

"Wow, high expectations, huh?"

"I told you, she's sassy."

Aiden grabbed a marker and started his own scribbles to impress the child. "Did your uncle braid your hair like that?"

"He alway does," Marissa proudly said.

"And why do I always braid your hair?" Jack asked.

"Because Uncle Jack does it best," Marissa looked up from her paper with a big smile.

Aiden gave Jack a smirk. "Yeah, I'm sure there was no coaching to that response at all."

"When you're the fun uncle, you get to coach whatever you damn well please."

For the next few hours Jack and Aiden went between the kitchen and the living room playing with Marissa and having private conversations about the night's event. Aiden was anxious about going to the police, but Jack managed to keep him from running away to hide and hope it would blow over. Finally, there was a knock at the door, raising Aiden's heart rate as he knew the time had come to go take care of business.

"That's my daddy!" Marissa chimed happily.

"Uh, do you want me to go downstairs or something?" Aiden asked.

Jack shrugged, "If you're too nervous, you don't have to meet him."

Aiden thought for a second. There was a sense that he did owe Jack for a lot of things recently. "I'll meet him."

"Really?" Jack asked in surprise.

"Yes, I'd like to."

Aiden sure loved when he could get that big smile to cross Jack's face.

"Daddy! Daddy! Daddy!" Marissa yelled as she jumped up and down. A man who could easily pass as Jack's twin walked inside.

"Hey boo, were you good for Uncle Jack today?"

"She was great," Jack said. "Hey I got someone for you to meet. This is my friend Aiden. Aiden, this is my brother Joey."

"It's nice to meet you," Aiden said as he shook Joey's hand.

"Nice to meet you, too." Joey smiled towards his little brother. "So what kind of friend is this? A friend or a *friend*?"

Aiden was surprised to actually see Jack blush a little. "We're still figuring it out."

"That's enough of an answer for me," Joey said. "If that's the case, we'll all have to get together sometime."

"Definitely, we'll talk about it. We got some things to take care of though, so you better take this crazy girl home."

"Let's go, Marissa. Thanks for watching her, Jack. It was great to meet you, Aiden."

"You too." Once the door closed, Aiden commented, "Wow, he really is supportive, isn't he?"

"Yeah, he is."

Aiden had to smile in his glory. "I don't think I've ever had the pleasure of seeing you blush."

"What are you talking about?"

"Oh okay. I got your weak spot now."

Jack laughed. "Okay, wise guy. Are you ready to go?"

Aiden frowned as he came back to reality. "No. That's why you're coming, so you make me go through with it."

"I know." Jack seemed to zone off as his eyes fell to Aiden's hoodie. That was the first time Aiden noticed Jack tug at one of his wristbands. Now that he knew the reasoning behind that action, concern came over him.

"What?"

"Let me see." Aiden bit his lip, understanding what he meant. He reached down, grabbing the ends of his hoodie and shirt, and slowly lifted them over his head. He winced in pain from the stretching, and he refused to watch Jack's expression as he looked him over. Jack let out a deep breath as he examined the injury around the abdomen and back. "Are you sure you don't want to go to the hospital?"

"They won't be able to do much. I can breathe fine, so it ain't that serious."

"You can barely move."

"I'm fine. I'm willing to go fill out a police report. That's all I want to do. That's all I can take right now."

Jack didn't like it but he wasn't going to push it. "Fair enough. Let's go then."

At the police station, Aiden relayed everything that had gone on with Brett to the police officer. Part of him regretted not keeping the notes as evidence, but part of him also didn't want to escalate things too much. The bruises on his ribs and lower back seemed to be enough. As he answered the officer's questions, Aiden was aware he was going back and forth on being completely truthful, and holding back enough to keep Brett from being arrested. Aiden could feel Jack's disbelief stare when he denied there being possible camera footage at his apartment from Brett pinning him to the wall in the hallway. In the end, the officer only had enough to arrest the guys who jumped Aiden at the restaurant, not Brett. Aiden kept a straight face to that response, but he was sure Jack could feel his relief.

"What about a restraining order?" Jack asked, finding his turn to chime in.

"You can file for one," the officer began, "a temporary order of protection will be granted immediately until the case can be heard for a possible permanent restraining order."

"Well then yes, let's do that, right?" Jack asked, looking at Aiden. He could tell Aiden was unsure about it as a lot of information was being thrown at him. "Aiden, this will protect you. You should do this."

"Just wait a sec," Aiden said, looking at the officer. "You mentioned that you or another officer is going to talk to him, right?"

"With these severe circumstances, yes. We'll let him know a report was made against him and give him a warning that he needs to stay away."

"So, do you think he'll stop once the police are at his door telling him to?" Aiden asked.

Jack's mouth dropped open in disbelief. "Aiden, come on. You can't give this guy a break."

"Just hold on, I want to hear the answer."

"He's not going to stop," Jack begged.

"Do you really think I need to file a protective order?" Aiden asked the officer, ignoring Jack's pleas.

The officer folded his hands and sighed. "I think you should listen to your friend, son. I've seen cases like this where people believe their harasser will simply stop if they don't react to the provocations, and then something really bad happens."

Aiden sank in his chair, not liking that answer. Now he really had nothing to argue against.

"Aiden, please. Take this seriously," Jack said, "I can't bear to watch that all happen again."

His foot began tapping fast. His fingernail found its way to his teeth to be chewed at. This was it. There may be little chance to turn back and let Brett come forward to fix their friendship, but there was a high chance that Aiden wouldn't survive the next beating. "Okay, fine. I'll...file for one."

"I think that's wise." The officer nodded. "I'll get the paperwork."

After filling out the order and getting the next steps for the future court hearing, Jack drove Aiden back to his house.

"I know that wasn't easy," Jack said as they walked inside, "but I'm proud of you."

"I feel so lousy," Aiden admitted.

"I know, but it was for the best," Jack pulled Aiden in for a long hug, "Want to go downstairs and watch a movie?"

"Yeah," Aiden sighed, "can you get everything ready? I'm going to call Jaxie."

Aiden stepped outside while he talked to his sister. He explained to her he had gotten seriously hurt and filled out a protective order against Brett. The only lie he told was the jumping happened outside his apartment and not at the restaurant. As frustrated as Jaxie sounded, she told Aiden she was happy he did something to protect himself. Even after hearing both Jaxie and Jack tell him they were proud of him for taking this big step, Aiden felt his heart sink into a frozen slumber. He didn't want it to be too late for him and Brett to ever fix things.

Jack helped Aiden get comfortable on the couch by placing a pillow on his lap for his head. There was undeniable exhaustion taking over Aiden as Jack took the initiative to hold ice on the bruises. The long running adrenaline had finally passed on. Even the chill from the ice couldn't keep Aiden awake as he gave in to the sleep and passed out on the couch for the night.

The warning from the police seemed to help. A couple weeks passed and nothing came from Brett. No notes, no beatings, no followings that Aiden picked up on. The injuries from the restaurant jumping were healing, albeit slowly. Aiden was grateful the injuries weren't obvious as they were under his shirt. The court date for the restraining order had been set, but Aiden was having a hard time feeling motivated to go through with it. If the warning took care of the problem, then he could let it go. He hadn't tried to talk to Jack about it yet because he already knew what his response would be.

Aiden and Jack didn't go on any dates in public the next little while, but Aiden was spending a lot of time at Jack's house. There were some days Marissa was over, so Aiden got to spend time with her too. Aiden even took Joey up on his offer, and he spent a day at the park with Jack, Joey, Marissa and Joey's wife, Amy. Snow didn't seem to stop Marissa from running all over the playground. It amazed Aiden to go into her perspective of what she was growing up with. Marissa was going to be shocked someday when she realized gay relationships weren't actually the norm, let alone accepted. A lot of other kids would ask her question after question once they found out, and she wouldn't understand why they would be so curious. Not until there would be one kid making a hateful comment and she'd ask her dad or Jack about it. Aiden hoped her sassy attitude would follow her when she'd need to stand up for herself for having a gay uncle.

As much fun as Aiden was having with Jack's family, he couldn't help but feel a little down; he wished he had the same support system. Joey and Amy were talking with Aiden, getting to know him, like any other person. They didn't ask questions regarding his sexuality. Their questions about him weren't worded specifically for him being the same sex as Jack. It didn't matter to them. They wanted to know Aiden as a person. He wished he could bring Jack around his family with the confidence they would treat him in a similar matter.

A few days after the day at the park, Aiden was home relaxing, and received an unexpected call from Jack.

"Hey, I have a favor to ask, and I hope it's not too weird," Jack began the conversation.

"What is it?" Aiden asked.

"I have a work emergency and have to go in. Normally, I could take Marissa, but this seems like it's going to take up some time and she's a little under the weather. Do you think you could come sit here with her?"

"Oh sure, that's fine. Just let me get dressed and I'll head over."

"Don't tease me like that," Jack said. "I can't spare time thinking about you undressed right now."

Aiden rolled his eyes at the remark. "Ha ha. I'll be there soon."

As Aiden pulled his car up to Jack's, he felt a sudden chill pass through. It put him on the alert and he looked warily up and down the street. He didn't see anything out of the ordinary, so he shook his head, trying to get rid of the feeling, but he just couldn't shake it and constantly checked his back as he walked up the driveway. Before knocking on the front door, he walked towards the other end of the porch and glanced down the side of the house. All he saw was a pile of snow that appeared to have fallen from the tree branches above. Walking back towards the door, Aiden knocked some snow off his boots while peeking down the road again. He didn't see anything, so he went ahead and knocked.

"I owe you," Jack said as Aiden walked in. "She's not that sick, just a little stuffed up so she's just been on the couch watching movies she's already seen a couple hundred times."

"Poor thing," Aiden said. He paused for a moment and looked at Jack feeling a little awkward. "Um, you did ask Joey about this, right?" he asked, still trying to pinpoint why his nerves were poking at him.

"Oh yeah, he's fine with you being here. He trusts my judgement." Jack walked over to the couch and leaned over his niece. "Alright honey, I'm going to leave. Aiden will sit with you, alright?"

"Okay," Marissa said softly.

For the next couple hours, Aiden tried putting his focus on taking care of Marissa. He held her until she fell asleep and then placed her on the couch before walking around the house. All the while he still felt on edge, so he'd subtly peek out the window every now and then. He wanted to believe he was overreacting and that he needed a more encompassing distraction, so Aiden made his way upstairs. He realized he hadn't been in Jack's room before and curiosity had gotten the better of him. It was a small room with the typical bed, nightstand, dresser, and TV. Aiden could tell Jack only cared for neatness for the rest of his house. His room clearly didn't get as much attention.

The dresser had a lot of books on it, not in any organized pile or order. Some were fiction stories, some were inspirational stories, and there was the Bible. Aiden liked to believe the Bible held comfort during the dark and unknown times, but the thick book brought mountains of memories of his parents drilling knowledge and judgement and rules into his head. He wondered if reading Jack's Bible would bring his, Lydia's, and Avy's interpretations within the text. Flipping through the pages there were areas that were highlighted, notes written, and some pages bookmarked. Taking a seat at the foot of the bed, Aiden opened to a random spot and began skimming. He waited until he found a spot to start actively reading.

The book of Proverbs. It was an area his parents brought up in plenty of life's scenarios as it was more of a teaching book than narrative. As the words went through his mind, the voice slowly went from being his dad's tough, to-the-point speech to Jack's soft, caring speech patterns. He could feel his heart being lifted at the new perspective being shown right in front of him. The words became soothing enough for Aiden to fall asleep.

"Aiden!"

The bloodcurdling scream caused Aiden to jolt awake. He had forgotten where he was for a moment as he shot up straight in the bed. Taking a quick look around, he saw he was still in Jack's room and the Bible was still open from him reading it.

"Aiden!"

It was Marissa. Her voice didn't sound curious as to his location. It sounded fearful. Aiden got to his feet and hurried downstairs.

"Marissa?" he asked, hurrying to the living room. The young girl was still on the couch, but tears were sliding down her face. "I'm sorry. I was just upstairs. Are you okay?"

"There was a lot of noise," she whimpered.

"Noise? Where?"

"Outside. It was loud. It was a lot."

Aiden had no idea what she meant. She was pointing towards the front of the house, so Aiden started going that direction. The feeling he had from earlier was coming back. That feeling that something wasn't right. Before he could reach the front door, there was a thud that came from the opposite direction.

"Aiden!" Marissa screamed. "It's in the backyard now!"

Rushing back to the living room, Aiden held his finger to his lips. "Shh, it's okay." He approached the shaken girl and helped her lay back down on the couch while pulling the blanket over. He wasn't sure how well he was pulling off the act that everything was okay when deep down he was panicking.

This time, Aiden walked into the kitchen to look out the window that faced the backyard. He wasn't able to see much, but he didn't find anything that seemed off. He attempted to dismiss the noise to something by nature as he was too nervous to truly investigate any further. Aiden grabbed the remote and turned on something for Marissa to watch. "You want to watch another movie?"

"What is outside?"

Aiden looked at Marissa with gentle eyes. "I don't think it's anything."

Another knocking sound came, causing both of them to jump. This time, Marissa was in full tears. "I want Uncle Jack."

"I know." Aiden sat on the couch and picked Marissa up, holding her tight. He needed comfort as much as she did. Another noise came from the direction of the front like Marissa had said. It sounded bad, but Aiden couldn't get himself to move.

"Is someone hurting the house?"

"I...I don't know. Maybe it's tree branches breaking from the snow." Aiden knew that wasn't the case. He was having visions of the restaurant when he got jumped. He couldn't risk stepping outside and leaving Marissa alone. What if he got hurt badly and couldn't take care of her?

The noises stopped then. An hour passed without anything else happening. Marissa had calmed down but Aiden was still on edge. He didn't dare get up to check anything out. He was nothing short of relieved when Jack returned home, but when Aiden looked up at him, his expression was anything but happy. He looked alarmed.

"Uncle Jack!" Marissa yelled, running straight for him.

"Hey," Jack lifted her in his arms, but looked at Aiden with concern. "Are you guys okay?"

"Yeah," Aiden said with a slightly shaky voice. "Why do you ask?" It was a stupid question and it worried Aiden what Jack may have seen to think him and Marissa were in danger. Jack carried Marissa back to the couch and sat her down.

"I'm still watching movies," Marissa said proudly.

"That's great. Keep watching it," Jack said quickly. He motioned for Aiden to follow him. Aiden felt his heart race as he walked down the hallway to the front office area.

"Jack, what's wrong?" Aiden asked nervously.

Jack put his hand on the doorknob, but didn't open it right away. "Someone busted up your car."

Aiden was unsure he heard him right. "What are you talking about?"

Jack opened the door and Aiden looked towards the street. Busted wasn't the correct term. His windows had been broken, his back tires were slashed, and someone had used something big to beat up the doors and front end. That was just what Aiden could see at the moment. He slowly walked outside to inspect the damage, still looking up and down the street expecting someone to jump out and get him.

"Oh my God," Aiden put a hand to his forehead. "That's what she was talking about."

"What? Who?"

"Marissa. She was freaking out, because she had heard a noise. Shoot, I was upstairs and didn't hear a thing. I came down and thought maybe it was nothing..." Aiden paused and looked towards the side of the house.

"What? What is it?"

"I heard something in the back. Marissa was freaking out, so I didn't want to go outside and really look. I blew it off."

Aiden wasn't able to explain further before Jack hurried across his front yard. Not daring to be left alone, Aiden was right on his heels. Blame was coming over him.

He shouldn't have fallen asleep, leaving the house and Marissa vulnerable. Once they got through the snow and at the back of the house, they both froze. It looked like big rocks had been thrown at the house, but nothing was broken. What really caught their eye was someone had spray painted on the house 'Die Faggots.' Aiden stayed in his spot while Jack took slow steps forward.

"J-Jack," Aiden stuttered.

"Let's go." Jack turned away from the words.

"I'm sorry," Aiden practically whispered.

"Get in the house," Jack said harshly. He grabbed Aiden by the hand and brought him around to the front and back inside. Aiden didn't have a chance to say anything as Jack kicked his boots off and marched away into the house. That action put Aiden on edge, but he followed along slowly. Once he entered the living room, he saw Jack on the couch holding Marissa. Aiden went back to his thoughts about Marissa's innocence at the park. Jack was well aware of what Marissa could have to see or hear people say about him. This was one of those times. If Marissa had been outside and saw Aiden's car getting wrecked, someone would have to explain to her why. If she saw the spray paint being put on the house, someone would have to tell her what it meant. They lived in a world where someday it would all have to be explained to her. They lived in a world where her normal really wasn't society's normal. And Aiden knew Jack would push that conversation as long as he could.

Aiden's car was undriveable. He wouldn't have wanted to take the risk anyway. As Jack put it to him, there's no telling what they did that Aiden wouldn't find out until his car was unwillingly driving into a ditch. He was able to get it towed but was sure it wasn't going to be worth fixing. Joey picked up Marissa but Aiden didn't talk with him. Jack explained to his brother what happened, and Aiden felt terrible. He had put Marissa's life in danger. He had scarred her. What if he hadn't woken up? What if whoever did this managed to throw rocks through the windows and hit Marissa? What if they tried getting in the house? These questions and more were swirling in Aiden's head and Jack's vibe wasn't helping.

After Joey and Marissa left, Aiden settled himself on the couch. Jack didn't sit with him. The TV was off and it was eerily silent. The only sound Aiden could hear was Jack walking around the kitchen clicking his knife.

"I can't believe Joey didn't strangle me," Aiden commented.

"It wasn't your fault," Jack said simply. Aiden could tell Jack's mood wasn't his usual cheery one, or even a soothing one, but he didn't blame him.

"I endangered his daughter, your niece." Aiden stood up and faced Jack. "I...I went upstairs after Marissa fell asleep on the couch. I was reading your Bible and I fell asleep. It's all my fault. If I had been up then maybe I would've caught them at my car. Even when she said she heard more noises, I didn't go try to look into it. I sat in here just letting it happen."

"Enough!" Jack barked. Aiden went silent and still. He glanced out the window and saw snow was falling heavily. It looked peaceful, but the house wasn't anywhere near peaceful at the moment.

Aiden turned back around and sat on the couch, placing his face in his hands. "God, I'm so sorry."

Jack didn't respond. Instead, Aiden heard a deep thud. It made him jump in his seat as he almost thought it was another rock thrown from outside. He was afraid to, but he turned and looked over the couch. Jack's back was towards him, and his knife had been shoved into the surface of the table. Aiden couldn't help it then. The tears fell fast and he headed for the front door, quickly getting his boots on. He barely had his jacket on when he walked outside and began going down the driveway. Marching through the snow, his cries mixed with the crisp air made him run out of breath. His legs were beginning to ache before he heard Jack behind him.

"Aiden, wait!"

Aiden turned to respond, his turn to yell. "No! This is why I didn't want you around me anymore! Something could have happened to Marissa today! Maybe nothing happened physically, but you can't convince me that she isn't affected somehow!"

"Aiden, stop!" Jack said, hurrying through the snow. "It's freezing out here. You can't walk home."

"You don't want me here right now. I don't want to be here right now."

"I'll take you home then. You can't walk in this. Come on. I'm not mad at you. I'm mad, but not at you. We both need to get some sleep, so just let me take you home."

Aiden stopped in his tracks. He knew walking through the snow was silly, so he gave in to Jack's offer.

"I can't believe you were going to walk in this," Jack shook his head as he drove to Aiden's apartment.

"I wasn't. I'm glad you came after me. I was going numb." Aiden let out a low chuckle.

Jack pulled into the parking lot and took Aiden's hand in his. "Really, I'm not mad at you. I care about Marissa a lot, so if Brett has anything to do with this...well, I'll leave it at that."

"I know."

"Do you want me to come help you look at cars tomorrow?"

Aiden shook his head, "I think I'll have Jaxie help. After I get one, I'll drive to the police station and tell them about this."

"Okay," Jack squeezed Aiden's hand, "Let me know how it all goes."

Aiden walked into his apartment and slammed himself into bed. The second his eyes closed, though, it all

181

came back to him. He heard Marissa's screaming cries. In his dream, though, guys got into the house. Jack was in the house and the men started attacking him. Marissa sat on the couch watching these men hurt her uncle. She screamed and begged for Aiden to help him. He couldn't move. He couldn't stop it.

Shooting upright, Aiden was desperately trying to breathe as he awoke from the nightmare. It felt like he had been holding his breath. His head and back felt drenched in sweat. Grabbing his phone to check the time, he saw most of the night had already come and gone. He hadn't realized he had fallen asleep at all. Even with the knowledge of the sleeping pills sitting on his nightstand, Aiden didn't want to go back to sleep. He couldn't bear to hear Marissa's cries again. Her begging him to make it all stop, and he wouldn't have been able to.

The next day, Jaxie drove Aiden to the car dealership. He kept his story to his car being destroyed at his apartment complex. It was hard to lie this time because his nightmare, Marissa, and Jack's reaction were really messing with him. Jaxie wasn't speaking as much as Aiden expected her to either. He could tell she was as enraged as Jack had been, but she seemed satisfied that Aiden had gotten the police more involved with everything. Once Aiden was able to find a car, he drove to the police station by himself to see what would happen next with Brett, even though no one saw him cause any of the damage from yesterday.

"I'm assuming there's no violation of the protective order since we didn't see him? Or if he uses other people?"

"I'm still waiting to hear from those who investigated the car," the officer responded. "Regardless, we'll be going to talk to him."

"So, what should I do?"

"Replacing your car was a good start. He won't know what you're driving anymore. Just hang tight and we'll see if we can get prints or something off your old car. We may get some sort of identification for someone."

"Alright. Thank you."

Aiden wasn't feeling satisfied after that conversation. His head was spinning while trying to find an explanation. He was trying to make sense of Brett willing to risk jail by continuing the harassment. That's when Aiden realized something. Brett may not be his best friend anymore, but that didn't change the knowledge Brett had of him. Aiden was aware of his habit of making choices. If he had seen Brett destroying his car, the chances of Aiden calling the police were slim. Part of that was from the lack of being able to stand up for himself, and the other part was from not wanting to watch someone who had meant a lot to him be taken away for potentially a long time. He would have sat inside watching, or, if he got brave enough, walked outside to try talking to him.

Brett knew Aiden better than anyone. If Aiden knew he wouldn't let Brett get arrested, then Brett knew that too.

-14-

That night, Aiden stood in his bathroom, staring at his reflection, deep in thought. He hadn't called Jack once that day, because of how conflicted his feelings were. Things were getting hideous, and he felt he was putting people in more danger. His nightmare and the what if's kept crossing his mind, interring with any other thoughts. The images he continuously saw were drowning him. Marissa's cries kept replaying in his head and stabbed him in the heart every time. He wasn't sure if he could ever face her again without being reminded of yesterday. His mind drifted back to the park, and his thoughts of how Marissa would view the normality of a gay relationship. Where he had once thought she was likely to think nothing of it, growing up with a gay uncle, now he couldn't help but think that she would begin to realize, all too soon, how ignorant some people could be about those who were gay. It brought trouble and harassment, just like Brett told him it would. Jack was right about a lot of things, but Brett was proving right too. Aiden felt solely responsible for ruining the innocent mind of a little girl. He couldn't bear to feel responsible about anything else happening to someone he cared about.

Disappointment and remorse filled him, and the tears flooded down his face. Aiden gripped his hair and pulled hard. He couldn't take it. He came to terms with what he had to do, what he knew he should do. It was breaking him apart more than the first time. He tried it once, keeping Jack out of his life for his own safety. Jack convinced him that they would be fine. Jack convinced him that Brett couldn't do anything to keep him away. This was taken too far though. Even if he did believe Jack would stand to the fight Brett would cause, that didn't mean the repercussions would be worth it to Aiden. Brett, and whoever else, had gone to Jack's house and were ready to harm anyone inside. There was no limit to what Brett was willing to do. This time, Aiden had to make the break off of this relationship permanent and he had to tell Jaxie about everything. He would need her support now more than ever.

Aiden sank to the tile floor. He didn't bother trying to get control of himself before calling his sister.

"Hello?"

"Hi, Jaxie," Aiden managed to choke out.

"Hey, what's going on? Are you okay?"

Aiden thought about the question as he let a couple cries fall through his lips. There was no point in trying to even convince himself he was at all okay. "No, I'm not okay."

"Aiden, what's going on?"

"I have some stuff to tell you. It's time I tell you some things I haven't been completely honest about lately. Not in a bad way, but...I just want to tell you things now.

It's going to be so hard, and I'm going to need your help. I need you here. Please."

"Yes, of course, whatever it is, I'll be there. I'll be off in a couple hours and I'll come over to talk. Is that okay?"

"Yeah, that's okay. Thank you, Jaxie, for everything."

"Always. I love you."

"I love you, too."

Once he got off the phone, he started typing a message to Jack. He couldn't bear to try and call him right now. There was no way he'd be able to get the words out, and he didn't want a back and forth argument. Each sentence he typed tore another heartstring. A heavy weight pushed against his chest, getting worse and worse.

Jack, I'm having a hard time dealing with what happened yesterday. I can't get it out of my head. What Marissa had to go through, and Joey, and you is breaking my heart. I can't stand it. I'm putting too many people in harm's way. I have a lot to figure out before I can move on. I really hate this, but we need to take a break from each other. It isn't fair to you...

Aiden was interrupted by a knock at his door. He hoped it wasn't Jack. That would add another layer of difficulty to this. At first, he decided he wouldn't answer the door. He would send the text and wait for Jack to leave. It sounded simple, but he knew it wouldn't be. Jack wouldn't give up that easily.

Aiden stood up, shoved his phone in his pocket, and looked himself over in the mirror. Another knock sounded. He turned the sink on and quickly splashed his face with water. Once he felt like he looked more alive, he stepped out of the bathroom. A third knock rapped the door. Aiden assumed his text was about to become an in person conversation. It would be near impossible to do, but Aiden knew what had to be done. He stared at the door for a moment, collecting himself on how to direct the conversation, and then grabbed the doorknob. His throat tightened up, nearly shut, when it wasn't Jack standing on the other side of the door.

"What are you doing here?" Aiden asked quietly.

Brett helped himself into the apartment, pushing Aiden aside.

"You...can't be here," Aiden managed to get out in a whisper.

"Don't even try calling the cops," Brett warned. "Don't get your panties in a bunch. I'm here to talk and get things through your head."

Aiden couldn't speak. He could only hope Brett was going to apologize, but his tone didn't say that was going to happen. Clearly Brett was going to talk, and Aiden was going to listen.

"Cops have talked to me quite a bit now. Asking me if I'm involved in the problems in your life. You're going to bitch this much after I warned you this would happen? You're the one who caused these problems. You knew what was coming. You were asking for it. Don't try to pin everything on me."

Aiden shook his head. "No..."

"I hear there was a child in that house." Aiden froze at the statement. Even though it was plainly obvious Brett had to be behind the incidents at Jack's house, hearing him practically admit it was still startling. "It's obviously not your little boyfriend's. Can't have kids when you're a fag," Brett sneered. "That poor little child has to go through some rough things just because you and this guy want your glory moments. How selfish can you be?"

"I'm being selfish?" Aiden asked. "You risked a child's life just to hurt me."

"Try that again. *You* risked that child's life. If anything would have happened to her, it would have been *your* fault. You got beat, badly, and sure as hell didn't take that seriously enough since you're still going over there. Your boyfriend could get hurt too. Y'all don't belong here. You never will. You're not meant to be here."

Aiden didn't say anything. He was too scared because Brett wasn't all wrong. A child had been put in danger. He shouldn't have been around Marissa with the knowledge of Brett's intentions. She was going to face some tough times when she gets older and people find out about her uncle, especially if Aiden was around him to prove anyone's suspicions. Aiden was also scared because he didn't know what Brett was capable of anymore. He clearly had no remorse over anything else that had happened.

"Did you sleep with this guy? Is that why you can't get away from him?"

Aiden shook his head, but that wasn't good enough for Brett as he smacked him across the face.

"You did, didn't you?" Brett asked in disgust. "You sick waste of life."

"No," Aiden said quietly.

"Huh? Speak up." Brett landed another smack across Aiden's face.

"No," Aiden said louder. "I didn't do anything like that."

"You liked it didn't you?"

"It didn't happen," Aiden argued, even though he knew it was pointless. Maybe it was as pointless as he was being proven to be.

"Okay, sure you didn't. You gave yourself up that easily to him, huh? That's it for you then. He knows you're not worth anything beyond the bed now. There's no way God's coming back for you either. You blew that one big time. You'll never have friends or anyone's respect."

"Stop," Aiden begged. "Why are you doing this? Why am I worthless to you now? Why!"

Brett shoved Aiden hard, causing him to stumble. "Don't act like you didn't know this was coming. I warned you about getting hurt, and you still stayed gay. That's what happens. I told you how some of the guys at RN's feel and we ain't about to let you fags do whatever you want."

Aiden's mouth dropped open. "You've...hurt people before over this."

"Maybe a quick hit or some nasty notes. You, well, it's a little more personal. It's what needs to be done. You had your chance to avoid it."

"No. This isn't okay. You guys can't do this to people. You can't do this to me!"

"You stupid little bitch," Brett grabbed Aiden by the neck and slammed him into the wall, slightly tightening his grip as he spoke. "I'm going to say this as clearly as I can, so listen up. Faggots don't deserve to breathe. There are dead people who deserve to have your life more than you. You aren't anything anymore. You see what happens to people who come out as gay? They get hurt, sometimes they get killed. No one protects them; not even God is going to help you. He wants you dead, too, so he can send you straight to Hell. Until that happens, all you're going to do is suffer. They are disgusting. *You* are disgusting."

Aiden didn't want it to happen, but the tears streamed down his cheeks as he gasped for air. No hit or kick Brett could throw would bring as much pain as those words just did.

"You really want to bring all this trouble into that child's life? Stop being the selfish prick you are. End this or get out of all our lives. No one wants it here. Your boyfriend would do us all a favor if he just killed himself." Brett slowly lowered Aiden so they were looking at each other. "Same with you."

189

Brett let go of Aiden, letting him fall to the floor hard. It was a repeat of the night Aiden came out to Brett. He was on the floor and Brett stormed out, leaving him there in confusion and fear. The door slammed shut as Aiden took in big breaths of air. It was hard to get in full breaths as he sobbed. There was no way he had heard what he just heard. There was no way Brett said all of that. Aiden desperately looked around his apartment to find a reason to believe this was a nightmare. Then something caught his eye. Something had fallen to the wood floor. There were pieces of glass sprawled around. It was a decor item, a glass sign he had gotten from his parents that had a prayer verse on it. His crying became louder as he looked to the ceiling, begging for a sign from God that Brett wasn't right. He didn't hear anything beyond his hyperventilating cries filling the room. That gave him the most unbearable feeling of solitude and abandonment.

Aiden couldn't control himself as he crawled over and started gathering the pieces into a pile. As the pieces got closer together, his crying slowed as his eyes fixed on the glass. The words from the prayer were now just broken pieces of randomly placed letters. The meaning they once had were now reassembling into another meaning. Aiden couldn't place the comforting words that the sign held just moments ago. Right before his eyes, the letters formed into the words Brett had just spoken to him. They became the words he had put into his head over and over again.

Faggot. Worthless. Disgusting. Hurt. Killed.

The letters wouldn't stop. They kept evolving into more and more words until sentences formed. Aiden couldn't watch it anymore. He swung at the glass to make it stop, not worried about glass getting in his skin. Simultaneously, his heart and breathing became rapid.

"No!" Aiden screamed, swinging over and over again. The glass had been pushed away and he was now just swinging at the floor. "It's not true! It can't be!"

Quickly getting up, Aiden rushed to the bathroom and looked at himself in the mirror. That's when he saw it. It was all true. There was a reason people reacted so strongly to gay people. It was a sin. They weren't meant to be part of life. Even when Aiden tried to do right, people were getting hurt. Everyone was struggling around him as he put them through the horrible things he was going through. He was selfish. He was disgusting. The life he possessed truly belonged to someone else, someone who would live it the correct way. No matter what he tried to do with his life, Brett would always be there to remind him of that. If not Brett, someone else would be there to tell him. There was no escape.

Aiden screamed. He screamed loudly. He grabbed the ceramic cup from the sink and smashed it on the mirror. Cracks went across the mirror, breaking apart his reflection. He couldn't bear to look at himself anymore. Anything that could be picked up, Aiden grabbed and threw against the wall or smashed against the sink. He yelled until his throat was raw.

When there was nothing else to throw, Aiden looked at the damage he had caused. This was the damage people wanted to cause him. He didn't feel better from breaking things just as people didn't feel they had done enough after hurting him. They would keep coming back. They wanted more to be done to him. They wanted him gone.

It didn't make any difference to Aiden anymore. He didn't cry anymore. There was a dull feeling in his hands, and that's when Aiden finally noticed the bits of blood from glass cuts. Wiping them down on his pants, he felt the pocket bulge of his phone. He took his phone out and walked out of the bathroom. The unfinished text he was typing for Jack was on the screen. There wasn't anything more to say though. There wasn't anything to reread or reconsider. Aiden typed one more sentence before hitting send.

I'm sorry.

Aiden put his phone on the coffee table. He knew he was done then. His battle was about to be finished. There were some nights Aiden wanted to go to bed and not wake up. Tonight he was going to make sure that happened.

Originally, Jack had started typing a long text back to Aiden. He couldn't let them end like this. He knew Aiden had witnessed a truly angry side of him, and it surely frightened Aiden, but Jack had gotten hit personally. When Marissa was born, Jack made a promise that no one was going to make her life hard because of him. He would do anything to make sure of that, and now there was a new level of anger Jack had for Brett. That didn't mean he wanted things over with him and Aiden, though. He cared about Aiden too much. He wanted so much more with him. The emotions were too out of control, though; and he wasn't thinking straight as he typed out the message. Jack tried calling, but as he expected, there was no answer. It wasn't worth putting more effort towards what could become an emotional fight, so Jack decided to go for a drive to cool off before trying to get in touch with him again. He would sleep on it and try calling Aiden tomorrow.

Jaxie parked her car. She was able to get off work early and hurried over to Aiden's apartment. She had no idea what he needed to talk to her about, but he sounded hurt. Not just upset, but hurt. She didn't think it was about

Brett, because she figured he would have just told her. When she reached his door, she knocked. A minute passed without an answer. She knocked again. Nothing.

"Did you really fall asleep on me?" Jaxie said to herself as she went through her keys. She grabbed Aiden's extra apartment key and put it in the doorknob. As she walked inside, she could feel that something was off. Something was wrong.

"Aiden?" she asked, setting down her purse and keys. She walked in further and noticed the broken glass on the floor. "Aiden? Where are you?"

As Jaxie made her way down the hall, she peeked in the bathroom and gasped at the sight. Things were thrown to the floor. The mirror was broken. The towel rack was broken. There were drops of blood splattered in places. She started to panic as she assumed Brett had been there.

Her protective mode kicked in as she backed out of the bathroom and rushed to the bedroom, banging on the door. "Aiden? What's going on? Are you okay?"

There was no answer.

"Aiden!" Jaxie yelled, immediately opening the door. Her knees went weak, her entire body almost collapsing. Her brother was on the bed, eyes closed. She immediately got the feeling he wasn't just sleeping. Her heart stopped for a moment when she observed that he seemed too still. Looking to his nightstand she saw three pill bottles. Jaxie picked each of them up and felt how light they were, and immediately threw them aside.

"Oh my God, no, no, no, no. Aiden!"

With shaky hands, Jaxie yanked Aiden up by the shirt. She used all her strength to support his limp body.

"Aiden! Wake up!" Jaxie screamed as loud as she could manage in an attempt to get a reaction. "Wake up, Aiden!" There was nothing. Panic pushed her quick thinking and Jaxie shoved her fingers down Aiden's throat.

His body lunged forward, vomiting on Jaxie, the bed, and the floor.

"Oh my God, oh my God, oh my God," Jaxie cried, pulling him close and gripping him tightly. She looked at him, seeing he still wasn't fully conscious. Quickly, she let his body fall onto the bed while she ran to get her phone.

Jaxie sat in the waiting room, unmoving. Her back was arched tight, her hands gripped the armrests of her chair, and her eyes locked with the tile floor. She was trying to understand what had happened at the apartment, but the only question she could focus on was if Aiden was going to make it.

As her parents entered the waiting room, Jaxie finally moved and she felt her body ache. She stood up but didn't move forward. Tears began to fall, blurring the image of her parents hurrying over.

"Oh my God, Jacqueline," Lauren cried as she approached her daughter, "What happened?"

"What was going on with Aiden?" Dalton asked, "Why did he do this?"

"I don't really know what happened," Jaxie said, wiping her eyes, "I was supposed to go over and hang out, and I found him unconscious."

"Is this about Courtney?" Lauren asked.

Jaxie froze. She even felt her tears freeze in place on her cheeks. This wasn't the way Aiden would have wanted them to find out, but she didn't have much choice now. Slowly, Jaxie took her seat with her mouth hanging open. "Mom, Dad, let's sit while we wait for the doctor. I have to tell you something."

"Have you talked to the police?" Dalton asked.

"No, they're in there with the doctors right now."

"Okay. Well, what do you need to tell us?" Lauren asked, sitting down, and pulling Dalton with her.

Jaxie prepared herself. "Well...something's been going on with Aiden the past few months. I mean...it's been longer than that. I don't know. Anyway, Courtney leaving really messed him up, and he...he came to some self-realizations. He's found himself on a different life path that...well, it sort of relates to that area of his life."

"What do you mean?" Dalton asked.

"I know this is going to be hard for you to hear, but," Jaxie took a breath before spilling it, "Aiden came out."

"Came out?" Lauren asked.

"He's gay," Jaxie said, quietly.

Dalton and Lauren didn't say anything, but Jaxie didn't see concern on their faces. They just looked at each other and their silence was pissing Jaxie off. She didn't want to blow her lid at the hospital, but she wouldn't be able to hold back.

"He's been going through a lot," Jaxie went on with a harsh tone, "He's been dealing with a lot of harassment, especially from Brett, and—"

Before she could go on, her father stood up and turned for the exit.

"Dad, where are you going?"

He didn't respond.

"Dad," Jaxie got up and followed him towards the exit, "Dad, don't you dare leave. Don't you do this to him!" Jaxie followed her dad outside, begging for him to stop.

"Dad! Don't do this to Aiden! Please!"

Jaxie stopped and watched her dad march through the parking lot. He never looked back. She wasn't sure if she should have expected this, but she was still feeling shocked and hurt. What took her through another turn was that her father didn't drive away. He clearly expected his wife to be following close behind. Instead of waiting inside

195

with her, though, he believed he had to leave the building his damned-for-hell son was in, fighting for his life.

Jaxie shook her head and yelled, "I'm not a virgin, Dad! I've exposed myself to guy after guy after guy! I don't care for a relationship, but I love getting in bed! Are you proud of me now? Proud of my temple I had to save for *the one*?" Jaxie spat the last two words in the direction her father had walked. She paused, waiting for some kind of response. A lump came to her throat and she couldn't force it away. "So...screw you, Dad. Just screw you!"

Clearing her throat, Jaxie turned and looked at the pavement. She took a kick at the snow. "And my name is Jaxie. Call me Jaxie or fuck off."

Jaxie hurried back into the hospital and marched up to her mom. "Your husband is waiting in the car for you. He wants to go home just so you know."

Lauren didn't respond.

"Well?"

"What do you want me to say, Jacqueline?" Lauren asked.

"I want you to chase down your husband and tell him that he needs to stay here and stand by his son," Jaxie demanded. "I want you to do something for Aiden! I want you to say you'll love him no matter what!"

"Well, this is quite shocking."

"Any other time, yes, this would be shocking. Right now, your son might be dead back there! You should be more worried about that than his sexual orientation!"

"Can I have a minute to think this over? You know your father and I have priorities to keep in order first. Our first priority will always be our relationship with the Lord."

Jaxie's jaw dropped and was at a complete loss for words.

"Jacqueline, think about it. If he didn't decide to be gay, he wouldn't be in this situation right now. He is being punished, and he'll be judged for this later."

196

Jaxie gritted her teeth as she muttered, "Bitch."

"Excuse me?"

Before she could have another outburst, Jaxie saw the doctor and a police officer come through the doors.

"Oh my God, is he okay?" Jaxie rushed over. She didn't even check to see if her mom followed.

"He'll be okay," the doctor said.

"Oh, thank God," Jaxie cried, nearly falling over. "Can I see him? Please?"

"Sure. He might be out of it, but you can come see him. Don't bombard him with questions, alright? Just be there for him."

"Of course."

"Can I talk to you first? It won't take long, I just want everything you remember as soon as possible," the officer said.

"Sure, yeah," Jaxie said, following the officer back to the seats. Lauren hadn't moved a muscle. Jaxie glared at her mother. "You really didn't come over to check on his status? They could have said he didn't make it. Do you realize that?"

"Let's not get worked up," the officer said, "I just have a few questions before you go see him."

Jaxie turned in her seat, facing her back to her mother. "Okay."

The police officer took out his notes and pen. "I understand this won't be easy. I'll try to keep it short. Take me through tonight's events."

"Well, I guess it started yesterday. Someone had destroyed his car and we had to go get him a new one. We did that earlier today. He had a feeling it had something to do with Brett, so he went to the police station, because he already had reports on file against Brett. He also has the protective order against him. He called me later on saying he needed to talk to me about something. I told him I'd be there after work. He said that was fine but he told me he would need me there for him. Whatever it was, it seemed important."

"How did he sound on the phone when he asked you to come over?"

Jaxie replayed the phone conversation in her head, "He seemed...very sad. He seemed frustrated and hurt. It didn't make me think this would happen though. I mean, he wanted to tell me something, but I don't know what it was. I have no idea what it was. I guess...at some point between that conversation and me arriving, things got out of hand in his own head. I don't know."

"And those pills he took?"

"Yeah, he got on a couple medications a few months back. He was having a hard time and started having panic attacks, so he was just on some stuff for anxiety."

"There were also sleeping pills in his system. Were you aware he was taking those?"

"No, not at all. I guess, in a way, it doesn't surprise me. He has been going through so much lately, and I'm sure there's things I don't even know about. I'm not surprised if he needed help getting some sleep."

"What happened when you arrived there?"

"He wasn't answering the door. I have a key to the apartment, so I let myself in. I walked in, and there was glass on the floor, and the bathroom was a mess. Things got thrown all over the place like something had really set him off, or maybe Brett was there and had attacked him. I walked into his room and he was on the bed unconscious. I saw the pill bottles. I couldn't wake him up, so I freaked out and shoved my fingers down his mouth and got him to throw some of it up," Jaxie explained. A realization came over her as she looked down, her lip quivering. "I still have vomit on my shirt."

"Here," Lauren stood up, taking her sweater off and handing it over.

"Thanks," Jaxie muttered, reluctantly taking it.

"Okay, I think that's all I need for now. At some point, we'll talk to Aiden and figure out what happened. You can go see him."

"Thanks officer." Jaxie stood up. "I'm going to change real quick."

She walked into the bathroom and slipped into a stall. Removing her shirt, she took a long look at it. She wasn't sure if she could ever look at it again without reliving the night.

"It's okay, it's okay," Jaxie said to herself with a trembling voice. She was ready to lose it, but put any strength she could into pulling herself together. "He's alive. Oh my God, he's alive." The shirt started feeling heavy and made her hands ache. She dropped it to the floor, unable to hold the cries back. "He's okay. Just relax, you can't do this in front of him. He's okay. You're okay. He's okay."

Once changed into the sweater her mother had given her, Jaxie left the stall and tossed the shirt in the trash.

Returning to the waiting room, she was surprised to still see her mom sitting there. Jaxie avoided contact as she snatched her jacket and turned for the doors leading to Aiden's hospital room. She didn't walk through them immediately. There was something she needed to say to her mother, so she turned to face her again. "I think you should leave."

"Why?" Lauren asked.

"For one, you haven't gotten up to even suggest you're about to follow me to go check on him. For another, if Aiden notices Dad's not here, he'll figure it out. He doesn't need that right now. So just go," Jaxie said firmly.

Lauren didn't say anything else as she stood up, gathering her jacket and purse.

"If you knew he was gay," Jaxie blurted out, "and you walked in on him unconscious from taking those pills, would you have tried to save him?"

199

Lauren gave a quick, unsure nod, then turned to leave without a fight to see her son. Jaxie was in disbelief. She expected this if Aiden had told them he was gay on his own terms. She didn't expect their parents to sink this low when his life was on the line. Once her mom was out of sight, Jaxie made her way to Aiden.

One of the scariest places to stand is on the other side of the hospital room door that separated you from your loved one. He was going to be okay, she was told, but she knew this was only the beginning. He wasn't going to leave the hospital and be okay. Jaxie was going to face every day afraid that her brother might consider this course of action again. She was going to have sleepless nights begging to hear from him the next morning.

"I know it's hard," a nurse spoke up from behind her. "He'll love knowing you're here though."

Jaxie bit her lip as she slowly opened the door. She was hoping Aiden would look better than he did when she found him, but that wasn't the case. He was pale and hooked up to multiple wires. He had an oxygen mask over his mouth and nose. His eyes were closed, but he groaned from time to time.

"Aiden?" Jaxie asked, quietly. She sat next to him and watched his eyes flutter but they didn't open. "It's okay, it's just me, Jaxie." She took his hand and gave it a squeeze. "I'm so glad you're okay."

Aiden began groaning to try and say something.

"It's okay, Aiden. Just relax. There is nothing you need to say right now. You just need to rest, alright? But don't worry, I'll be here all night." Jaxie leaned over and kissed Aiden on the forehead. "I love you so much."

Aiden slowly opened his eyes. He was in a heavy amount of pain. His head hurt, his stomach was jumpy, his throat was raw, and his hands felt achy. It scared him to think about what he was going to see, so he cautiously looked around while his vision adjusted. There were wires and tubes, but he didn't try to figure out what they were meant for. He felt something going in his nostrils pushing air in. He licked his dry lips multiple times. His jaw felt sore as if it had been forced to sit in a position for some time. He remembered hearing a lot of different voices last night, but he hadn't been able to make out the words. Looking towards the window, Aiden saw Jaxie asleep in the chair.

"Hey," Aiden's voice cracked, his throat ringing in pain. "Hey...Jaxie." She didn't budge. He grabbed a piece of paper off the side table, balled it up, and threw it at her.

Jaxie jumped, looking alarmed as she took her surroundings in. "Aiden. You're awake." She walked over and pulled her brother into a tight hug.

"Easy," Aiden said in a hoarse voice. "It hurts."

"Sorry. I'm just happy to see you awake."

"Everything hurts."

"Well, they pulled glass shards out of your hands. Thankfully nothing deep, so just bandages. They also had to pump your stomach," Jaxie explained softly.

Aiden looked out the window. He was grateful Jaxie was by his side, but he could barely face her right now. "Who found me?"

"I did. I was coming over, remember?"

Aiden nodded. "I remember. I'm sorry, Jaxie."

"Don't say you're sorry. You have nothing to apologize for," Jaxie assured him. "You don't even have to explain right now, okay? I just want to help you feel better."

Aiden continued to stare out the window.

"I wanted to be here when you woke up, but I do have to go get things from your apartment. I forgot to grab your wallet. I can also get you clothes or whatever else you need."

"Phone?" Aiden asked.

Jaxie sighed. "Aiden, I don't know if that's a good idea. I don't even know why this happened, so I don't want you seeing anything that could..."

"Please?" Aiden asked. "Just bring it."

"Okay, but I'm monitoring before you see anything from anyone you don't need to see."

"Thank you, Jaxie."

"Okay. I'll be back in a couple hours. I love you."

"I love you, too."

-15-

Jaxie's body and mind had settled enough for her to realize how disgusting she felt, so she stopped at her place first to take a brief shower. She mainly scrubbed at her chest and stomach where the vomit had been, and then gave her hair a quick wash. That was all she cared to do. The goal was to keep herself moving. She wanted to avoid losing focus and becoming weak. Upon arriving at Aiden's apartment, she became on edge to relive anything. She wanted to only focus on what she needed to grab. Her eyes couldn't be allowed to take in the view. She couldn't let her brain register anything and risk bringing her back to last night. The only thought she allowed to repeat itself was her list of things to pack. As quickly as she could, Jaxie walked through the living room, internally yelling that list to keep her mind from wandering to anything else. She kept things in a pile on the coffee table, then made her way down the hall. Keeping her head down, she grounded her mind before entering. To keep from going far into Aiden's room, Jaxie slid through his doorway, refusing to look at the bed, and rushed into the closet. She grabbed a backpack sitting on the floor, and, without paying much attention, shoved clothes in there. Her feet ran back to the living room, threw the other items into the backpack, and bolted out of the apartment.

As Jaxie returned to her car, she sat for a minute to recollect herself. She wanted to get herself more in control before even thinking about going back to the hospital. She wanted to be able to focus only on Aiden, and not let him feel any tension off of her. Unzipping the backpack, Jaxie shuffled through to make sure she didn't forget anything. Aiden's phone was on top of the clothes, which brought a thought to her head. Maybe she could find answers on her own. She turned it on with some hope, but as expected, the phone was locked.

"Damn," Jaxie muttered, tossing the phone onto the seat beside her. None of this made sense to her. He hadn't talked to her like he was planning this. She was sure something happened after her phone call with him. That's when last night began flashing in her head. Her brother's lifeless body. The bottles and pills scattered about. Jaxie screamed. She almost lost her brother, the most important person in her life.

"Aiden, why?" She began bawling, choking on her words. "Why? You can't do this to me. For God's sake, don't do this to me!" Her fists slammed against the steering wheel as she yelled. It felt good to do, but it wasn't enough. She wanted to find something, anything, to point her in the right direction. There could possibly be something more in the apartment, but Jaxie refused to go back in there.

Another idea popped in her head, but she didn't sit to think about the details. Jaxie turned the key and hurriedly drove out of the parking lot. She drove down the road and approached another apartment complex. Her eyes wandered as she parked her car, and then she found it. Brett's truck was parked there. He was home.

Jaxie had no idea what she was going to do, but she didn't care. She only knew that she was done. She no longer could sit around and listen to what Brett was getting away with. It didn't matter how crazy she was about to become, she knew Brett had something to do with what happened, and she was going to make him admit it. Her fingers wrapped around her key, ready to turn and pull out of the ignition.

A loud ringing sound made Jaxie jump in her seat. She panicked, wondering if the hospital was calling her. Her screen was black though, causing a moment of confusion. Peering down at the passenger seat, Jaxie saw Aiden's phone was ringing.

"Who's Jack?" Jaxie was desperate for anything, so without hesitation, she answered, "Hello?"

"Uh, hello?"

Jaxie cleared her throat but couldn't stop the crying in her voice. "Who is this?"

The voice on the other end took a second to respond. "This is Jack. Is Aiden there?"

Jaxie took a deep breath as she tried to pull herself together. Her first thought was that this was his new boss or a coworker from his new job. "I'm...sorry," she swallowed the emotion down, gaining a bit of control. "This is his sister."

"Jaxie?"

She was taken by surprise at the response, "Yeah, how did—"

"What's wrong? Did something happen to Aiden?"

Jaxie swallowed again. She was feeling the frustration of not being able to get the lump to go away. "He's, um...he's not okay. I'm sorry, who are you?"

"My name is Jack. I met Aiden back in November. We've...been spending some time together."

"Oh," Jaxie said, getting the picture.

"I'm...sorry you had to find out like this. I was just trying to reach Aiden. What's going on with him?"

Jaxie's crying lightened up, as a little hope seemed to present itself. She looked over at Brett's truck again, and then up at the building where he was. The opportunity was right there for her to go confront him. "Jack, would you mind meeting me somewhere to talk?"

"Yes, absolutely. Name the place."

It took a lot for her to do it, but Jaxie ended up leaving without seeing Brett. She drove to a small restaurant that wasn't far from the hospital. She felt better thinking she was still close to Aiden if there were an emergency. As confident as she felt in meeting Jack, she had many scenarios going through her head on how to go about the conversation. There were questions to be asked, but it was hard to consider asking them with the seriousness of the situation. She had no idea what Jack even looked like. While she waited, Jaxie tried passing some time by calling the hospital, and told the doctor to let Aiden know she had to run an errand and she'd be back soon. She didn't want to talk to him herself and accidentally spill what she was really doing.

After she hung up the phone, Jaxie stared down into her water. She grasped the cup, tapping her nails against it, trying to count the ripples that moved across the surface.

"Jaxie?"

Jaxie quickly looked up at the man escorted to her table. She wasn't sure why, but her body reacted by standing up to greet him. There was a desire to hug him, a need for the feeling that things were going to be okay.

"Yeah, Jack?"

"Yes," Jack responded. He turned to the hostess. "Can you just bring me some water, please?"

"Sure. Anything else for you?"

Jaxie shook her head. "No, thank you."

As the hostess walked away, Jack held his hand out to the table. "Shall we?"

"Yeah." Once they sat down, Jaxie's foot tapped against the floor. She knew what she wanted to ask, but didn't know how to lead up to it. "I'm sorry if this is blunt, but you've been spending time with my brother? Like, more than just a friend's type of time?"

Jack's mouth hung open for a second as his hand reached for the back of his neck. "Well, kind of. Testing the waters, I guess, is the right way to put it."

"That's...actually comforting to hear. I'm sorry if I seem out of the loop, but it's just...Aiden never mentioned you," Jaxie spoke quietly, not wanting to offend him.

"I know. He was unsure where things were going to go with us, so he didn't want to say anything and I didn't push him to," Jack explained. His hand came back down and played with his gray wristband.

"So, are you guys...a couple?"

Jack cleared his throat, chuckling a little. "Not exactly. We've spent some time together, got close, but I wouldn't label us...yet, I hope."

"How did you guys meet?"

"He went out to The Color Band one night and we met there."

"That's great." Jaxie watched as Jack seemed nervous. "I'm sorry if I'm hitting you with questions. I got a little hopeful."

"No, don't be sorry," Jack said, playing with his fork now. "I'm sorry to jump topics, but I'm worried something is wrong. Where's Aiden?"

Jaxie closed her eyes tightly, already feeling the tears push through her eyelashes. Even though Jack was bringing some hope to the situation, Jaxie had to face reality again that they weren't in the clear yet. She nearly jumped when she felt Jack's hand grab hers.

"It's okay," he said softly. "You don't have to tell me where he is. Just tell me he's okay."

Jaxie wiped her eyes furiously. "Yeah, he's okay. As okay as he can be."

"Okay," Jack nodded.

It was impossible now to switch topics. Formal conversation was no good, it was becoming a barrier between them. Jaxie could see the concern all over Jack's face. She could see that he cared deeply for her brother.

"I'll tell you what happened."

"You don't have to."

"I'm not going to make us pretend to have a casual conversation. I can see how worried you are. He's in the hospital."

Jack ran a hand down his face. His mind bounced between two reasons that Aiden could be in the hospital. He wasn't sure which he preferred. "What happened?"

"Last night I was supposed to go over after work. He was going to tell me something important." Jaxie looked at Jack. "I think I know what that was going to be now. Anyway, I walked inside. His bathroom was a disaster, things were broken. I found him unconscious in his bed. He overdosed on pills, or at least attempted."

Jack looked down, shaking his head. He wished it had been the other scenario.

"I don't know why he did it," Jaxie went on, "he seemed like he really wanted to talk to me. I really think something happened between him calling me and me getting there. I just don't know what."

"I'm so sorry this happened," Jack said. "If you need anything, please let me know. Please."

"You guys got really close?"

"Yeah, we did," Jack said. "I felt like we were having a breakthrough. I was ready for something with him, but he wanted to take it slow. He did send me a text last night about us taking a break, because he was worried

208

about me getting hurt. I was going to try and talk to him about it today."

"You should come see him," Jaxie blurted.

"I don't want to impose."

"It's not imposing. It's very obvious how much you care about him. I'm happy he's had you around, and he may be really happy to see you. He needs all the support he can get right now."

"You are right about that." Jack looked down, uncertain on his decision. "This is so hard."

"I understand if you don't want to. If there's something personal it hits, I don't want to make you come see him. I just want him to have anyone he can get. Right now, I'm all he has. He's all I have."

"He's got me, too. I want to help him. He's got a long road ahead of him." Jack shifted uncomfortably in his seat. "I'll come see him. I should. I have to."

"Great. If you want to come now, you can," Jaxie said, standing up. "I should get back to him."

Jack followed Jaxie to the hospital and they walked into the building together. Jaxie hoped she was doing the right thing by bringing Jack along. She didn't know who else to bring or what else to do to help Aiden. This opportunity came along, so she wanted to take advantage of that. It was better than Aiden hearing she got arrested for assaulting Brett. Jack stayed a little behind while Jaxie entered Aiden's room first.

"Hey, hun," she walked over and gave Aiden a kiss on the cheek. It was relieving to see more color to her brother's face. He was sitting up a little and appeared more awake. "How are you feeling?"

"I'm okay."

"Have you eaten?"

Jaxie watched as Aiden looked like he could vomit. "Please don't talk about that."

209

"I'm sorry. Well, I brought some stuff for you to do. Cards, games, magazines. I just sort of grabbed anything. I brought your wallet since the doctor's needed it last night, and I brought your phone. I'm going to hold onto it, though."

"Thanks. I may need to check something on my phone. I need to talk to someone."

"Well, about that, something came up while I was gone."

"Hmm?"

"I ran into somebody." Jaxie walked over to the door, waving for someone to walk in.

Aiden's eyes widened in horror as he watched Jack take steps into his room. "Oh no."

Jack didn't waste a second as he hurried to the other side of the bed and wrapped his arms around Aiden. "I'm so glad to see you're okay."

Aiden wrapped his arms around Jack. It hurt to do so, but he used any strength he had to hold onto him. He hadn't realized how much he wanted Jack by his side until now, but he was worried about Jack's feelings towards him. Once they broke the hug, Aiden looked over at Jaxie. "Are you mad?"

"About what?"

"Not telling you."

"No, of course not!" Jaxie assured him. "I was very happy to meet him."

"How did you guys meet anyway?"

"He was trying to call you," Jaxie explained. "We met up and talked."

Aiden could barely look at Jack. "You told him what happened."

"Don't worry about it," Jack said as he took Aiden's hand. "We're just going to be here to help you now."

Aiden looked between the two. "Neither of you deserve this."

"Aiden..." Jaxie said softly.

"I told the police and the doctor what happened," Aiden said, leaning back against his pillow, "but I told them I wanted to tell you myself, Jaxie."

"I'll go outside," Jack said.

"No. I want you to hear it from me too. Please stay."

Jack sat in a chair and scooted close to the bed, holding Aiden's hand. He had to mentally prepare himself. Jaxie sat in another chair, trying not to show how afraid she was. It was getting more difficult to bury any negative vibes.

Aiden took a few deep breaths before spitting out. "Brett came over."

"What?" Jack asked. It took a lot for him to hold back on his tone.

Jaxie looked across the bed at Jack. "You know about him, huh?"

"Uh-huh," Jack responded.

"Well, did you call the police?" Jaxie asked, looking back at her brother.

"I...tried, but...no, that's not true. I really didn't try. Shit, he knows how to get me to cower away. He just started telling me things...I was disgusting, my kind doesn't belong here, and...I should just..." Aiden's voice shook and his eyes watered. A dark, trembling fear took over the room and everyone could feel it.

"Shh," Jack soothed, rubbing Aiden's arm. "You don't have to go on with that part."

Aiden looked up to the ceiling, "I don't know. It all just got to me. I had a panic attack in the bathroom, but I didn't feel like *I* had to stop the attack. It was different. It stopped on its own; instantly. And then...I was just done. I saw myself in the mirror as someone who really had nothing going for him. I went and grabbed all those pills—"

"That's enough," Jaxie interrupted. "You don't have to go on."

"I'm so sorry you guys. I feel like I failed you both."

"You didn't," Jack said firmly. "That's not at all what you have done. We're going to get you through this, alright?"

Before anyone else could go on, a voice near the room's door interrupted the three.

"Oh my God."

Everyone looked towards the door to see Lauren standing there, looking pale.

"Mom," Aiden said, surprise clear on his face. Jack quickly took his hand away from Aiden's.

Lauren cleared her throat and took a couple steps into the room. Jack being in that room was equivalent to a deadly virus to Lauren, and she was going to be cautious. "I thought I'd come check on my son. If you don't mind," she said, looking to Jack, but not with eye-contact, "this is a family matter."

"Of course," Jack said, standing from his seat. "I'll come back later."

"No," Aiden begged, "you don't have to leave."

"I'm not going to make anyone uncomfortable," Jack insisted.

"Please don't."

"I'd prefer it," Lauren said firmly. She walked along the wall, deliberately leaving plenty of space for Jack to leave the room without getting near her.

"Jesus, Mom," Jaxie muttered, shaking her head.

"Really, it's okay," Jack assured before looking down at Aiden. "I'll be back, alright?"

Once Jack was gone, Jaxie glared at their mother. "Mom, do you really think that was the way to help Aiden?"

Lauren ignored her daughter as she walked closer to the hospital bed. "How are you feeling?"

"I'm okay, Mom."

"What made you do this? What happened?"

"There's too much to tell you. I've just...had a lot going on."

"I told them everything," Jaxie admitted. "I told them about the things going on and you coming out. I'm sorry you didn't get to tell them, but I didn't have a choice."

"Well, your father and I could have told you what would happen after going down the Devil's path. It's no wonder our prayers for you and Courtney weren't working. Quite frankly, we're surprised God spared you. It means you're getting a chance to redeem yourself."

"Mom, shut the hell up!" Jaxie barked.

"If you didn't follow him, the Devil wouldn't have put the pills down your throat."

Aiden shook his head. He had heard his parents talk this way about other people, but Aiden never had his mother talk to him like this. "Mom, please."

"No, Aiden, you need to listen to me now. You should have told us you were having these feelings. We could have stopped it sooner. God could have taken care of it."

"No. No one could have stopped this," Aiden stated firmly, anger slowly boiling in the pit of his stomach.

"It's not the righteous way! You were straying from the Lord and we could have fixed that for you. Since you are still here, you need to turn yourself around, fast."

"Mom, God is not going to hate me for being gay. I'm so sick of people saying I need to fix myself."

"God may not hate you, but he will judge you."
Their mother glanced towards the door before meeting her
son's eyes. "Look at yourself. You've already gone as far
as exposing yourself to that man and doing unspeakable
things behind closed doors."

"Mom!" Jaxie stood up. "Do you hear yourself
right now?!"

Aiden looked out the window, hearing Brett's voice
repeat the same thing, calling him disgusting after accusing
him of sleeping with Jack. "First of all, I haven't done any
of that stuff. Is that all you think gay people do?"

"Well, they certainly like to show off in public."

"Maybe some, but not Jack. Straight couples show
off too, but you don't notice it. Jack is a great guy..."

"Mom, this is really the last thing Aiden needs from
you," Jaxie argued. "You need to leave."

"Why didn't Dad come?" Aiden spoke up.

His mother sighed and looked at him
disappointedly. "He'll be ready to see you when you're
ready for our help."

"So...his love for me isn't unconditional?" Aiden
asked. Hearing that question broke Jaxie's heart. She hadn't
thought of it like that, and it really stung. How could a
father be so awful to his own son?

"I'll see if I can get him to come visit. I am happy
to see you're okay," Lauren said, "I love you." Aiden
didn't respond as she left the room.

"She couldn't even hug me. The idea of Jack just
being near me made my body too vile to hug."

"Don't worry about it," Jaxie said through clenched
teeth as she wiped at her eyes.

"I really haven't slept with him. We've never
kissed."

"Aiden, why are you telling me this? Do you think
I'd see you differently if you had?"

He slowly shook his head. "No."

"Our parents are going to believe what they're going to believe. Even if you had proof you didn't do anything physical, it wouldn't change their minds." Jaxie watched as Aiden's head sank low. "If you go that far with Jack, do you believe you're going to be vile? Is Jack vile if he's done things with another man?"

"Jack doesn't have a vile bone in his body."

"And neither do you," Jaxie said, walking over to the bed. She sat on the edge and took Aiden's hands into hers. "Just keep being you. Be with Jack if you want to be with Jack. Do whatever you want to with him. Do whatever is going to bring your happiness."

Aiden squeezed Jaxie's hands. He had been wasting time worrying about them meeting each other. Now he wished he had done it sooner.

There was a knock at the door and another doctor walked into the room. "Excuse me? Hi, Aiden? I'm Dr. Holm. I'm the psychiatrist. Your doctor said now was a good time to try and talk to you."

Jaxie squeezed Aiden's hands. "Alright, I'll leave you to this."

"Do you have to go?" Aiden asked.

"I'm not leaving the hospital. I'll just be waiting outside. I'll go see if Jack is still here if you want him to come back in later."

"Yes, please."

"Okay. I love you." Jaxie gave him a soft smile as she walked out. She headed to the waiting room where she found Jack.

"I'm so sorry about my mom," Jaxie said, taking a seat.

"It's really okay," Jack assured her. "I'm just sorry Aiden had to go through it this way. Is he okay?"

"I don't know. He's talking to a psychiatrist right now."

215

"That's one of the harder parts. He's going to finally have the word suicide thrown at him."

Jaxie gulped. "Oh my God..."

"He needs to hear it. They'll figure out his thinking process, if he wants to do it again, how he's viewing life right now, just everything."

As Jack went on, Jaxie sensed the sincerity and personal touch to his explanation. "You've...been through this before."

"Don't tell him. I haven't figured out how to tell him about that part of my life. It's a lot."

"I'm sorry you had to go through it. Do you...ever think about..."

"Doing it again? I used to. It's...it's just a really long story."

"Of course. I'm sorry. I shouldn't be prying."

"It's fine. I know you're curious for Aiden's sake. I may have to face it a little bit anyway to help him."

They were quiet then. Jaxie had heard of hard times people can go through when they've been made to feel different, specifically in a bad way, but she hadn't ever been face-to-face with it. Each time she took a glance at Jack, he had changed into another position and had found another object to mess around with. Sometimes he was pulling on his wristbands. She could see the wheels in his head spinning, taking him back through memories of his own struggles. She could see him attempting to find his own inner comfort. It was heartbreaking. It infuriated her. It scared her, wondering what was to come next for her brother.

"What are those?" Jaxie asked, attempting a distraction for him.

Jack looked at her, then back down at his arm where his fingers were under a black wristband. "Bible verses."

Jaxie became intrigued. "You believe God loves you? I mean, even though you're gay?"

"Of course. I know other people might not, but that's okay. I can only worry about my own relationship with Him."

"Can I read them?"

"Sure," Jack said, extending his arm and pulling his jacket sleeve higher. Jaxie turned each one, hoping for some comfort to come from reading them. She read the first three; they made her smile and feel a sense of empowerment. As she turned the black wristband to read it, something under the wristbands caught Jaxie's eye. She flinched slightly as she noticed two small scars. Once Jack noticed, he retracted his arm and embarrassingly pulled his sleeve all the way down.

"I'm sorry," Jaxie said quickly.

"No, I'm sorry. I don't know why I did that."

"If you're worried about what I'm thinking, I can promise you I'm the last person in this family you have to be even a little concerned about judging you."

"I know. It's stupid. I'm sure Aiden has seen them some. He's just too shy to ask."

"Yeah," Jaxie said, feeling bad she made it obvious that the cuts caught her attention. "Well, I'm going to go see how it's going. Do you want to come with me?"

"Are you sure?"

"Yes, of course. You can go in with him while I go talk to the doctor."

Going through the double doors was proving to be a difficult task for Jack. He hadn't expected to be in this situation with Aiden. Hearing about what happened with Brett had only been a vague statement, but Jack didn't need to hear the rest. He already had a good idea how it all went down, and, unfortunately, he knew Jaxie wouldn't be able to fathom it all. He was already putting work into keeping his anger aside.

Jack walked into Aiden's room, finding him turned away from the door.

"Hey," Jack said as he walked around the bed, "how did it go?"

"It was okay," Aiden said softly.

"Were you honest with them about everything?"

Aiden nodded slowly, "I didn't want to hurt you."

"Aiden, please don't..." Jack pulled Aiden's hand into his. "Not right now, okay? Right now, we just need to focus on helping you."

"As soon as I did it, I regretted it. I swallowed those pills, and I thought I'd just go to sleep. That'd be it. Then it hurt...my stomach hurt so bad. Then I realized I didn't want to die anymore." Aiden wiped his tears away. "It was too late, though. I couldn't get out of my bed or anything. I couldn't stay awake."

"Stop," Jack said, a little harsher than he meant to. He couldn't figure out what to say next. Nothing seemed right. Instead, he went to the other side of the bed and climbed in next to Aiden. It was uncomfortable, but he didn't care. He just wanted to hold him.

Both of them almost fell asleep as there was quite a bit of time that passed before Jaxie walked into the room. She couldn't keep the smile off her face at the sight. Her brother appeared to be in some peace. "Aiden, I spoke with the doctor."

"Yeah?"

"He thinks you could come home tomorrow with heavy supervision."

"Oh."

"What's wrong? That's good news, right?"

"I'm scared to go back there, Jaxie. I don't want to see any of it. I don't want to go back to that apartment. Even if I'm not there alone. I just can't. What if it makes me try again?" Aiden asked. "I don't want to try again, but what if I have a panic attack? I just...I can't go back there."

218

Jack sat up and got off the bed, rubbing the back of his neck. "It might be worth it to break the lease."

"I can't afford that," Aiden shook his head.

"Maybe we can talk to the landlord and let him know the situation?" Jaxie suggested.

"They won't care. They just want their money."

"We could...try asking Mom or Dad to help out."

"Mom may be willing to, but Dad won't let her. You know that. It honestly doesn't matter. If I can't break it, I'm still not going back. I'll keep paying rent, but I'm not going back."

"Okay, hold on," Jack said, "Aiden, don't stress about it right now. Jaxie and I will talk about it and figure something out."

Jaxie nodded in agreement. "Where do you want to go if you get discharged tomorrow? You can take my bed and I'll sleep on the couch."

"If you don't have the room, he can come stay with me. I have a guest room he can stay in," Jack offered.

"I can't do that." Aiden shook his head.

"Stop with that. I wouldn't offer if I didn't mean it. It's up to you though. Wherever you're comfortable going."

Aiden settled against his pillow, staring at the ceiling. "I'll think about it. I'm really tired right now."

"We can let you rest some." Jaxie patted her brother's arm. "Jack and I can go to your place and start packing some of your stuff if you'd like."

"Yes, please. I want...need to be out of there."

Jaxie followed Jack down to his truck. "Thanks for helping with this."

"Yeah, of course."

"Actually, I should probably also thank you for calling Aiden's phone when you did."

"How come?"

"Well, you seem to know about Brett, so you'll understand this. I was getting Aiden some stuff from his place and I was desperate to figure out what happened to him, so I drove to Brett's apartment. I wanted to confront him and demand answers, maybe hit him a couple hundred times. When you called, it stopped me and I came to meet up with you instead. I would've gotten in trouble and Aiden definitely didn't need that."

Jack slowly nodded as he gripped the door handle. "You know where Brett lives, huh?"

"Yeah, but I'm not going to show you."

"Probably a good idea."

They both got in the truck and began driving to Aiden's apartment to empty out as much as they could.

"I wasn't going to bring this up in front of Aiden and put more worry on him," Jack said, "but I'll help pay for his breaking the lease."

"Jack, we can't ask you to do that," Jaxie told him, shaking her head.

"I don't want to hear it. He can't go back there and be reminded of everything, and Brett won't know for sure where he is anymore if we get him out of there. It needs to happen. You know it does."

Jaxie didn't say anything else. She had seen the fear in Aiden's eyes as he talked about not going back to his apartment. She would get all of his things out if she could. As long as she didn't have to risk her brother going back there, she'd do anything.

"Let's take care of this first." Jack motioned towards the glass on the floor. The day had been so long already and it was only the afternoon. Jack took a garbage bag and the two carefully grabbed every piece they could

220

find. Jaxie had to put most of her focus on holding herself together, knowing there was more coming their way.

As Jack set the trash bag near the door, he couldn't help but look around the living room and begin imagining how things happened with Brett. It enraged him. He lightly tapped his fist against the wall, having a strong urge to punch right through it. He easily would if Jaxie wasn't there, clearly needing his support. Neither of them could be doing this alone.

Jaxie stared down the hall, but couldn't move forward, so Jack took that as his cue to lead the way. He let out a low whistle as he took in the sight of the bathroom. "He really did have a moment. I think we should throw everything away and get him new stuff."

"Alright," Jaxie said quietly, going to get another trash bag. They filled it with as much stuff as they could. It was hard not to try and imagine step-by-step how Aiden's meltdown happened. It was hard not to try and put themselves in his head, imagining what he was thinking. Jaxie brought the full trash bag next to the other one. She turned and saw Jack waiting to go into the bedroom.

"Ready?"

"Never," Jaxie whispered. She took soft steps towards the bedroom, as if she were trying not to wake a sleeping monster. Slowly, she stepped into the room, Jack right behind her. They stayed put as they took in the view. The pill bottles and pills were still scattered around. There was dry vomit on the sheets and floor. The smell had become awful. Jaxie's will gave up. She couldn't stand in there. She had no idea how she managed to do what she did last night, because she couldn't get herself to think straight being back there now. Her body sank to the floor, hard cries escaping her lips.

Jack joined her on the floor, hugging her tight. "It's okay. He's still here, and that's because of you. You saved him."

"Not really," Jaxie practically yelled through the choked tears. "I helped him not die, but that doesn't mean he's saved."

"We're going to help him, alright? He'll be okay. We will make sure he's okay." Jack broke the hug and held her shoulders, looking her in the eye. "He will be okay."

Jaxie bit her lip and closed her eyes, attempting to calm herself.

"I'll try to clean this up, but it'll be easier to pay the landlord a carpet cleaning bill instead. We'll throw out the bed stuff. Would it be easier for you to pack the rest of his clothes?"

"Yeah," Jaxie whispered. The closet did seem to be an easier spot for her to be in. Jack got to his feet and helped Jaxie up.

Jack walked to the kitchen to grab anything he could find to try and clean the carpet. He knew he couldn't stay there much longer before he ended up breaking something himself. He was already fighting with himself, trying to hold himself back from finding Brett and giving him a piece of his mind.

Reaching into his pocket, Jack pulled out his knife and began flicking it in and out. "I'll be damned if anything happens to him."

-16-

After packing up what they could manage, the two drove back to the hospital. As they entered the waiting room, Jaxie saw the police officer from last night. He was wanting to speak with her. Jack took a seat to wait while she got an update.

"What's going on?" Jaxie asked the officer.

"Brett claims he wasn't at Aiden's apartment last night. There's sufficient evidence though, so we took him in."

"That's good news then, right?"

"For now. He could still bail out, but hopefully this arrest sets him straight. Encourage your brother to go to that court date. A permanent restraining order is what is going to keep him safe in the future."

"I will, of course, but what about other people? Brett has used other people to hurt him."

"Same procedure: give us a call. The best thing he can do is report anything, so we can arrest Brett when it's necessary. Even if he isn't sure who it is, tell him to report everything. We don't want to see him here again."

"Neither do we." Jaxie nodded. "Does Aiden know Brett's in jail?"

"Not yet. He's been asleep, so we've talked with his doctor."

"Okay, I'll talk to him about it. Thank you, officer." Jaxie felt some relief after hearing Brett was in jail. What worried her was he could have already bailed out, but it would be difficult to ever know. She walked over to where Jack was seated to relay the news. "He said Brett was arrested. He can bail out, so I don't know how good of news that is."

"It's something at least. Brett's getting something he deserves, finally."

"He was saying we need to make sure Aiden goes to his court date."

Jack nodded in agreement. "Aiden is going to argue with himself over and over about going through with it. He already has. Even when he hears that Brett's been arrested, he's going to wonder if that's punishment enough."

Jaxie put her hand over her mouth, trying to keep herself from crying. "I hope he doesn't skip it. I...he can't get hurt again. I can't let him get hurt again, Jack. I just can't!"

Jack pulled Jaxie into a hug. He didn't say anything. He let her have his shoulder to cry on. It was all he could do as he wasn't sure he could promise anything.

The next morning Aiden had another appointment with Dr. Holm. Jaxie and Jack joined towards the end and agreed to supervise Aiden, ensuring he wouldn't ever be left alone. With their assurance, the doctor agreed to discharge Aiden that evening. He was thankful for that. He didn't feel like sitting at the hospital was helping him heal much.

"I don't want to keep your prescriptions from you," the doctor explained to everyone in the room, "but, I don't want you in charge of them, Aiden."

"That's fine," Aiden nodded.

"I want to add an antidepressant and make only one of the anxiety medications a priority. The other one should only be for a serious need."

"Okay, I understand."

"Good. I'm going to get some paperwork filled out. I'll be back."

After the doctor left the room, Aiden stared at his hands, playing with the sheets. "I decided where I want to go. If it's okay with you guys, I want to stay with Jack."

"That's fine with me," Jaxie said and glanced at Jack. "Is it okay if I come with you for a little bit tonight?"

"You're more than welcome to come over," Jack answered.

"Is that okay, Aiden? Or if you want to just go there and go to bed, I can wait until tomorrow."

"No, I'd like you to come." Aiden looked up at Jack. "Thank you for letting me stay with you."

"Of course," Jack said. "Now go on and get dressed. You'll be out of here soon."

Once the discharge was complete, Aiden rode with Jack. They didn't say anything to each other. Aiden felt like he had failed Jack, and even if he had, Jack didn't seem to be holding anything against him and Aiden appreciated that more than he could express. He was feeling a little better now that he was out of the hospital, but he was becoming nervous thinking about staying with Jack. There were a lot of feelings going through him, thinking about what he could be ready for. He had taken Jaxie's words to heart, about doing what he believed would bring him happiness.

Aiden didn't expect it to happen, but he started crying at the first step inside Jack's house.

"What is it?" Jaxie asked, grabbing his arm.

"I don't really know," Aiden said, walking further into the house. "It's a lot of changes. When I think about what I tried to do, I just...I can't believe I did that. I can't believe I did that to you guys."

Jaxie hugged her brother, holding him while he let the emotions out.

"I'm going to make some dinner," Jack said.

"Alright. I'll help you get organized, Aiden," Jaxie said, lifting a bag in each of her hands. Aiden brought his sister downstairs to the guest room, and they began sorting his clothes.

"You're not mad that I chose to stay with Jack instead of you, are you?" Aiden asked, sitting on the bed.

"Of course not," Jaxie said, "I think it's great you feel comfortable enough to stay here. Honestly, he can probably give you the best support in this situation."

"Yeah." Aiden nodded as he looked out the window.

"Jack really cares about you, you know. From only the couple of times I've been around him by myself, I can tell. He's a really great guy."

"He is. Even through all this, I can't believe I was lucky enough to meet him."

"I know Mom and Dad wouldn't agree, but it was clearly in some higher power's plan for you to meet him."

"I like to believe that," Aiden agreed.

As she watched her brother continue to unpack, Jaxie felt her heart lift. She hated thinking about what she could be doing right now if things had gone a different way, but those thoughts couldn't ruin her happiness at seeing Aiden awake and breathing. "I'm so happy I get to be having a conversation with you right now."

Aiden thought about what she meant and smiled back at her. "I am too."

"I love you so much, Aiden."

"I love you too. Thank you for everything." Aiden glanced towards the door. "I hate to end yet another sentimental moment between us, but I smell food. I'm really hungry."

Jaxie laughed, "Let's go upstairs."

Jaxie was in the kitchen making small talk with Jack, and she noticed Aiden sitting on the couch in silence. He was settled in a corner spot, hugging his legs to his chest, and letting his head rest on his knees. She tried not to let it concern her too much as she expected there would be high moments followed by sudden low moments. However, it was those low moments, when he was being quiet, that she would worry about him the most. She would only wonder what he was thinking about, but she didn't want to pry.

"It's ready," Jack said from the kitchen. "Everyone grab a plate and we can just sit in the living room, watch some TV. Unwind." Aiden didn't move. Jaxie slowly made her plate, looking at Jack for assurance to not worry. Jack didn't appear to be concerned as waved her to the living room. "I got his plate."

Aiden ate slowly with his stomach still having sensitive moments from the pumping, but he was relieved to have a nice, hot meal. Relaxing on the couch watching mindless TV was a nice change of pace in itself.

Jack noticed Aiden only touching a few bites of his dinner. "Is it okay?"

"Yeah. My appetite is still off."

"Do you want Jaxie to stay the night? She is more than welcome to."

"No, it's okay," Aiden said, looking at his sister. "You should really get some sleep in your own bed."

"I will sleep much better knowing you're in good hands." Jaxie smiled. "I'll come by tomorrow and we can go talk about your lease, okay? I figure the sooner we can get it done, the better."

"I'm plenty ready to do that as long as I don't have to go in there."

After dinner, Jaxie could sense Aiden being tired and possibly overwhelmed, so she excused herself for the night, as hard as that was. The boys walked Jaxie outside, and Aiden gave her a long hug before she got in her car. He was having the realization that he didn't need a bunch of family to support him like Jack had. Having one family member be there for him made up for the rest that wouldn't be. As Aiden watched her car disappear he felt how grateful he was to have her in his life. If she hadn't been, he would have been more lonely through all of this. Lonelier than he could imagine. He did feel edgy with the idea of her not being with him for the night, but he was still comforted knowing he wasn't alone.

"What do you want to do now?" Jack asked as they returned to the living room, sitting back down.

Aiden watched as Jack leaned his head against the couch, his eyes barely open. "You look very tired."

"I am." Jack yawned. "I don't know if I'm comfortable with you sleeping downstairs by yourself."

"I'm not going to try anything," Aiden assured. "Besides, I don't know where you put my pills."

"Still, when your mind wants something badly enough, you could try anything."

"What will make you feel better?"

"If I sleep downstairs. I can sleep on the floor or the couch."

Whether Jaxie or Jack knew, picking Jack's house wasn't a random decision by Aiden. He had thought long and hard about it, and had decided he wanted something further with Jack now. More than just spending time together. After what Jaxie said at the hospital, Aiden felt the hard push to move forward. He finally wanted to bring some light to his fantasies. But first, he had to get the courage to speak. This seemed to be the perfect time to bring it up.

"No..."

"Aiden, it's not me accusing you or not trusting you. It's about being there to help you through anything you can't get yourself out of. That's all."

Aiden felt butterflies in his stomach, enough to make him sick, while he tried to form the words he wanted to say. "Can...can I..."

"What?"

"Can I...just sleep upstairs with you?" he asked quietly, looking towards the wall.

"No, I don't want you sleeping on my floor. That won't be comfortable."

Aiden shook his head, still not looking at him. "No, that's not what I meant."

Jack paused, realizing what Aiden was hinting at. "Are you sure? You don't need to do that. I'm helping you out, because I care about you. Not because I expect anything from you."

"I know that. I want to. I really want to be next to you."

Aiden couldn't see it, but Jack was smiling big. "Alright. Well, let's head up there then. We both need our rest."

"Yeah. Can I use your shower first?"

"Yeah, go ahead. I'll be up in a bit."

As inviting as the hot water was, Aiden was too exhausted to stay in the shower long. He quickly rinsed himself off, stepped out, and got in a clean t-shirt and sweats. Everything was going smoothly until the steam started coming off the mirror. That's when he became alarmed. The cracks he had caused on his apartment mirror were starting to appear, spreading across the glass. The damage he caused to himself back then and shortly after were right in front of him. The damage he may have caused to Jaxie and Jack from it all. He wasn't proud of the man he was right now and didn't want to see himself.

Desperate to get away from his reflection, Aiden quickly grabbed a comb to pull through his hair. He wanted to do that one task and then get out before the mirror cleared itself. He wasn't fast enough. His reflection was appearing right before his eyes. The mirror was breaking more. There wasn't a chance for him to try and breathe through it. It was happening too fast. He dropped down to the floor to hide. His breathing became rapid and his stomach jumped to his throat. He grabbed the counter tightly, leaning his head against the cabinet with his eyes shut tight.

Aiden felt alone in the battle that was coming before him.

That's when it hit him. For a second, he could clearly think and tell himself that he wasn't alone. This time he wasn't by himself during a panic attack. There was help on the other side of the door. Aiden crawled to the door, keeping the mirror out of his view, and reached for the door handle, pulling it open. "J-Jack?"

Jack walked into the bathroom but didn't say anything. He got down to the floor and pulled Aiden into his arms, squeezing firmly. His arms stayed in a tight grip. Aiden could feel his own uneven breathing as he buried himself in Jack's chest. He was scared and desperate to find protection. Jack used his hand to make circular motions against Aiden's back. That was slowly helping regulate his breathing. At first, Aiden couldn't make out what Jack was whispering to him so he did his best to rein in his focus, trying to quiet his mind to hear the words.

"You are okay," the words slid through, "You are safe."

Jack repeated the phrases until he felt Aiden's body relax. He slowly moved back to look Aiden in the eye and asked, "What happened?"

Aiden glanced up where the mirror was. There were no cracks and the steam had barely moved. He couldn't believe how much his mind had tricked him during his panicking. "I didn't want to look at myself."

"Okay," Jack put his arms around Aiden, holding him while he collected himself. After a moment, Jack helped him to his feet. He walked Aiden out of the bathroom, not giving any impression that his episode had been ridiculous. Aiden sure felt it was. "Are you okay?"

"I think so. Thank you."

"I'm glad you had me come help. Ready for bed?"

"Yeah." Aiden watched Jack walk to one side of the bed. He felt his heart skip a beat as he didn't notice Jack had been shirtless the entire time. The recent panic attack seemed to disappear from his mind as other thoughts crawled in. Jack sat down on the bed, noticing Aiden wasn't moving.

"Aiden, if you're not comfortable with this, we can go downstairs. I'll take the couch or whatever you want."

"No, no. I...want to be up here. I know I do." Aiden wasn't sure who he was trying to sound convincing to, Jack or himself. He took his time sliding into the bed and sinking into the pillow. "This is a lot more comfortable than the hospital."

Jack yawned as he was being taken over by the comfort of his bed. "I'm sure it is."

As he looked over and saw Jack settling, Aiden felt a question come to his mind. He tried to force it away, not thinking it was the right time. That wasn't working though. It was lunging upward more and more, trying to force its way out. He was sure Jack had already fallen asleep, at least he hoped so, but his voice spilled out anyway. "Jack?"

"What?" Jack mumbled out.

"I have a question."

"I feel like you were about to ask, but chickened out and just said you have a question instead."

"Yeah, sort of."

"What is it?"

"Nothing."

"Are you sure? You can ask me anything."

"I won't sleep if I don't ask," Aiden admitted more to himself than Jack.

Jack tensed. The first thing that came to his mind was Aiden wanting to ask about any personal experience he may have, and he wasn't confident about answering honestly. He reluctantly responded, "Go ahead and ask."

"Okay...God, this is stupid...can," Aiden took a deep breath. "Can we...well, can we kiss?"

Jack sat straight up and looked at Aiden, not expecting that question. "Really?"

"I want us to. I had thought about it before, and I've had a lot of time to think about it the past few days. I want to. I really do."

Jack looked Aiden in the eyes. "Come here." His hand wrapped around Aiden's head and pulled him close. He moved slowly in case Aiden changed his mind. Aiden closed his eyes as he felt Jack's lips against his own. As he sank into the kiss, Aiden let his hand slide up Jack's arm and to his shoulder, taking in every muscle. There was no regret or shame.

When they parted, Jack gave Aiden a tight hug. They both lowered back down against their pillows, Aiden immediately shying away as he turned his back towards Jack.

"Worth it?" Jack asked.

"Yes, it was."

"Good," Jack said as he pulled Aiden against him, holding him close.

"Get it out of your system?" Aiden asked jokingly.

Jack chuckled. "Not even close, but I'm happy I got to do that much."

"Me too," Aiden grabbed Jack's hand and held it. He may have been exhausted, but he wanted to take this moment in as long as he could. Jack's words about him being safe felt truer the longer he stayed against him.

Aiden woke up the next morning alone in the bed. He sat up, stretched, and made his way downstairs where he found Jack at his computer working, so he helped himself to the kitchen and grabbed some coffee. Next to the coffee maker was a napkin with a couple pills on it. The sight of them brought a disgusting taste to his mouth. Worries rushed through his head at the idea of taking them. He didn't want them to relax him too much. He didn't want them to put him to sleep. He didn't want to sleep forever. He didn't want to die.

"Morning," Jack said, walking into the kitchen. Aiden broke away from his running mind. His fingers cramped as he had been clutching the handle of his coffee mug tight. The back of his neck crawled with sweat, yet he felt cold. "How did you sleep?"

Aiden blinked hard in an attempt to ground himself. "Fine."

"Good. You found your medicine?"

"Uh, yeah." Aiden refused to look at the pills again as he stared at the coffee maker.

"You can take them."

Aiden quickly shook his head. "I can't."

"I know what's going through your head right now." Jack approached Aiden, turning him around to face him. "Listen to me. You can trust me. I'm telling you you can take these pills and you'll be okay. They are going to help you. I promise. One at a time."

Jack picked up one of the pills and placed it in Aiden's hand. He patiently waited for Aiden to make the next move. As soon as it touched his tongue, Aiden felt his stomach leap up to his throat. He was choking. He wasn't in the kitchen anymore. He was in his bed, tossing back pills, letting them fly down his throat. Not again. He had to stop it.

"Calm down." Aiden heard Jack talking to him. "You're not in danger. You're here with me. Focus on where you are."

Focusing on his surroundings, Aiden saw his room slowly vanish. He looked around as it gradually transformed back to Jack's kitchen. He was safe. He was okay. His throat opened up as he swallowed the pill still sitting in his mouth.

"You okay?"

Aiden nodded as he rubbed his eyes, making sure he couldn't see any more of his bedroom. "I think so."

"Alright." Jack picked up the other pill and handed it over. Aiden was able to take that one with ease. He used the counter to support himself as he was feeling slightly lightheaded. Jack didn't say anything. He simply stood there and waited for Aiden to collect himself.

"Thank you," Aiden said as he took a cleansing breath.

"You're welcome. Do you know when Jaxie is coming to pick you up?"

"In an hour. I should go get ready."

"Okay. Listen, I already talked to Jaxie about this at the hospital. I'm not going to hear any argument. I told her I'm going to help you pay to break the lease. I want to get you out of there, so I'm going to help with it. Now don't argue with me on it."

Aiden nodded. "Can I...at least voice a concern?"

234

"I guess, but it won't change my mind."

"I figured that. I know we've had some big steps for us, but we still haven't officially established what we are. What if we don't become...anything?"

"What about it?"

"You're just doing so much for me."

"I don't expect you as a reward, Aiden. I'm doing this because I care about you as a person. That's what you are, a person. If we don't become anything, I'd love to still be your friend. I'm not going to regret anything I've done for you."

Aiden grinned as he looked down at his coffee. "Thanks."

"Now I have a question for you. Feel free to say no if you aren't ready for it."

"What?"

"Well, Lydia and Avy sort of know what's going on. They want to check up and make sure you're doing okay, so they want to come by and see you. It wouldn't be a long visit. Is it okay if they come tonight, or do you want to wait?"

"Yeah, they can come. I could probably use some help from Avy."

"I figured as much. I'll let them know they can come. If it ever becomes overwhelming, though, just tell us and they'll leave."

"Sure, sounds good. I'm going to get dressed."

Aiden went upstairs and got ready to go out. He had no idea how much it could be to end the lease, but he knew it had to happen. It was too dangerous for him to be there by himself. And if Brett had bailed out of jail, it was dangerous of him knowing where to attack Aiden without anyone else around. The biggest thing causing him to tense up at the moment was the worry he'd have to go inside the apartment during this meeting.

"Jaxie is here, so I'm going to head out," Aiden announced, coming down the stairs.

"Alright." Jack walked with him to the door. "Good luck with it all. Call me with the amount."

"Thanks. Hey, would it be okay if I invited Jaxie over tonight too? She can meet Lydia and Avy."

Jack smiled. "Of course."

"Thanks." Aiden grabbed the door handle to leave.

"Come here," Jack hugged Aiden, giving him a peck on the cheek. "Go get this taken care of."

Jack continued to work while Aiden was gone. It had been a long couple of days, but he was feeling a lot of relief. The memories from his own past had tried knocking at his head, but with Aiden's attempt and him now staying at his house, he managed to focus on those enough to ignore it. He was also feeling ecstatic about Aiden feeling more comfortable with the relationship. There seemed to be lighter days ahead, but Jack knew it wasn't time to let his guard down; Aiden wasn't out of the woods yet.

"Hello?" Jack answered Aiden's call.

"Hey, we're at the office for the lease."

"Okay, what did they say?"

"Well, we explained the situation to them. We showed them the protective order and told them everything that has happened. They are willing to let me end the lease early without pay, but they want me to pay for the broken mirror, clean the carpets, and any other damage that there might be."

"Alright, tell them to send the bills for those here and I'll send a check."

"Jack, I'm sure I can afford that much. They are letting me out of the lease."

"Don't argue with me about it. You haven't been at work for some time, so I'll pay for it." Aiden was quiet.

"Don't give me the silent treatment, Aiden. I'm happy to do this, and that's the end of it. Just give them my address for the bill and come back."

"Okay, fine."

About an hour later, Aiden and Jaxie returned, this time Aiden bringing his car with him. He was relieved to have that done and over with. He felt a certain sense of freedom knowing that that apartment wasn't his anymore.

"So, everything got taken care of?" Jack asked.

"Yeah, with all the problems, I guess it allows me to break the lease," Aiden explained, "It actually benefits them if I leave, because Brett won't cause them problems either. I admitted I broke the mirror and there would need to be a lot of cleaning on the carpet, so they said I just need to pay for that and we'll be good. I'll just need to get everything else out by the end of next week."

Jaxie chimed in. "Well, Jack and I can get everything else."

"Yes, we will," Jack agreed. "I'm happy to hear it went well."

"Yeah. I'm still pretty tired. I slept okay, but also didn't feel like I slept at all," Aiden said. "I want to take a nap before Lydia and Avy get here."

"Alright, I'll come check on you in a bit," Jack said, watching Aiden walk towards the stairs.

After Aiden was long gone, Jaxie turned to Jack, her expression tight. "How was it last night?" she asked. "Did he do okay?"

"Well," Jack said, "he did have a little panic attack, but he got out of it okay. Then he kissed me. Then we went to bed. So, it was quite a night to say the least."

Jaxie had to catch up for a moment before smiling. "Was that...the first kiss?"

"Yes, it was." Jack smiled back.

"Wow. That must have been a decent change of pace."

"Very much so."

"What about that panic attack?"

"He handled it right. He asked me for help instead of trying to go through it alone. That's all we can ask him to do."

"It scares me what a panic attack could lead to," Jaxie admitted.

"That's why he's not alone. I'm here to guide where it leads to as best I can. He had a little moment this morning too, but I expected that one. I know him taking those pills is going to bring him back to his attempt."

Jaxie shook her head sadly. "It's going to get better, isn't it?"

"I'll do everything I can to make that happen."

-17-

Lydia and Avy arrived that evening. They immediately hugged Aiden and told him how happy they were to see him. Aiden could feel a shift in the atmosphere of the house. Avy's enthusiasm and Lydia's lively spirit seemed to make everyone instantly relax. Aiden didn't want to get ahead of himself, but he could feel his problems vanishing just from them being there. Jack and Jaxie even appeared to be loosening up, which was nice for Aiden to think they weren't worrying about him. He was glad his sister was going to finally meet the people who had become important in his life.

Everyone gathered in the living room to socialize and for Jaxie to get to know the girls. Jack, Avy, and Jaxie had beers to drink. Aiden was grateful that Lydia didn't drink, so he wasn't the only one drinking water. He wasn't desperate for alcohol, but he wouldn't have minded something to help him become more social. From his incident, though, he had to take a break from his usual whiskey.

It didn't take long for the conversation to go from small talk to a discussion about the social status of being gay. Aiden stayed quiet about it, and he sat close to Jack on the couch for support. He knew he shouldn't have gotten too excited about his troubles disappearing in the presence of Avy and Lydia. Now he was feeling slightly restricted. Jaxie was interested in the conversation though, so Aiden didn't want to interrupt.

"I just can't believe all the harassment that still goes on," Jaxie commented. "It's hard for me to understand there's still people that hate something that's harmless to them. It's not illegal or anything."

"There may not be laws against it here," Lydia said, "but that doesn't mean people are going to accept it. When it's that big of a change, people who don't agree with it feel higher up than us. They believe they have more rights than we do and think they can tell us who and how to love."

"Avy has quite the story to tell," Jack said. "She's probably the only one of us that has reached a milestone to be able to talk about it to anyone."

"She sees it as a self-growth story instead of a painful one now," Lydia smiled, squeezing Avy's hand.

"I can't wait to be able to say I can do that," Jack sighed, surprising Aiden. He knew he had to be talking about what happened in high school. He had forgotten Jack still hadn't told him the details.

"What is your story, Avy? I'd love to hear it if you'll share," Jaxie said.

"Absolutely. Well, about eight years ago I found a music producer who wanted to give me a record deal. It was really exciting and I was looking forward to starting my music career. Then he found out I was gay. He didn't make it a big deal. He just asked me one day if it was true because he had heard some things. I told him yes. He thought I was trying to hide it, but then I gave him the whole speech that it's not me hiding it, it's just nothing I need to say upfront. It doesn't change my talent. It's not like straight people go around introducing themselves and including their sexual preference," Avy explained.

"That's true," Jaxie nodded.

"So anyway, some time passes. I've got lyrics written and figured out the music behind them. The producer wants to take me out to celebrate. We were one day away from beginning to record. I expect everyone to be coming out with us, and I expect we're going to some nice restaurant or maybe the producer's house. Neither was true. He took me out to a club, like a real club, and it's just me with him. I ain't the clubbing type, but I figure a couple drinks won't kill me," Avy sighed. "This...well, I guess every song being played was loud, a lot of bass, sort of erotic-type for close dancing. There was one particular song that was more erotic and suggestive than others and when it came on the producer asks me to dance. I figure sure, one dance, and I can probably get out of there and get some sleep. He starts dancing in a very touchy-feely way. His hands are all over me and he's holding me really close. I was uncomfortable, but again, it seems to be the club thing to do so I went along with it. He knew I was gay, so I'm thinking he knows he's not getting anywhere with me. Then he brings me to this private room with another woman. He told me to...start doing stuff with her."

"What?" Jaxie asked in shock. She looked around at everyone. Lydia looked sad and Jack looked angry. It was Aiden's first time hearing this story, but he was too distracted to react. "Why would he want you to do that?"

"He said it was something I should get used to for the business I'm getting into. That was bullshit and I knew it. It was for his own pleasure. That's just the stigma." Avy shrugged. "If you're a gay man, you're disgusting. If you're a gay woman, you're fun to watch. Don't get me wrong, it can be the other way too, but that is what people typically think. Anyway, I refused, got smacked around, and I got out of there. I didn't show up the next day for recording, and when he called me, I told him there was no way I was coming in. I'm done. I quit. I even tried a sexual harassment claim, but he was a rich music producer with good lawyers."

Lydia butted in. "Which also means he's probably done this type of thing before."

"Right," Avy said, "but, being gay was a much different thing even eight years ago. I was seen as whining because I wasn't actually raped or assaulted by a man. I was just being difficult with something I could change if I wanted to."

"That's awful." Jaxie shook her head. She was getting a glimpse of how bad things could be, and she was imagining how things might have gone down for Aiden that she may not have been aware of.

"Things have improved some, but not a lot," Lydia frowned.

"I was scared to try and get into music again because I didn't want to go through something similar." Avy's firm, serious expression turned into a smile. "But with Lydia's support and Jack's protectiveness, I found a great team and am finally making my dream come true."

"Ten weeks away from performing on a big stage," Lydia said, excitedly, "but who's counting?"

"I hope it helps smash the stigma of being a gay Christian," Jaxie said.

"It's a step," Avy agreed. "That's all we can do for the years to come. Take steps."

Aiden wasn't able to focus clearly on the story. He was feeling himself tuning in and out as his brain was feeling jumpy. Whenever he got a glimpse of the story, he felt weight on his chest. He remembered Jack mentioning earlier about tonight possibly becoming too much for him.

At the time, he didn't understand why that would happen. Now it was making sense. There were inner dilemmas still going on whether he realized it or not. Aiden felt his head become heavy and slightly dizzy, so he leaned against Jack's shoulder. Jack glanced over, taking his hand and placing it under Aiden's chin, caressing it as they locked eyes. Looking into Jack's eyes soothed Aiden like a silent lullaby. After a moment, Jack put his arm around Aiden and pulled him close.

"Alright guys," Jack spoke up, "it's been a long day. I think we could all use some rest."

"Of course," Avy smiled as she stood up. "Let's head out, babe, and give Aiden his space."

Lydia followed suit, walked over to Aiden, and put her hand lightly on top of his. "You'll be in our prayers tonight."

"Thanks." He smiled weakly.

"I'll talk to you tomorrow, Jack," Lydia said, "It was great meeting you, Jaxie!"

"It was a pleasure. I'm glad I got to talk with you girls," Jaxie smiled.

"Anytime," Avy smiled back. "Good night everyone!"

"Night girls," Jack said.

"Well, I can head out too." Jaxie stood up and looked at her brother. She took the same hand Lydia just held, and gave it a squeeze. "You do look exhausted. Are you feeling alright?"

"I'm okay. It's a lot."

"I'm sure. I'll call you tomorrow, okay? I love you."

"I love you too, Jaxie," Aiden said.

"I'll show my way out, Jack." Jaxie walked across the living room. She didn't want to interrupt the comfort her brother was in. "Have a good night you two."

Aiden and Jack were alone on the couch. It was quiet. Jack kept his arm around Aiden's shoulders, using his hand to caress his hair. With the room less full of people, the heaviness seemed to lift off Aiden.

"You doing okay?" Jack asked.

"Yeah."

"Did it become a little much?"

"Yeah. I just didn't know why."

"Your mind is dealing with a lot."

"I guess. I'm glad Jaxie got to meet them."

"Me too."

"Avy really did have an inspirational story. I didn't know she went through all that. That wasn't fair to her."

"It wasn't. She has come so far, though."

Aiden could feel his eyelids getting heavy as Jack's hand stroked through his hair. It wasn't distracting enough to push his curiosities away, though, he hoped it would have. With everyone gone, he could try and get some more answers to Jack's past. His mind was pushing him to take that opportunity. He knew the conversation wouldn't be easy to make happen, but he wanted to try. "Hey, Jack?"

"Hmm?"

"You've seen me at my worst in more ways than one."

"Yeah, I suppose."

Aiden gulped, preparing himself to be put in an uncomfortable position again. "Tell me."

"Tell you what?"

"What happened to you in school?"

"What?" Jack asked quietly, his hand stopping mid-stroke.

Aiden sat up and looked at Jack. "Something really bad happened. You wouldn't have acted the way you did on New Year's Eve if it wasn't. You wouldn't have acted the way you did for a lot of things if it wasn't something terrible."

"Aiden, this isn't the time."

"Jack, I want to know," Aiden begged. "Please."

Jack shook his head.

"Please, Jack. You can trust me."

"It's not a matter of trust, Aiden."

"Whatever it is that's holding you back...just, please. Please know I'm here for you as much as you've been there for me. I want to be, but I can't if you don't open up to me."

"You couldn't sound any more like Lydia there if you tried." Jack could tell Aiden wasn't going to let this go. Not this time. Something was pushing Aiden past his usual unassertive ways, and Jack had a feeling he wouldn't be able to avoid it. It was also undeniable that Lydia was right about being open with Aiden. This was going to have to be faced if he really wanted something more intimate. "It was...that guy."

"The guy who had the little brother?"

"Yeah," Jack said quietly. "He beat me up plenty of times. I couldn't seem to do anything without him finding an excuse to hurt me. I didn't even know him or his brother. He just had it in for me."

"That's...wow. At least I knew Brett. Being hurt by someone random just seems...I don't know if I can even find the right word."

"Yeah." Jack zoned off and stood up from his seat.

"Where are you going?"

"I told you what happened."

Aiden gave him a disbelieving look. "That's the stuff Lydia told me. There's more."

Jack sat back down, silently cursing. Out of frustration, he took off his purple wristband and started stretching it. "Okay. There was one specific incident that I'll never forget."

"What happened?"

"It was after I told the school what was going on. I didn't tell the school I was gay, but I told them I was getting picked on relentlessly. It didn't matter. They knew why I was getting harassed. The guy said he wanted to make amends though. It was similar to Brett pretending he wanted to talk to you at the restaurant."

"That's why you told me not to go."

"Yep. I knew better."

"So, you got beat by some guys for tattling?" Aiden asked.

"Not exactly," Jack said, staring ahead. "We were outside, at this little tunnel thing at the back of the school. It was him and two of his friends. The friends hit me a couple times, just enough to get me on the ground. Then that guy...he reached into his backpack..."

Aiden quickly felt sick to his stomach. "What? What was it?"

Jack stared down at the wristband he was holding. His grip was tight. He tried to push out the next sentencing, but couldn't get it through his lips. In a hasty manner, Jack got up from the couch and walked out of the living room. Aiden groaned to himself, assuming Jack had gone upstairs. He got to his feet and turned for the hall, preparing to go to bed without success, but stopped short when he saw Jack hadn't headed that way. Jack had walked down the hall into his office area. He was standing, facing the wall where a cross was hanging. His arms were out in front of him, his hands against the wall for support, and his head hanging low in defeat.

Aiden saw his opportunity to keep this moving forward. Jack was not giving up on the conversation yet, but yearning for strength to keep him going. Strength to help him face this. Aiden walked into the office and put his arms around Jack, laying his head against his back. He didn't know what to say. He just hoped the embrace would speak for him.

"He pulled out...this vibrator," Jack suddenly started speaking again. Aiden kept his cheek on Jack's back, listening as he went on. "It was a big one. They...said things about me wanting it so bad. I was held down and they...started shoving it in my mouth."

Aiden could feel his eyes widen. He lifted his head slightly and looked up at Jack. His head was still hanging.

"They forced it in and...yeah. I gagged a lot and got sick on it," Jack paused. He lifted his head up and looked at the cross.

"Oh my God," Aiden said quietly.

"They just left me there. They shoved me down. I just stayed there for a long time. It was dark by the time I walked home."

"Did you...ever try to...do what I did?" Aiden was surprised the question came out. He hadn't thought of that, but it came to his head quickly after hearing that story.

Jack let out a harsh breath, turning around to face Aiden. "I don't know if that's a good idea to talk about right now."

"Jack, please. I want to know the truth."

Jack let a half-smile slide across his face. He brought his hands up and roughly ran them up and down his face. "What happened to the shy guy who was afraid to ask me stuff?"

"You said I could ask you anything."

Jack shook his head. "I liked it better when you asked me to kiss you."

Aiden gave a small smile. "Maybe we can get back to that after this talk."

"I don't appreciate the blackmailing..." Jack sighed in defeat, closing his eyes. "Okay. Twice."

"What..." Aiden said, his voice trailing off.

Jack's hands were now intertwined behind his head. "Yeah. The first time was sort of an accident, the second time wasn't."

"I'm...so scared to get the thought of trying again."

"Hey," Jack said, grabbing Aiden's shoulders and looking him in the eye, "just because it happened to me doesn't mean it will to you. You have a big support system all around you. You can be honest with any of us if a feeling like that comes back."

Aiden nodded. He was scared to hear about Jack's attempts, but he needed to know. "So, what happened?"

"The day of all *that*, after my mom and Joey went to bed, I grabbed a knife. I made these cuts on my arm," Jack frustratingly slid his wristbands off his arm and let them fall to the floor. He flipped his arm over, and showed Aiden different scars. There were a few short ones and a long one. "It was these smaller ones. I did those first. I liked how it made me feel. It just numbed everything for a few seconds. I wanted more, but I had no idea what I was doing. So, then I tried it again—this bigger one—but I went too far. Technically, too deep. I began bleeding all over. I freaked out and tried to get it to stop, but I couldn't. My mom took me to the hospital and...well, if I hadn't gotten help, I would've bled out."

"Then what happened?"

"That's how I came out to my mom and Joey. My mom was instantly furious, but not at me. She was furious at the school and these kids. Her and Joey were nothing but supportive of everything. It was suggested I switch schools, but I didn't want to leave Lydia alone, even if it was just for senior year. My mom fought and fought for the other kids to get expelled, but it was a battle..."

"Because you were gay?" Aiden asked.

Jack nodded. "It was never said that way, but like you getting fired from your old job, you can just tell. They made it sound like I was asking for it. Those guys got suspended for a couple months. They had to promise to leave me alone. They sort of did. It went from physical bullying to verbal, but sometimes that's worse."

Aiden cringed at that last statement. He remembered sitting on his floor, looking at the glass letters of the broken sign. They had formed into the hateful things Brett had said to him, and each one felt like those glass pieces were being shoved through his skin. He remembered thinking how no amount of punches could come close to the pain of Brett's words that night.

"Whenever I complained, the school said to just ignore it and get through the rest of the school year," Jack continued. "That guy was a senior that year, so he would be gone for my senior year. It didn't stop people from saying other things though. As I'm sure you can imagine, it got around quick that I took a...yeah, that thing in my mouth. Everyone said things about me liking it or that I was putting it elsewhere. One time my backpack was taken and got filled with them."

"Oh my God."

"I also got a lot of comments that I should've bled out and died."

Aiden felt chills as Brett's words forced their way into his mind again. Those words that told him he wasn't worth a life. "What happened the second time?" he asked reluctantly.

Jack took a deep breath, clearly regretting he had mentioned him attempting twice. He patted Aiden's shoulders a couple times and walked past him to head for the kitchen. "I'm sorry, I know you're supposed to be taking a break from drinking, but I'm going to need one."

"That's fine." Aiden followed Jack into the kitchen, taking a seat at the counter. "I like to drink, but I don't need it."

Jack grabbed a tall glass, put a little ice in it, and then filled it with liquor. It was a lot of drink, and Aiden knew Jack was going to be drunk in no time. "Well, I'm sure it helps that the whiskey is gone."

"I don't know how you drink tequila," Aiden said, looking at the glass with disgust.

Jack chuckled as he took a drink. "It's my drink of choice during these types of talks."

"Well?"

Jack leaned his glass side to side, letting the ice clink back and forth.

"It wasn't an accident that time?"

"No. After high school was over, I decided I needed some protection. Outside of school, in the real world, it wouldn't just be bullying making me feel bad. People will kill you if they perceive being gay as something...well, worth killing over. Some people think murder is justified then. So, I got a gun. Lydia isn't a fan of them. She doesn't even like carrying a knife. Like Avy said, though, when people hear a girl is gay, they don't really beat them up. They just ask to watch them shove their tongues down another girl's throat or up their...well, yeah. Avy carries a gun anyway, because things can happen. Anyway, I was about twenty and I went to this party. I still wasn't very open about being gay when I hung out with people. At that point, I just wanted somebody to be my friend since I had lost so many. So, I'm at this house party and someone was there who had gone to school with me. I didn't really know them or anything, but they sure remembered me. They started telling people about how I was this kid who sucked down male sex toys behind the school. Other people joined in with their comments. The ones who weren't joining in obviously didn't care that I was gay but they didn't have a reason to stick up for me either. Finally, I had had enough and made my way out the door, but I heard one more statement that rang through my head the entire way home. 'Why don't you just kill yourself?'"

Aiden was quiet, not realizing his fingernails were digging into his arm. Brett had said the same thing to him.

"It's not like I hadn't heard it before, but something was different that night. I thought I had escaped the high school stuff, but I realized that wasn't the case. I could run into these guys any time anywhere and they'd throw it all back at me again. I could run into any person that wants the death of gay people and it'll always be thrown at me. Some guy could have a great conversation with me, and that's all it is, just me making a friend. Once they find out I'm gay, though, they instantly assume I must want to get in bed with them. I just wouldn't be able to escape it. That was my mindset then. I drove home from the party and sat in my car. I sat there for a long time. I decided I was done. That's it. I was done. There was no point in me being around if I was going to get hurt all the time, and I wasn't going to pretend to be straight all my life. I was done. So...I took my gun, and..." Jack took a slow sip of his tequila. "I held it to my head."

Aiden drew in a sharp breath.

"Then, right before I pulled the trigger, someone ran into me."

"What?" Aiden asked, confused.

"Another car hit my car. I had parked in the street and someone hit the side of my car. The impact made me drop the gun. This poor woman; she had had a seizure and lost control of her car. The damage to the cars was minimal which was amazing. Anyway, after her car had hit mine, I got out and was helping this woman, keeping her calm and telling her everything was fine; I wasn't mad at her. An ambulance arrived to take her in. I stayed on the scene a while longer; I wasn't hurt or anything. The woman's sister eventually comes by to take her car. When she found out who I was, she thanked me profusely. She said if I hadn't been there, her sister may have died just sitting in the car if no one got her help. She was really nice and very grateful. Everyone parted ways and things got cleaned up. I go inside and go to bed, completely forgetting about what I had been about to do. I was in shock, I suppose. The next morning I drive to a shop to get my car fixed up. When I'm about to leave my car, I see the gun on the floor. Then it hit me. I had almost killed myself and there would have been no coming back from it." Jack chugged the rest of his drink. "I got rid of it that day. I also got rid of that car shortly after and got my truck. Now I just carry my knife around for protection. Thankfully I've never had to use it beyond threats."

Aiden felt a pinch, and looked down, seeing the deep lines he had scratched into his arm. "I...I think I'm ready for bed."

"Me too," Jack said. "Are you coming upstairs again?"

Aiden nodded. "I think we both could use each other's company."

"I agree."

"I'm sorry." Aiden shook his head as they walked towards the stairs. "I didn't mean to respond to that story by going to bed."

"It's not easy to have a conversation like that."

"I'm glad you told me everything. It was hard to hear, but I think it'll help."

"I think it will too. For both of us."

They laid in bed together, both quiet. Neither of them were asleep yet, but weren't sure what to say. Jack's arm hung around Aiden, holding him close. It was as comforting for Jack to hold Aiden as it was for Aiden to be held.

"How have you been feeling?" Jack asked, breaking the silence.

"Fine, I guess." Aiden shrugged in the darkness. "How do you mean?"

Jack sat up with his elbow propped on the pillow and his hand supporting his head. "Have you thought about trying it again? Or have you thought that things are hopeless or anything like that?"

Aiden kept his eye on the window, looking at the stars. He began wondering how many other people were looking up at the stars, searching for the hope to keep moving forward until things got better. How many times did Jack look at the stars and wish for a better day? Just one better day.

"I don't know if hopeless is the word."

"What *is* the right word?"

"Wonder, I guess."

"Wonder about what?"

"After hearing your story, Avy's story, and Lydia's story, I know things will get better. They have to. I just wonder how long it'll take."

"Start small. Don't think about how long it could take, just think about how you can make tomorrow better. Then tomorrow night, think about how you can make the next day better. Then build up to bigger goals."

"I think the bigger goal is getting my life on track as soon as possible. I need to go back to work, find a new apartment."

Jack looked down at Aiden's eyes fixed towards the window. "I'm not kicking you out you know."

"I know, and even though we're moving forward with things, I still want to work on myself."

"That's good, but don't rush it. You still shouldn't be alone yet."

"I know, but I am going to go back to work. I'm going to talk to Toby tomorrow."

"Good." Jack nodded. "Can you look at me?"

Aiden turned his head. He looked up at the slightly drunken glossiness in Jack's eyes. Even in the dark, with only the moonlight and stars shining in, Aiden could still see his green eyes stand out.

"I hope your feelings towards me haven't changed after hearing all these stories. I had my weak moments, but I don't let them define me today."

"Of course I don't think any differently of you. I don't know if I ever could. You've done so much for me, and never expect anything in return. You didn't do anything just because you were hoping for a lay. You just did it, because you're a good guy."

Jack shrugged. "I try to be better than the ones who were against me."

Aiden watched Jack's eyes lower to his lips. He turned the rest of his body around, inviting Jack to satisfy his craving. Their lips locked with confidence this time. Aiden's fingers slipped their way into Jack's soft hair, his skin getting goosebumps as Jack's hands ran down his back. His hands grasped hard when he let Jack's tongue seduce its way through his lips. Aiden didn't even mind the tequila taste. It didn't last much longer as Jack's weight became heavy.

"I think the alcohol is winning," Aiden laughed.

Jack nodded, already half asleep before he laid back against his pillow. As hard as it was to hear Jack's story, Aiden was happy to see he had come out strong, and that he got to be in his life. No matter what direction they went, the time with Jack was something Aiden would cherish forever.

-18-

Spring was coming around, and Aiden was excited for it. It had been a long winter, but the snow was finally melting away with the warmer days. The air was smelling like dew in the morning, the trees were becoming full of leaves, and the sun was brighter than ever. Aiden spent the last month living with Jack, working at The Color Band, and seeing a therapist. Jack had slowed down his own life to help Aiden. He didn't go out with friends or have anyone over. They kept any special time together small and would spend them at home. As everyone expected, Brett had been bailed out of jail within days of his arrest. It put everyone on edge once the word got out, but no one saw or heard from him. Aiden was starting to insist on apartment hunting, but he hadn't really spent any time alone yet, and that made Jack nervous.

"Are you sure you don't want to just rent out from me?" Jack asked.

"That'd be pointless. I haven't slept downstairs once since I've been there," Aiden said. "I don't want you to take offense. I just need to do this for myself. It's only going to be a year lease, and then we can see where we are. I still want us to work on our relationship too, but I can't give you my best if I'm not at my best. I'm pretty sure you've told me that once or twice."

"Biting me in the ass now."

"Oh stop. You know this will be good for me."

"I know, I know. It's just not going to be much fun sleeping alone again," Jack said.

"I'll miss that too." Aiden smiled. "Don't worry, I'll be coming for sleepovers."

Jack didn't seem satisfied, even though he knew Aiden was right, but quickly put a brightened look on his face. "Well! Joey told me they were taking Marissa to the park later. Do you want to go?"

"I don't know," Aiden said quietly.

"You know they don't blame you for anything, right? They never did."

"I know."

"Remember what the therapist said about you facing things? You may have to face things that happened by being around Marissa again."

Aiden thought for a moment. "I don't want to keep you from seeing them. You should go. You haven't seen them because you've been too busy keeping an eye on me."

"They want to see you too. Come on, please? You were just saying how you need to do things that would be good for you even if it breaks my heart." Aiden gave him a nasty look. "I'm kidding. For real, though, I think this would be really good for you."

Aiden sighed in defeat. "Okay, sure. I'll go look at a couple places and then come back."

"You're going right now? Do you want me to come with?"

"No, Jack. I'll be just fine. I can't have you babysit me forever."

"I know, I'm sorry. I know I've been watching you like a hawk. I'm sure it's becoming annoying."

"Maybe a little. I understand why you have been, and I do appreciate it." Aiden took a deep breath to keep from getting too irritated at Jack's overprotectiveness. "I'm sorry I'm being a little hostile. I'm just a little excited because I finally feel good enough to go out and do something by myself."

"Well, that is great. I'll leave you to it then, so good luck. We'll go meet them at the park in a few hours, okay?"

"Okay. I'll be back soon."

The entire time Aiden was gone, Jack sat in his chair, staring out the front window. He wasn't working and the house was quiet. He couldn't get himself to do anything but think about the past month. There were great times, and there were plenty of hard times. He understood why Aiden wanted to move out, and he understood why Aiden would be excited to feel strong enough to be independent again. It was just going to be hard for him to get used to living alone again. Jack couldn't help going through each day wondering if there was anything wrong he did, or if there was some irritating habit he had causing Aiden to want to move out. Deep down, he knew he was being ridiculous, but it was hard not to wonder. His hopes had gotten too high from their time together, and Jack had imagined over and over again Aiden deciding to stay with him for good. Even though it was hard to accept things not going the way he had wished for, Jack couldn't be selfish and could only support Aiden's decision.

Once he saw Aiden's car pull up, Jack walked to the front door to meet him.

"Good news, I found a place," Aiden announced.

"Oh, that's good," Jack said with a small smile.

"That's the fakest smile I have ever seen."

"I'm sorry. I am happy for you. When do you move out?"

"In a week."

"Okay." Jack turned and grabbed his shoes to get ready for the park.

"Come on, Jack. You can't be that torn up. I know it seems like the backwards way of a relationship, but anyone else you've had move out never came back. I'll be back plenty."

Jack subtly rolled his eyes as he grabbed his keys. "I've never had anyone else live here. I told you I never had a serious relationship."

Aiden's face fell. "I'll still be back. I still want us. You have to know that. I want us."

"Ready to go?" Jack asked, ignoring Aiden's comment.

"Yeah, I guess."

During the drive to the park, Aiden shifted nervously in his seat many times. He didn't know how this was going to play out. Joey and Amy weren't holding anything against him, and Aiden believed that, but they didn't speak for Marissa. Aiden didn't know how he would handle it if Marissa denied him or talked to him about that day. It wasn't helping that Jack wasn't in the happiest mood. Aiden wasn't trying to hurt him by moving out. He felt he had to do this for himself.

"Are you really that worried about me living on my own again?" Aiden asked, breaking the silence.

"I don't know. I have a lot of feelings towards it."

"Like?"

"Maybe a little bit worried. Just sort of sucks. You do what you have to do and I'll support it. You know that." As Jack parked his truck, Aiden looked towards the park and spotted Marissa coming down the slide and running quickly for the stairs to go down them again. Her mouth movements were clearly her laughing. He couldn't hear the laughter though. Flashes of her screaming and crying played in his head instead. His nightmare of her screaming out the word 'help' dragged through his ears. Aiden closed his eyes, breathing deeply, attempting to ignore it all.

"Ready?"

"I won't ever be," Aiden responded, slowly opening his door. He let Jack walk ahead of him while he continued breathing his worries away. The instant Marissa saw Jack walking towards the park, she took off running.

"Uncle Jack!" she screamed.

Any troubles going through Jack's mind disappeared at the sight of his niece. He hurried over and scooped the little girl up in his arms. Aiden could see how much he had missed her. "Hey boo! I've missed you so much. You look like you've gotten bigger."

Marissa was giggling in her uncle's arms. Aiden could feel himself relax as he was hearing the laughs instead of the ghost cries. "Where have you been? I had to go to Grandma's a lot. She's not as fun as you."

"Oh, you know you love her. She's just old and slow. I've been pretty busy."

"Daddy told me Aiden was sick."

"He was. I've been taking care of him. Look, I brought him with me today."

Marissa smiled big as she watched Aiden walking closer. "Hi, Aiden! You're not sick anymore?"

Aiden felt his heart warm up at her cheerful tone. "I'm feeling a lot better."

"Good, because you were sick for the longest time ever, and I need to come back to Uncle Jack's house to play."

Aiden grinned. "I forgot how brutally honest she can be."

Jack laughed. "I'm sure you can come visit soon. Is it okay if we play with you at the park today?"

"Yeah!" Marissa responded excitedly. "Come on! Let's play hide and seek!"

Aiden had to keep himself from crying at the little girl's excitement. The traumatic memories that threatened to take over were easing away from her contagious laugh. Aiden had expected he'd only be able to handle a short time there with everyone, but they ended up being there until it got close to dark. Marissa kept everyone plenty busy. Each of the adults had their turn chasing her and racing her down the slide. Aiden was full of joy when Marissa asked him to push her on the swing. He was glad he took this leap to be face-to-face with her. There were moments Aiden would start to remember that day, but he took the grounding techniques Jack and the therapist used on him and would stop his mind from wandering further to the what if's. When Aiden would watch Jack play with Marissa, he hoped there would be many, many memories with her for years to come that would make it easier to be around her and not immediately think of that day. That was the first time Aiden really thought about a far future with Jack, and it filled his heart with joy.

Even though Aiden thought about that day during their time at the park, Marissa never once mentioned the incident at Jack's house.

The week flew by too fast for Jack to keep up with. It was the day Aiden was moving into his new apartment. He specifically picked a place that looked nothing like his old one. Jack was helping him, and much to Aiden's amusement, was taking his time doing so. They got Aiden's furniture from a storage facility and got it in place. Now he just had to organize everything from his boxes. The one thing Aiden was still uncertain about was having his medications with him. He decided to keep the bottles at Jack's for the time being, and only bring enough to his apartment to last for a few days.

"It's a nice place," Jack commented.

"Yeah, it'll do for the year."

"If you feel like you start having a hard time, just come over. I always have that room for you."

"You mean your bed."

"Well, yeah, whatever you want."

Aiden smirked at the comment. He knew Jack would try anything to keep him from moving out. If he was honest with himself, Aiden knew he'd still spend nights at Jack's house, and he was okay with that. He needed more alone time, though, to work on things for himself in his own environment before making any further, permanent commitments.

Once they got the last of the boxes in, Aiden took a deep breath before telling Jack some news. "So...something came for me."

"What's that?"

"The hearing for the restraining order. It's next week, so I got everything for it. The temporary protection order is going to expire on that day for them to possibly grant a lifetime restraining order."

"That's great." That was the happiest Jack sounded all day, and Aiden knew he was about to ruin it as he gave him a blank stare. "Aiden, no..."

"I'm thinking about dropping it," Aiden blurted.

Jack muttered syllables, trying to form a single word, before finally snapping, "Have you not learned anything?"

"Jack, he hasn't tried to do anything ever since my attempt. Maybe he didn't think I'd actually do anything to that extreme, and it opened his eyes after he heard that I did. Or maybe the cops really spooked him from that arrest."

"Yeah, maybe he's following the order for now to not end up in jail again, but that doesn't change his feelings."

"And it's now been over a month since all of it. Maybe he's moved on by now."

"Big, big maybe. And if you don't show up to that court date, you won't have another chance. The courts won't take you seriously next time. Then Brett has free range and doesn't have to worry about jail. If he plays his cards right, like at the restaurant, he knows nothing will happen to him." Aiden was quiet as Jack raised his voice. It wasn't shocking that he was reacting this way, but Aiden wanted him to try and understand his thought process. "I'm sorry, Aiden. I just don't want you to get hurt again. I know that it may seem like a waste of time now, because time has passed without any problems, but you have to do it. You have to."

"What about forgiveness?"

Jack grabbed his hair as he threw his head back, looking up at the ceiling in frustration. That question told him that Aiden had thought long and hard on how he could make it sound reasonable for him to give Brett a lesser punishment. Jack knew that anything he said right now, Aiden had an argument ready. So many nights he would have his arm around Aiden, their bodies caressing each other, and Aiden may have been thinking only about Brett deserving mercy. Jack looked back at him, choosing his words carefully. "You can forgive people without excusing them. You can still go to court and make this official. He doesn't have the right to hurt you. You can still forgive him

262

while you do all of that. You can forgive while moving on with your life without him."

"How?"

"Forgiving him is just saying you're not going to let the pain he's caused run your life anymore. It doesn't mean you have to let your guard down."

"I guess so. I just can't help but think what if one day he comes around and wants to fix our friendship? Maybe it won't happen soon because he clearly has strong feelings about me. But what if years from now, he wants to fix it, *truly* fix it, and he can't because I went through with the restraining order?"

Jack shrugged and shook his head. "Honestly, Aiden, I don't know. All I can say is, you can't worry about that right now, because right now he wants to hurt you. I can almost guarantee he's not thinking about what if he feels differently in the future. He's in the now, and in this current moment, he wouldn't have batted an eye if you didn't make it."

Aiden let out a long breath and tapped his fingers against his arm, keeping himself grounded. Jack's voice was continuing to get louder and aggressive. "You never got a restraining order against the guy at school."

"That's different. They weren't trying to kill me. They got their one good prank on me to make my school life hell and were done with me. Brett has a personal attachment to you that makes him hate you, not just dislike or think you're a freak, he *hates* you. He'll keep coming for you."

Aiden turned away, crossing his arms and looking at the floor. He was beaten. Jack was telling all truths, but was it enough to push Aiden to that courtroom? "Will you be mad at me if I don't go through with it?"

"I won't be happy. It's your choice though. I'll be here no matter what. If you decide not to go through with it, then I guess I have to wait until you learn on your own,"

Jack said, tapping his fist against the wall. "Do you want me to stick around and help you get settled?"

"No thanks, I'm going to my parents' house."

A look of surprise crossed Jack's face. "Really? Did they finally reach out to you?"

"No. I talked to Jaxie, though, and I guess they've checked on me through her. It's too sinful for them to talk directly to me. I'm just going to show up there."

"What are you going to say?"

"I'm going to tell them this is how things are now. It's up to them if they want to be part of it or not."

"What do you expect them to say?"

"I have no idea. I'm not going to expect them to be comfortable with it, but I'm hoping they're willing to try."

"Okay. Well, I would like to talk about this whole court thing again. Call me later and let me know about this visit."

"I will."

Jack started for the door, but turned around and hugged Aiden. He held on tight for a minute, not saying anything. There had been quite a bit of anger in the conversation. The last thing Jack wanted to cause was Aiden to overthink the brutally honest warnings into a panic attack. When he backed away, he looked into Aiden's eyes, caressing his cheeks. Aiden didn't want to look at him, knowing there was only hurt in his eyes. Not knowing what else to say, Jack gave him one quick kiss, then left.

Jack's recent reactions and moods towards his decisions on moving out and possibly dropping the court hearing were bothering Aiden, but he was trying to let it go for now. The neighborhood that Aiden grew up in and had driven through time and time again as an adult became different territory. He felt an intruder label on his back. However, he was feeling confident; more and more he was coming to terms with the fact that some people weren't going to accept him, and possibly weren't meant to be in his life. It was hard, but he was slowly learning to accept it.

"Aiden," Lauren said in surprise when she opened the door and saw her son standing before her. She stepped outside and pulled him into an awkward hug. "I'm so glad to see you here."

"You could have called or come to see me anytime, you know."

"Jacqueline told us you moved out of your old apartment and I wasn't comfortable going to that man's home."

Aiden tried not to let her wording upset him. "His name is Jack. And yes, he and I lived together temporarily. I could have met you guys for coffee or dinner somewhere else. I...can I come in please? This should be a conversation I have with both you and Dad."

A small, unsure smile crossed his mother's face. It was obvious his father had told her not to let him inside. "Okay, come in."

Aiden sat on one side of the kitchen table and his parents sat across from him; the silent judgement clear on their faces. But he kept himself upright and met their eyes. He wanted to see this conversation through.

"Aiden has informed me that he is in a sexual relationship with another man," Lauren said towards her husband.

"Hold on, hold on," Aiden said. "If we're going to have this conversation, you'll need to *listen* to me. Not just hear the words, but really listen to what I'm saying. And Mom, I never said that. I am in a more-than-friendship relationship with Jack, yes. Is it a sexual relationship? No. I've been too busy focusing on myself to think about any of that."

"You shouldn't be in any type of relationship with him either way," Dalton said firmly. "Not even friends because he's living a sinful life. That's not how we raised you."

"I'm not going to get into a religious argument with you. I know you won't budge on your opinions, you won't be open-minded and see my take on it, so a religious debate would be a waste of everyone's time. All I want to say is that I believe Jesus still loves me and knows what's in my heart." Aiden bit his lip as he glanced up to the wall where a cross was hanging. It had been there for years, and he couldn't help but take note he never once prayed to it. "Anyway, I've been through a lot. I don't feel like I'm at a comfortable point in my life to go through everything that has happened to me, especially with you guys. Jack's been there for me, though. He's helped me a lot. I can't even break the tip of the iceberg in how much he's helped me. He cares for me in a way that a significant other would care for their partner. The crazy thing about that is that he did it when I wasn't ready to be that significant other to him. He did these things for me without question. I don't know why or what first drew him to me, but I'm so grateful for him. Doesn't that count for something in your mind? Doesn't it matter more who he is as a human being or what's in his heart?"

The immediate response was silence, then Lauren said, "Aiden, as much as I disagree with it, I am thankful that someone was there for you. I know we weren't there for you at your most desperate time, and I hope someday you can forgive us for that. I know our priorities didn't align with yours at the time. We want to be able to forgive you as well, but I can see you haven't realized your wrongdoing yet. There's no abandoning though. We'll always be here when you're ready."

"Uh, well, okay." Aiden shook that off, figuring that was the best he was going to get. His mom gave a hidden apology in the beginning of her statement, but had to retract to how things could come in full circle if Aiden cooperated. "I just want to add that I'm not asking you guys to be okay with all this. I'm not even asking you to meet Jack. I'm not ready for that. I'm just asking you to be willing to try. I don't care how slow the process is, but please don't believe that my life has become less significant because of who I'm choosing to be with."

Lauren nodded slowly. "It would certainly take some time."

"That's okay, Mom. It wouldn't be right of me to ask you to be okay with it right now. I understand your beliefs and that's not always easy to change or reshape."

"I don't want to lose my son," Lauren said, tears brimming in her eyes. "It's just...you aren't him. I know who my son is, or was, and you aren't him."

"Of course I am."

"No. You've let the Devil in too much and he's taken over. I'm not sure how much we can try for something that that man is seducing you to do." Lauren looked over at her husband. "Is there anything you want to add?"

Dalton couldn't even make eye contact with his son. Aiden could tell his father was adamantly refusing to accept any of this and it was breaking his heart the longer he waited for his father to speak.

"You know this will only go in circles. There's no agreement we'll be able to come to."

Aiden looked to his mom waiting for her to say anything else, but she stayed silent.

He stared at the two of them for a moment longer, then nodded. "I'll show myself out." Aiden stood and left his parents' house. He got in his car and called Jaxie to relay what happened.

"Hey."

"Hey, Jaxie," Aiden said. "I just spoke with Mom and Dad. I decided to show up and try to talk to them about everything."

"Wow, really? How did it go?"

"The first thing Mom said to Dad was that I'm having sexual relations with another man." Aiden sighed. "She wouldn't even refer to him by name."

"Sounds like it was off to a great start," Jaxie said sarcastically.

Aiden let out a humorless laugh. It felt good to do that, not giving his parents power over his emotions. "I told them that I don't expect them to accept this or be comfortable, but just be willing to try. Mom...I don't know, at times she seemed like she wanted to try and then she'd sort of have conditions. Dad couldn't even look at me, and all he said was that we weren't going to agree on anything. That's when it all went quiet, so I left."

"I'm sorry. I hate to say I'm not surprised. Are you going to try again?"

"I don't know. I'm going to leave it be for now. I did my part; the ball is in their court."

"Well, I'm proud of you. Just know that."

"Thanks. I just wanted to catch you up on that before I drive away. I don't know when I'll be back here. I'm going over to Jack's now. Love you."

"Love you, too. Call me if you need anything."

Aiden hung up his phone, and looked at his parents' house. The house he grew up in. Now, there was a good chance this was the last time he'd be there. He wasn't going to try and go back, not anytime soon, and he didn't know if he'd ever be invited back. He shrugged it off, started his car, and drove away, taking one last look at the house in his rearview mirror.

Aiden arrived at Jack's house and told him how the conversation with his parents had gone.

"I don't even feel that bad about it. I feel more...good about myself that I at least did it."

"You should. I know that took a lot, but it was a good step. You're doing rather well with these independent strides," Jack said. "So, did you think about the court thing at all?"

"Jeez, we only talked about that a few hours ago."

Jack simply shrugged.

Aiden walked into the living room and slammed himself onto the couch. "I can tell it's going to bother you a lot more than you're letting on if I don't go through with it."

"It just worries me, rightfully so," Jack joined Aiden on the couch and had a nearly defeated look on his face. "I've been the one who's wanted my life to be over. I've never been on this side of it, though. Seeing someone I care about wanting their life to be over. Being the patient in the hospital is nothing like being the one worried sick."

Silence fell between the two. Aiden looked up at Jack and saw the fear in his eyes and the tears ready to come down his face. "Jack..."

"When I called your phone that day, I thought I'd be trying to convince you not to take a break from us. And now I wish that were the conversation we had. When I heard you were in the hospital, I thought it was Brett and I'd be going to give him a taste of his own medicine. I wish that was what happened. Instead, Jaxie answered the phone. Instead, you tried taking your life. I was scared to death, Aiden. I prayed over and over in each corner of that hospital that I wasn't going to lose this guy I had fallen for. I had never wanted to be with someone so much, and I felt like I had failed if you thought there was nowhere else for you to go."

If there was anything Aiden wanted Jack to understand it was that he hadn't failed him. He wanted Jack to understand that he never meant to hurt him by his suicide attempt. He wanted Jack to understand that he didn't mean to put him through all of that. There had to be something he could say for Jack to know. "I am sorry you went through that. More importantly, I'm sorry I put you

269

through that. Because of you, though, I am in a much different place than I was at my attempt or around the holidays or when I first came out, and even before I started wondering if I was gay. You've done so much. I couldn't possibly list everything you've done." Aiden looked at Jack, thinking back to that night he first met him. Those green eyes. They were so lively and they caught him before they exchanged words. The leaves on the trees couldn't beat the vibrant color his eyes held. They had pulled Aiden into a welcoming, warm trance that night at The Color Band. Aiden couldn't look away from them. "Do you know what's the most important thing you've done for me?"

"What?"

"You've proven to me that unconditional love exists."

Jack smiled, releasing some tension between them. Aiden brought himself closer, leaning against him. Jack's arms wrapped around him, giving him that protected feeling. Aiden closed his eyes as he sank against Jack's chest, listening for his heartbeat. It had become his secure place. He felt Jack's lips plant kisses on his head, and then lay his cheek against his hair. "I'm glad you've got to experience that. Just please do this for yourself. Please go to that court date."

Aiden kept his eyes closed as his hand searched for Jack's. Once he found it, he intertwined their fingers. "I promise."

"Are you nervous?" Jack asked.

"I'm scared to death to see him there. I haven't actually seen him in what seems like forever. At least not the him I knew."

"He can't get you there. You are the victim. Just be honest with them."

"What if they don't grant it?"

"We'll figure that out if that happens," Jack said.

"Are you sure you don't want me to come with?"

"I'm sure."

"Is Jaxie going?"

"No. I want to go alone. I feel like it'll be less pressuring."

"Okay, good luck. Call me as soon as you get out."

The entire process was slow. Aiden didn't do as much talking as he thought he would have to do. Brett didn't talk much either, which Aiden was grateful for. The little bit he did speak, Aiden was surprised to not recognize his voice. It sounded like a stranger. The lawyers talked, and the police were examined. A couple other guys had to be examined too; the police found them to have been the ones who jumped Aiden at the restaurant. He had looked at each of them for a split second, but couldn't bear to look much longer than that. As the judge went over his decision to grant the restraining order and the terms attached to it, Aiden felt one weight lift from his chest only for another one to settle in its place. He never once looked at Brett, but he could feel him staring him down the entire time.

Aiden went back to his apartment after the hearing. He was unsure how he felt. He expected to be happier with the result. He was supposed to be feeling a sense of peace and safety, wasn't he? Instead, he felt like he was giving up on working things out with someone who had been his best friend for years. Any real chance of things going back to how they used to be was gone and Aiden couldn't help but feel bitter about it.

"Hello?" Aiden answered his ringing phone.

"Hey, are you out?" Jack asked.

Aiden was laying on his couch, unable to stop going over the hearing. "Yeah, I got done a couple hours ago."

"Where are you? Are you coming over?"

"I came home. I needed to think about things."

"What ended up happening?"

"They granted it," Aiden said, not able to cover the resentful tone in his voice. "It's a lifetime restraining order. He can't come near me, can't contact me, nothing."

"You don't sound happy..."

"I'm not sure how to feel. I would have felt a little more hopeful for a timed restraining order, but they made it permanent. Forever. There's no chance for us to ever try and reconcile this."

"He may never want to anyway." Jack sighed, a hint of sadness in his voice. "Why don't you come over? I don't want you sitting alone thinking about all this."

"I'm not going to do anything, Jack. I just don't want to be around anyone. I think I'm going to take a nap before I go into work."

"Okay, do you want me to come by tonight or just stay home?"

"It doesn't matter. Either way, I'm coming back to the apartment after work."

"Okay...well, call me if you need anything."

Jack did stop by the bar that night, but Aiden didn't talk with him much. He didn't like the way he was feeling about Jack after the court hearing. He was starting to feel like he had been forced to go through with attending the court date and the assignment of the lifetime restraining order without getting to really think about it and make the decision for himself. It wasn't until it had gotten late into the night that Aiden wanted to talk to Jack about it, but he was already gone.

Aiden never admitted his harsh feelings towards Jack, and things went on as normal. He tried moving on without worrying about never getting the chance to repair things with Brett. A week after the hearing, Aiden had started hearing rumors from customers at The Color Band, but he hadn't paid much attention to them. He caught the whispers about Brett, his job, and people being mad at him. Aiden's focus was trying to move forward and not look back on Brett, so he would tune out of any details. It wasn't until he got a phone call from Jaxie confirming some of the stories that he started to worry.

After the call with his sister, Aiden drove to Jack's house to tell him all he had heard.

"Hey, I didn't expect you tonight," Jack said, letting Aiden inside.

"We need to talk."

"What's going on?"

"You've been hearing the stories going around, right?"

"Yeah." Jack placed his hands in his pockets. "People heard about the hearing between you and Brett, which was expected."

"And people started protesting RN's as an anti-gay establishment. It wasn't everyone there, it was just Brett."

"Yeah, but after everything Brett did, they kept him employed there. People get pissed off about that sort of stuff. And let's be real for a second. There is no way he was the only one. How many times did you see a gay couple at that bar?"

"Okay, admittedly, not much if ever."

"The demographic there is aligned with his beliefs, so gay people didn't go there, which is fine. But then he became more outspoken about it, and now it's coming back to kick him."

"He got fired," Aiden stated.

"What are you talking about?"

"Jaxie called me and told me. She found out he officially got fired, because he was bringing too many problems to the place."

Jack shrugged, clearly not feeling sympathy for Brett. "I don't understand why you seem mad."

"I didn't realize this was all going to happen. He was just supposed to stay away from me but now he lost his job, and I have no idea what else may happen to him."

"That's not your fault. You can't worry about what happens to him from now on. You had to do this."

"Did I?"

"Why are you sticking up for him?"

"Why did you force me to do this?" Aiden snapped.

Jack shook his head, his eyes wide. "I didn't. I may have been pushy, but I had to be before you ended up dead."

Aiden scoffed. "I don't think he would've killed me. If he wanted to, he would have by now."

"He almost did kill you. You may have attempted it, but he caused it."

"You know what I mean! If he wanted to shoot me or something, he would have already!"

"But you don't know that! The more chances you would've given him, the more he would've done. I couldn't watch that, Aiden! There's no way..."

"You didn't have to!" Aiden barked. "I didn't make you stay around to watch. You could have left if it was too much. I could have worked things out with Brett, maybe not right away, but eventually. Then he'd warm up to you and I could have you both in my life! I should have made my own decision on how to handle this!"

"Fine," Jack said, walking to the front door in frustration. He opened it and stood aside. "Go handle it yourself. Go over to Brett's and fix this. Go put your plan into action."

Aiden stood where he was. He revisited the night Brett held the door in the same manner at RN's, right before he got sick in the bathroom. Brett cared about him at the time. Brett wanted to help him at the time. Looking through the opening, he could see his car parked in the street. It was where his old car had been before getting damaged, and

Brett was possibly the one who caused it. The streetlight was shining on the dry, yellow-green grass recovering from the winter. Aiden started to see himself in the street, that first time he walked up Jack's driveway months ago. It was someone so broken, so defeated he couldn't even lift his head to look at himself. Now, he was about to lose the person who had tried to help him put the pieces together again.

When Aiden didn't move, Jack slowly closed the door. "I know you're mad at me. I know you're mad at a lot of things and I'm easy to blame. I'm willing to let you throw the anger my way. It's fine."

Aiden slowly walked over and fell into Jack's arms. "I'm sorry."

"It's okay."

"You weren't going to let me walk out, were you?"

"Maybe not." Jack smiled.

Aiden pulled away and looked up, keeping his arms around Jack's waist. "If I hadn't gone through with the restraining order, you weren't going anywhere. No matter how ugly things would have gotten, you were always going to be around to help."

"Yep."

"But why?" Aiden asked. "I know you do things because you have a good heart, but there is more to it with me. Why did you come up to me that night at the bar? What made you so confident that I was the guy you wanted a relationship with?"

"I wasn't. I took a chance. I came up to you because you looked like that guy who needed a drink to escape whatever was going on in your life. Just thought I could help, and then I...I don't know, while we talked that night, I became more interested. You let me just talk your ear off, so that was a good quality right off the bat." Jack laughed. "I got a really good feeling about you, so I went for it."

Aiden let a wide smile come across his face. "I'm really glad you did."

"I know you're going to go back and forth on this restraining order and being mad at me. Just keep in mind that you did do the right thing." Jack brought his face closer to Aiden's, looking him in the eye. "And you can try and say any angry things at me all you want. You won't push me away that easily."

"No matter how hard I try, huh?"

"Exactly." Jack winked.

-19-

The time had arrived. It was the night before the "He Still Loves Us" festival. It was the night before the big day of Avy's performance and her album release. Aiden was expecting himself to be more nervous, but he was eagerly counting down the hours. He had a lot to be happy for and was optimistic about what was coming in his future. In the few weeks that passed since Brett was fired, no one seemed to know what he was up to. The protests at RN's settled down and the hearing was old news already. Aiden was moving on as best as he could without worry of Brett's future intentions, but he kept his guard up.

Aiden was at Jack's house and Marissa was with them spending the night. On occasion, Aiden would check out the windows for anything suspicious. There were also a couple of times he'd step out on the front porch and take a look around. The intention being out of concern for

Marissa's safety, not his own. Nothing was ever out of place and he wasn't sensing any feelings being off. It was one of the more relaxing nights Aiden had in a long time.

"So, what's the plan for tomorrow?" Aiden asked. He was laying back on the couch with his legs spread out across Jack's lap. Marissa was running around the living room playing in her own imagination.

"Lydia and Avy will be here early, so I can do their hair. Then we'll head over to the grounds."

"Are you going to do my hair tomorrow?" Marissa asked.

"Of course! I'll spike it up real good like a rock star."

"I want it to be purple."

"Sorry bug, I can't do that without actually bleaching you. I don't have the color spray. Next time."

"Fine, I guess."

Jack chuckled as he got to his feet and swept Marissa up in his arms. "It's time for you to go to bed though. I've already kept you up too late. Let's go get your sleeping bag."

"Sleeping bag? I always sleep in your bed with you."

"Well, that's not entirely true. Aiden's sleeping there tonight though."

"That's not fair," Marissa said in her ready-to-argue tone.

"You get to sleep on the floor next to us. Won't that be fun?"

"How is that fun?"

"It will be, because you can watch videos on the tablet until you fall asleep. Now say good night to Aiden."

"Good night, Aiden!" Marissa smiled, waving her little hand.

"Good night!" Aiden smiled and waved back. He heard Marissa jumping all around upstairs while Jack got her sleeping area ready. The noises would get quiet and Aiden would catch snippets of Marissa attempting a rebuttal to the sleeping arrangement. He started shaking his head once he heard Jack coming back down the stairs.

"What?" Jack asked.

"You spoil her," Aiden laughed.

"I'm the uncle. It's in my job description."

"I can sleep downstairs if she's going to make a fuss all night."

Jack laughed, "No, no. She's being dramatic. She sleeps in her sleeping bag plenty here, because she takes up all the space in the bed."

"How?"

"I ask myself that a lot." Jack walked into the kitchen and grabbed two glasses. "Want a drink?"

"Wow, I haven't had a drink since my incident..." Aiden trailed off.

"I know. It's been over two months, so I think you deserve one."

"Yeah." Aiden walked into the kitchen, watching Jack open a fresh bottle of whiskey and pour it into the glass. "I've missed it."

"I don't doubt that."

Before Jack could add soda to the drink, Aiden took the glass and savored a long sip of the straight liquor. "Oh yeah, that hits the spot."

"Alright, I see you're hitting it strong tonight. Good deal," Jack nodded, taking the soda to make his own mixture. "Here's to tomorrow!"

"Absolutely. Tonight was fun. It's very tiring playing with Marissa. It's cute how much she adores you." Aiden smiled into his glass before adding, "She does really have you wrapped around her finger."

"Yes, she does. She's the best though. I've told Joey they can't have another one, because I don't know how I could possibly handle one more, especially if it was another girl."

"What about you?"

"What about me?"

Aiden ran his finger around the edge of his glass. "Have you...I mean do you want kids? It's pretty obvious you'd be great as a dad."

Jack smiled. "Thank you. I think so, yeah. I think about it from time to time."

"Do you ever worry about the obstacles of having them?"

"Sure. There's a lot of options though. There's adopting, hiring a surrogate. There's ways to make it happen. What about you? Did you ever picture having kids with Courtney?"

"Yeah, I did."

"And now? You still want any?"

Aiden didn't have to think too hard before nodding. "Yeah, I think I would."

"Well, maybe someday," Jack smiled.

Soon after their drinks, Aiden and Jack went upstairs to bed. The night was longer than Aiden had expected it to be. Everytime he felt himself relax and about to fall into a deep slumber, Jack rolled into a new position. Aiden wasn't typically a light sleeper, it would take more than a person moving around to keep him from getting any sleep, but he could sense Jack on edge.

"Jack?" Aiden whispered. He nudged at the restless body, wanting to check if Jack needed to talk. "Jack? Are you awake?" There was no answer except Jack rolling onto his side.

A conclusion was reached that Aiden wasn't going to get to sleep anytime soon. He carefully got out of bed, not wanting to wake Jack or Marissa, and went downstairs. He didn't know what he was going to do, but it felt wasteful to lay in bed at the time.

The first thing Aiden did was look out the front window. His car was in the same spot with no harm to it. No one was outside. It was so still out there anyone would question if time was stopped. Aiden hoped one day the small inconvenience of needing to check outside for danger would subside. He went for the kitchen next, still not having a plan in mind. On the counter were some boxes that held copies of Avy's CD. Jack was helping Avy by letting her store some of the CD's at his house. Aiden hadn't had a chance to look at them yet, so he reached for one. The cover was Avy in her usual jean jacket, she was holding onto the neck of a guitar, and she had one leg coming up in a straddle-like position around the body of the instrument. There was a fainted cross in the background, and she had the biggest smile on her face. Aiden wouldn't have expected anything less badass from her.

Aiden placed the CD back in the box. He debated having another glass of whiskey to help him sleep, but that wasn't sounding too appetizing. Next he tried looking through the fridge. He settled on trying to eat a quick snack, aiming to put himself into a food coma. Aiden made a plate of carrots and vegetable dip, which he had become accustomed to as it helped him stay away from cigarettes. It had been quite some time since he had one, ever since Jack asked him to stop, but the cravings still creeped up in uneasy situations. As he ate, he felt his mind wander to anything else he could do to help him sleep. He was coming face-to-face with a regret from his incident, aside from the regret of trying to take his own life. The sleeping pills. He was starting to wish he hadn't used the sleeping pills that night. They could come into use right now. They were gone though, having been pumped from his stomach and disposed of somewhere. He had to rely on other methods now. Aiden figured he could come to terms with that and would go back upstairs.

That didn't happen. Aiden's mind didn't seem to think that was it. Just like that night at RN's when Aiden was trying anything to not leave, he took his time cleaning up while he continued thinking about the sleeping pills and an alternative. He put each part of the snack away one by one, wiped the counter, got a drink of water, wiped the counter again, and rinsed out his glass. It didn't take much for his body to start walking towards a small cupboard above the microwave. There was a sense he was doing something wrong, so he checked behind him to make sure Jack wasn't there. The coast was clear, so Aiden proceeded to open the cupboard. There were different medicines, the usual symptom relievers and headache pills, but as Aiden searched through them, he couldn't find his own pills. He wasn't surprised Jack would hide his medications in a not-so-obvious spot. They weren't what he was after anyway. There was a small hope that maybe Jack used sleeping pills, but even if he did, they'd be hidden from Aiden too. He glanced at the other bottles, wondering if any of them could help him at least relax enough. He landed on a bottle of cold medicine. That had to be harmless enough. When he originally lied to Jaxie about using cold medicine, she didn't seem that concerned over it. He wasn't thinking about the consequences that could come out of it. He was only thinking about sleep as he grabbed the bottle and took the lid off.

Aiden was able to sleep in some, but he woke up feeling like he had a terrible secret. He wasn't worried about taking the cold medicine when he went back to bed, but now he was trying to tell himself it wasn't that serious. It hadn't knocked him out. It relaxed him from being so jumpy at Jack's movements. Now he was wondering if he had made a mistake doing that. Would he be labeled at-risk of harming himself again? He didn't want to go back to the hospital.

Aiden didn't want to sit in that worry, so he went downstairs to find Avy, Lydia, and Marissa in the living room. Avy was on the couch, appearing to be talking quietly to herself while looking at papers and tapping her foot. Marissa was coloring; her hair was sticking in different directions just as Jack had promised to do. Aiden couldn't muffle his laugh at the sight.

"What are you laughing at?" Marissa asked.

"Your hair looks crazy," Aiden responded.

"So does yours."

Aiden ran his hand through his hair he hadn't bothered combing yet. "I really didn't think I could ever have my feelings hurt by a tiny human."

Lydia was coloring on her own piece of paper, laughing at Aiden's comment. "She said you took her spot in the bed last night."

"Oh you heard about that, huh? She'll never let me live that down." Aiden took a seat on the couch next to Avy. "Are you ready for today?"

"I think so."

"Wow, I think that's the first time you've ever sounded unsure of something."

"This morning it all hit, that's for sure," Avy said with a nervous laugh.

"Where's Jack?"

"He's cleaning downstairs before doing our hair. I'm not going to lie, I'm already nervous enough as it is, and him being nervous doesn't help." Just then there was a knock at the front door and Avy yelled, "Come in!"

"Morning everyone!" Jaxie greeted, balancing a wide box in one hand.

"Morning," Aiden looked over at his sister. "What is that?"

"Donuts! I figured everyone would enjoy one, or I could eat them all."

"I want a chocolate donut!" Marissa said, loudly.

"A girl that knows what she wants. I like it," Jaxie laughed. She set the box of donuts on the counter and placed a donut on a napkin for Marissa. "I got you the chocolatiest one."

Jack walked up from the basement then and quickly helped himself to his own donut. "Good morning to you, Jaxie. This is very much appreciated."

"You're very welcome."

"Alright, Lydia, I'm ready for you," Jack said with his mouth half-full.

"Sweet," Lydia said, getting to her feet.

"By the way, guys, Joey should be here soon for Marissa, so just let him in and tell him I'll see him at the festival," Jack said.

"Got it," Aiden replied.

"You seem to be having a busy morning," Jaxie commented.

"Ain't that the truth?" Jack said, heading for the stairs.

Aiden watched Jack bouncing between conversations and walking as if he was in an unknown house. He got up from the couch and walked towards him. "Hey," he said, stopping Jack in his tracks.

"Sorry," Jack smiled, pecking a quick kiss on Aiden's cheek. "I meant to say good morning to you too."

Aiden chuckled. "It's not that. I was just going to tell you to relax a little."

Jack let out a nervous laugh. "If I wasn't keeping busy doing everyone's hair I'd probably be having some tequila for breakfast."

"That's disgusting."

"Yes, but I'm nervous enough to."

"I'll let you get back to doing hair then, because I'm not dragging your drunk ass out in public. I'll go get myself ready," Aiden turned away and walked back to the living room.

Jaxie followed her brother to the couch, nodding towards the basement. "Wow. He's nervous, huh? He seems quite on edge."

"Oh yeah. He was tossing and turning all night. That's why I slept in a little."

"He's not even the one who has to perform!" Avy laughed.

"No kidding." Aiden turned to Jaxie. "Come in the kitchen for some coffee and the donuts?"

Jaxie got the hint that he needed to talk to her about something, so she led the way. "What's up?"

"Have you heard anything else going on with Brett?"

"No. Why? Have you?"

"No." Aiden shook his head.

"That's good, right?"

"It is. I just wonder if he knows about this festival. I mean, I'm sure he does; everyone knows about it. I'm just feeling edgy that he's going to try something, you know?"

Jaxie shook her head. "I don't think so. He could face serious consequences, and that would just be for causing something at a public event. Then you add on the restraining order side of it. Plus, this is a big festival, there'll be loads of people around," Jaxie said, sipping the cup of coffee Aiden handed her. "Maybe him losing his job woke him up a little bit. Maybe he finally realized he can't pick and choose who is worth what."

"Yeah. Don't tell Jack this, but I still worry about Brett sometimes. There's times I'm mad at him too, but I worry. I don't even know what for."

"He was your best friend, Aiden. The memories you guys had are the reason you worry. It just comes naturally to you, you know?"

"Yeah. I sort of wish it'd just go away. I asked Jack if losing his old friends ever stopped hurting...and he said no."

Jaxie put her coffee cup down and took Aiden's hand into hers, "I know there's not really anything I can say to fix everything, so I'll just tell you that I love you, and I'll be here for you whenever you need it."

"You always are." Aiden was glad Jaxie was joining him at the festival. He was thankful for her support, especially in the matters of Brett. Jack saw Brett in a hateful manner and made it difficult for Aiden to talk to him about his feelings in that regard. Jack would try to sympathize, but he struggled to. Aiden didn't blame him. Jaxie had strong feelings towards Brett too, but she knew the old Brett. That left a bit of an open door for Aiden to lay out any of his feelings to her.

"There's something else I want to tell you. I know you'll tell me to tell Jack, but I don't want to make him jumpy."

"You mean jumpier than he already is?"

"Well, for now," Aiden sighed. "I was having trouble sleeping last night with all of Jack's tossing around. I was getting too awake to stay in bed so I came down here. Then I...well, I took some cold medicine."

Jaxie's eyebrows furrowed. "Okay?"

"I took it to help me go back to sleep. I wasn't thinking at the time. After I took it, it relaxed me enough to sleep. Then this morning, I was hit with the thoughts of how I used to rely on sleeping pills so much to help me sleep. It became a problem, I'll admit that. Then I used them to...I don't want to depend on something else to get through the nights. This morning I couldn't stop imagining myself getting too desperate and going to a pharmacy to get my own sleeping pills."

"Okay, slow down. Tell me something honestly. Was the one and only purpose of you taking that cold medicine to help you sleep?"

"Yes, honest. I just wanted to get some rest for today. I guess I could have just gone to the guest bed downstairs, huh?"

"I don't know. Maybe you wouldn't have slept then not being next to Jack. I think you can relax though. If that's the only intention you were having, I'm not going to get too worried. People take stuff like that when they can't sleep. It is sort of normal. If you start becoming dependent or start considering sleeping pills, tell me or Jack. Please just tell us before you take any actions."

"I will. I just...I feel like I relapsed or something."

Jaxie shrugged. "Maybe in some shape or form you did, but it's okay. Don't let it eat you up. Just don't do it tonight. If you can't sleep tonight and you're here, try talking to Jack instead."

"Should I tell him about this?"

"Maybe not right away. You told me and I think that's good enough for now. I'll even talk to Jack for you if you aren't sure." Jaxie watched Aiden look down at the counter. "Are you okay?"

"Yeah, I think I'm okay. I just needed to hear someone say I didn't mess up too bad."

"You being this aware of it is a good sign. Now come on, let's enjoy these wonderful, circular, glazes of goodness."

The rest of the morning went as smoothly as it could have. Things happened on schedule, but everyone's nerves were jumpy anyway. There was a lot of anxious excitement. The boys got in Jack's truck while the girls piled in Jaxie's car, and they all drove to the "He Still Loves Us" festival.

The festival was going great. There were booths of fun activities, games, and food. There were a lot of people around. Lydia and Avy walked around the festival some and then had to go get to work. Jack spent most of his time with Marissa, Joey, and Amy. Since Marissa wanted to spend a lot of time at specific games, Aiden and Jaxie went their own way around the rest of the grounds. Aiden couldn't help himself and would occasionally stare off at a group of people who were smiling and embracing one another. There were family members and friends happy to be there to support their loved ones. There were groups of people who didn't personally know anyone that was gay, but they were there in support anyway. Sometimes it made him think about who he wished could be supporting him. He didn't feel right letting it bother him though. Not today. There was a great support system for him, whether they were blood-related or not. He tried to be optimistic and thankful for who he did have.

The sun was beginning to set, signaling that it was almost concert time. Aiden and Jaxie found the table Jack was sitting at with Joey, Amy, and Marissa. Lydia was backstage helping Avy get ready. Marissa was excited, unable to stay in her seat as she jumped around the table. There were six stuffed animals on the table, Aiden certain they came from Jack winning them for her. He was ready to make a joke about the spoiling again, but Jack was the only one at the table sitting quietly. He was staring at the stage with more focus than was necessary when there was no one performing on it. He had one finger spinning his red wristband around his arm.

"Jeez, Jack, you really *are* nervous," Jaxie commented.

"This is just such a big deal for Avy, and for the gay community. We'll get backlash of course, but what else is new? I'm going to go back there and see how she's doing." Jaxie watched as he made his way towards backstage. "He's so excited and so scared."

"Playing a lot of games for prizes was keeping him a little distracted," Amy said.

"I see he was successful." Aiden nodded towards the toys.

"I'll make him keep these at his house." Joey chuckled. "We knew he'd be jumpy here. That kid has been through too much."

"I hope this doesn't come off wrong," Aiden began, "but I thought your mom would have been here."

"She would have in a heartbeat. She's just too old for this type of stuff. She called him earlier and talked to him some."

"I'm going to take Marissa on a quick walk until it starts," Amy said, getting to her feet.

"I'll come with. We'll be right back," Joey said.

Aiden watched Marissa pull her parents along, asking how she could get another stuffed animal. He glanced back at the stage and said to Jaxie, "I'm used to Jack being super confident. I don't even know how to handle this part of him."

"Be a boyfriend," Jaxie winked.

"What?"

"Okay, this will sound weird, but think back to the times Courtney or any other girlfriend was tensed up about something important. This relationship may not be a guy and a girl, but it's the same in this situation. Be a boyfriend to Jack in his time of need."

Aiden thought about what Jaxie said, trying to determine what he could do. Not only what he could do as a boyfriend, but what would Jack specifically need from him? It wasn't long before Jack returned to the table, not appearing any calmer.

"How is she?" Jaxie asked.

"She's ready." Jack nodded. "She's very ready. Lydia will come sit with us in a minute."

Aiden looked around at the people supporting the event. There were straight couples and gay couples. There were families and friends. Some people had arms around each other, others were hand in hand. People were talking excitedly and people were laughing. Everyone was able to be affectionate in their own way, with who they wanted, without judgement. No one cared what other people were seeing them do. Outside of this big circle, people could be wishing death on them, but that didn't stop anyone. He imagined Lydia and Avy in the back. Lydia had to be holding Avy close, whispering supporting words in her ear. Love had no limits here.

Aiden scooted his chair closer to Jack and took his hand, intertwining their fingers.

Jack looked down as if caught off guard, then looked back up at Aiden and smiled. "Thanks for coming."

"Of course." Aiden glanced back at Jaxie, who gave him a supportive smile and a tiny thumb's up.

When Avy came on stage, the atmosphere took a switch. There was a new presence emerging. No one could see it, but everyone felt it. As Avy's words rushed through Aiden's ears, he could feel them sink in, becoming a personal meaning. He didn't realize it, but he was squeezing Jack's hand tight. His eyes followed her around the stage, unable to look anywhere else. She wholeheartedly meant what she was singing to everyone, and wanted everyone to believe in it too. Even though everyone was loud and cheering her on, Aiden could only hear Avy singing. The music even seemed tuned out. It was just her voice singing what needed to be said to him. Tears came to his eyes as the once unsure path of his life was appearing right before him, clearer than ever.

The moment Avy finished, there was a second of silence, and then an uproar of cheers. Lydia couldn't contain herself as she ran up on stage and hugged Avy tight. Aiden watched as everyone around got to their feet, applauding, cheering, and shouting for an encore. He looked next to him. Jack wasn't standing, nor had he taken his hand from Aiden's to clap. He stayed seated and still, Avy's words sinking into him, and the tears trying to break free. Joey walked around and hugged Jack from behind, whispering something in his ear. Whatever Joey said, that made the tears escape Jack's eyes fast. Aiden knew how much this night meant to him, and even though Jack was crying, Aiden felt his heart leap joyfully for him. It was a night neither of them would ever forget.

The festival ended late into the night, but that didn't stop anyone from still wanting to celebrate. Jaxie had to go home for an early shift in the morning but Aiden, Lydia, and Avy all got in Jack's truck to triumph at his house. The four were exhausted, but too pumped to relax. They settled in their usual hangout in Jack's basement, ready to celebrate the best way they knew how, card games.

"That was such a big turn out!" Lydia said excitedly.

"You did amazing, Avy," Aiden said smiling at his friend and squeezing her shoulder.

"Thank you. Now everyone get your glasses up," Avy said, raising her drink, "I just hope you all know how grateful I am that you're all in my life. You all had a special part in making this a success, and it was. Here's to a new chapter for everyone in the gay community and to spreading love, not hate. I love you all and can't wait to see where the rest of this year brings us."

"Amen to that!" Jack smiled. Each of them cheered and tapped their glasses together. No one could contain their excitement as they continued to talk about the event. They could barely get a decent card game going as they were distracted in their conversations.

"Okay, I'm ready to switch from beer and have one good drink," Jack said, getting up from his seat.

"Perfect timing. I need a refill," Aiden smiled.

Jack took Aiden's hand, pulling him to his feet. He laced their fingers with one another and they began walking up the stairs. Once they reached the kitchen, Jack switched from holding hands to putting his arm around Aiden's shoulders.

"Tell me honestly, how was it for you?"

"It was amazing. It really was."

Jack gave Aiden a kiss on the cheek. "I'm really glad. Last summer when all this was announced, I didn't expect to actually have a date to bring."

Aiden set his empty drink glass onto the counter. He wasn't sure what triggered him as he quickly brought his hands up to Jack's face and pulled him into a kiss. It was a long kiss. There wasn't a built-up confidence boost that pushed him to do it. It just felt right to go for it this time. It was fitting right in place. Jack was caught off guard as he clumsily found a safe spot to set his beer bottle without letting the contact go. Once his hands were free, he placed them on Aiden's waist, guiding them into a deeper kiss.

There wasn't a point for Aiden to stop, but a faint sound went through his ears. He broke the kiss to listen closer. Jack hadn't caught on as he kissed down Aiden's cheek and went across his jawline towards his neck. Aiden was ready to blame his nerves given what was happening at the moment and turned to lock with Jack's lips again. The noise happened again. This time Jack slowed down.

"Did you hear that?" Aiden asked.

"I think so."

"What was it?"

"Sounded like someone yelling." Jack turned away to listen closer.

"You don't think someone is here making a fuss about the festival and Avy, do you?"

"Maybe. We sort of expected that could happen. It's awfully late, so I don't know." The faint yelling was heard again. "I'll check it out."

"Are you sure?"

"It'll be nothing. We see if someone is out there directing their tantrum at us and then call the cops to make them leave. It'll be done and over with. Then," Jack replaced his hands on Aiden's hips and pulled him close, "I'll be back for you."

"You know the girls are still in the basement, right?"

"They know where the door is," Jack chuckled. "Make me whatever you're drinking."

Jack turned to go down the hall while Aiden composed himself enough to move from his spot. Another noise rang out, this time it sounded closer and clearer, causing them both to freeze. Both of their hearts skipped a beat, wondering if they truly heard what they thought they heard. They glanced at each other, confirming what they believed was going on.

Aiden was now at Jack's heels quickly going down the hall and approaching the front door. There was no doubt they heard the same thing from the outside.

"Aiden!"

"Go back in the kitchen," Jack ordered, his mood instantly changing.

"No. Let me see. I'm not scared." Jack wasn't willing to argue as he grabbed the doorknob and opened it. They both peeked outside. Brett was standing in the yard, yelling at the house.

"Brett?" Aiden asked, walking past Jack.

"Don't even try it," Brett said with a slight stagger. He had been drinking.

Aiden stopped in his steps on the porch. He glanced back at Jack, who was keeping his eye only on Brett. Aiden could see Marissa flashing in Jack's eyes. There wasn't going to be a civil conversation. He knew Jack would strangle Brett right now if the chance was given.

"Hope you don't try running off this time," Jack said. "I've been waiting for this opportunity."

"Jack," Aiden whispered desperately.

"Look at me, Aiden!" Brett snarled, ignoring Jack's warning.

Aiden slowly turned back around, barely looking Brett in the eye. He didn't know what to do. The words Brett had said to him threatened to run through his head, but he tried fighting them off.

"Because of you, I lost my job and I got people giving me grief all over the place. All because you had to have your little dramatic moment. That's all you gays are good for is making a big deal out of everything." Brett shook his head. "I didn't make you do anything that night. You chose to take those damn pills. You want to blame me for that? You have to ruin my life over it?! You had to take me to court and cause hell everywhere! Oh well. Since you couldn't even successfully take pills, I got other means to do what needs to be done."

Before Aiden could even think of how to respond, Jack stepped forward, getting in front of him. "I'm the one who pushed him to get that restraining order. He wanted to give you a chance, but I convinced him not to."

"Jack," Aiden said.

"Shut up," Jack barked, "I'm the reason it all happened. I'm the one you should have a problem with. And believe me, you do. You came to my house and could have hurt my niece. If you think you're going to get away with harming her or Aiden, you are mistaken."

"Jack, please stop."

"Go inside," Jack said firmly.

"Listen to your fag, Aiden," Brett sneered. "This won't take long anyway."

"Ever have your teeth kicked in by a fag?" Jack snarled in response. "That will be a fun story to tell your 'big man' buddies."

"Jack, please," Aiden begged.

"I'm not going to tell you again. Get inside now! It's about time he fights someone who's ready to defend himself."

Aiden couldn't listen to them argue anymore, and he didn't want Jack mad at him. His heart was attempting to push through his chest as he hurried inside. Before he could turn to look outside again, Jack reached for the door and closed it. He didn't want to stand there, but his feet were stuck. It was seconds before the voices got louder and Aiden could tell one of them gave a shove. Aiden ran for the kitchen and leaned over the sink, waiting to get sick. When that didn't happen, he started hyperventilating. He ran downstairs, not knowing what else to do. Something bad already started outside and it was only going to get worse.

"Aiden, what's wrong?" Avy asked.

"Brett's here," Aiden gasped through tears. "Him and Jack are getting into it. He made me come inside."

"I'll go out there," Avy stood up.

"Should I call the police?" Lydia asked.

"No," Aiden butted in, "please, can we just try to get him to leave?"

"Okay, okay. Just stay down here," Avy said, heading upstairs.

Aiden paced the basement, feeling himself begin to lose control. He didn't want to see it, but his mind flashed images of Brett hurting Jack. Even though Jack was considerably larger, Aiden wished he hadn't left him out there by himself. Lydia took Aiden by the arms and did her best to soothe him, sitting him on the floor.

"Jack doesn't deserve this," Aiden whimpered, "I should be dealing with whatever Brett is doing right now."

"Aiden, you can't..."

Lydia couldn't finish her sentence as they heard a gunshot from upstairs.

-20-

How could it be that only four hours ago Aiden was at the festival with everyone? How could time be so slow? Time could not be passing correctly. This had to be a nightmare. That would explain what was wrong with time. Only four hours ago Aiden was at the festival and now he was pacing the waiting room of the hospital. That doesn't happen. It wasn't supposed to happen. It was almost one in the morning, and he was alone awaiting answers. He was supposed to be laying in bed right now. That's why this was a nightmare. Time was wrong and he wasn't where he was supposed to be.

The helpless feeling tugging at him wouldn't ease up. Truthfully, Aiden could be in the back if he wanted to. It was offered. He could be getting information quicker and hearing what the police were discussing. But he couldn't get himself to move through the doors. It was almost easier to walk out the exit doors and not be given answers at all. He didn't know which answer or result he wanted to hear. Now he understood what Jack meant by being on the other side of things, being a patient versus being a worried loved one.

"Aiden?" a voice cracked, stopping Aiden in his steps. He watched Jaxie hurry over to him and land in his arms.

"What's going on?" Jaxie asked. She looked around for anyone else there with him, but she didn't see anyone. "What happened?"

Aiden had called Jaxie to meet him at the hospital, but he didn't give her any information. He couldn't spill it out on the phone. So much had happened in a short amount of time, he almost questioned his own memory. "Brett showed up at Jack's place."

"What!" Jaxie shouted. "I don't understand. Why? What did he do?"

Aiden sat down in a chair, unable to speak as he broke down. He leaned forward, his face hiding in his hands. Jaxie wanted an explanation, but she knew Aiden wouldn't be able to provide them right now, so she took a seat and held him while he sobbed. She was convincing herself that she'd have to find everything out from someone else, but who? She didn't know the current status of anyone else. The one thing Jaxie did know was she wasn't going to like what she heard.

"Relax, Aiden," she soothed, "you gotta tell me what happened. You gotta tell me something."

Before Aiden could answer, Lydia was next to arrive at the hospital. Jaxie looked at Lydia, not able to place the expression on her face. Was she sad, angry, or scared? Why was she just arriving at the hospital now? Where was she before?

Lydia walked over calmly and sat next to Aiden and Jaxie. "Hey," she greeted the two solemnly.

Aiden got enough control of himself to ask, "What happened with Avy?"

Lydia shrugged. "She's still at the police station. They told me I might as well leave because I didn't witness anything anyway."

"Why is Avy at the police station?" Jaxie asked. "Where's Brett and Jack? What *happened*?!"

Aiden turned away, tapping his foot, his nervous energy not allowing him to keep still. "They got in a fight."

"Oh my God," Jaxie said softly. If they were at the hospital, Jaxie could come to the conclusion that there was a winner and a loser. But who was which?

Aiden tried to continue but he couldn't go on. He was conflicted in how he'd tell the story. There was a side of him that was going to tell it from a side of anger towards Brett, and there was a side of him that would have anger towards Jack.

Lydia spoke up, which Aiden was thankful for, to explain in detail what had happened. "Brett came to Jack's," she started. "He was very angry about everything that has happened to him. Jack made Aiden go inside. I wasn't there for this part, but I guess Brett was blaming Aiden for where his life was heading. Jack told Brett that he was the one that pushed Aiden to go through with the restraining order so Brett should be dealing with him. I mean, Jack had a lot of anger built up for Brett, so he wasn't about to shy away from a fight. Avy went outside to help while me and Aiden stayed inside. Avy was going to see if she and Jack could maybe reason with Brett and get him to leave without involving the police, or, you know, limit Jack's hits before getting Brett to leave." Lydia took a deep, shaking breath and her eyes were brimming with tears. "Then Aiden and I heard a gunshot."

Jaxie could barely gasp before they heard the doors from the hall open, all three of them turning to look. They saw Jack walk out, his head hung low and his right wrist wrapped. Lydia got to her feet, hurrying over to hug him. Even with holes still in the story, Jaxie was relieved to see Jack up and walking fine. She was ready to stand, expecting Aiden to go over to Jack as well, but he didn't move. Instead, he went quiet and leaned forward, keeping his back to Jack. He stared at the floor, awaiting to get the answer he wasn't sure he wanted to know. Jaxie took Aiden's hand in hers, ready to support him.

"Well?" Lydia quietly asked Jack.

Jack didn't answer as he glanced towards the chairs. Seeing Aiden working hard to avoid his gaze, he nodded at Lydia, then walked over to the seats.

"What happened?" Jaxie asked as Jack sat across from Aiden.

Jack let out a low sigh. "Brett and I got into it."

"Are you okay?" Jaxie asked, nodding towards Jack's wrist.

"Yeah, I'm fine. The coward—" Jack stopped, knowing this wasn't the time. "Anyway, it got ugly quick. Avy got involved. He pulled out a gun...but Avy was faster."

"She...she..." Jaxie placed a hand over her mouth, getting the picture.

"Aiden," Jack took Aiden's hands in his, but he still refused to look up from the floor.

"Please don't..." Aiden whispered.

"Aiden..."

"Don't say it," Aiden's eyes squeezed shut, tears falling to the floor as he knew what had happened. "Please don't say it."

Aiden felt Jack's hands squeeze while the words flowed out. "He didn't make it."

Instantly, Aiden yanked his hands from Jack's. He looked at Jaxie with pleading eyes, "Please tell me it's not true."

Jaxie stared at Jack, also hoping what he had just said wasn't true. He looked down in response and Jaxie shook her head. Tears filled her eyes, but not for Brett. As relieved as she felt for her brother's well-being, she only imagined what conflicting feelings were about to hit him. "I'm sorry," she quietly said to Aiden, "it's true."

Aiden's reaction was unexpected. He didn't begin crying uncontrollably like Jaxie prepared for. Instead, he began rocking back and forth, his face instantly going from sorrow to resentment. He looked ready to explode.

"I'm so sorry, Aiden," Jack said quietly.

Aiden's eyes darted at Jack, finally looking at him. Immediately, Aiden jumped up and pushed Jack. The emotional buildup made Aiden shove as hard as he could, causing Jack to fall back onto the floor. There was an uncontrollable fire inside of him. He got down on top of Jack and grabbed him by his shirt collar, pulling him up close. It wasn't long ago he was holding this man in a passionate embrace, and now he wanted to slam him into the floor. Jack grasped Aiden's hands, trying to pry him off. "Is that all you can say about this is sorry?!"

"Aiden, stop! You don't want to do this!" Jaxie yelled, trying to pull her brother off.

Aiden didn't have time to think about what he was doing as two security guards quickly pulled him up. "Sir, is there a problem here? We will escort you out if you can't control yourself."

"No, no," Jack said, quickly getting to his feet. "I'm sorry. We're fine. He just found out his best friend died, okay? It'll be fine. We're cool."

The guard looked at Aiden. "Sir?"

"I'm fine," Aiden mumbled.

"Consider this your warning then, all of you," the guard said firmly before they both turned away.

The four of them were on their feet, silent. Jack had his eye on Aiden, unsure what else to say. Aiden kept his eye on the floor, shoving his hands in his pockets. The next several minutes dragged on. No one knew what to do next. Finally, Aiden took a deep breath and looked at Jack. "Don't act like you're not happy about this."

Jack's jaw dropped in shock. "Aiden—"

Aiden didn't give him a chance to finish. He stormed for the exit, Jaxie at his heels.

"Aiden, hold on!" Jaxie said, hurrying outside.

"I need to be alone."

"I don't think that's a good idea."

"Jaxie, please..."

"Let me come with you," Jaxie begged.

"Oh my God!" Aiden turned screaming. "Do you not hear me? I need to be alone!"

"Yes, Aiden, yes I heard you!" Jaxie yelled back. "I just don't get it! This guy was your friend. And then he turned on you for being honest with him, for wanting to be true to yourself! He hurt you! His friendship was conditional, it had limits! He destroyed any significance you felt you had, and made you believe you weren't worth shit! He tore you up so bad, you wanted to end things! And here you are, getting ready to mourn his death! How?!"

Aiden shook his head in frustration. "I understand all he did to me. In fact, you can say what he did all you want, but you'll never understand how I felt because of that bastard! Everything that asshole did to me! I just—there are still memories. Everything we did in our lives before all this and how things officially ended from me..." Aiden waved his hand around as he searched for the word, "changing! He's gone now. I should be so happy. But what a surprise, Brett's making sure I'm *still* hurting!" Aiden paused as he looked towards the hospital. "Was this worth it? Was it worth not lying about myself? Was it worth losing him? I don't know. I really don't know."

"Don't say that..."

"Don't give me the right or wrong speech. I need to be alone," Aiden repeated. "Please."

Jaxie slowly crossed her arms, nodding. There was nothing else she could do. Anything else she said or did would only push him away, and she couldn't risk that right now. Jaxie reluctantly watched as her brother got into his car and drove away.

"He left," Jaxie announced. "I'm not going to go after him. I gotta let him be. I'm sorry he pushed you, Jack."

"I'm fine, really."

Lydia looked towards Jack. "Did they really call it? He's gone?"

Jack slowly nodded. "How's Avy?"

"Things seem to be leaning on her side. She may be there most of the night anyway."

"They were telling me it was looking like self-defense. I know they aren't done talking to me either though."

"I'm so sorry this happened," Jaxie said quietly. "Jack, what happened during this fight?"

"Once Aiden went inside, Brett came up on me. He shoved me, I shoved him. Then it was mostly grabbing and him trying to hit me, but he couldn't land one because he was so drunk. He also tried rattling me up by calling me names and accusing every gay stereotype. This was about Aiden, though. Brett couldn't get to me personally no matter how hard he tried, and he didn't like that. He got frustrated with himself and reached into his jacket. I expected the worst, so I grabbed him and threw him aside. He fell against a tree and onto the ground. I'll admit, the next thing I did was stupid on my part, but I was so pissed off. Instead of leaving him there, I grabbed him by the shirt and brought him to his feet just shaking him and yelling at him. I'm sure his head hit the tree from me shaking him. I had a lot to get out but I left myself vulnerable, because he reached for his gun again. The first thing he did was bring it up high and hit my wrist with it, breaking my grip and letting him go. For a second he tried to aim it at me, but the next second Avy took her shot." Lydia wrapped her arm around Jack's, leaning her head against his shoulder, grateful both her best friend and girlfriend were alive. Jack brought his other hand up and ran it through her hair. "I wasn't going to kill him."

"I know," Jaxie nodded. "I know you wouldn't have done that."

"I don't know what all Aiden saw. Him and Lydia ran out, and I got over to him as fast as I could. I didn't want him to see the body there. I was holding him tight, keeping him shoved against me, no matter how hard he tried to look," Jack bit his lip. "I just wanted to protect him."

"You did as much as you could," Lydia assured.

"If Brett didn't have a gun, he'd still be alive. Avy wouldn't have shot him without the reason to. And even if he didn't have a way to fight back, I wouldn't have beat him to death. I would not have killed him. I just wanted to blow off my own steam and give him what he deserved."

"You don't need to go on, Jack. You don't need to convince me," Jaxie said.

"I need to convince Aiden," Jack shook his head. "You heard him. He thinks I'm happy about this."

"He's talking out of many, many emotions. Don't take it too seriously," Jaxie said softly.

The doors opened, and two police officers walked out asking for Jack. "Okay, hopefully I can finish this up soon." Jack got to his feet. "Try texting Aiden, alright? He doesn't have to talk to me or any of us, but just ask him to message us and let us know he's alright."

Jaxie looked at Jack with alarm. "You don't think he'd try...*that* again, do you?"

"Like you said, he's on a bunch of feelings right now. I'm not sure what it could lead to," Jack admitted. He turned away to talk with the police.

"Oh God, no," Jaxie whispered, leaning her face into her hands. "No, no, no."

"Jaxie, don't freak out yet," Lydia said. "You were right to let him go. That was the right choice. Us going after him and being all over him would make it worse. Jack was right, we just need to let him know that we want him to check in so we know he's okay. We don't want to make him think he has to talk to us."

"How can I just sit here without knowing what he's doing right now?" Jaxie asked, near tears.

Lydia took Jaxie's hands into hers. "We are going to pray and ask for God to hold his hand tonight while we aren't there with him."

Aiden was at his apartment, sitting on his couch. There was a cold glass of whiskey in his hand, and an even colder feeling in his heart. The only sound was that of his phone constantly going off. There were many texts he hadn't given a glance at. Jaxie would call. Jack would call. Even Lydia called a couple times. The only thing Aiden got up for was to refill his glass over and over again, though, it didn't matter how much liquor was inside of him. Nothing was helping his feelings subside. Not the feelings of sorrow, not the feelings of anger, not the feeling of being entirely crippled by everything.

As Aiden expected, there was eventually a knock at his door. He looked up at the clock. It was 2:26 in the morning.

"Aiden?" It was Jack. "Aiden...I just want to make sure you're okay and not doing anything drastic. Can you please just tell me you're okay?"

Aiden looked towards the door, but didn't get up.

"Aiden? If you don't answer me, I will call the police. I just need to know you're alright and I'll leave."

"Go away," Aiden said. There was a long silence. He didn't hear footsteps walk away, so he got up from the couch and approached the door. "You said you would leave once I answered. Now go!"

There was another pause before Jack responded, "Okay."

After Jack was gone, Aiden knew he wouldn't hear from anyone else the rest of the night. He gently leaned his head against the door. His foot kicked at the bottom. Lifting his head up, Aiden tapped his forehead against the door over and over, gradually growing in intensity. Once the spot on his head started becoming numb, he backed away and turned for the kitchen. He half threw his drink into the sink, hearing some glass break off. He couldn't seem to let that go as he angrily grabbed at the sharp pieces and got them in the trash. It didn't make him feel better. He picked up the remainder of the glass and tossed it into the sink, broken pieces flying upward. Aiden furiously grabbed the small pieces and threw them into his trash.

"Shit," Aiden muttered as he saw small lines of blood appear on his hands. He turned the faucet on and immediately hissed at the stinging sensation. A dull feeling was coming on and he wondered if this was what Jack felt during the night he cut. There was pain but it also felt good to let out anger and hate in a damaging approach. As the water ran clear, Aiden checked for any glass in his skin and bandaged the small cuts. Even though there was a high going through him, Aiden was aware Jack ended up nearly dying from his cuts. That didn't have to be his route. He could be smarter than that if he kept going. This opportunity was in front of him, and Aiden had a choice to make. He could keep relieving the high emotions with the glass. He could distract his mind with this pain until the other pain from the night's events went away. He could go to sleep numb.

Aiden couldn't overlook the truth. Even the numbness would only be temporary.

No matter what he did, nothing was going to change from that night, and he didn't want the hateful feelings overwhelming him. He wanted to sleep and get past the now. Once he finished cleaning up, Aiden went to his bedroom. Exhaustion was finally overcoming him.

Sitting on the edge of his bed, Aiden was staring outside. There were clouds in the dark sky. He couldn't see any stars. That didn't seem to change the fact that Aiden felt watched right through the clouds. He could feel Brett looking down at him. It wasn't in a comforting way. Getting to his feet, Aiden walked up to his window and opened it. There was a gentle breeze. Still, he wasn't comforted; he felt like something was advancing on him.

"Why?" Aiden asked out loud. "Why couldn't we just keep being best friends? You didn't have to hate me. Nothing had to change!"

Jaxie's words at the hospital rang in Aiden's mind. Brett destroyed his significance, yet he couldn't handle his death with a simple good riddance. Why couldn't he? With Jack's blessing he had forgiven Brett. He forgave Brett a thousand times already trying not to let any pain from Brett run his life. There was a pain happening right now, though, but forgiveness wasn't going to take care of it. Aiden was revisiting childhood memories. All the good memories that were before this domino mess. Those were causing a different ache. Heartache.

Was it worth it?

He thought this heartache would have happened after the restraining order, after it was too late to fix their friendship. But now, Aiden was feeling a different meaning to this ending. He knew it was truly over. Brett wasn't coming back, in any way. If Aiden had never come out, Brett wouldn't have despised him. If he had never met Jack, Brett may not be dead right now. There wouldn't be a heartache to feel.

Was it worth it?

Jack. If he hadn't met Jack, there wouldn't be a heartache. If Jack wasn't involved, there wouldn't be a heartache. If Brett didn't know the truth, there wouldn't be a heartache. It didn't matter which way Aiden put it, he knew it was a lie. If he didn't tell Brett the truth, or if he told Brett he would stay straight, their friendship wouldn't have gone back to normal. There would be a heartache of him being fake and only imagining a guy like Jack in his life.

Aiden turned away from the window and saw the book Jack gave him for Christmas sitting on his dresser. He hadn't opened it in some time. Then a noise was heard from behind and Aiden turned back to look outside again. It was beginning to rain. An old saying came to his mind about rain being angels crying.

"I can't let you cause me pain anymore."

Aiden started closing the window, but left it cracked open. He picked up the book and climbed into bed. Curling himself into a ball, Aiden hugged his pillow, and opened the book. He started back at the beginning. Tears streamed down his face, and he didn't try stopping them. He needed to cry. He had to put his sorrows to rest. Brett was gone. Truthfully, the Brett he once knew had been gone for a long time. There would be grief in his days coming, but he wanted to pick and choose what to put that energy towards.

With that thought, Aiden made a promise to himself. This would be the last time he was going to shed tears for the Brett that got himself killed.

-21-

Aiden spent the next three days by himself. He would send messages to Jack and Jaxie letting them know he was doing okay, but didn't lead on any further conversation with them. He knew he needed time to figure things out. On that third day, Aiden finally left his apartment to go to work. At first, he was unsure about going in, but as the night went on he was glad he did. Jack didn't go into the bar that night. Neither did Lydia or Avy. Aiden heard that Avy was let go on self-defense, but he wasn't certain on the details. He was okay with them not being at The Color Band. It helped his thinking process further.

"How are you holding up?" Toby asked.

"I'm doing alright," Aiden replied while pouring a beer.

"You know you didn't have to come in. I would've understood."

"I needed to come out."

"Well, if you ever need to take time for yourself, you'll always have a job here. Just know that, alright?"

"Thank you, Toby. I appreciate that." Aiden paused while he handed the beer to a customer. "Toby, can you do me a favor?"

"Yeah, anything."

"Can you let Jack know I was here tonight? I've messaged him some the past couple days, but I know he's still worrying. Can you just let him know I came to work? I think he'll feel a little better."

Toby nodded. "Yeah, sure. I can do that."

"Thanks."

When Aiden got home from work, he went straight to his bedroom and slammed on the bed. Bartending wore him out. He definitely felt like he was out of his game. He undressed down to his boxers and settled under the covers. The book was sitting on the other side of the bed. The night of Brett's death, Aiden read the book from cover to cover. The past couple nights, Aiden read different parts over and over again. He wanted to think about what the book was saying and he wanted to understand what it personally meant to him.

Aiden wasn't sure if he'd stay awake long enough to read that night, but he sent a message to Jaxie, asking her to let him know where she'd be the next day.

The next morning, Aiden saw a response from his sister that she would be at work. Aiden showered, dressed, and headed to the diner. Even with how tired he was, Aiden ended up taking time to skim the book until he couldn't keep his eyes open. That was the first morning he was feeling refreshed and renewed. He walked into the diner and pulled his sister aside to talk, feeling empowered to move forward on the right foot.

"You know that night you kept me up all night worrying," Jaxie said. "I mean, you've kept me up every night worried."

Aiden could see that her eyes looked puffy and tired. "I know, I'm sorry."

"Jack told me he went to your place that night and you were fine, but I still worried. We've been texting back and forth the past few days to let each other know whenever we would hear from you."

"That doesn't surprise me."

"I'm glad you came by to see me. How are you doing?"

"I think I'm okay right now. I'm doing better."

"What happened to your hands?"

Aiden looked down. There were multiple tiny scabs along his hands. "Don't worry, I didn't do anything stupid."

"I'll be the judge of that."

"I threw a glass in the sink and I may have been a little hostile in cleaning it up. That was it though. I'm fine."

"Alright," Jaxie said quietly.

"Do you want to strip search my body for self-harm?"

"No. I'm not trying to sound like I'm accusing you. I'm sorry, I haven't slept."

"It's okay. I know you've been worrying nonstop. I just wanted to come talk." Aiden paused. "I'm sorry I blew up at you at the hospital."

"I understand why you did. I really do. I'm sorry I got so pushy about how you were handling it all. My own frustrations got the best of me."

"They may have, but you were right. I was stuck in the past, thinking that I could relive it, that Brett and I would be the same as we once were. I don't want you to argue this next thing I'm about to say. Just listen. I know you and Jack won't admit it to my face, and maybe you

312

guys don't realize it anyway, but I know you guys will
shake off Brett's death. I don't blame you guys. I did have
a realization last night, though. Maybe multiple realizations
from the past few days. I still don't think I understand it
completely, and I still have some doubts to work out in
time, but I'm...feeling good about where I'm going."

"I'm happy to hear that."

"All I could think about was what if I hadn't gone
back inside when Jack and Brett were going to fight?
Maybe Brett wouldn't have attacked if it had been me
talking to him instead."

"Maybe he would've shot you then. But we can't
change what happened, and we won't ever know. I'm sorry
we can't, though, because I know it's causing so many
confusing feelings for you."

"Yeah." Aiden nodded. "I'll figure it out. I know I
will. I just had to make the choice that I wasn't going to let
the pain run things anymore. Part of that is going to be
letting Brett go, including the old Brett. I know I'll go
through that process many, many times."

Jaxie smiled and gave her brother a hug.

"Do you know what happened with Avy?" Aiden
asked.

"It took a long time, but she was able to leave by
claiming self-defense. She won't get charged with
anything."

"Thank God," Aiden let out a sigh of relief. "She
wouldn't have deserved that." Aiden looked to the floor for
a moment, then back at his sister. "Anyway, I can let you
get back to work. I just wanted to come apologize and truly
let you know that I'm okay. I'm going to be okay," he
assured. "I have other matters to take care of now."

"Okay. And just so you know, I am hurting from
Brett's death too." Jaxie's lip quivered as she continued,
"I'm not just walking away from it like he meant nothing to

me. He was like a big brother to me all those years. I've cried for him."

Aiden hugged his sister and held her. "I'm sorry. I don't want to sound like I'm calling you heartless or something."

"No, you're not. I just thought you should know. We can both grieve together if it's something you need."

"Do you need that?"

"I wouldn't mind it."

Aiden pulled out of the hug. "You don't feel like I deserted you, do you?"

"No. I've actually been at Jack's house a couple of times. I'd be worrying over you and crying over Brett. He just let me pour everything out on him. I know you had to do what you needed to do."

"I'm happy he was there for you. I'll be here now too. We can both go through this together."

Jaxie smiled at her brother. "I'm glad to hear that. I should get back now and I can let you go do what you need to do. I love you."

"I love you, too, so much."

After speaking with Jaxie, Aiden drove to Jack's. He sat in his car for some time, staring at the house. There was some difficulty having that talk with Jaxie, he knew he had put her through hell, but now he wasn't sure how he could face Jack. That night began playing out in his head, the time that Brett showed up. Even the moment after he had gone inside the house, Aiden's mind tried putting together how he thought everything may have happened. If Avy hadn't gone out there, Jack would have been shot instead. Then who would have stopped Brett from shooting him next? Aiden didn't want to think about it. As Jaxie said, they couldn't change what happened.

Aiden stepped out of his car and walked up the driveway. His eyes stayed on the grass, wondering where Brett's body had collapsed from the bullet. He tried remembering the moment when he and Lydia ran outside to see what had happened. Was Brett already dead? Aiden wasn't sure. He remembered someone rushing over, grabbing him, and holding his head down. They were refusing to let him go. At the time, he had no idea if it was Jack protecting him or Brett trying to hurt him. He remembered fighting to get out of the grip, unsure if he was in danger or not. It wasn't until he managed to turn his head upward and catch a glimpse of Jack's face did he know he wasn't in harm's way. Then he remembered Jack walked him back into the house, still shielding him. Aiden managed a quick glance, but he only recalled seeing Brett's shoe. He had no idea if he was dead.

Aiden got out of his memory and finished his walk up the driveway. He approached the porch steps and turned back around to look at the grass again. There weren't any signs of a fight. There wasn't any sign of a body being there. From behind, Aiden heard the front door open. He looked up the porch steps and saw Jack walk outside.

"Aiden."

"Hi. Can I come in?"

"Yeah, of course."

Aiden followed Jack inside, closing the door behind him. "I'm sorry about what happened at the hospital. I shouldn't have said what I said and I shouldn't have pushed you down."

"No need to apologize," Jack said. "I understand why you said it. I just hope you know I didn't wish for Brett to be dead. I know I had harsh feelings towards him, but—"

"I know those feelings were for good reason."

"Yeah...but I never hoped he'd be dead. I would've hoped he'd change, even though I knew he wouldn't. I had anger to get out and that's all I intended on doing." Jack shook his head. "I know this is all going to hurt and take time to get past."

"Yeah, it will." Aiden nodded. "But I realized something last night while I was reading the book you gave me."

"You read the whole thing last night?"

"I read the whole thing that night after I got home from the hospital. I've read parts of it over and over again the past few nights too. I needed to. It helped me think. And...I'll never regret having Brett as a friend for the years that I did. He was great for that time of my life. He was what I needed for that time of my life. I am going to miss him...I'll miss him from those times."

Jack nodded. "I know you will."

"I will, a lot. His fault was that our friendship had this weird limit. I don't even think Brett knew that because he never would have pictured me as gay. When he was faced with it, though, he couldn't handle it. He had this vision of gay people in his head and even I, his best friend, couldn't change that," Aiden explained. "This next part may hurt to hear and I hate that I even thought about it. I tried convincing myself that if I never met you, I wouldn't have to deal with this. Brett wouldn't be gone and I'd be okay. Because of you, there is this brokenness I'm trying to handle now. I was putting all sorts of blame on you and thinking about how different things would be if I hadn't met you. The better things if you weren't around." Aiden took a deep breath. "I was picturing my life if I faked everything and just played a part as a straight guy to keep my old life around."

Jack was sliding his teal wristband up and down his arm. It was unclear where Aiden was going with all of this, and it worried him.

"But those better things wouldn't be worth it. Dead or not, Brett wasn't meant to be in this part of my life, as much as that hurts to know. I have no idea what you saw in me from that night we met, but you didn't have limits from the beginning. Even if I wasn't interested in a relationship with you, you made it clear that you'll always have my best interest at heart. You are an incredible man, Jack." Aiden smiled. "I'm nothing short of grateful that I met you."

Jack couldn't contain it anymore as he hugged Aiden. He couldn't find any words to say. He didn't have to. Aiden returned the hug, resting his head against Jack's chest, searching for the heartbeat he desired to listen to now and always. Jack ran his hand through Aiden's hair, giving small kisses upon his head.

When the hug broke, Aiden took Jack by the hand and smiled. "I need to ask you something."

Jack chuckled. "Did you chicken out of asking again?"

"No," Aiden shook his head. "It would've been weird to just come out and ask."

"Alright, shoot."

"Should we make this official then?"

Jack looked surprised, like he misheard. "What?"

"Our relationship. You've been working so hard at this for me to become your boyfriend, right?"

"Really?"

"Yes, really."

"Don't tease me. You're serious?"

Aiden laughed. "Would you answer the question?"

"Yes! Yes, yes, yes. A million times yes," Jack replied, unable to contain his excitement. He pulled Aiden close and deeply kissed him. Aiden missed that, even if it had only been a few days since their last kiss.

Jack backed away from the embrace. "I'm taking you out to dinner tonight, and making it properly official."

"I like the sound of that."

Jack smiled as he cupped Aiden's face, locking their lips again. Aiden wrapped his arms around Jack and held on tight. There wasn't any sign either of them were going to let go.

Aiden couldn't help letting out small laughs as he attempted to talk through the quick pecks. "I'm enjoying this...but I do want to get ready if we're going out tonight."

Jack backed away and sighed. "I guess you have a point." He brought his hands down to Aiden's waist and looked down at him. "Want to meet me at six?"

"Yeah," Aiden smiled, and unwillingly got out of Jack's hold to leave.

Aiden was going to wait until after Jaxie got off work to get ready for his date. Until then, he decided it was a good idea to catch up on some sleep and take a nap. He knew a long night was ahead of him.

Jaxie's shift ended after the lunch rush, then she and Lydia met Aiden at the mall. He was nervous about tonight, but it was different. Last time, Aiden was on edge because he cared what people might have been thinking at the time. He was on edge about what people would be thinking when they saw him with Jack. This time, though, it felt like a true first date. It was first date jitters. Aiden was ready to finally take this relationship somewhere. He was ready to be happy.

The three had met by the pretzel stand. "I know you didn't bring me here for just pretzels," Jaxie commented. "Although, I have no argument against it either."

Aiden chuckled as he looked between Jaxie and Lydia. "I want both of your help."

"With what?" Lydia asked.

"I went to see Jack this morning. We talked things out. I told him everything I thought about. It's a long, happy story. Anyway, I met you guys here, because Jack

318

and I are going out tonight. We are going on a real first date and we are going to make this relationship official."

Aiden didn't have to look at either of them to see how big their smiles got. There was also some shock, as their heads were spinning trying to figure out why Aiden wanted their help at the mall.

"Clothes!" Lydia said cheerfully. "You need new clothes."

"That is why I brought you two here, yes," Aiden smiled.

"Yes, let's go!" Lydia leaped up. Her and Jaxie each took one of Aiden's hands and excitedly brought him through a couple clothing stores.

"Okay, go try these on and model for us," Jaxie smiled, half-shoving her brother into a changing room. She took a seat on the bench next to Lydia.

"Our boys are finally going out," Lydia said with a cheesy smile.

"About time," Jaxie laughed.

"You're telling me. Jack hasn't had a boyfriend in...gosh, it has to be close to four years now. He'd be working, at the bar, or hanging out with me and Avy. I love him, I do, but damn he needs a guy in his life. I need more alone time with my girl," Lydia said. "What about you? Are you trying to find someone?"

Jaxie shrugged. "I don't know. I sort of like just doing my own thing right now."

"You're still pretty young."

"Are you and Avy ever gonna get married?"

Lydia got a big smile on her face. "I hope so."

Jaxie returned the smile, then got up from the bench. She walked to the changing door and impatiently knocked on it. "Come out and show us! Not like it needs to be perfect, Jack is gonna take it off later."

The door opened and Aiden walked out, slightly blushing. "Really? Can't have a filter?"

"I don't think I'm wrong," Jaxie said, taking Aiden's hand and pulling him out further.

Lydia stood up in a giggle-fit and started looking over the outfit. "I love your sister."

"She certainly knows how to get her point across," Aiden grinned.

Once they were done at the mall, Jaxie and Lydia went with Aiden to his apartment to help him finish up. He didn't really need help getting ready, but he didn't mind the company. It was helpful to get time moving along. Aiden showered, got in his new clothes, and let the girls help him with his hair.

When everything was finished up, the three were standing in the kitchen, taking a moment to finally breathe from the nonstop few hours.

"Okay, so I gotta ask," Lydia began saying, "how did it get decided you guys were going out tonight as a real couple thing?"

"I went over there and talked to him about what I had been doing the past few days to try and heal from everything. I told him some harsh truths about what had gone through my mind about him. It was all me talking about the ugly side of things." Aiden paused. "Then I asked him out. He didn't see that part coming, but that was the conclusion I came to after thinking about all those hard things. I do want to be with him."

"I'm so happy for you guys. You look amazing and I can't wait to hear how it goes," Lydia smiled.

"Thank you," Aiden said, "and thanks for helping today."

"Of course! I'm excited for you guys." Lydia gave Aiden a hug. "Thanks for asking me to come hang with you and Jaxie. I'm glad I could be of some assistance. I should head out and go be with Avy now."

"How is she holding up?" Jaxie asked.

"She's doing better. She's still a little shaken," Lydia sighed sadly. "She's carried around a gun for so long, but never had to use it. She'll be okay."

Aiden looked down at his shoes. "I'm sorry she had to do that. I'm even more sorry because I didn't really see anything traumatizing. She had to go through this trauma because of me. I don't know what happened outside that night, and I can only imagine what she's going through from what she had to do."

"You don't need to say you're sorry, Aiden. She'll get through this. I know she wouldn't rather be sitting at home wondering why she didn't do it, and dealing with another scenario that could have played out. But you just focus on having fun tonight. I'll take care of Avy and you take care of Jack." Lydia slightly smiled before turning for the door. "I'll see you guys later."

"Hey, Lydia?" Aiden grabbed her arm. "Just...tell Avy I'm not mad or upset or anything. I know why she had to do it. She'll be in my prayers and I hope to see her soon."

Lydia smiled with a slight hint of tears. "Thanks, Aiden. Bye, Jaxie."

"Bye, Lydia. It was great seeing you today." Jaxie smiled at her brother as Lydia left. "Well, are you ready?"

"As ready as I'll ever be."

"You guys will have a fantastic time. Did you tell Mom or Dad?"

"No."

"Alright. I won't say anything."

"I don't care if you do. If they find out, they find out."

Jaxie grinned. "You have grown."

"Yeah, for now. What if...I don't know, what if bad thoughts or something pop into my head? What if my anxiety gets the best of me during the date?"

"That's okay. Maybe they will. No one honestly expects you to be over everything right away. You're confident and handling everything amazingly today, but tomorrow you could be in bed all day full of resentful thoughts. You'll be up and down, but that's okay. Just be honest with Jack about your feelings. If you need to cut the date short, cut it short. You know that ain't gonna change what Jack wants."

Aiden nodded, really hoping there wouldn't be a grieving episode during the evening.

"You'll be okay. And I don't mean for tonight. I mean in general. You will be okay."

"Thanks, Jaxie. For everything. I know I've said that a lot lately but you've been my rock this entire time. You've kept me grounded and never once made me feel like there was something wrong with me, even if I was sure there was."

Jaxie wrapped her arms around her brother. "I love you."

"I love you, too."

The siblings held the hug for some time. Jaxie was the first to back away and patted Aiden's shoulders. "I'll head out so you can get going. Just remember to have fun. And I expect a call tonight to tell me all about it."

"Definitely."

"Unless you two get a little too busy, then call me in the morning."

Aiden shook his head with a silly grin, looking away as he felt his face get hot. "Night, sis." He heard the door shut and he slowly walked towards the living room window. He opened it, closed his eyes, and took a deep breath. He kept his eyes shut for a moment, taking it all in. It was clear out, but the smell of rain was lingering in the air. Aiden focused, letting his thoughts slow down and letting his feelings level out.

For the final minutes he had left Aiden looked over himself in the mirror numerous times. Once he was satisfied, he got into his car and started driving to the restaurant. During the drive, he wasn't feeling nervous. He wasn't feeling confident. He was feeling calm. He was feeling accepting of everything that had happened. He knew it wouldn't stay that way forever, but he hoped it would stay that way for the night.

At a red light, Aiden looked up towards the sky. It wasn't as clear as it had been earlier. Some dark clouds were drifting by. He thought about Brett looking down at him again. Did he picture Brett being happy for him? No. Did he picture Brett smiling down at him, maybe an apologetic expression? No. He couldn't even fake the old Brett feeling resentful for how things ended between them. He only saw Brett looking at him in disgust. He saw Brett spewing hate towards him. But that was okay. Aiden was okay with that. It didn't matter anymore. He wouldn't let it matter.

Aiden pulled up to the restaurant, the nerves now creeping up on him. He checked his pockets a couple of times for his phone and wallet. He looked himself over in his rearview mirror. Unexpectedly, he smiled at himself. He couldn't seem to help it. Taking a quick look around, he spotted Jack's truck in the parking lot, and his heart raced.

"Here we go." Aiden stepped out of his car. His feet quickly carried him to the doors. He walked inside and took a look around, spotting Jack at a table towards the corner.

Once they locked eyes, Jack stood from his chair, smiling wide. Aiden hurried over to him, anxiously ready to be near him. Jack opened his arms, feeling warm as Aiden accepted the hug.

"Wow, look at you," Jack commented as he looked over Aiden's outfit.

"Thanks. Lydia and Jaxie helped."

"They did great. Are you ready?" Jack asked, motioning to the table.

"Ready when you are."

They each took their seat across from each other. Aiden made the first move by reaching across the table and taking Jack's hand into his.

Aiden wasn't worried about what was going to come out of that night. He wasn't worried what tomorrow would bring. He had no idea where he would be with Jack in the next month or year. Their label was of no concern to Aiden. No matter where they were, or what the relationship became, it would all be worth it.

Made in the USA
Las Vegas, NV
21 November 2021

34963318R00184